The House on Cheyne

To
Barbara and Lettice Cooper

The House on Cheyne Walk

Perry Organ

HEINEMANN : LONDON

William Heinemann Ltd
15 Queen Street, Mayfair, London W1X 8BE

LONDON MELBOURNE TORONTO
JOHANNESBURG AUCKLAND

First published 1975
© Perry Organ 1975
SBN 434 55400 6

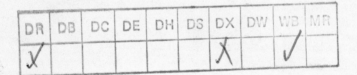
Printed in Great Britain by
Northumberland Press Limited
Gateshead

ONE

Once upon a time I lived in a house by a river that ran into the sea. It was a house much like this one, old and dark and full of the river's dampness. There was a bridge, too, as here, lines of lights looping across the water, the faintest of beacons on foggy nights. Sometimes the fog lasted longer than the night: we hardly knew that morning had come, except that suddenly the lights were gone and the bridge loomed like the hulk of some giant ghost-ship sprawled across the channel. The Charles, the Thames, the same ocean, the same person— a year, a century ago.

The vicar will be getting up in a few hours, looking over his notes, trying out on his tongue the names to be called in the marriage banns. The Anglican Church still observes this practice, though I gather it is not so burdensome a duty as it used to be. The couples are fading out—in Chelsea, at least— who are so trusting or so foolhardy as to make public promises to love for ever. But the sense of family and of property remains as strong as ever in some of them; I met one young man who looked on Cheyne Walk itself as a kind of family domain. His family's, not mine, I might add. The Pierces settled long ago for a few hundred marshy acres in Massachusetts, since shrunk to a compact but elegant strip along the Charles just before Cambridge slides into the detritus of Somerville and East Boston. Two new Harvard houses have gone up on our land in the last twenty years; skyscrapers, very modern, very airy. The Master's dog, in one of them, jumped or fell from the penthouse roof where the Master was holding his inaugural cocktail party; a student reported seeing the dog as it went past an eighth-floor window. They keep an eye on things at Harvard.

Here there is not much to see, though the night is going. Soon someone somewhere will throw a master switch, 'Put out the light!', and the lights will go out on Albert Bridge, on Cheyne Walk, on streets all over London. It is quiet now, the traffic at an ebb, the darkness not quite total. My satin

1

dress is hanging on the door, its folds making watery shadows in the mirror. It looks like an old-fashioned wedding dress, but it is pale green, not white, not quite virginal. Patrick likes it. He says it looks like the dresses that princesses wear in fairy tales. I wonder if he has a particular fairy tale in mind. I have read to him the story of the twelve princesses who danced all night, clandestinely, night after night, and wore their shoes and stockings to shreds. All that secret, frenzied, unavailing gaiety! It was the sort of thing one might have expected Sophie to do, not me.

Those months on the Riviera before her marriage she lived full tilt and devil take the hindmost. Not that we in the family knew it then, for my sister to all appearances was a proper young lady, but we had our suspicions. I still have the snapshot she sent to us in Cambridge that summer, taken in one of the little hill towns behind Nice: Sophie, beautiful as always, sitting demurely on a pile of crumbling, peach-coloured stone —'some ruin, no doubt,' my mother sniffed, 'appropriate enough'—her lap full of flowers, Charles bending over her, his face in the shadow. In fact, I never saw Charles' face till I arrived in Europe six years later. There had been other pictures, but only of Sophie, and then of Patrick—the hasty, abundant snapshots of a first and, as it turned out, an only child.

Patrick will be getting up soon and hunting for his Sunday clothes. Jane usually forgets to lay them out on Saturday night, being in a hurry to get to her Scottish dancing. I have seen her dance dress, taffeta, with paper flowers crushed into the waist. Jane Burrows! She does very well, though. She has never endangered Patrick's safety, and what more, really, can one ask? There are those to whom safety is the last concern.

'Madam,' Jane said to me last month—she nearly always calls me 'Madam', perhaps not knowing a fitter title—'I don't know what to do about Master Patrick. He wouldn't go near the garret last autumn. Now he's always running up there, racing round and trying to tear open the doors, just to devil me. Does he know what happened to his mother?'

'Yes, he knows. His father told him. He says that truth is best for children.'

'Then he ought to play in his own room, or downstairs. I don't like following him up there, wondering what he's going to do next. It makes me nervous, the responsibility.' Jane's face had flushed at this unusual outburst of spirit.

'It makes me nervous, too, Jane. Perhaps we ought to ask Mr Vivian to close off that attic. It's a pleasant enough place to sit, with the french windows overlooking the garden, but there's no cause now for keeping it open.'

'No, Madam, no cause.'

No cause, no, none. Oh, Jane, what shall we do, and what does it matter? There is no accounting for our lives. And yet if I go over in my mind everything that has happened, perhaps I will get at the cause. Or rather, if I am lucky, perhaps it will come to me; for I have found that if one wants anything too much, struggles for it, it escapes, dissolves, melts into something else. I think it was Dr Johnson who said that the mind can only repose on the stability of truth. Well, I would welcome a little repose, but how does one establish the truth? It is not a matter of assembling facts; I have all the facts I am likely to get; it is finding out the truth they represent that baffles me. Does death always have a reason—and can it be found? I know something, but not all. I know enough to make my nights broken and my sleep haunted, enough so that, in these small hours of the morning, when I try to write down and sort out what has happened, I become afraid of the very shadow of my hand upon the paper.

The mist is thinning now, there is a freshness in the air, my satin dress glows more distinctly against the door. Will we ever be ready to go? It seems so long ago, and yet it was only—what? A year? No, not so long, October then, June now—nine months ago that I sat by this window for the first time. I looked out at the Thames and felt half homesick for New England and half beguiled by London. I sat here for a long time that night, watching the lights on Albert Bridge, letting the breeze from the river blow on my face. It had been a long journey, by sea...

TWO

Paddington that day was a greenhouse, sun streaming in through the arched, glassy roof, magnifying and heightening the press of faces and voices and rumbling trains. Viewed from the recesses of the boat-train where I had spent the last five hours en route from Plymouth, England had been remote and soundless, no more than a painted landscape. I felt dazed as I stepped from the carriage into the station. Passengers swirled towards the ticket barriers and were met by a countersurge of travellers, friends, families, guides, porters. The sun glittered on the glass panes; the day was very warm. I had expected England to be cold in October, but the air had the warmth and softness of summer. Beyond the gates I could see stalls and barrows heaped with flowers. My heart rose. I could not resist the thought that perhaps someone had come to meet me after all.

Among the descending passengers was the robust, balding, ginger-moustached young man with whom I had eaten, danced, played deck tennis and bridge for the past five days at sea, in one of those curious affinities that shipboard life invites or necessitates; we had talked of meeting in London, had exchanged cards and addresses. While I watched, he was rushed upon by four young children, plainly his, the ginger of his moustaches having transplanted itself on to each small head; a moment later a handsome woman in a cerise suit embraced him and led him away in a convoy of children. He gave me a slight nod and smile as he swept past, but his face was already remote as his life shunted off on to another track. His wife looked back for an instant, her eyes resting on some point beyond me. Then they were gone, lost in the crowd, though I could make out here and there four russet-coloured heads in the throng that pressed forwards. I felt tired. The shafts of sunlight that fell from the glassy roof were filled with dust. I side-stepped a puddle of spilled beer, got a firmer grip on my two bags and began walking towards the distant archway. I knew there would be no one to meet me. Well,

4

that was what I had wanted, wasn't it? what I had always wanted, not to make trouble for anyone.

My low spirits did not last long. London, seen for the first time in the rush hour of a bright October afternoon, was irresistibly exhilarating. The taxi swerved south towards Chelsea, and I had my first sight of the great city, of streets and parks and monuments that I had known by name since childhood. We must have moved slowly, the streets were clogged with traffic, but I was unaware of time. We swung into Hyde Park; people flowed everywhere, coatless and happy on that glorious afternoon. We inched our way towards Knightsbridge, down Sloane Street, and into an unexpected square where a fountain splashed and gurgled noisily above a kneeling bronze maiden and the roar of encircling traffic.

'Sloane Square, Miss. Chelsea. We're not far now.' The cab driver's voice brought me out of my trance. 'I'll go along King's Road to Beaufort Street before cutting down to the river, to be sure to be on the right side of the street to let you off. Just about impossible to turn round on Cheyne Walk at this time of day—unless you want to get killed.' A gold tooth flashed in the sun as he grinned amiably.

'Any way you like. It's all new to me,' I replied. I would not have minded if he had driven ten miles out of the way so long as we remained in London, and so long as I did not have to face too soon the house that I was bound for. But the journey was almost over. We turned south onto Beaufort Street and there, all at once, was the Thames. It was so inevitably there, gracious and assertive, more purposeful-looking somehow than my meandering old Charles. Warehouses and smokestacks lined the farther shore; red and green barges waited serviceably at their moorings; a handful of gulls flapped and wheeled over the bridge before us, one of many that leaped the river in marvellous arcs as far as my eye could reach.

I was still looking at the river when the cab pulled to the left and stopped. 'Here we are, Miss.' The driver helped me out and handed down my bags. I sorted out the unfamiliar coins in my hand and paid him, gave him all, my heart racing as I looked up at my new home.

A tall, narrow house of reddish-brown brick faced me; an elegant house, its long windows finely proportioned to the height of its four and a half storeys. Sophie had said in one of her few letters that the house was mid-Georgian, built in the 1760s. Its graceful windows and doorway, the door of panelled oak surmounted by a carved fanlight, were similar to

5

those of the buildings I knew in the old sections of Boston and Cambridge, but I had seen none in a setting comparable to Cheyne Walk. The air of the neighbourhood was not unfamiliar, though; the houses here had an austere, well-kept reticence that I had met before, in Boston, in Newport, in North East Harbor. The houses of the rich are the same everywhere.

The sun had sunk perceptibly in the last few minutes, and only a faint golden arm of light lingered over the Battersea chimneys to the south. I saw no lights in the house, though, no figures moving. Again, as at the station, I felt expectant, but of what? A band, flowers, welcoming orations? Whatever, there was complete silence. And that was fitting enough, I supposed. My sister Sophie, flamboyant Sophie, was dead. She had died in late August. I was here partly in response to her last letter, partly on my own whim, never having ventured beyond the sacred family preserve of New England before. I would have cancelled my visit on learning of her death— my inclination had been to refuse her invitation on first receiving it—but her husband had renewed the summons and asked for my help, for so I interpreted his letter despite its formal and even chilly tone, in accustoming young Patrick to a life without his mother. I had given up my teaching position for a term to come to England. Leave was certainly owing to me, anyway. Headmistresses—notably Mrs Lofting, I reflected—have a way of preying on the *noblesse oblige* instincts of their long-time employees. I was reluctant to look on my trip as a mission of mercy. The truth is, though it was a truth I did not then admit to my conscious mind, I felt less bereaved than liberated by Sophie's death. I was both resentful and fearful of approaching this house of the dead and the duty that awaited me.

So there I stood, on a fading October afternoon in Cheyne Walk, staring at a darkened house. There was nothing for it but to go up the short gravel walk, the three shallow steps, and lift the heavy, lion-headed knocker that bared its brass fangs at all intruders.

There was no response. I waited, wondering what I would do if no one came, when a movement at the window on my right caught my eye. A small boy was twisting his face sideways against the pane to look at me. He was straddled precariously on the hump of a camel-back sofa, and I instinctively motioned to him to get down: six years of herding young children about had left its mark. The boy slid over backwards, heels flying, and vanished from view. The door swung open. We were face to face.

6

'How do you do? I'm Sarah Pierce. You must be Patrick.'

'I *am* Patrick.' I could see his mother's combative spirit already shining out of him.

'I'm very glad to meet you.' We shook hands, though perhaps I should have kissed him. In spite of my years in the classroom, small children could still discomfit me, which was not hard for anyone to do, for that matter.

'Jane Burrows' down in the kitchen getting tea. Mrs Chalmers' at her sister's. Daddy's away. But we knew you were coming.'

'Well, that's good.'

'Want to have some tea?'

'Thank you.'

And so I walked into the house on Cheyne Walk for the first time. I followed Patrick through a panelled hall into a room that was dark as a cave except for a single eye of light glowing at floor level some feet away.

'Don't you want any lights on?' I asked, bewildered.

'Well, all right, if you want them. I'm running my train. It's more fun in the dark.'

He flipped a switch, and we were surrounded by shapes and colours as grotesque as the darkness. The room was filled with massive furniture from a hundred years ago: the hump-backed sofa I had seen from the walk, several gargantuan chairs upholstered in olive and crimson velvet, ruby-hued lamps, a black library table and several smaller ones, their clubbed legs twisted about with pineapples, gargoyles and drugged-looking dolphins. A Persian carpet, patterned with undulating vines and arabesques, overlapped the room from wall to wall like a great red ocean. Miniature train tracks ran in and about the furniture, curving off in a dozen directions before disappearing into the blackness under the sofa. My senses reeled; I sank down on the nearest solid object.

Patrick set about laying down more track, following the curves of the carpet. He put the links down slowly and joined them meticulously, as if performing a ritual, and I had a sense of *déjà vu*, of Sophie at home in Cambridge, years ago, setting out dolls' teacups, saucers, cutlery. This little boy had something of the same intentness, though if he was like Sophie his concentration on any one object would not last long. Physically between him and his mother I could see little resemblance. Where Sophie had been raven-haired and sapphire-eyed (truth rather than kindness compels these tributes), this child was hazel all over—hair, eyes, complexion—more in my image than hers, the worse for him, I reflected wryly.

7

He felt me watching him. 'I'd better tell Jane you're here.'

'Don't hurry. I've been travelling all day. I'm glad to sit still and rest.'

'Did you come on a boat or a plane?'

'Boat, and then the train from Plymouth.'

'We knew you were coming today, but you didn't say when.'

'I didn't want your father to go to any trouble. I didn't know if we'd dock on time or how long it would take to get through customs and so forth.' The words tumbled out blithely, as they always did when I was not telling the whole truth. While it was true enough that I did not want to cause any trouble, I also resented fiercely that six years had passed before Sophie and her husband had seen fit to offer me their hospitality, and then when it was to their purpose, not mine.

'I would've liked to come to meet you. We never go anywhere any more.'

His words, spoken in a low voice, pierced me. How could I have visited my own perplexity and hostility on a five-year-old child, his mother not two months dead, and he living alone with a middle-aged father and a pair of servants? I looked down at him, but he said nothing more, only scowled intently at a bent siding. I had been little used myself to spontaneous affection; it seemed that Patrick and I already shared the same benumbing consciousness of its lack.

'You have met me, now, and I am very glad to be here.'

Patrick looked up and smiled, and perhaps I would have hugged him then and there, as I had failed to do earlier, if at that moment a harried-looking girl had not shot into the room:

'Master Patrick! Oh, begging your pardon, Madam!' The speaker, who looked to be twenty years old but was no higher than my shoulder, stopped short, and the tea tray rattled and teetered on her spindly arms.

'Good afternoon, I'm Patrick's aunt.'

'Oh, you're Miss Pierce, then! How d'you do! If we'd known you were coming this early, we'd have laid a proper tea.' There was no answer to this, I being as nonplussed as she, and she hurried on: 'I'm looking after Master Patrick these days, ma'am. My name's Jane Burrows. I tidy up, and keep an eye on Master Patrick—sort of a mother's help.' So saying, she blushed and broke off, remembering that there was no longer any mother to help.

'My sister mentioned you in her letter, Miss Burrows.'

'Did she now?' The girl looked pleased. 'He's a good lad,

8

doesn't need much looking after. Smart for his age; in school now, of course.'

Jane poured out the tea while she talked, and Patrick handed round a plate of cake and biscuits. I began to relax. My nephew was not the whining child I had feared, and Jane Burrows was not intimidatingly capable and aloof. The head of the house was still unknown to me, but he failed to weigh on my spirits. I watched Patrick as he sipped his mug of cocoa. Perhaps, I thought, there is a providence that shapes our ends, after all. Perhaps it was my end to make up to Patrick for Sophie, not only for her absence but her presence, for I could imagine Sophie maternal about as readily as I could imagine a cat swimming the Charles. My sister's vision of life had excluded females and children, other than herself. 'I shall have one,' she had said, 'as soon as I'm married, just to show that I can do it.' And she did.

We were getting along quite easily now. The siding had been straightened out, and the green locomotive was running smoothly in a maze of tracks; Patrick lay on his stomach, monitoring it. Jane Burrows, encouraged to join us at tea, was chatting away about her five younger brothers and sisters in Gravesend, scattering crumbs expansively over the velvet sofa as she ate and talked. I began to feel drugged with sugared tea and the warmth of the room and her high, chirruping voice.

A sharp thud, the sound of a heavy door being swung shut, roused me. Jane jumped up, sending the plate of biscuits flying off her lap. 'Mrs Chalmers!' she cried, whether by way of announcement or alarm, I was not sure. In a moment the intruder walked into the room, a rush of outdoor air accompanying her. She was a large woman, broad and tall, dressed in black, her hair pulled into a knob at the back of her neck; she had a stern and sallow face, with hooded black eyes that seemed not to blink. There was a long moment in which no one spoke; we might have been the frozen figures of a Seurat painting. Realizing that Jane was unequal to introductions, I introduced myself for yet a third time in this strangely ordered household.

'And I am Mrs Chalmers,' the woman replied. 'I am housekeeper here, as I presume'—here throwing a reproving glance at Jane to indicate that she did not so presume—'you have been told. I am sorry you were not better received. Mr Vivian is abroad this week on business; he will be back on Wednesday. He asked me to convey his regrets that he could not be here. I myself was called away unexpectedly to attend my sister, who is ill.'

'She's had her womb taken out,' Patrick threw in, 'so she won't have any more trouble than she's already got, Jane said.'

Mrs Chalmers ignored him. 'I hope you have been given tea and shown your room.' There was more of command than of cordiality in her remark. Jane looked down, abashed.

'I have had tea, thank you.'

'We had dinner at midday, Mr Vivian being away, but you may have your dinner this evening, if you wish me to prepare it.'

'No, thank you, that won't be necessary. I had a meal on the train.'

'A pleasant journey, I trust?'

A pleasant journey! To come as the last mourner to my sister's grave, to an alien house filled with strangers? Mrs Chalmers' frigidity repelled me. It struck me that not one of them had spoken of Sophie—but then, neither had I. I answered quietly:

'Yes, pleasant enough.'

'I shall show you to your room now, if you like.' Without waiting for an answer, she added, 'Jane, take Miss Pierce's things,' casting an eye at my two suitcases. They, at least, could stand her gaze, being the best of Louis Vuitton stock, solid, moneyed. Would I always rely on possessions to make an impression that I myself could not make? I recollected myself:

'Yes, thank you, that would be fine.'

Patrick, who had not moved from his stomach, bounded up and started through the doorway.

'You will wait here, Master Patrick,' said Mrs Chalmers, drawing him back by the tail of his jersey. 'Miss Pierce wishes to rest now.' I had not meant to exclude Patrick from my company, but something in Mrs Chalmers' tone kept me from saying anything.

We stepped out into the hall. The rubies that had burnished the living-room were gone; the house seemed shabbier, darker. I saw that the walnut wainscoting was warped in several panels; a spindle was missing from the staircase half-way up; the edges of the stair-carpet were worn through. This did not seem like Sophie's house at all. A faint scent of decay hung over the stair well. The house was old, I knew; but the atmosphere struck me as being less the decay of age than the loss of vitality, the result not of use or abuse but of a curious moral indifference, though what moral indifference had to do with threadbare carpets, I had not then the slightest notion.

10

Suddenly my ankle twisted under me and I gasped with pain. I looked down: a cut across my left instep, no more than a slit, was widening into a red stain.

'Watch out, Miss Pierce. The third step from the bottom. The wood has given way there, and the men have not yet come to repair it. Stay to the right.'

I could barely make out Mrs Chalmers' black-clad figure on the landing. Her words floated down to me detached, imperious; the cut stung. When had following where Sophie led ever brought me anything but trouble? I took hold of the banister wearily and, withdrawing my foot from the rotten step, made my way up the stairs.

THREE

The door closed behind me, and Mrs Chalmers was gone as abruptly as she had come. The room I found myself in was large and light, and I felt at once what had been lacking below: the presence of Sophie. The furniture here was small-scaled and delicate, covered mostly in silks of light blue and lemon-yellow; the walls were also blue, except for the white frames of the panelling; three tall windows opened to the south, their white silk curtains blowing inwards with the breeze off the river. It was a pleasingly decorated room, in keeping with the eighteenth-century origin of the house. But amidst the graceful French and English furniture, I saw with surprise the homely pinewood rocking-chair from Sophie's bedroom in Cambridge, and sitting in it a lumpily stuffed white cat and a china-headed doll, familiar companions from earliest nursery days. And there, too, was the hand-crocheted bedspread, yellowed with age, that had lain on our parents' old four-poster for as long as I could remember. Sophie had draped it, shroud-like, over a Louis Seize chaise-longue; the effect was somehow blasphemous.

I examined my foot and wiped the blood off as well as I could. The cut was not deep, but it struck me as the final insult of an exhausting day. I sat down on the chaise-longue, after carefully removing my parents' bedspread, and lay back, too tired even to think of unpacking. Facing me across the room was an ample dressing-table, the large mirror above it reflecting a welter of perfume bottles, silver-framed photographs, and a shining, vermeil-enamelled vanity set. That vanity set! Aunt Avery had sent it to Sophie from France, and it had arrived on the morning of her sixteenth birthday. Sophie had rushed up to her bedroom with it, not even waiting to finish breakfast.

'Handsome is as handsome does, my dear.' My mother stood behind Sophie as she held up the new mirror to herself and whirled round to view herself on all sides in the full-length mirror of the wardrobe.

'Oh, Mama,' Sophie replied, 'where do you drag up those

12

old sayings from, anyway? Nobody talks like that anymore. Anyway, it's a wonderful present! Something that will last, not like a bottle of cologne or'—throwing a glance at me— 'a book.'

'Why not a book?' I always rose to the challenge, though I seldom met it.

'Because if you read a book, Miss Know-it-all, you're done with it, but you can pick up a mirror and look in it every day of your life.'

Since, even then, there were days I did not look in a mirror from morning to night, I could not agree with her. Besides, I thought, no one, not even my sister, could get the same thrill from looking in a mirror as from reading Tolstoy. I said as much to her.

'Depends what you see in the mirror, doesn't it? And besides, I have never read Tolstoy.' She spoke with the triumphant air of Oscar Wilde's young lady who had never seen a spade.

'Now, now, girls,' my mother scolded, her arms folded across her chest as she rocked back and forth on her heels, her greyed fair hair frizzing about her head like an imperfect halo. 'We can't stand here all morning preening and squabbling. And you, my girl'—to Sophie—'need a brush more than you need a mirror.' She picked up the new hairbrush and began to brush Sophie's tangled dark hair, lovingly, caressingly.

My mother was almost forty and had been fifteen years married when she first conceived a child. My parents had grown used to their own lives, lives that were spent separately in large part, except for the domestic rituals of meals, bed, and visiting back and forth with the clan. Once my parents had got over the shock of my mother's being pregnant, they quickly decided it was a boy that frisked about inside her; it disappointed them, though I did not discover this for some time, when I came to light as a girl. By the time Sophie was born, four years later, it did not seem to matter, they were ready to enjoy a daughter. They certainly did not enjoy me, though I was anxious to win their approval and they were not intentionally hard-hearted or neglectful. But they were at ease with Sophie. Perhaps it was her vivacity and her good looks; perhaps it was her conviction that she was the most important person in the world. Whatever, they responded to her eagerly, like desert plants to water.

My father's family, the Pierces, had been successful textile manufacturers for more than a century. Their mills were scattered up and down the Lowell and the Merrimac, the Taunton and the Connecticut, puffing out sheets and pillow-cases and

13

tons of waste that had done much to choke up those great New England waterways.

My father, as if in reaction against generations of money-makers, took up the study of the Orient and ended as Professor of Far Eastern Languages at the university. He kept his scholarship and his family life as separate as the T'ang and Ming dynasties, and except for a few pieces of *chinoiserie* flung at random up and down the halls of our riverside mansion we would not have guessed that any civilized world existed, any more for him than for us, outside of Cambridge and Back Bay Boston.

My mother—I think now in looking back—would have preferred a husband who was a figure in, if not business, then politics or at least something 'useful', one of my mother's favourite words. Not that she, so far as I could see, had done anything useful. She, too, was of old New England stock, but in her the tree-felling, God-worshipping energy of her forebears had frittered itself away to a nervous, fussy compulsion to order and arrange everyone and everything within her grasp. My mother's mind had tightened and narrowed with the years; my father, beneath his stiff collars and precise habits, exuded hints of a relaxed and yielding aestheticism. I suppose the two complemented each other. Together they were the last New England salmon, leaping the falls, weary unto death. Sophie and I were the products, at times perhaps the victims of their union.

I picked up one of the silver-framed photographs from the dresser. It showed the four of us, sitting on the verandah of the Cohasset summer house: I about seven, Dutch-bobbed, squinting into the sun, wearing a sailor-dress that looked too hot for the season; my father, also heavily clad, in a gabardine suit with a waistcoat—did men still wear waistcoats in the height of summer?—one arm folded behind him, only the elbow jutting out, stiff and exact as the line of an obi, and holding, undoubtedly, in that hidden hand, a Filipino cigar (my mother would only let him smoke it out of doors); my mother, sitting up stiffly in a wilting organdie dress, though undoubtedly (strange how often one is tempted to say 'undoubtedly' of one's parents!) it had been crisp and newly ironed a half-hour earlier, my mother not being one to under-work her Irish laundress; and Sophie, about three, sitting on my mother's knee, well forward, her curls tied up in a top-knot and her bright eyes staring fearlessly ahead, like the figurehead at the prow of an old clipper—

'Miss Pierce!' The imperative voice accompanied a rap at

14

the door and Mrs Chalmers' large head thrust into the room. 'I forgot to mention that supper is at eight. Would you like it in your room, or will you be coming down?'

'What? Oh—well ...' I focused with difficulty on what she was saying, my mind being miles away, years away. 'Yes, yes, I'll come down, thank you. Thank you for telling me.'

She did not turn away immediately, nor did I want her to, for whatever the strangeness of this house and housekeeper, they were not so unnerving as the past that sprang up at me from the mementoes in this room. I looked about for something to say to hold her; my glance fell on the large bed. 'Mr Vivian—'

'Yes?' Mrs Chalmers looked at me, curious.

'Mr Vivian, is he—doesn't he—am I—' I stumbled along, not knowing how to finish. 'I hope I am not disturbing his arrangements. They ... he and my sister ... shared this room, I presume?'

Mrs Chalmers smiled slightly, her head cocked on one side, her eyes unblinking.

'Mr Vivian moved his things to the study.'

'The study?'

'Yes, off the drawing-room on the first floor. You haven't seen much of the house yet. It's a beautiful house, a magnificent house.' Was I imagining it or did she say this defiantly, as if expecting opposition, though I had given no sign of any? She went on: 'There are four storeys, a basement and a garret, and the stairway running up one side. There are two large rooms on each floor, the front one facing the street and the river, the other the back garden; and a third, smaller room on each floor at the back of the hall. Mrs Vivian had most of those converted into bathrooms.' Mrs Chalmers sniffed disdainfully, as if a smell of sewers had suddenly floated into the room. 'The kitchen and my rooms, which give on to the back garden, are in the basement. On the ground floor is the drawing-room where you took tea—we call it the parlour—and a dining-room behind. The main drawing-room and the study are on the first floor. Then you come to this room and Mrs Vivian's dressing-room—it was meant to be a guest room—on this floor. The child's room and Jane Burrows' are on the floor above. And then the garret, which looks over the garden, no windows on the street side.' She paused, breathing hard. 'It is a beautiful house.'

I looked at her, but she was gazing off into space, her mind as far away as mine had been.

'Have you been here long, Mrs Chalmers?'

15

'Thirty-nine years. I came to this house as upstairs maid. I was fifteen years old. Mr and Mrs Vivian were newly married then. I held young Mr Vivian in my arms, and his sister, when they were no bigger than that'—pointing at the doll that stared blankly from the rocker. 'Oh yes, I know this house. I know its ways.' She frowned at a panel on the east wall as if it held some ineffable secret. Suddenly she advanced into the room and snatched up a photograph from the dressing-table. 'It's not the same, you know. It's not the same.' She held the picture out to me threateningly. I did not recognize the subject: an old man with bursts of white hair at the temples, stocky, stooped, both hands on a cane. 'When Mr Vivian senior was master of this house, and the mistress alive, this was a house to be proud of, no nonsense here.' She shook the picture angrily, as if the violence of the gesture would rid the house of its subsequent failings. 'Everything the same then, always, no changes, no newfangledness. A solid house. Everything in order.'

Her vehemence startled me. I waited for her to go on, but she said nothing as she replaced the picture quietly on the dresser.

'Well, Mrs Chalmers, that's all I wanted to be sure of, that I wasn't turning Mr Vivian out of his own room.'

'No, he moved into the study. He put all the old things back in there last month. Everywhere in the house. His father's and grandfather's furniture. Grand pieces they are, too. Solid. Don't give way beneath you.' One could not say as much for the staircase, I thought. 'I believe that Mr Vivian preferred not to be reminded of'—she paused delicately—'the newly deceased. He left this room, and he left it the way it was, the way she had done it. He thought you would want to sort things out, dispose of her clothes and jewellery and the like.'

'I'm sure he knew her better than I—' I broke off in confusion. I did not mean to get into a discussion of the respective worth of husbandly and sisterly knowledge. 'Yes, thank you, Mrs Chalmers. I will look over my sister's things. Eventually.' My voice was prim; I could hear the echo of my mother's in it. My mother was always good at closing interviews.

Mrs Chalmers turned to go, but paused at the door and said to me coolly: 'You're not much like your sister, if I may say so.'

She withdrew and pulled the door shut behind her.

My face felt flushed. I sat down on the bed. Not much like my sister! I looked down at the photograph I still held in my hand. Sophie looked back at me, unrepressed by the cover-

16

ing glass or twenty-two years of intervening time, sitting saucily on Mama's knee, fingering the ribbons—they were blue, I remembered—that fell from the yoke of her gauzy baby-dress. Ribbons, always ribbons, a blue-ribbon baby ...

My parents gave a christening party for her when she was two months old. It is one of my earliest memories. Tables with blue-and-white-striped umbrellas dotted the lawn. It was a day in late May, when Cambridge looks its best: the sun was bright but not hot, the oaks and beeches cast new-leaved shadows on the grass, the scent of late-blooming lilacs filled the air. Any spiritual meaning the occasion was intended to commemorate was forgotten; everyone was drinking champagne and talking. Raised on a wooden platform under a striped canopy was Sophie's white-skirted bassinet, its blue satin ribbons fanning out in the breeze. People all afternoon stepped up to look, and their voices drifted to me in fragments as I played behind the bar, watching Jess, our houseboy, fill and refill trays of long-stemmed glasses:

'Oh, isn't she pretty!' ... 'What a darling!' ... 'Look at the eyes!' ... 'A real beauty!' Sometimes someone, usually a woman, would lean over to me to say a word or two: 'Aren't you lucky to have such a sweet little sister?' 'It must be just like having a big new doll!' The crowd, the voices, the sips of champagne from glasses left standing, confused me. Were they talking about that little thing that yelled for most of the night and left wet patches on Mama's dresses? I nudged my way to the bassinet and pulled myself up to look. Just as I thought! It was nothing but a little rabbit, white and fat. At that moment the rabbit opened its eyes and smiled and waved two round fists in my face, the cradle rocking with the gusto of the movement. I stared down. They were right. She was like a doll, like my favourite Snow White doll, at that—blue eyes, a cloud of black hair, pink-and-white cheeks. I backed away slowly and jumped off the platform and hurried back to Jess.

I had been shown the light. I had been converted. As the months went by and Sophie began to crawl and then to walk, I was willing if not eager to play the rôle of helpful big sister that my mother promoted. But Sophie would have none of it. I was prepared to protect her, to teach her, to be the leader; but for all her fragility and docility in the eyes of our parents, it was she, not I, who was the leader; and she got us into many scrapes, though I was the one who generally took the blame. One day, a morning in winter when we were bored and had nothing to do, she dared me to wrestle with her on

17

top of the big sofa in the bay-window alcove. I scrambled up, she leaned backwards out of reach to taunt me, lost her balance and fell through the window—which was shut. The glass breaking brought my mother and the maids running; Sophie was rushed off to hospital, where she remained for three days having bits of glass picked out of her back. I actually prayed for her, I was so anxious. She came home as saucy as ever and loaded with gifts, including a white rabbit-fur muff, of which I was intensely jealous and which I considered hardly a just return for her sins and my prayers.

She was decidedly prone to accidents and, as I think back on those childhood years, perhaps even then of more than normal recklessness. Trees, swings, ponies, bridge railings were magnets to her. A sense of danger did not operate in Sophie; she thrived on self-imposed perils. I have read, or heard it said, that the wish to live strenuously is allied to a wish to die. The truth is, I have never believed or even understood that theory. It was excitement and gaiety that my sister craved, not death. Everyone was too serious for her, she said, too solemn; she said this to me in almost a panic-stricken way, as if she wanted me to reprove her and agree with her at the same time.

The breeze was colder off the river now. I looked out at the river and the bridges, glowing with strings of lights in the deepening sky. I felt immensely tired. I fell back upon the bed and pulled the blue-and-yellow silk eiderdown over me. It was a huge bed compared to the one I was used to, and had three layers of pillows shored against the headboard. The sheets and cases were of fine, sweet-smelling linen—such things do not go unnoticed by a textile manufacturer's granddaughter —and kneading them between my fingers, I felt the slightly raised surface of embroidery, monograms, I supposed. Sophie liked to have her name on everything; I had always considered it a vulgar trait. And she had liked lolling in bed; she would have been in her element as an eighteenth-century Belinda, disposed on a heap of pillows, proffering chocolate from a Dresden pot to a circle of morning admirers. How could the tomboy have turned, and overnight it seemed, into an accomplished coquette? One day it was all ponies and snowball fights, the next it was dances and mascara and conversations whispered in the dark.

I stretched and put my arms under my head and stared at the ceiling. There was an elaborate design in plasterwork, a kind of five-pointed star, beaded like a jelly-fish, with chains of moulded fruit and flowers radiating from it. Another Vic-

18

torian improvement, I supposed, to the Georgian severity of the house. I gazed idly at the flowery chains that looped their way to the dark corners of the room. When had Sophie not had admirers?

Her power as a woman was made clear to me early on. Rob Warner, the boy I liked best—my only boy-friend then, my second year in college—was coming up from New Haven to spend a couple of days with us. It was the second week of June, and already as hot as August; my father's rose bushes had burst forth all at once and hay fever had attacked me in full force. Sophie, then fifteen, said she would be glad to help me out by entertaining Rob. I well remember that weekend. I spent most of the time sitting under the oaks with my parents, wheezing, sneezing, and wiping my watery eyes, while Sophie played croquet with our guest, she looking as cool as a cucumber, though much prettier, and chatting with an easiness that belied her years. And it was she who accompanied Rob to the theatre that night with the tickets I had bought. They did not get back till well after midnight. Sophie said blithely that she had wanted to walk home—all the way from Tremont Street—the night being so fine. My mother was angry but held her tongue for Rob's sake, my father philosophized vaguely about the undesirability of late hours, Sophie laughed pertly and went up to bed.

Rob did not ask me out any more after that; or rather, he asked me perfunctorily to the Connecticut Valley Agricultural Show, which no one in his wildest moments could have associated with romance. Later, when Sophie was officially allowed to go out with young men, Rob was among her first suitors. I could have told him to save his breath, he would not get anywhere with her. He did not, either. Sophie did not want to hold onto a man. She hunted for pleasure, not for need, and abandoned her prey as soon as she had secured it.

There had been many men after that fifteenth summer; we were never free of them. I remember that once, even, on a winter cruise to the West Indies, an African prince or pasha had proposed to Sophie when we were not three days out of Boston harbour. He had promised her rubies and pearls and—what thrilled her most, I think—some ten thousand subjects to rule over in his particular corner of sub-Saharan Africa. My father had put an end to that prospect, but it was plain to me, if not to my parents, that Sophie could not be reined in for ever. She took exemplary care to tell me about her various liaisons while we were still living under the same roof, knowing that I lacked the audacity to tell our parents

19

and that she would have lied her way out of it if I had. I am not sure if all the encounters were sexually oriented; Sophie implied that they were, that she was the devil's own mistress. Perhaps she was. But I can also see, in retrospect, that along with her natural sensuality she possessed an innocent air that might well have evoked, at least occasionally, an answering innocence. Who knows? And why did Sophie have to play the temptress with an ever-changing succession of men? It was certainly from no lack of early affection; I can think of no one, male or female, so adored by parents, teachers and friends from her earliest years.

But I have learned a good deal of immoderate desires and destructive impulses in the last few months. They exist, though the reasons for them may never be found.

Outwardly, Sophie was a discreet young lady, obedient to her parents' wishes and to the conventions of her society. Yet she had an absolute if well-hidden indifference, amounting almost to revulsion, towards the New England aristocracy, towards the generations of Pierces, Websters, Averys and Childecotts that had woven themselves into our family tree. And in the end it was she, not I, who had cut loose from that dying tree. I was in my last year at Mt Holyoke when Sophie, seventeen, graduated from Mrs Lofting's School for Girls. The family expected that she would enter college as I left, sustaining the procession of Pierce females through the Holyoke halls. But Sophie put her foot down; no ladies' seminary for her. Nor would she engage in the series of balls, dinners and *thés dansants* that then constituted an introduction—granted, of course, only to those who needed no introduction—to society. Instead, Sophie asked for and received, so flabbergasted were my parents who flapped around like land-locked seals, an allowance to study painting and design at a school in Brooklyn that nobody had ever heard of. The following summer she hired herself out as a night-club waitress and with her earnings departed in the autumn for a year of study in France. She charitably acceded to my parents' request that she should at least 'live decently' and moved in—for her savings were not inexhaustible—with our one expatriate relative, Aunt Avery Vassallo, who in the only previous instance of female rebellion in the family had married a French musician and gone to live in a sun-washed villa on the edge of Nice, where for some fifty years she had been 'paying the price of her sins', as my mother put it, though Sophie and I were never able to discover what the price, much less the sins, might be. In the midst of the year of the 'Grand Tour'—so my parents airily referred

20

to it when the subject came up in company—Sophie up and married an Englishman we had never met. Sophie notified us of the marriage by a singing telegram.

My parents did not have to endure the shock for long. They were killed in a car crash a month later. I alone was left in the big house beside the Charles, its rooms heavy with generations of living and dying, its garden overborne with oaks and roses and weeping Concord vines.

It was a strange feeling, lying in the room of someone I had known so well yet had not seen for most of her adult life. Now six years had passed since she had married, and she was dead. What had her life been like with Charles Vivian? He apparently had fallen for her as quickly and as hard as the rest of her men; the two had no sooner met than married. Had he been able to keep her in line and to make her happy, or had she played him sweetly false as she had so many others? But perhaps I wronged her, for there was in her, despite her recklessness, something that belied the sensualist—perhaps it was her ambition and her desire for independence. But for Sophie, was marriage itself not a denial of independence?

I did not know. Seven years ago she had sailed from Boston; she had married, borne a child, ruled a house and died. She had died dramatically, as she did all things, falling to her death from the top-floor balcony of this house onto the iron railings and the flagstone terrace of the garden below. A terrible death.

I put my hand over my eyes involuntarily. I felt overcome with strain, and with an unexpected sense of loss. The bed was soft and yielding under me. I knew I must get up and wash and dress before supper, but those were my last waking moments on the thirteenth of October last. I dreamt much that night, I remember that. I dreamt of Sophie and my mother and Rob, and something soft was twisting and billowing under me, over me; a lion-headed locomotive was bearing down on me, white-faced dolls were leaning out of the carriage, blue ribbons fluttering; something was pressed against me, holding me down, suffocatingly. I awoke in terror, to find the eiderdown covering my face and entwined with my arms and legs. I was trembling and sweating, though the windows were wide open and the stars clear and bright in the cold midnight sky.

FOUR

It is curious how, without cause, a mood can vanish overnight. When I awakened, the monsters of the night had fled. The sun fell on the chairs and coverlet, on the silvery knick-knacks of the dressing-table, with a mild and gentle light. I stretched, feeling the luxury of having all time before me. At home at this hour on most mornings I would have been rushing around looking for my watch, my notebooks, gulping a too-hot cup of coffee, and wondering if the day in the classroom would be won with honour or otherwise. After serving faithfully if without distinction for six years, it was becoming clear to me that I had no call to the teaching profession, nor, despite much self-questioning, any marked desire or ability to do anything else.

'Aunt Sarah!'

'Yes? Come in!'

Patrick skipped into the room, the belt of his bathrobe trailing behind him.

'I thought you'd never get up! Jane said not to bother you, but I've been up for hours. I have to have my piano lesson this afternoon, but can we go to Battersea this morning? Please?'

'Battersea?'

'Battersea Pleasure Gardens. The Fun Fair. Over there.' He pointed out the window, across the river. 'You walk over Albert Bridge, and it's right there.' I pulled myself up and followed the line of his finger. All I could see was a line of trees, leafy-green as a bunch of celery. 'There's a carousel and a ferris-wheel and a water chute and everything.' Patrick was bouncing up and down now at the foot of the bed. 'Jane said she'd take me if you said it was all right.'

I lay back, smiling. 'Jane did, did she? Well, maybe I'll just go myself. Jane can have the day off. It's Sunday—everyone should have the day off! You and I together. How about that?'

'Oh, yes! Super!'

22

Within the hour we set off for Battersea. We whirled about on a variety of neck-jerking rides and ate popcorn and candy floss, as Patrick directed, and eventually we found ourselves in the midst of the trees that I had surveyed from Cheyne Walk. We were truly in the midst of them, high off the ground, on the tree-walk, a rickety contraption of swinging planks and rope railings that wove its way aimlessly among the trunks and branches, carrying us far above the crowds below. I felt free, swaying there among the leaves and the webs of sunlight, free of demands, questions, commitments. America, the land of opportunity, where anyone can do anything, had been for me, I saw in a rare moment of perception, as binding as a strait-jacket. Schools, friends, career, attitudes—all had been deter-mined for me by wealth and breeding from the day I was born; the choices, which had once seemed so endless as to exhaust me, were in fact as limited as the moves in Chinese chequers. Unless one fought, unless one was not afraid. Sophie had not been afraid; born into the same circumstances, she had torn herself free. I had looked on her defiance at the time as an act of ungrateful violence; now, for a moment, I knew that all severings were painful but necessary. And if she had wrenched free, so could I. Watching the changing patterns of people below me, hearing children laugh and shout, I felt an irrational happiness. ('Irrational' because, according to the Calvinism I had imbibed from my mother, there was no valid and perma-nent cause for happiness in this world; unhappiness one could always find reasons for.) Yes, I was happy! There was no happier lot than swinging in the treetops on a sunny October morning, with a five-year-old beside me!

I turned to Patrick—he was gone! I had no idea which way to look for him. The tree-walk coiled away to left and right, high and low; the leaves were full of voices. I saw a light brown head a few feet below me; the child turned; it was not Patrick. 'Patrick!' I called, and called again. My legs were trembling; I could hardly walk. 'Patrick! Patrick!' There was no answer, though faces turned to look up at me wonderingly. Patrick had not wanted to come up here at all, at first. I had cajoled him out of my own childishness. His little mouth had shrivelled into a thin line, and he had clutched my hand tightly when we began to climb. Of course! What had I been thinking of? His mother had fallen to her death from such a height. 'Patrick! Patrick!' I was running now on the narrow boards, heedless of other people. 'Patrick!'

'Hullo, up there!'

I looked down, my head spinning. A man was waving at

23

me and grinning. And hand in hand with him was Patrick.
I made my way down to the ground, my knees still shaking,
my hair undone and loose about my ears. Patrick did not look
at all abashed. He led his friend forward.

'Here's Fergus, Aunt Sarah.'

'David Fergus Llewellyn Howell. But Fergus will do.'

He smiled and held out his hand. I shook it, pronounced
my name, but did not return the smile. I felt I had made myself
absurd, and that it was their fault.

'Did you think you'd lost the old chap? He just came down
to pay his respects—spotted me at the snack bar.'

That was plain enough, I thought, as the two of them stood
there placidly licking ice-cream cones.

'Fergus is a friend of the family, Aunt Sarah.'

'Oh?' I said, sceptically. In Boston a friend of the family
was at least twenty years older than I and did not eat ice-
cream cones. Patrick's friend was my age, I guessed, in his late
twenties. He had light blue eyes, a thin beaky nose, no chin
at all, and curly, crinkly, flaxen hair. His pale eyes were magni-
fied by the thin, gold-rimmed spectacles he wore. He had the
look of a cherubic hawk.

'Yes, that's right, Charles and I are old cronies. In politics,
you know.'

I did not know. Sophie, so far as I could recall, had never
mentioned anything about Charles and politics. I knew only
that he was a solicitor.

'Charles has moved up in the organization a bit faster than
I have. Connections and all, you know. He'll probably be
standing again this time.' He pulled a used handkerchief from
his pocket and mopped at some drops of ice-cream. I saw that
the middle button was missing from his jacket; his turtle-neck
jersey might once have been white. I suspected that Fergus
did not have much in the way of either connections or money.

'I see. I haven't heard anything about that. What do you
do in politics?'

'Oh, I give lectures here and there for the Central Office.
Tory, of course. You know old Charles would never be on the
other side.' He chuckled. 'I go out to different places. I was
in Somerset last week. I go all over. All these little places in
the bush—they want someone from London to come and talk
to them. Rouses the constituents up a bit. Not that I'm an
orator. I give them facts. Facts go over best. Statistics. You
can't beat statistics.'

'No, I suppose not.'

'I don't get much out of it, of course. Train fare, lunch, a

24

few pounds. I write articles once in a while, too, analytical pieces.'

'Analysing what?'

'Oh, statistics.'

'Oh.'

'I worked for a branch of the UN Association for a while, but they were a prickly lot, very prickly. No getting along with them.'

His expression was fierce, though his voice kept its affable, sing-song lilt. I wondered if he might be a bit prickly himself. We were walking along the path now, following Patrick, who had set a fast pace towards what I took to be the carousel. Calliope music coursed towards us in loud-soft waves.

'Have you always been a Londoner?'

'Me?' He looked at me incredulously. 'Wales. Penclawdd, near Swansea. What about you?'

'America. Cambridge, near Boston.'

'Like it here?'

'I hope to.'

'Terrible thing to walk into. Strange, can't imagine someone like Sophie finishing up that way. Can't imagine anyone finishing up that way!' He grimaced.

'No,' I agreed. 'Did you know her well?'

'We had our romps. Charles left her alone a lot of the time.'

I stared at him. He was looking straight ahead at the carousel where Patrick was whirling round at a dizzying pace on a yellow ostrich. He must have felt my stare, for he went on:

'Romps, childish pleasures, picnics, that kind of thing. Sophie was a great one for games. My kind of girl.' He turned to me as he spoke, and his eyes were mischievous and wary. He looked older than I had thought, and less cherubic.

'Oh, Lord, I've forgotten Foxie. Left her at the Ladies'. She'll think I've run off with another woman. Got to run. Back in a minute.'

He galloped down the path we had taken, and I was left looking at the merry-go-round, which was revolving at an ever faster speed. Or was it I who was revolving? Fergus' words swam in my head; he had dropped plenty of facts, if not statistics. Charles Vivian had political ambitions. He had often left Sophie alone. Sophie and Fergus shared romps and games. She was his kind of girl. The leopard does not change her spots?

Fergus reappeared, leading a sulky-mouthed girl who even in a fit of sulks was something to look at. A tangle of auburn

25

curls, wide amber eyes in a narrow face, and curves the rest of the way down. This was Foxie, all right.

'Miss Pierce, Miss Fox.' Fergus introduced us with a gallant sweep of the arm.

'Gillian will do. Don't call me Foxie. He does'—jerking her thumb rather high-handedly, I thought, at Fergus—'but I don't like it.'

I had not thought of calling her Foxie, or even Gillian. However, I responded in kind:

'Call me Sarah, if you like.'

We eyed each other. Her sulky mouth relaxed into a smile.

'You're Patrick's auntie. How nice for him. How's Charles?'

'I haven't met Patrick's father.'

'Patrick's father? Never thought of him that way before. Why don't you say, "Sophie's husband"?' Gillian smiled and her voice was innocent, but the question had an edge to it I did not like.

'Are you a friend of the family, too?' I asked, none too sweetly.

'You might say so.' Her smile widened. 'How about you? Visiting for a while? Good time of year to be in London. In summer we're overrun with foreigners.'

'Is that so?' I thought it unlikely that she could ever be overrun by anything.

'Oh, yes, it's quite unbearable. Mostly Americans.'

'They must be a considerable help to the economy. I gather it's on the verge of collapse.'

'Oh, it's always that way. You'll get used to it.' She smiled again—I had not understood before just what a Cheshire cat smile was. 'Ever been here before?'

'No, I haven't.'

'Well, we really must show the girl about a bit, Fergus. Who'd want to be shut up alone with Mrs Chalmers and—Patrick's father?'

'You, for one,' returned Fergus.

At this the Cheshire cat smile split and broke into a laugh.

'Come on, come on,' said Fergus, twisting her arm. 'Don't be your usual bitchy self. I bet you haven't done any work all week.'

'Ah, but I have.' She wrenched her arm free and slid it around his waist. The situation was getting beyond me. I tried another tack:

'Are you in politics, too, Gillian?'

'No, I don't do anything political at all. I work'—she

nibbled at an astonishingly long, pearly-coral thumbnail—'as a script writer. Free-lance. Television.'

'Oh, I see!' I was impressed. That certainly beat being a junior history and geography mistress at Mrs Lofting's School for Girls.

'She writes commercials, advertising jingles,' Fergus said, and Gillian frowned at him. 'What's your latest, Foxie—you know, the Fluffywhip one? Oh, yes, I remember: "Try Fluffy-whip for a really rare topping: No one eats it west of Wapping."'

'That's not how it goes at all,' Gillian said petulantly. We waited. She opened her mouth, closed it. 'I've forgotten how it goes, as a matter of fact.'

We both laughed, and Fergus consoled her:

'Never mind, old girl, I know you don't do it for the money. There is no money in it. Tell you what, I'll treat you birds to lunch—lunch being bangers and bitter at the pub.'

Gillian sighed. I would have declined this ominous-sounding repast because Patrick was due at his music teacher's at two, but just then the carousel faded to a stop, Patrick bounded towards us, and Fergus immediately put the invitation to him.

'Oh, Aunt Sarah, could we?' Patrick's face was alight with expectation. I remembered the gloom and stillness of the house on Cheyne Walk.

'All right,' I said, 'if Fergus wants us. But your music lesson's at two. And—' to Fergus—'I thought children weren't allowed in pubs?'

'Ah, we know one right on the Embankment, with a garden. It's all right if they're outside. This one has tables, benches and about fifteen neighbourhood dogs. Just the place for a spot of orange squash and a big, fat sausage, eh, Pat lad?'

'Oh, yes!'

So off we went, the four of us, back over Albert Bridge, the gayest of bridges, its sturdy blue pillars and red-and-white portholes seeming but an extension of the Fun Fair we left behind. The Thames glittered; ducks bobbed like corks on the incoming tide. Fergus and I padded along behind Gillian and Patrick, and even the impressive sight of Gillian's bottom, moving insouciantly before us in glove-tight plum-coloured corduroy trousers, in a walk I could not hope to emulate, did not dim my cheerfulness as we neared the Chelsea shore.

FIVE

Patrick's music teacher lived at the top of Danvers Street, a short street running north off Cheyne Walk into Paulton's Square and King's Road. We barely got there on the hour— I dragged Patrick along at a fast trot after our leisurely lunch—and we were both panting when I handed him over to his teacher. I was to come for him at four she said. Two hours seemed to me a long time for a five-year-old's piano lesson, but I learned that part of the time was given over to a group lesson with other children and part to tea, an arrangement that considerably enhanced the appointment in Patrick's eyes.

I leant against the front railing to catch my breath. Paulton's Square was a pretty place, with rows of white-fronted nine-teenth-century terrace houses facing a fenced garden in the centre. The doors of the houses were painted in an assortment of bright colours, and the window-boxes spilled over with low-growing plants and flowers that crowded each other for survival. Space, light, room to breathe—it seemed that the struggle to survive never ended. London had come to terms with the problem better than most places, I reflected, at least in Chelsea. I was struck by the remarkable quiet of these small back-streets; once one was out of the bustle of King's Road, Chelsea was almost village-like. I walked back towards the river, north again up Lawrence Street, across Upper Cheyne Row and Phene Street, and down to the river once more by Chelsea Manor Street. The streets were not only quiet but almost empty. In the course of my walk I saw only three people: a charwoman putting out milk bottles, a man in salmon-coloured trousers walking a dog, a mechanic lying under a car.

I turned west and headed home. The traffic on the Embankment was noisy, but somehow it did not disrupt the peaceful-ness of the mellow brick houses that bordered it. I saw that some of the houses had round blue plaques embedded in their walls: George Eliot, I read; Rossetti; Swinburne; and some-where in the neighbourhood, I knew, had lived Carlyle, Henry

28

James, Leigh Hunt, Oscar Wilde, and Turner and Whistler. These houses had known acts of creation and destruction that I could hardly conceive of; the blue plaques were like badges conferred, delayed seals of respectability and acclaim. Across the Thames loomed the distinctly non-Georgian towers and chimneys of Battersea. The four lean smokestacks of a power plant shot up in the air like the legs of a dead sheep on its back. Elsewhere the buildings were squarish, blunted. A sign rampaged across the front of a paper company's warehouse, declaring its waspish message to the opposite, richer shore: 'Thousands of Pounds Wasted Daily. Save Your Waste Paper.' Means and ends facing themselves, I thought; but for once the disparity between servant and master, labour and idleness did not trouble me.

Chelsea on that autumn afternoon was more welcoming, more golden, more promising of civilized pleasures and surprises than any place I had yet known. I felt extraordinarily light-headed and happy as I strolled along, touching each bar of the wrought-iron railings that ran along the front of the neighbouring gardens. The house on Cheyne Walk was mine for the afternoon; Jane and Mrs Chalmers would not be in till evening. I looked up at the house, sun-lit and stately in the full glow of afternoon. Was it only yesterday that I had found it so forbidding?

I stepped inside, tossed my bag on the hall table, walked into the parlour and threw myself with a self-indulgent sigh on the old velvet sofa.

'Do make yourself at home.'

I sat up with a start. My eyes were unaccustomed to the interior darkness. Then I saw a very tall man leaning against the library table at the far side of the room, his head cocked to one side, examining me.

'I ... didn't know anyone was here,' I said in confusion.

'Obviously.'

'I live here,' I added, hesitantly, as if in fact I did not.

'Oh?'

'I'm Sarah Pierce, Mr Vivian's sister-in-law.'

'How do you do, Miss Pierce.'

The coolness of the man! He continued to loll against the table, interrogating me with his eyes. His glance wandered up and down my body, appraisingly, and yet so aloofly that I felt not so much insulted as patronized.

'And whom did you come to see, may I ask? And how did you get in?' I spoke quickly. My chagrin was giving way to anger.

29

'Through the door, to the second question, and you, to the first,' he said, stepping forwards.

I jumped to my feet. There was no doubt now that the man was being insolent.

He stopped in the middle of the room. 'I'm sorry. Perhaps I have startled you. But then, you startled me. You were not quite what I expected from Sophie's description. Allow me to introduce myself: I am Charles Vivian.'

My previous dismay was nothing to what I felt then. A sinking feeling came over me, I had blundered once more. But I had also been provoked. What right did this man have, no matter who he was, to play such games?

I did not have much chance for reflection. He gestured that I should sit down again, and the gesture was as compelling as if he had drawn me down with both hands. I found myself holding a large glass of sherry and listening to an amiable monologue about his trip to the Continent, where his business had been concluded earlier than he had expected, about Patrick's schooling, the house, the garden, the deplorable increase of traffic on the Embankment, as if our coming together had occurred in the most routine manner. I sank back against the velvet cushions helplessly.

He had seated himself at the other end of the sofa, full in the afternoon sunshine, and I could see him plainly now. He had a long face with a strong chin and a large but well-shaped nose; his features were more coarse than fine, but undeniably handsome; his hair was dark and thick, with no trace of grey in it, though I knew him to be in his late thirties; the eyes, which I took to be black were, I saw, when he turned towards me, a glowing hazel; intelligent eyes, unexpectedly merry, I thought, considering all he had been through. In spite of his age and his air of complete self-possession, there was something about him that made me think of the pictures of English schoolboys in my childhood books: perhaps it was the eyes, or the unruly hair falling over the forehead.

'... quite lost.'

'Excuse me?'

'I was saying that until now—until you—Patrick and I have been quite lost.'

'Oh?'

'We aren't used to living without women.'

They were ordinary words, spoken casually, but to me they had an explicitly sexual ring. I felt him looking at me; I stared in embarrassment at the arabesques in the carpet.

'What's the matter? Have I said something wrong? You are a woman, aren't you?'

I looked up at him then. He was smiling faintly, mockingly, and my confusion increased. 'I don't know how we ever got onto this subject. In regard to you and Patrick being "lost", Patrick seems perfectly all right to me. In fact, I hardly see why my presence here is necessary!'

'Don't be taken in by his ebullience. He may seem to be taking things in his stride, but he often wakes up screaming at night, and he has developed a tremendous fear of heights. Not that you've been here long enough to know.' I thought guiltily of the morning's adventure on the tree-walk. 'Jane Burrows means well,' he continued, 'but she's hardly more than a child herself. And Mrs Chalmers—to put it kindly, she doesn't have much warmth to spare for anyone.' He shrugged. 'No, you provide Patrick with a link with his mother. You give some continuity to his life, and that's what he wants and needs. Besides, what am I to do? Send him off at his age to a boarding school or hire some stranger from an agency? And my sister can't stand children; she keeps dogs. No, I can assure you that you could not be any more useful in Boston than you are here, if that's what's worrying your conscience.'

'Well, whatever continuity I provide for Patrick won't last long. I have to be back in Boston in January. That's when the new term starts.'

'Oh, come now, why do you have to go back so soon? Will Mrs Lofting's female school crumble without you?'

'I can hardly stay here.'

'Why not? You don't take up much space, and you don't look as if you'll eat us out of house and home.' He was referring, I knew, to my 'spareness', as my father called it, and his smile taunted me again. 'Or perhaps you think that staying in the same house with me would be improper—or unusual?'

'Both.'

'Perhaps you're right. And neither of us can afford a scandal, can we? Not that I suppose you have any vices, have you, Miss Pierce—or may I call you Sarah?'

His joking offended me. 'No vices that I care to make public.'

'Private vices, public virtues. Or vice versa. Which is better?' His eyes were very bright, the pupils mere pinpricks. 'Do stay, Sarah!' He leaned forward suddenly, his eyes holding mine. 'We could stand a little New England uprightness here. One tires of the bohemian life. Chelsea breeds sinners—it always has.'

31

'Patrick doesn't strike me as a sinner, nor do you. And the life in this house can hardly be called bohemian. Mrs Chalmers runs a tight ship, I can see that.'

'Yes, she does, alas. Well, then, we must do what we can to liven things up a bit, so you won't leave us too soon. There must be a man or two lurking about—why is it that personable men are so hard to find, compared to personable women? I'll have to give it some thought. Let's see, perhaps ...'

'How can you talk so frivolously?' I burst out.

'What? Have I touched on a delicate subject? Perhaps there is someone at home ...?'

'I mean, how can you talk about such trivia with Sophie not two months dead!' My voice was trembling with the anger and bewilderment this man stirred up in me. We had sat here bandying words, drinking sherry, fencing. The whole encounter filled me with distaste. I felt the need to shake myself free of it and to get hold of what had happened, of what I had been putting off, putting off ever since I had learned that Sophie was dead. I put my glass down hard on the table and stood up.

'Tell me exactly what happened. I want to see where she died.'

He replied coldly, without moving: 'Look in the back garden, then. We don't keep resident bloodstains.'

'I want to see where she fell from.'

'The garret? Sophie's attic we called it. There's nothing there—an old desk, an easel, some books.'

'I don't want to see her belongings. I want to know what happened—where, how, why? No one has told me anything. Your cable, your letter gave only the barest facts.'

'It was not a fancy death, Sarah.'

'Show me where she fell from.' My voice was as hard as his. This stubbornness was unlike me.

There was silence. I looked at him. He was staring straight ahead, not at me. I felt a pang of conscience. How could I know what he had gone through in putting to rest memories of Sophie? Now I had stirred them up, blundering again. I was about to speak, but he pulled himself up from the sofa and, still without looking at me, walked to the door.

'This way.'

He started climbing the stairs, and I followed. His long legs took the steps two at a time. Two, three, four flights without pause, the crimson of the stair-carpet darkening as we mounted to the uppermost reaches of the house. At the top a black door faced us, slightly ajar. He pushed it open. We were in a

32

narrow, slant-ceilinged room that ran the width of the house. The only light came from a pair of french windows cut into the wall on the north side, overlooking the garden. The furniture was sparse: a large, old roll-top desk with a green-shaded bulb hanging from a cord above it; a gaunt sofa and chair covered in black horsehair and separated by a small, hooked rug, its colours faded past recognition; a full-length easel leaned against one wall, and piles of books were stacked on the floor on either side of it. The room was cold, monastic. I felt as if I were inside a coffin.

'This was Sophie's attic?' My voice rose on a note of incredulity. Charles was looking at me with the suspicion of a smile on his face.

'Yes, it was her favourite room, her retreat.'

'Retreat from what?'

'My dear Sarah,' and the note of mockery had returned to his voice, 'it is quite clear that you have never been married, or you would know how desirable and indeed necessary it is to retreat at times from the mayhem of married life, even from a most loving husband and son.'

'You were happy together, then?' I could have bit my tongue off after asking the question, but he only replied:

'*Pourquoi pas?*'

The twisting away into another language was both a withdrawal and a reprimand. I returned hastily to the subject that had brought us to this chilly room:

'How did she die? Tell me exactly.'

'You make everything sound so easy. It's the way of you Americans. So abrupt and direct, yet so rhetorical.'

'Had she been sick?' I persisted. If I was going to be typed as an ugly American, I would live up to the name.

'In the best of health.'

'Depressed?'

'Depressed? No, not at the time. She had her ups and downs, of course, like the rest of us. She did seem under a strain, I think, or as if her mind were ... elsewhere.'

The latter I could well imagine. I knew Sophie's span of attention and her willingness to devote herself to any one object to be brief. Had something—or someone—other than Charles and Patrick come into her life?

'These questions—' Charles' voice cut through my meditation—'are you suggesting that her death was not an accident but a suicide?'

His words startled and shocked me, though surely my own mind had been drifting unconsciously in the same direction.

33

'I'm not suggesting anything. I'm simply trying to find out what happened. The truth.'

Charles looked at me levelly. His eyes held no hint of mockery in them now: 'It has occurred to me that her death may look like a suicide, but I reject the idea. I have never known anyone so tenacious of life as Sophie. Through all her moods, her anxieties, she lived with extraordinary gusto.'

We fell silent. Both of us had known that gusto. Motes of dust floated in the air over the roll-top desk, making it into a giant, golden honey-hive in the rays of sunlight. It looked like the old desk in our grandfather's study in Quincy; Sophie and I had often climbed up on it and slid down its shiny, corrugated surface. Yes, suicide was unlike the Sophie I had known. But what was it about this house that filled me with morbid thoughts, overbore me with a sense of conflict and violence?

I walked over to the windows. Charles sat down in the horsehair chair and began to speak in an expressionless voice:

'It was a Sunday night in August. Sophie and Patrick had gone to our cottage in Sussex a few days earlier; they planned to stay there a week or ten days while I was on business in Brussels. Jane Burrows was on her annual leave. Mrs Chalmers, who had spent the week-end at her sister's, came in early on Monday morning. It was she who found Sophie, at about nine o'clock. Sophie had fallen from there'—he pointed to the balcony that I could just make out on the other side of the veiled french windows—'to the flagstone terrace that joins the house and the garden, a drop of some sixty feet. The coroner said that she had been dead about eight or ten hours and must have died instantly, neck broken and skull fractured on the flagstones. She was spared death by impalement, at least— her dress ripped on the iron spikes of the basement railings, but her body fell free.'

I shuddered, though I had got what I had asked for, a graphic description. And yet—

'How could she have fallen? You say it was her sanctuary. She must have known this attic and the balcony like the back of her hand.'

'Oh, yes, she did. But it was easy. There was no balcony.'

'What!'

'We were in the midst of alterations. Sophie had been worried about the balcony for some time. The flooring was thin and uneven, and the railings were low; she wanted the balcony strengthened and widened, both to make it safer for Patrick and to accommodate her easel and painting equipment. She had directed the builders to remove the old balcony and to

34

put up a new one during the period we were to be out of the house. The night she returned and came up here, she must have opened the french windows by habit and stepped out: she always preferred to sit outside, as well as to paint outside, in warm weather. There was virtually nothing there. The workmen had taken down the old balcony but hadn't put up the new one yet. The scaffolding was there, the skeleton, but no floor, no railings.'

'How terrible!'

'Yes.'

'But since she had ordered the work herself, she must have known what to expect. She would not simply have walked out unthinkingly.'

'No, it doesn't seem likely. But the clue must lie in what you just said, "unthinkingly". If she was not thinking about the alterations to the balcony, if she had her mind on something else, was distracted, anxious, she might very well have thrown open the windows and stepped out—and off—to her death.'

I reflected on this and could see the likelihood of it. Sophie's mind had often juggled several things at once, and none for long. But there was something else. What was it? Oh yes—

'But why did she come back to the house at all? You said she planned to stay in Sussex till the next week, yet she returned to the house only a few days after she left it.'

'I don't know why she came back. She left Patrick with the Baileys, our neighbours in the country, early on Sunday evening. Sophie told them only that she had to go up to London and asked them if they could keep Patrick for her. Ann Bailey said that she seemed nervous, tense. She didn't give any reason for the trip. She gave Patrick a last hug and then drove away in her little sports car, a mile a minute. Of course, she always drives fast, like a gangster making a getaway.' He smiled, remembering, then recollected himself. 'Sorry!'

I was not thinking about the speed of Sophie's driving. I was thinking about the suddenness of her trip to London. Had she come to keep an appointment? If so, it must have been a very private sort of appointment, for she had disclosed nothing of it to the Baileys despite leaving Patrick with them. Had she come to the house to meet a lover in her husband's absence? But why would she have come to the attic—to this bare, austere room? Still, adulterers had no doubt bedded down on harder spots than a horsehair sofa.

But why should I suspect her of adultery? Except that from the time she was a young woman Sophie had always 'had'

35

men—her term for her relationships. But is it fair to judge
of present by past behaviour? Perhaps it was my own innocence that made me imagine sexual intrigue whenever I thought
of Sophie. But what else could have brought her to a deserted
house in the middle of the night?

Charles had opened the french windows to let some fresh
air into the dank room. I walked over to the balcony and
looked out over the brick-walled garden. Roses, dahlias and
chrysanthemums were still blooming thickly in the beds that
bordered the lawn, and a knotted, looping hedge of blackberry
brambles was heavy with fruit at the western wall. Lilac shrubs
bordered the entrance to the path that curved its way lazily
to the bottom of the garden. Next to the house were the black
iron spikes of the basement fence and, adjoining that, the
flagstone terrace. The horror of the event, remembered, made
me recoil. I stepped back abruptly and rammed into Charles
—the jolt threw me forward again and I clutched at the balcony railing. He caught me under the elbows and held me
firmly.

'Let's not make it two of you, please. I can't have you both
on my head.'

I hastened to free myself and withdrew into the safety of
the garret. I was shaking, but I could not let the subject rest:

'Does Patrick know what happened?'

'Yes, I told him that his mother had fallen to her death.
Truth is best for children, don't you think?'

'Not only for children.'

'You demand a lot of people, don't you, Sarah?' Was it
amusement or contempt that I heard in his voice? He looked
at me warily. 'Well, anyway, Patrick knows as much as anyone. He didn't know right away. The Baileys offered to keep
him in the country for two weeks, until term began. The day
I brought him home I told him what had happened. He's very
young; he couldn't take it in at first. After school he would
burst into the house, Jane tells me, and go bounding up the
stairs to the attic, expecting Sophie to be here to welcome him.
They used to have tea here every day. In the past fortnight
he has stopped doing this; he refuses to come up here. He's
afraid, I suppose, of what he won't find.'

Their loss sank into me for the first time.

'How have you managed?'

'How does anyone manage? We go on doing the same old
things.' He sighed. 'Patrick's only five, you know. He's forgetting, I think.'

There was a tiredness and a gentleness in his voice that I

36

had not heard before. I closed the windows and turned back to him. He was sprawled in the small armchair, his long legs stretched wearily before him, his arms dangling over the edges, like some stranded Gulliver in a shrunken land.

'But he has not forgotten yet, nor have I. So we need you, Sarah ... both of us.' His voice was soft now, barely audible, his large head thrown back on the chair, his eyes closed.

What reply I would have made was not made, not then, and what new level of understanding we might have entered on, I do not know, for that moment chimes reverberated through the house: the clock at the bottom of the hall was striking the hour.

'Four o'clock! I've forgotten Patrick! The music lesson is over!'

I ran down the stairs, my pulse racing faster than my feet.

SIX

Patrick sat on a low hassock, solemnly eating chips, dipping each in the yolk of a fried egg that had grown cold on his plate. I sat across from him on Sophie's pale blue chaise-longue, sewing buttons on a blouse. We were silent, but it was a companionable silence. A full day of school is exhausting for a five-year-old, I mused; and the days were cold now, darkness dropped early as the end of November neared. We seldom moved far from the fire on these bleak afternoons. We had taken to having tea together—supper for Patrick— in Sophie's bedroom, my bedroom I should say. The room was warm and bright, and the child seemed to like it here, removed from the reach of Jane and Mrs Chalmers. Here he was never scolded for spilling milk on the rug or not sitting up straight—I was not much of a disciplinarian with children, though I tried to be. Patrick liked to look at the photographs on the dresser, and Sophie's knick-knacks, and the books I had brought him from America with pictures of cowboys and Indians and astronauts.

With six years of teaching under my belt, I had prided myself on knowing how to deal with young children, but living with a five-year-old night and day, entertaining him, consoling him, was more of a job than I had bargained for. Patrick had no playmates outside of school hours, and he did not know how to read yet. I bought him blocks, cars, puzzles and joined him in running his train, but somehow our diversions petered out very quickly. There was no television set in the house— Sophie had always hated television—and even if there had been one, I doubt that it would have held Patrick, for his span of attention was short. We muddled on as best we could, though, and I reminded myself of Charles' words, that what the child needed was simply the semblance, failing the substance, of a mother.

Although Patrick could not read, he liked being read to— I have never met a child who does not—and books served better than anything else to pass the hours. Sometimes, too,

38

he would spread the book before him on the floor and try to copy the letters or pictures. He had a strong sense of design and a delight in colours, much as his mother had had. I looked up from my sewing and saw that he had finished his tea and was down on the floor once more with his crayons and paper, copying out letters of vastly uneven size from a magazine beside him.

'Mama was always writing things, Aunt Sarah.'

'Writing things? What sort of things—letters, do you mean?'

'No, not letters. I don't know what they were. She wrote things down in little blue books, the kind we have at school.' He drew himself up on his elbows and looked at his work appraisingly. 'She said it made her feel ver-chus.'

'Ver-chus?' I supposed he meant 'virtuous'. I smiled, not so much at him as at the unconscious, uncanny mimicry of Sophie's voice, at once petulant and complacent. It occurred to me that the little blue books must have been diaries, which Sophie had been in the habit of keeping, faithfully and meticulously, since she was a schoolgirl. It was a habit that surprised me, for Sophie did not take pains over many things other than her painting; and certainly as a correspondent she had been cursory and erratic. Still, her own thoughts, activities and feelings had always mattered most to her, and she saw no need to share them, least of all with her family. What had she shared with Charles, I wondered? If I had a husband, I would share everything with him. Especially if I had a husband like Charles, so abrupt, so difficult to please, and yet—I sensed—so responsive to women. To one woman, anyway ...

'But he whom I seek is a King.'

'What?' I looked down at Patrick in astonishment.

'But he whom I seek is a King—how can this poor babe be he? Those are my lines, Aunt Sarah. I forgot to tell you. We're having a play at school, and I'm the Second King. I brought my lines home. Miss Trimble says I have to learn them by heart. I know the beginning already. I've only got one more. The Inn-keeper and the Angel have the most.'

He took a crumpled piece of paper out of the pocket of his grey-flannel shorts and handed it to me. I read a few lines. It was a simple dramatization of the Christmas story. Ah, I thought, now this was something I could do—how often I had coached my schoolgirls in the rites of the Nativity!

'I have to have a costume, too. You have to make one,' said Patrick, with something of his mother's peremptoriness.

'Well, now—what do kings wear?'

'Crowns and bathrobes. That's what they wore last year,

39

Miss Trimble said. We can make the crown out of cardboard and aluminium wrap. That's what John Woodleigh did. He's First King. The robes have to be long and soft, and red or blue would be best. Mama had something like that. Let's see . . .'

He jumped up, walked over to the wall of cupboards lining one side of the dressing-room, and pushed the sliding doors apart. That vast closet, I was sure, had been Sophie's doing: she had loved clothes. I had not touched the cupboard since I came, despite Mrs Chalmers' injunction. Patrick stared up gravely at the rows of dresses, shoes, coats and scarves laid out in shining order.

'That's for you, and this is for me,' Patrick said with decision. He had climbed upon a chair and pulled down a blue velvet dressing-gown and a red silk cape. 'You're Jesus' mother, just pretend. And this can be Jesus.' He took the china-headed doll from the rocker and wrapped it in the eiderdown from the bed. 'You hold it on your lap, and I'll come with my gift of frankimmense.' He examined me critically. 'You have to looked tired. Mama said babies make you tired.'

I laughed and held out my arms obligingly for the doll and arranged the blue robe around my shoulders.

'Now I'll get ready. Would you fasten this, please?' I fastened the red cape around him. 'All right, now you sit still with the baby and I'll come with my gift. What can we use for that?' I handed him my sewing kit. 'All right. Now, what do I say again?'

We went over the lines together, and he carried them off well, though 'frankincense' repeatedly came out 'frankimmense'. He wanted to get it exactly right. 'One more time,' he said, and marched towards me: 'I bring a gift of frank-imcense to lay at his royal feet.' I smiled in what I hoped was a demure and properly tired manner and lifted the swaddled doll to see the offering.

'Bravo!' came a voice from behind us. Patrick and I spun round. Charles was leaning against the doorway, still in his overcoat, cheeks red from the cold. 'You're trafficking in exotic stuff, Patrick. Frankincense. And bringing it to children, too —disgraceful! But then, what a fair lady you have to serve, the Queen of Heaven, no less.'

Patrick, confused, jumped up from his kneeling position. Why did Charles have to use that ironic manner towards the boy, I wondered angrily? Indeed, with almost everyone. I had seen too much of it.

'It's a play for school, Daddy. For Christmas. It's about—'
40

'You don't have to tell me,' Charles interrupted. 'I know the story. The infant King was born to Mary and Joseph. But Joseph wasn't really the father, was he? Who was the father, Patrick? Do you know?'

'God.'

'Of course. Or so the rumour went. In any case, Joseph went along with it. He was only an old man, and protective of his wife's honour, not to mention his own. But what about the Virgin Mary? A lovely young woman, and yet so hypocritical.'

I stared at him, aghast at his flippancy.

'We're finished now. I know my lines,' Patrick murmured. Then: 'Will you and Aunt Sarah come to the play, Daddy?' The child was resilient, undaunted by or perhaps hardened to his father's habitual irony. How distant they were, for father and son!

'If I'm free that day, we'd be delighted to come—wouldn't we, Aunt Sarah?' Charles said 'Aunt Sarah' in the same derisive tone as 'Virgin Mary'.

'Yes, of course.'

'But you'd better get "frankincense" right. I don't want a son of mine bungling things. Words are important. "Frankincense." Say it.'

'Frankincense.'

'Right. Now run along to Jane. It's bedtime, and she's waiting for you in your room. I want to talk to Aunt Sarah.'

Patrick left the room with a quiet 'good night', not even asking for a bedtime snack or story—much more docile with Charles than he was with me. What tyrants parents are, I thought!

'Why do you treat the child that way?' I burst out.

'What way?' He looked at me in astonishment.

'With, oh, coolness amounting to contempt.'

'I'm not contemptuous of *him*, God knows, only of the foolish way that most people treat children, and the nonsense —like that Nativity rot—that they hand out to them.'

'By "most people" you mean me, I take it?'

'Don't flatter yourself, my dear Sarah. I do not mean you. You strike me as rather a mild Christian. There is more of the prig than of the fanatic about you, and I have never found priggishness unsusceptible to cure.'

'What's the cure?'

He smiled down at me, an unexpected dimple coming and going in his cheek, his long body leaning towards me. I had

41

never before been so aware of his physical presence. I sat up with a start.

'Don't worry, Sarah, I'm not about to pounce on you. That chaise-longue you're sitting on is too fragile, for one thing. Sophie and I tried it once.'

He laughed and turned away, picked up the fallen cape and tossed it in my lap.

'You're ... impossible!'

'When I think nastily, I speak nastily. We must give some token to the world of what we are. Your man Hawthorne said that, I believe.'

'He's not "my man Hawthorne".'

'American, that is to say. New England, Puritan. But no, not your man. He whom you seek is a king—and you wouldn't settle for less, would you? Sophie was less—fastidious.' He laughed again, but there was no merriment in it.

I was silent. His words confused and wounded me. What had I done to provoke them? I could not look at him; all I wanted was that he should go away.

'Before you throw me out, I'll leave. I came up here to give you some news: we're having company for dinner tonight.'

'Tonight!' Then I did look at him. 'But it's seven-thirty already!'

'Don't worry. He won't be here for another hour, and Mrs Chalmers has everything in hand. It's one of my old school friends, Henry Hobbett-Gore. Not that I invited him for that reason—I can't stand my old school friends these days. I honoured him with an invitation because he's the most influential member of the selection committee.'

'The selection committee?'

'In the constituency where I have a chance of standing as candidate for MP in the next election. Which is probably not far away, if you've been able to plumb Britain's entrancingly complex economic situation.'

'I read the papers, if that's what you mean.'

'A good start, by all means. And it shows perseverance— the print of *The Times* is hard on the eyes. Now, I should like Hobbett-Gore to leave our house this evening with the impression that I have more wit, charm, intelligence and zeal for the public good—'

'Including morals?'

'—Including other people's morals—than any other potential candidate. In short, he must go away convinced that I have what it takes to get a Tory into that particular seat, which is

42

now held by Labour. Am I not winningly zealous already?'

He was, indeed, and I realized that it was the prospect of securing a nomination that had made him so jaunty. He had not raised the subject before with me of his political ambitions; it was only from Fergus' hint that first afternoon in Battersea that I had any inkling of it. It occurred to me that Charles was a man who did not like to fail at anything, so that only when a goal was within his reach would he talk about it. Nor did he discuss his work as a solicitor. When I thought about it, it was hard to say what we did talk about during the few hours that we spent together each week: books, the day's headlines, something that Patrick had said or done; whatever the subject, it somehow ended up smaller than life, reduced by Charles' ironic and slighting manner. He would undoubtedly make a very clever MP with his knack of 'putting things in perspective'.

'So that's the challenge—and you will help me, Sarah.'

'I?'

'Yes. I could have taken Hobbett-Gore to my club for dinner, but it's not the same as a home-cooked meal, is it, with a female face to look at over the wine?' He smiled at me. 'So, I should like you to dress carefully and charmingly— as you always do, of course. And moderate your New England twang, please. And don't go on too much about how things are done in Boston. We don't feel the same way about the colonies as you do, you know.'

It was typical of Charles to flatter a person in one breath and flay him in the next. Like Patrick, though, I was beginning to acquire some protective armour as the weeks went by.

'Perhaps you'd rather I didn't come downstairs at all. Why don't you and Mr Hobbett-Gore dine *à deux*? I'm not sure I can alter my accent in so short a time.'

'Oh yes, you'll manage. We'll dine at eight-thirty, as usual. I rang Mrs Chalmers at noon to tell her there'd be a guest for dinner.'

Oh, you did, did you, I thought? Well, Mrs Chalmers had not said anything to me—but that was only one more indication of my unnecessary presence in this house. My expression must have registered my feelings, for Charles added, almost kindly:

'I want you there, Sarah. I like to see you sitting across the table from me. You're much prettier than Hobbett-Gore, I can assure you.'

With that he walked out of the room, and I was alone. I sat there despondently, a velvet-shrouded figure in the mirror

43

across the room. The hands of the clock on the dresser moved silently onward. A dinner to dress for, a face to prepare.

And what about dinner? Should I see what was going on in the kitchen? Probably Mrs Chalmers had gone on a shopping spree during the afternoon and come home with her capacious shopping-cart bulging in all directions; she preferred doing her own shopping to having orders sent in. She was undeniably a good cook. Once, when my mother was complaining about some squabble in the kitchen, my father had said that from his experience in the army (he might as well have said in a Chinese opium den, so unlikely did that circumstance seem) he was convinced that all cooks were irritable and all good cooks were bastards. The word 'bastards' had trembled in the air over the family dinner-table, and Molly, the serving-girl, had poured a ladleful of gravy into my mother's lap. Oh yes, best to keep away at all times from cooks and kitchens. Still, Charles had designated me as hostess for the evening, and I probably ought at least to check on the meal—or would that be a reflection on Mrs Chalmers' capabilities? I could not decide. For the daughter of a family that prided itself on decorum (my father's saying 'bastards' aloud was the exception that proved the rule), I was a sorry product. Out of no stronger feeling, in the end, than curiosity, I decided to have a look below.

As I descended to the basement, the mouth-watering smell of lamb roasting with rosemary and garlic came up to meet me. I thought of Patrick already tucked away in bed. It was a pity that children were shut out from the pleasures of a grown-up dinner. Oh well, he would get some lamb tomorrow, cold or warmed-up, for supper. At the bottom of the stairs, the kitchen came into view, a brightly lit cauldron of steam and odours. The brightness made me blink; I paused in the short, dark corridor that led to it. Mrs Chalmers was poised above a large stock pot, a spoon held critically to her nose. Jane Burrows was peeling onions and sniffling. Suddenly Mrs Chalmers lifted her head and addressed Jane:

'Mr Vivian will have to watch his ways if he's going into Parliament. That girl was here last night again. Till three in the morning!' Her low voice smouldered into a laugh.

'Hmmn,' said Jane, wiping her eyes.

'She's good-looking, of course, and not too bright. Vulgar, I'd say.'

'Hmmn,' said Jane again.

Mrs Chalmers took the lid off a saucepan and the smell of cauliflower filled the steamy room. She prodded the large white head reflectively. 'Miss Pierce is not vulgar, I'll say that for her. Pity she's short on looks.'

'Oh, do you think so?' cried Jane. 'I think she's lovely! So tall, and all that long, silky hair and the way she twists it up, like a Danish pastry—I wish she'd show me how to do it!'

'Well, depends on your taste, I suppose. I can't imagine she's much to the master's taste!' She hooted again, and began to grate a hunk of cheese violently. 'She seems to be getting on all right with the boy, at least. Surprises me—I thought he'd need someone with more vim and vigour. Someone like his mother—not that we want *her* sort in the house again!' A pile of pale yellow shreds mounted beneath her hand. 'I tell you this, my girl'—she shook the grater at Jane, and bits of cheese exploded in all directions—'whatever he's up to now, he's only getting his own back!'

'Oh, Mrs Chalmers, don't speak ill of the dead!' Jane dropped her knife, and the strength of her emotion made her eyes water more furiously than ever.

'No,' Mrs Chalmers subsided, 'it was a hideous way to die. Those french windows were locked, though, and bolted. They can't blame *us*.' She stirred a pan of white sauce firmly. 'Three months now, seems longer. The boy's taken it pretty well, considering. He's as unpredictable as ever, though. Nobody ever disciplined him except me. He's more mine than hers, in a way.' Jane wiped her eyes on her apron; Mrs Chalmers smiled to herself. 'She let him do anything, so long as they had good times together, laughing and carrying on, the two of them, like a couple of babies. A child can't learn too early that life's a business, not good cheer.' She pursed her lips as she stirred a cup of milk into the pan. 'That was a good idea, keeping him in the country for a while afterwards. Boys like country. Which reminds me, Jane—Mr Vivian's going down to the country tomorrow. We'll save the pudding till Sunday supper. It's his favourite. He's having company at the cottage, I suppose.'

'Strange time of year to be having company, in that cold place.' Jane sniffed. 'Did he say who it was?'

'He never says who it is. You know that.' She dumped the cheese into the white sauce authoritatively. 'I have my suspicions, though!' She laughed knowingly and bent over the stove, peering at the sauce with her huge, black, near-sighted eyes.

Suddenly I was filled with panic. I wondered if I could get back to my room without being heard; I dared not be found out now. My mind went back over the conversation as I crept

45

up the stairs, and the stabs of shock did not subside. I reached the bedroom and closed the door gratefully. I felt as if I had been bombarded from all sides.

It was after eight now. Hobbett-Gore would be here at any minute. I bathed and dressed hurriedly. I could not have felt less in a mood for entertaining. I looked in the mirror: my face was pale, and there were shadows under my eyes. Even my favourite necklace of cairngorms did little to brighten the reflection. I brushed my hair and put on some mascara. I looked like a sleep-walker, and my lashes felt sticky. How did other women ever get themselves put together? Short on looks —yes, Mrs Chalmers, despite Jane's tribute—and brains as well. Why had I stood there so stupidly, neither walking right into the kitchen nor retreating at once? Passive, indecisive; a born ditherer. I deserved what I got.

I looked around the room. The clothes we had used in our masquerade lay scattered across the rug. I began picking them up; I had always felt a need to put things in order, a compulsion that Sophie had never shown. How could two children born of the same parents be so different? Her blue velvet dressing-gown lay in a heap beside the chaise-longue. I scooped it from the floor and held it up to me; blue was Sophie's colour, not mine, but it was a lovely gown. I smoothed the shoulders over a coathanger and tied the gold-tasselled sash around the waist. There was hardly room in the clothes-cupboard for it; I wedged it in as best I could, and tucked the sleeves in carefully towards the centre. As I did so, I felt something flat and hard against the soft fabric. I pulled out the robe and shook it, but nothing fell out. Then I saw that the full sleeves had slits at the wrist making deep pockets, like a Japanese kimono. I put in my hand and drew out a thin, blue book, the sort that children use in school as exercise books. I recognized the round, childlike script on the cover at once, but the words were hard to decipher, blurred by coffee rings. I made out:

HOW I SPENT MY SUMMER HOLIDAYS

by Sophie Pierce

'Pierce', not 'Vivian' ... she had not been married, then. And the title was that of the composition we had been required to write at the beginning of every school year in Cambridge. But Sophie had not owned this robe when she lived with us in Cambridge, I was sure of that. Could this be one of the little blue books that Patrick had mentioned—a diary, perhaps?— and was the title a joke on Sophie's part?

I turned over the cover and read half a page. The doorbell

46

rang, but it hardly distracted me. Yes, it was a diary. I closed the notebook and stood there holding it, wondering what to do. I had already been burned once that evening, eavesdropping on a private conversation. And Sophie and I had been brought up very strictly not to read other people's mail or to interfere with each other's belongings, and I, at least, had observed the stricture. Sophie had hoarded things like a magpie—bits of jewellery, odd buttons and ribbons, dance programmes, notes from her boy-friends, bleached shells from Cape Cod summers —and shrieked if I so much as borrowed a pin from her. I looked down at the blue notebook with the familiar hand-writing. The impulse I had had to read it was gone. I did not really want to hear about Sophie's life at all. It was not mine, and it was finished. It came to me, viciously, that I would be happy not to see, hear or speak her name again.

I tried to shove the notebook back into the sleeve of the robe but could not get it through the opening. I dropped the book and the robe in disgust, and went downstairs. I was already late, but for once I did not care. The evening, I thought, could not hold any more rebukes or surprises for me than it had already provided.

SEVEN

Low, male voices were coming from the drawing-room as I reached the first floor. The smell of a wood fire and freshly cut chrysanthemums was strong in the air. Charles, or Mrs Chalmers, was entertaining in style, I thought cynically—the guest of the evening was getting more of a welcome than I had received on my arrival at Cheyne Walk. I did not pause but walked straight into the room. The two men rose at once.

'Good evening, Sarah. I was beginning to wonder if you had forgotten us?' Charles' voice was cool. 'May I present Henry Hobbett-Gore? Henry, my sister-in-law, Miss Pierce, visiting us from America.'

I held out my hand, and Mr Hobbett-Gore bent so low over it that for one awful moment I was afraid he was going to kiss it. I saw thin strands of sandy hair combed carefully over a ruddy scalp. He straightened up to all of his short height and beamed at me.

'A pleasure to meet you, Miss Pierce. May I say, I was so sorry to hear of your sister's death? It must have been a terrible shock for all of you. I met her only a few times. A charming woman—so original.' He quirked an eyebrow at me, as if afraid that I might display a like tendency.

'Yes, Sophie generally made her presence felt.' The words came out more vindictively than I had intended. Charles frowned, twisting a glass of Scotch in his hand, but Hobbett-Gore rattled on, unnoticing:

'Oh yes, she certainly had a great deal of presence. One felt it immediately. I must admit, we're not used to such flair, if that's the word, in our little constituency up north. She certainly would have turned a few heads up there!' He grinned broadly, his small, grey eyes narrowing to slits.

'Where is your little constituency up north, Mr Hobbett-Gore?'

'In Nottinghamshire. There's no really big city in my part of the county, just a cluster of small towns. But Charles has told you all about this, I'm sure?' He looked round at Charles

48

for confirmation. Charles smiled but said nothing.

'We've exchanged a few words on the subject,' I volunteered.

'Ah, he's a modest man, our Charles.' Hobbett-Gore leaned towards me confidentially. 'I think he'll get the nod up north. I pull considerable weight with the rest of the committee, y'know.'

'It's not a Conservative seat at present, I gather?'

'Well, no, it's not. Been in Labour's hands for twenty-five years, as a matter of fact. A Labour "lord" holds the seat, no less, a knight, an old veteran. "A knight there was a-pricking on the plain"—who's that? Byron?'

I smiled. 'Somebody old, anyway.'

'Well, that's what this fellow is. Old. But the old knight is standing down this time, so we have a chance, a chance. They have a majority of only six hundred, and that's not impossible to swing. Given the right issues, the right candidate. Someone who's really keen.' He turned to Charles and winked.

I turned to him, too. He had sat silent, seemingly removed and indifferent, while we had discussed him and his prospects. The man nettled me; I wanted to hold him to account.

'Are you really keen then, Charles? Why did you go into politics in the first place?'

'*Pour le sport,* my dear Sarah. *C'est tout.*'

Hobbett-Gore blinked at him, then at me, a small owl revolving its head. I should have known better. I had gotten a similar evasion, also in French, when I had asked him whether he and Sophie had been happy together. When would I learn that Englishmen could not be tackled head-on?

'Ah, he's always joking, our Charles. You're too modest, old chap,' Hobbett-Gore offered obligingly. 'I can tell you why, Miss Pierce. Just between you and me'—he dropped his voice —'Charles likes power. Power with prestige, that is. So do we all—the difference is, he's the right sort to exercise it. He'll go far, y'know. Our constituency has been a stepping-stone for more than a few men. As Charles knows.' Hobbett-Gore winked at him again. I began to wonder if it was a tic. 'You see, he knows how to treat people.' This was news to me. 'Knows who should get what, and for what. Natural know-how. He got a First, y'know, at university, and I only got a Third. He's always been the fair-haired lad.'

'The fair-haired lad of whom?' I asked.

'Oh, well, of the younger Conservatives, you might say. Liberal but not too liberal; can be counted on not to buck the party line. But has his eye on things, knows what's going on in the world, and locally as well.' It was clear that Hobbett-

Gore was already sold on Charles—he certainly needed no help from me, I thought to myself. 'Does his homework—immigration, the health services, the drug problem, the energy crisis, the coal miners' disputes—that's what most of our people do in the constituency: mining, along with some light industry and engineering. The thing is with Charles, you see, he knows more than he's saying. That inspires confidence.' It occurred to me that Hobbett-Gore and I had different ideas of what inspired confidence. 'And all those years with a top law firm. And no scandal—not even a traffic violation—which is more than can be said for some of our members. Yes, ambition, ambition—that's the last spur of noble minds, y'know.'

Charles looked at Hobbett-Gore with the faint, sardonic smile on his face I had seen so often.

'I think I'll get you taken on as an agent, Henry. You're wasted on the selection committee.'

'Not wasted, my boy, if I get you the nomination. What about it, Charles, have I hit the nail on the head?'

'Not only hit it but flattened it,' Charles said good-humouredly. 'Politics is just another form of soliciting, of course.'

I was not sure what he meant, and I doubt that Hobbett-Gore knew, either, from the look on his face. At that moment Mrs Chalmers entered the room and announced dinner, and the men did not resume the subject as we walked downstairs.

My thoughts were not much on eating, though Hobbett-Gore sighed appreciatively when Jane brought in the saddle of lamb and handed round a steaming dish of cauliflower mornay. When I saw the cauliflower, my appetite vanished completely, replaced by a vision of Mrs Chalmers stirring the sauce and muttering about three a.m. visits and 'getting his own back'. I spoke as little as I ate, but my quietness put no damper on our guest. He was virtually a non-stop talker, and without the aid of wine. I had noticed that he had been drinking nothing before dinner, and at table he turned his wine glasses over as if he were at a state banquet and could not trouble himself to speak to the help. Though I felt Charles looking curiously at me several times in the course of the meal, he did not try to draw me out but gave himself up to listening to Hobbett-Gore, encouraging him now and then with a question or nod. The talk turned on the differences between various countries and nationalities, a subject that Hobbett-Gore seemed to find of extraordinary interest because, apparently, all the differences served to bring out the superiority of the English. There was nothing malicious in his remarks; indeed, I believe
50

he thought the choice of subject a compliment to my presence and an invitation to me to speak on the glories, derived from England, of my homeland. But I would have none of it. I was tired of the whole business of sociability.

I hoped that the formality of the dinner pointed towards the observance of one old English custom that I had been prepared to dislike—the women leaving the men after dinner to their port and cigars—but that was not to be. Whether on account of Hobbett-Gore's abstemiousness that evening or the fact of our being only three, the men rose with me from table and we returned to the drawing-room together, Hobbett-Gore drawing his arm through mine as we went up the stairs and telling me, rather sweetly and protectively, that I ought to eat more or I'd simply fade away and that he wished I'd call him Henry. I promised to oblige him on both counts.

The drawing-room, with its blazing fire and red-damasked chairs, was welcomingly warm after the chilly dining-room. Mrs Chalmers had set out a Meissen coffee service, and as I poured coffee from the exquisite pot, I hoped the company would equal the china in grace and seemliness. I could not take many more surprises that day.

'I say, Charles, do you still put your fivers on the nags?' I over-poured Henry's cup, but he took it without noticing. 'Looking at those prints on the wall makes me think of the way you and Dillon used to go haring about from meeting to meeting—Cheltenham, Chester, Goodwood—don't know how you found time to open a book, much less come out with a First.'

'Yes, we had some good times,' Charles responded, after a pause, his face clouded.

'You still keep up with the horses, then? Or have you been thoroughly domesticated over the years, old man?'

'Oh, thoroughly domesticated, of course.'

'Well, we like a man who's versatile, but perhaps it's just as well if you've given up the gambling. Might not sit too well up there with the voters. Inflation's bad; times are tight. Too many problems. Mining, miners, always a problem, always a sticky bunch to conciliate. Remember last winter? Current member hasn't been able to do much about it, probably our best chance to win the seat. Have to take the hurdles—if you'll forgive my choice of phrase!' He laughed merrily.

'Is the miners' situation the main problem in the constituency, Mr Hobbett-Gore?'

'Henry, Henry.'

'Henry.' I had forgotten our compact.

51

'Yes, I'd say so,' he resumed, placated. 'But it's not only the miners. The hosiery and boot manufacturers are having their troubles, too. You see, they've got to change their machinery to suit the times, and that's an expensive business. Apparently women don't wear stockings any more: they wear tights. And other items of intimate apparel are having their ups and downs, too.' He winked at me, his round face beaming in the fire-light. 'And the people who make wireless components and the like, it's hard going for them. The Japs have come into the market in a big way since the war. Wish they'd stay on their own side of the water—we've got enough to handle with the European competitors, God knows. And then there's drugs. You wouldn't believe it in the heart of England, Sarah, but we've had some shocking cases up there amongst the young people, simply shocking.'

'I see. Well, it certainly sounds as if you and Charles have your work cut out for you.'

'Oh, that we do, that we do, but it can be done. It'll take money to get our man in, of course.'

'I thought that the amount a candidate could spend was strictly limited by law.'

At this, Charles joined Hobbett-Gore in his laughter.

'My dear girl,' said Hobbett-Gore, 'my dear girl!' He wallowed farther into the red cushions and let out another burst of laughter. I began to wonder if some hidden spring in his chair triggered laughter whenever he shifted his huge thighs. 'Yes, yes, yes,' he resumed, when he got his breath back, 'money is useful. And a wife. Those are two very desirable things for a man who wants to be an MP.'

I froze with my coffee cup half-way to my lips; I dared not look at Charles. Even Hobbett-Gore sensed his error:

'Sorry, Charles—wasn't thinking when I said that.' He paused. 'What I mean is, every man needs a wife, not just you in particular, of course, Charles. I mean, of course, every man needs a wife, that is ...' He gazed at us helplessly.

I broke in: 'Do you have a wife, Mr Hobbett-Gore?'

'Henry, Henry.'

'Henry.'

'Oh, no, no, my mother's enough to keep me busy. She's almost eighty now, lives in Nottinghamshire. I've got a lovely little flat fixed up for her up there. Part of our old manor house; too big to keep the whole thing going. I go up every Friday like a faithful husband and come back to London on Monday mornings.' He laughed again. 'I go out on the town quite a bit, though. I've quite a string of fillies in my stable.'

52

He winked at me. 'By the way, Sarah, do you like to dance? I do like a spot of dancing now and then.' He leaned over to me confidingly. His cheek, close to mine, was pale and puffy, and I could smell talcum powder mixed with the garlic of the lamb. There was something about him that was faintly effeminate.

I drew away from him and looked to Charles for help, but his back was towards me. He had crossed the room to pour himself more brandy. I turned back to Henry.

'I'm not much of a dancer. That was more in my sister's line.'

'Oh, I know, I know,' he said enthusiastically. My imagination ran wild; I had a vision of Sophie dancing with this man, a bright little bird fluttering just above and beyond a dinosaur wrenching itself out of the mud. 'But really,' he went on earnestly, 'we must get together soon. I know a delightful calypso club in Soho. Smashing. Clears the blood, y'know, dancing.'

'Oh, well, really, I don't think I could—'

'Dance with Henry?' Charles had picked up our conversation. 'Yes, why not, Sarah? It sounds—smashing.'

I felt the blood rush to my face; first Charles could not be bothered with me, then he meddled outrageously. I felt I was being used, by both of them.

'We didn't do much dancing at Mrs Lofting's. Where I taught,' I added, seeing Henry's puzzled look. 'I taught history and geography to nine-year-olds.'

'Oh, indeed? Charles didn't mention that,' he said with raised eyebrows. 'That surprises me. I understood you were an heiress.'

I looked at him in astonishment. I did not like the idea of people discussing my private affairs behind my back. Was it Sophie or Charles who had told him this, I wondered? But it was true, I was an heiress. The Pierce mills had spun wool and cotton into gold. Since the age of twenty-one I had received a sizable annuity. And when my parents died, they left an estate of three million dollars net. It had been halved between Sophie and me, each to receive an enlarged annuity until reaching her twenty-sixth birthday; then each came into her full half of the principal, to do with as she liked. Why our parents had chosen the twenty-sixth year for the great showering, I am not sure, whether to support inevitable spinsterhood or to secure a hesitating suitor. If Sophie had lived, she and Charles would have been immensely rich; or if she had lived at least till her twenty-sixth birthday, Charles would have been immensely rich, for I knew from the terms of the will she had filed with our family lawyers during the first year of her marriage that she had made him her sole heir. But she had died in August, seven months short of her twenty-sixth birthday at the end of March. Her half of the estate passed, by the terms of our parents' will, to her descendants, if any, and if none, to me. Patrick, therefore, was her heir, and I, as sister, rather than Charles as husband, had been appointed executor until my nephew came of age. I had come into my own share of the inheritance three years earlier and had, on the advice of our lawyers, ploughed it all back into stocks and bonds, which had without exception proved healthy and vigorous. So Henry spoke the truth, wherever he may have picked it up: I was indeed a rich woman. Yet it was a circumstance I often found more irritating than gratifying. I said to him in an irascible voice:

'You don't approve of teaching school? Perhaps you think I should stay at home and count my gold pieces?'

Charles looked at me sharply, and Henry was, for once, speechless.

I could not stem the familiar resentment rising in me when people alluded to my wealth; it seemed to turn not only my money but me into a commodity. Yet I knew, too, that some of the resentment was what I felt against myself, a feeling of being superfluous and over-privileged in the midst of a suffering world. I had discovered that the Puritan and the money-maker make a powerful but uncomfortable alliance in one's soul. The souls of the Pierces must have been hard as nails for generations.

'Sarah quite enjoys her teaching, Henry. She leads me to believe that she can hardly tear herself away from it for the pleasures of London and the needs of her sister's family.' Charles' voice was suave; Henry recovered his composure.

'Oh, well, yes. I suppose that teaching's as good a way as any to while away the time. For myself, though,' he laughed, 'I certainly wouldn't work if I didn't have to!'

'What is your work, Henry, may I ask?' I was glad to get off the subject of myself. I knew I was close to saying irretrievable things.

'Oh, a little of this, a little of that. I'm in investments mainly. Put other people's money to work.' He frowned. 'I think, mostly. That's what investments mean, thinking.'

'That must be taxing.' I almost added, 'for *you*', but caught myself. What was wrong with me tonight? A few hours earlier, with Patrick, I had felt perfectly happy and at peace with the

54

world. Then the day had started to disintegrate, from the moment that Charles had walked in on us. If only I could leave this room and go upstairs and sleep!

Charles must have read my mind, or else he felt that the conversation was getting out of hand, for he said suddenly: 'Are you feeling tired, Sarah? Henry and I have plenty of business to discuss; I'm sure he'd understand if you wanted to leave us to ourselves.'

Henry looked from one to the other of us and sighed. 'Can't tell you how much I've enjoyed meeting you, Sarah. It's been a marvellous evening. But don't let us wear you out. I know how tiring it can be—entertaining—I do a lot of it myself—mostly at my club, of course. And I can see you've certainly put yourself out for me. Splendid dinner—absolutely marvellous.'

'Do come and see us again soon, Henry,' I heard myself saying. 'It was a pleasure for us, having you here.' The same old phrases, and in this instance, lies. Charles was right, most of us are hypocrites. But what was the alternative? At that moment I saw the choice as decorum or anarchy, not falsity or truth.

The two men rose as I said good night, Henry reminding me jovially that we were going out on the town soon. Charles' eyes were enigmatic; he made almost a mock bow as he opened the door for me. The evening had not gone very well, I thought, as I climbed the stairs to my room. There were words I would have taken back if I could; I was given to too quick a resentment of remarks that were probably quite innocent—Sophie and I had been alike in that respect, at least. Still, despite my flat-footedness, Henry had repeated his invitation to go dancing: the uglies of the world flock together, world without end. But Charles was not pleased with me, I imagined. But why should I mind what he thought, damn him! And yet I did mind.

I undressed and got into bed but could not sleep. I turned on the light. The china-headed doll stared fixedly from the rocker. Did she curse her fate, I wondered, her endless, doll's existence? What did life offer to a woman not smitten by love or gifted with talent? I could see my life stretching before me at Mrs Lofting's, my students growing to womanhood, to blossom or shrivel as fate directed. Or did one make one's own fate? No, for all the seemingly self-willed acts that individual beings make—such as my forebears flinging themselves across the Atlantic three hundred years ago—we are all more driven than driving.

I had drifted in gentle, familiar channels all my life. Nothing had been expected of me, and I had fulfilled the expectation. For a time, in my last year at college, I had thought of going on to law school, if any would accept me, but that winter my old school-mistress, Mrs Lofting, had offered me a teaching position that would fall vacant soon at her school, and I had taken it, being rather tired of the whole business of being a student after sixteen unbroken years of it. Nor had my father's attitude done much to spur me on to any more daring or ambitious course. He, unlike my mother, had not discouraged specialist study on the ground that I would forfeit or endanger the married state; rather, and this, I suppose, was more telling, he imparted wordlessly, by his manner, a suggestion of the ugliness of pursuing any goal too strenuously, whether one was man or woman. (For Sophie, intent on painting, he made an exception; for art, one could excuse even passion.) My father's mind was like a Saryk carpet; there was no dominating centre, only beautiful geometric shapes repeating themselves right off the edge, with no beginning or end. He was, despite his being a university professor, a lotus-eater in Boston, of which there were, heaven knows, few in his generation.

So for the last six years I had held on, treading water, not knowing I was treading water, but mistily hoping that fate might choose to vary the monotony it had so far imposed on my life. I taught at Mrs Lofting's from Monday to Friday; I went to the Symphony on Saturday nights (the same seat every week); I lunched occasionally at the Copley-Plaza with an old school friend or two; on the odd, warm-weather Sunday I rambled with the Massachusetts Audubon Society about stretches of the countryside where my grandfather's mills lay deserted and silent, reflected in the glassy waters of backwoods rivers and ponds. In short, I led the life of a well-bred Boston spinster nearing her thirtieth birthday, till Sophie again reached into my life, disrupted it, and pulled me across the ocean by her dying.

So here I was, and still adrift, letting others, strangers now —or was it fate itself?—decide my course and rôle. How suffocating the bedroom was! I got out of bed and opened a window wide, in spite of the fierce November air that rushed in. I wondered what they were talking about downstairs; I wondered if Charles would go out after Henry left, or whether, perhaps, the visitor of last night would return. I walked about the room restlessly, picking things up and putting them down again. Sophie's robe and the blue notebook were lying beside the cupboard where I had dropped them. For a long moment

56

I stared at the writing on the cover. My earlier resolution crumbled; I needed reassurance; I needed to take hold of something familiar in this alien house. It was a novel sensation, but for the first time in a quarter of a century, I needed Sophie. I picked up the notebook, got into bed and began to read.

EIGHT

HOW I SPENT MY SUMMER HOLIDAYS
by Sophie Pierce

Saturday, 17 June. The train got into Fréjus-St-Raphaël at
4 p.m. Free at last! Avery will be chewing her pearls in Paris,
wondering where I am. I suppose I'll have to wire her and
tell her I decided to come back a day early. Silly old bag!
What a wad of fat. I'd die before I looked like that. Not that
I look so hot at the moment. My hair's filthy. I wonder where
the bathroom is in this crummy hotel. Maybe I can wash it
in the bidet. My legs itch. I bet that train was full of fleas.
Gianfranco was cute, though, trying to teach me Italian—
'*Uccello, uccello,*' flapping his hands and pointing at the sky.
He says he drives a taxi in Rome and I ought to come and
see him. I bet! He looks like Burt Lancaster. So innocent.
We got through a lot of cigarettes standing in that corridor.
The French trains rock like crazy!

Monday, 19 June. Back to the old grind. Oh well, all for art.
Anyway, I think my painting has improved since I've been
here. A different scene from Brooklyn, that's for sure! Made
it up with Avery pretty well. Told her I had to get back early
to get ready for exams. I did get ready, sort of, lying on the
beach at St Raphaël. Nice has such a crummy beach, all little
rocks, 'cailloux', they call them here. Anyway, I told Auntie
I'd take her out to Cap Trois Mille tomorrow afternoon to
pacify her. You'd think somebody seventy years old would
know how to drive a car! Maybe the car wasn't invented when
she was born, or even the wheel. *Quelle vieillesse!* She loves
all those shops out there; it's the biggest shopping centre in
France, I guess. They make me dizzy. I like that restaurant-bar
part, though, 'Drug 3000', with the glass-bottomed swimming
pool over it. I'll swim and drink beer and she can paw through
the counters at the Nouvelles Galeries to her heart's content.

Tuesday, 20 June. I met the cutest Englishman today in Drug 3000. I was sitting there at the bar after a swim minding my own business (more or less!), waiting for Avery as usual, and leaning back to look up at the swimmers, when a waitress side-swiped me and I went right over backwards. I really bashed my elbow. This man picked me up—he really did pick me up, it was marvellous—and plopped me down on the stool again and bought me another beer. His name is Charles Vivian. He's here in Nice for about two weeks. He lives in London. He looks sort of dissipated, he was really putting the booze away, and he certainly doesn't 'stand on ceremony', as Mama would say. He's a lawyer and he's going to be in Parliament some day, he said. Isn't that exciting! We were getting along fine till Avery turned up, the old bag, winking and blinking and shaking her pearls. She was awfully cool to him. I suppose she was afraid I was getting myself picked up. Of course, that's what I told her—'Hi, Avery, this nice man just picked me up.' That didn't go down so well; I had to tell her then just what happened. I can't believe that she actually eloped with somebody when she was barely nineteen, no older than I am. Charles was quite charming to her, but he looked so seedy, I could have told him there was no hope there.

Anyway, Avery started talking about all the meal-planning she had to do this week because the cook was off—mostly this means going down to one of the *traiteurs* on the Rue de la Californie and buying about fifty bucks worth of *pâté, fonds d'artichauts, jambon, ratatouille, salade niçoise,* cooked chickens and two hat-boxes' worth of *patisserie.* I reminded Avery that just about the best pastry in Nice was right here at the Toute au Beurre counter, so why didn't she go and get some while she was here? I was thinking that maybe she'd leave me alone for a while then with Charles. He hadn't even gotten my phone number yet. But she said, 'All right, come along then, Sophie, that's a good idea.' I told her I'd be there in a minute, I hadn't finished my beer. That was a mistake. She thought I'd been drinking ginger ale; she doesn't approve of alcohol though she indulges herself in every other way. 'No, right away,' she said, or we'd be late for her television programme, so I had to go, but I said in a loud, clear, looking-down-my-nose voice, imitating my mother: 'Do come to see us, Mr Vivian. Villa Blanchesfleurs, Avenue de la Lanterne.' Avery didn't second the invitation but at least she kept her mouth shut, except to say good-bye in a very cold voice.

Wednesday, 21 June. He came this afternoon, about six. What a transformation! He wore a cream-coloured linen suit, a Graham-Greeneish straw hat, a wide silk tie, everything but gloves, and maybe he had those, too, I wasn't looking. I told him he had a split personality. He said, 'Which of the two do you prefer?' And I said, 'Who said I liked either?' Avery simmered down a lot when she saw him. Appearances mollify her when they don't petrify her. She had Josie bring iced tea into the garden and we sat down under the pear tree. The garden's looking sort of weedy, things starting to dry out with the heat. But the laurier-roses are blooming, and geraniums as high as my shoulder, and the hibiscuses that look like great big orchids are just beginning to open. We drank our tea and talked, and Avery began to act less like a hen afraid her one egg is about to be snitched. Of course, she never had any kids of her own, so that makes her worry about everybody else's. Things took a lucky turn when she asked him what brought him to this part of the world (as if she owned it), and he said he was visiting his father, who's bedridden with arthritis and lives in a nursing home near Vence, having found England too cold and damp. 'Oh, quite, quite, I understand perfectly. My husband suffered so, too. He passed away twenty years ago'—she always sniffs when she says this—'We could never have lived in New England, where the rest of the family live, it's so cold.' I felt like saying, you couldn't have lived there anyway, after running off like that. How can people change so? She can't always have been this way, full of clichés, so untrusting, so convinced that the only good experience is no experience. Does life really change us all? I hate to think of it. Well, anyway, Charles had struck the right note with her, and they chatted on about the ills of old age and the healing *soleil* and how fine it was that he came to see his father whenever he could 'before it was too late'. He'd told me yesterday in Drug 3000 that he came only when his law firm sent him—they have quite a few rich, expatriate clients down here—and then mainly *pour le sport*. Sometimes he'd look in at the Casino and the Hippodrome, but mostly, he said, he just fooled around, because he didn't have much money. I told him that my family had lots of money, but that I just fooled around, too. We laughed at that. Isn't it funny how people end up doing the same things if they're at all alike in personality? I don't think money has anything to do with it. I'm sick of money. You always feel the presence of it at home, though it isn't much talked about. I don't mean *it* is there but the *thought* of it is there, like an old perfume bottle lying under the sheets, smelling up the whole linen-closet. When I'm

60

a painter, I'm never going to have any money, or just *pour le sport*, as Charles says.

Anyway, tea went swimmingly, and when Charles got up to go—after precisely twenty minutes, so formally, I wondered if he'd left a calling card on the silver plate in the hall—Avery was positively drooling and giving him the old Boston and China-tea blend of bracing cordiality. 'Do call on us again, Mr Vivian. It's so dull, I fear, for Sophie here. Nobody to keep her company but those scruffy art students and an old lady like me'—simpering, fingering the rope of pearls she wears like a hair-shirt. Charles said he'd be delighted. I walked him to the gate, taking the twisting path that goes all the way around the *parc*. The ground is already breaking into cracks with the heat, but the daisies on either side of the path at the back of the house are still going strong. They look like they've been there for a hundred years; you couldn't break those clumps apart with a pick-axe. I picked a flower and twirled it in my fingers; he reached out and took it from me—she loves me, she loves me not, she loves me ... It came out, she loves me. 'If she loves me, she'll have to give me another flower. There's nothing left of this one.' 'She doesn't *have* to do anything,' I said. I picked another daisy and reached up to put it in his pocket. He caught my hand and held it and kissed me on the lips. It was a good kiss. '*A toute à l'heure*,' he said, smiling. '*A toute à l'heure*,' I said. I opened the gate for him and watched him saunter down the drive, for all the world like a proper Englishman.

Thursday, 22 June. I was thinking about Charles in life class this morning, though it's hard to think when you're supposed to be concentrating on drawing muscles. But I kept seeing the curve of his neck and shoulders in the model—they're both slightly stoop-shouldered. I've noticed that tall men often are, unless they're athletes or have been in the military. I don't think Charles has been either; he's too much his own person. I can't tell what he's thinking. He was so different yesterday —until we got out of sight of Avery—from what he was the day before at Cap Trois Mille. But why shouldn't he be different? Besides, he is rather old—thirty-one—twelve years older than I am! It'd be awfully dull to be the same person all the time. I can't imagine he cares much about being a lawyer, all those deeds and wills and things. It must be politics that gets him wound up. He looks like a gambler. He's so tall.

Friday, 23 June. We drove out to Vence to see his father this

61

afternoon. Charles drives as fast as I do. All the way up those crazy hills, one-handed, the Peugeot leaning on its side on every turn, his arm round my shoulders the whole time. I put my hand on the wheel some of the time, and then his hand sank lower till it was under my arm and touching my breast. It made me feel sort of soft and sleepy. If it'd been Gianfranco in his taxi, we'd just have pulled over to the side of the road for a while, I bet! I wanted him to kiss me. I'm beginning to suspect that Charles likes to tease me, string me along, and I'm the one who's supposed to be the expert at that—so Sarah says, anyway. She always thinks she knows so much! She's so sure of herself, and critical of everybody else. Anyway, we got through the drive with no stops and no mishaps. He knew where his hand was, though, I knew that.

His father was a sweet old dear. Kind of shook me up, though. The room was so dark after the sunshine and it smelt awfully clean, but it's a very nice nursing-home, an old villa converted. Charles' father—his name is Leo—is very pale, with a big bony face. His eyes are set deep in his head, and they're very dark brown, almost black. His hair sticks out in white tufts. He can't sit up straight, but he put out his hand and shook mine. What a shock! It felt like the dry, webbed foot of a dead chicken. It didn't have any strength in it, it was all curled up. That's the arthritis; Charles had warned me about it, but it was still a shock. He asked about my family and my painting and how did I like being in the South of France, Provence, the cradle of the arts? I said I liked it fine, and how did he like it, and then I wondered if I should have said that because of course he came here to die, not to put too fine a point on it. But he smiled—his teeth are all yellow—and said he liked it fine, too.

He told Charles to go down to the kitchen and see if he could get some wine for us from the cook, and Charles left. And then he said, 'How do you like my son, Miss Pierce? He has talked about you a good deal in the past few days. I haven't seen him so distracted from himself for a long time, in fact, never.' That flattered me, I can tell you, because I had begun to doubt my own powers. I didn't say so to Charles' father, of course. I said, 'Oh, I do like him. He seems so grown-up compared to the boys I know at home. All they think about is money and booze.' He laughed and said, 'Well, Charles is not perfect, my dear, and he may not be so unlike the others as you think. He has always wanted to get on. Perhaps it runs in the family. I was ambitious, too, when I was young. My father was only a joiner—a carpenter, as the Americans
62

say—Polish by birth. His name was Wywynowski. He changed it when he came to England in the 1880s. He found work, married a London girl and raised a large family. I was the fifth of ten. We all had to scrounge and scavenge and hang on by our fingernails. 'Oh?' I said; I never know what to say when people start to rattle on about the past. But I didn't have to worry because he went right on talking. 'I was apprenticed to an ironmaster when I was very young, and because I worked hard and because I was lucky, I bought into the firm eventually and in the course of time made quite a lot of money. We bought a house in Cheyne Walk and we made money in the City, especially during the Second World War. But the post-war business went downhill fast, trying to diversify, and even after we retrenched and laid off a lot of people, we never regained the old prosperity. I sold my share of the firm twelve years ago—just after my wife died—it was either sell then or go bankrupt later or perhaps both. There was very little money even to see Charles through university. Fortunately, his sister married about that time, and that was one less burden to worry about.'

His head fell back on the pillow then, his face crumpled in like a broken kite. I could see that speaking was a great effort for him, but I couldn't think of anything to say. I didn't say anything right away, being pretty well knocked out by all that family history. He looked at me and said: 'I tell you these things, my dear, that you may understand Charles somewhat. Charles does not care to talk too much about the past. He lives for the future.' 'He likes girls, though, doesn't he?' (Why on earth did I make that idiotic remark?!) 'Oh, yes, he likes girls,' he said, giving me a big smile, and I guessed he liked girls, too, in his time. 'I can see that he likes you, in particular, very much.' I wanted him to go on talking about Charles, but I guess his mind was wandering, because he didn't talk about him any more. He said: 'Sometimes I wish I had been a carpenter, like my father. He did beautiful work, gave as much care to a garden bench as he did to an inlaid sideboard. He loved intricate designs, puzzles; he'd put something hidden and clever in the most utilitarian pieces. Strange how some people are born with a need to simplify things and others with a yearning to complicate them, to elaborate on them. He was a complicator, I was a simplifier—drive, drive, drive, straight ahead all the time. Which are you, my dear?'

'I don't know. I haven't thought about life like that. I guess I'm probably a simplifier. My parents make life very complicated. My father's a professor of Oriental languages, not very

63

simple. My mother doesn't *do* anything, but she's always fussing about something, worrying. So's my sister, Sarah. I don't know what they have to worry about, everything's laid out for them. The past hangs so heavy in our house, the whole sickening New England bit—do what you're expected to, live up to your sterling ancestors.'

'I doubt that's limited to New England.'

'Well, all I want to do is paint some pictures. And be able to play all of Chopin's waltzes.'

'And marry?'

'Well, love somebody. Maybe lots of people.'

'Oh, I doubt you'll do that!' He laughed.

'Do *which*?' I wanted to ask him, but just then Charles walked in with a bottle of Gigondas and three wine glasses speared on his fingers like a pawnbroker's sign, and we got on to other things.

Saturday, 24 June, midnight. Two nights in a row interrupted— it's not fair! When we got back from Vence yesterday, Avery cornered Charles for dinner and we spent the whole evening playing three-handed bridge with her. She didn't stop talking all evening, and it's no use trying to stop the flow. Why are old people so selfish? But Charles' father isn't like that. I'd better try not to simplify. He was really awfully nice. I wouldn't even mind playing three-handed bridge with him, but I suppose he couldn't hold the cards. He managed to hold the wine glass all right, though—we got through that whole bottle of Gigondas with no trouble at all! And then tonight, Charles asked Avery and me out to dinner and the movies— he's really buttering her up—but Avery couldn't go, because this is her bridge night with *les girls*, the old biddies down on the Promenade. So it looked as if Charles and I were going to have an evening *à deux*, at last!

We went to one of the restaurants at the Old Port where you eat outside. It's super at night-time, the lanterns, and the lights from the harbour boats, and the fishermen twisting their nets and talking and yelling and happy with the end of the week's work. It was windy and fun. The paper table-cloths were flapping and blowing, and the basket of bread tipped over and blew off the table. I said, 'Oh, there goes the bread! Why don't they do something about that?' And Charles said, 'Would you rather they made it *heavier*?' And we laughed. He knows I adore the French bread, I could make a meal off it, with a few olives on the side. It was a very happy dinner somehow—even the red peppery stuff they spoon into the

64

soupe de poissons didn't make me choke the way it usually does, and we drank lots of wine. At the end Charles said, 'Are we going to the film now?' I looked at him. Was he reading my mind, or was I reading his? 'Do you want to?' I said. 'I asked you first,' he said. I don't think he likes to be pinned down or be forced into taking the initiative. I know how he feels, but it makes me kind of uneasy, because then it puts the finger on me to say how the game's going to be played, and that's not a very endearing position to be in, in the long run. So I said, 'Sure.' 'All right,' he said, 'let's go.' But when we got to the theatre there was a line two blocks long. 'Never mind,' he said, 'I've got some pictures we can look at, at my place.' 'Etchings?' I said. 'Yeah,' he said, making fun of me. He likes to kid me about my American accent, but one thing I never say is 'yeah'. 'No thanks,' I said, 'I'm not interested in etchings.' 'What are you interested in?' 'I haven't decided.' 'Well, come up and have a night-cap and think it over.'

So we got to his apartment—it's really only a room in a little *pension* off the Boulevard Gambetta—but when we walked into the building, there was a man standing in the hall. A fat young man in a dinner jacket, looked like a penguin. He said, 'Good evening, Charles, I've been waiting for you. And good evening to you, mademoiselle.' He looked French, but he spoke English English—I would've thought his voice was Charles' if I'd had my eyes closed. 'Dillon,' Charles said coldly, 'I thought our appointment was for Tuesday.' 'It was,' the man said, 'but things have changed—*mais, plus ça change, plus c'est la même chose, n'est-ce pas*?' Charles had dropped his arm from around my waist, but he wasn't giving any ground. 'Sorry, Dillon, but I have other plans for the evening.' 'So I see. Aren't you going to introduce me to your lovely friend?' Charles looked as if it was the last thing he wanted to do, but he said, 'Sophie, may I introduce Aubrey Dillon. Dillon, Miss Pierce.' '*Enchanté*,' Dillon said, but then not another word to me; I think he just wanted to score a point against Charles. 'It won't wait, Charles. So sorry.' He smiled at me. 'Run Miss Pierce home now. I'll wait for you.' Charles scowled and turned around and hustled me out the door. I asked him about Dillon on the way home, but all he said was that he was an old school friend and a pest. He kissed me hard when we got to the villa, though. There was no fooling around about it. I think the preliminaries are finished.

Sunday, 25 June. Well, it had to happen and it did. I can't think of anybody but Charles. I could blame it on the lunch,

65

I suppose. Those French lunches, they really get you into trouble. It's not just the wine; it's how everything is strung out and savoured, course by course, sense by sense, so that by the end of the meal—two hours—the touching of fingers on a sugar bowl, the brush of legs under the table, makes you tremble. We were at the beach at Juan-les-Pins. We had only to step from our table and we were on the sand. We didn't go in the water right away. We lay on the sand on those blue-and-white striped mattresses. There's something sweet and private about lying so close yet separate, bits of hairs trailing over your eyes, eyes all but closed to shut out the glare, the sweet shared smell of wine on our mouths, the curve of his back, his legs. He is a very big man, stealthy, unused. Then we went in the water and swam around for a while and played. We were like otters, splashing, diving, dunking each other. But then at some point it wasn't just playing any more. I didn't think it would be, not after last night, not after the very first moment that he picked me up off the floor of the bar really. We got out of the water at the same time, and got dried off, and I put my dress on over my bikini, and he took me to his room in the *pension*. The shutters were closed against the heat of the day; it was cool and dark after the beach. He put his arms around me, and I pulled his head down to mine, and lower. I let him undress me, I wanted him to undress me. He put me down on the bed and lay down beside me. We made love. I didn't want to get up. I didn't want him to get up. I could have lain there forever, our legs intertwined, his arm under my neck and his hand resting on my breast. It seemed so final, so fixed, so lasting, like the paired figures on the royal tombs that we copied in class last week. His skin, our skin tasted salty from the water, his hair was still wet under my cheek.

He got up first, and put his clothes on quickly. I was watching him button his shirt when I said—I don't know what came over me—'Now you'll have to marry me, you cad.' He looked down at me with that funny, give-nothing-away smile and went on buttoning his shirt. Then he sat down on the bed and took hold of my wrists and forced them backward onto the pillow and kissed me again. I can't bear having anyone hold my hands down, it really makes me panicky. 'I just might do that,' he said, and let me go.

Monday, 26 June. I can hardly wait to see him tonight. I couldn't draw a thing in class today, couldn't concentrate. I kept thinking about him, and getting married, and—only a

66

little—what the parents will say. Imagine me proposing to a man! Sarah would never believe it; I'd never have believed it myself a week ago. I was always telling myself that I wouldn't fall into that trap: matrimony. I know what it does to people —look at Mama, and Avery. But it's all very easy to make theories when you haven't got Satan in front of you—not that Charles is Satan, of course! I never met anybody until now that I wanted to be with all the time, anybody that I could even consider sharing the future with. With most people, little doses are enough. I've got to write to Mama and Papa today; Charles said I ought to when he was driving me home yesterday, and I knew it myself, anyway. They won't like it, but it could be worse. They always love anything English, and Charles is about as English as you can get. They'll find him respectable, even if he isn't rich. The law has always appealed to Mama; I'm sure she thinks Mandarin very wispy stuff compared to good old English statutes. Sarah will be green with envy; but she'll find some fault with it, I know, she always does. Always analysing and criticizing everybody else's life. If she'd relax, she'd enjoy life more. The trouble with her is, she thinks she's too good for any man, won't put herself out for anybody. I still remember that time with poor old Rob Warner—that week-end would've been a disaster if I hadn't rescued him. Of course, he *is* a ninny. Still, if Sarah keeps her nose so high in the air, she'll fall and break her neck one of these days—or something more 'poi-sonal', as my Brooklyn friends would say!

Well, I'd better get busy and write that letter!

Friday, 30 June. We've been out every night this week. The usual!

Charles told his father about us a couple of days ago. He said that he'd known I wanted to marry Charles as soon as he'd talked to me for five minutes, that first afternoon. Can you beat that? It made me angry at first—I don't want to be *that* transparent—but Charles said that he'd been very pleased and that he wanted to see me again soon. We were going to go out there this afternoon, but apparently he's having a weak spell and has to be left completely undisturbed. I hope I don't ever get in that state—when I go, I want to go *fast.*

Charles asked me again if I'd heard from my parents, though I only wrote to them on Monday. Does he think we run our own airline? We may be rich, but not that rich—Onassis is in no danger yet! I think Charles is more worried than I am

67

about what they're going to say. I said to him, 'What does it matter what they say? I already gave you an answer—yes, yes, yes.' 'To set the record straight, sweetie, I believe it was I who gave you an answer.' 'Oh, all right, don't remind me. I'll never live that down. Anyway, I don't see why our future has to depend on my parents.' 'Oh, it doesn't, but one does well not to alienate them.' 'Are you afraid they'll disinherit me or something?' 'No, I think they're too fond of you, as I am, but I'd like to be sure.' 'You've got a nerve! You fortune-hunter!' 'Indubitably.' 'Well, you ought to know, then, that I don't get any of the family fortune till they die—except, of course, for a pretty big annuity when I turn twenty-one.' 'I'll wait. I think I can just manage to put up with you till then.'

He's impossible! But I guess he meant it. He's already started going through all the legal procedures for a Niçoise wedding. He says the French marriage law is rather *compliquée*—like everything else here!

Oh, I do want to get married right away. I can't bear the thought of him going back to London alone next week. And how can I stick out the year with Avery when I'm thinking of him all the time? She drives me out of my mind. I haven't said anything to her yet; Charles said I should wait and see what the parents say before telling her. He brought her a whole lot of red and white carnations when he came to pick me up tonight—there must've been about five dozen of them. They grow all over the place here, just like milkweed and goldenrod at home. We didn't have enough vases for them, so I rounded up some old milk bottles and plunked them in. They look like a row of torches along the portico. Avery thinks he's the living end, a real gentleman. It is nice to get flowers.

Saturday, 1 July. The letter was waiting for me when I got home tonight. They'd sent a night letter but the Côte d'Azur mail service being what it is, it got here at 8 p.m. instead of 8 a.m. I bet Avery was dying to know what was in it. Fortunately she'd fallen asleep by the time I got in. It wasn't quite what I expected. They—or I should say Papa, for he's the one who wrote it, with Mama standing over him probably —fussed and fumed a bit, more than a bit, about the 'precipitateness of the romance', but then their fuss sort of collapsed, and the last few paragraphs were kind of sweet:

'But in the end, dear Sophie, the decision is indeed yours, as you make plain to us with an air of wilful defiance that

68

rather saddens us. We had not known that we were such tyrannical parents; in fact, it is hard for us to recollect a time that we denied you, or Sarah, anything. Perhaps we should have: the pattern of wanting and getting, with no struggle, is pleasant but dangerous, for the break, the fall, comes harder when it comes. Your mother and I shall not always be here to make things easier for you, and the world is not likely to stand in our stead.

Apart from the impulsiveness of your emotions, there is also the matter of your intended career. A year ago nothing could stand in your way; now you seem ready to throw it all over. Despite your optimism, we very much doubt that you will have the incentive, the time or the stamina to continue professionally with your painting once you have the responsibility of a household. We should prefer that you at least see out your first year of studies in Nice; or, if that young man is so precious to you, that you complete your studies in London and try some work on your own before marrying or even committing yourself to an engagement. (We have arranged to let your annuity begin this summer instead of on your twenty-first birthday, should a need for money be influencing your decision.) Best of all, of course, would be your coming home to us. But let that be. Your mother is not well enough to travel at present, as you know—at her age a broken hip is no light matter— but within a few months she should be sufficiently mended for us to travel to London and meet your Charles Vivian and talk to you both.

So, could you not hold on for a little while longer to your own individual life? It cannot be recovered, as your mother has brought home to me many times, once you are a married woman. Surely if this man loves you, and if you value yourself, there is no call to rush into marriage. You are barely nineteen.'

And then, as if they'd read the letter over and weren't quite happy with it or with themselves, they added a postscript: 'In any case, dear Sophie, nothing that happens will ever estrange you from us. We think of you always with fondest love.'

So what do you think of that? I thought they'd kick more, give me something really to rebel against. I thought my mind was made up, but that letter's enough to make me start biting my fingernails again. I've got to read it to Charles. We're going out to Renoir's house in the country, 'Les Collettes', tomorrow

—I mean today! It's 2 a.m. on Sunday morning already! Oh, dear! I kind of wish he *could* meet my parents.

Sunday, 2 July. I read the letter to Charles this afternoon. We were sitting under the olive trees at 'Les Collettes'. I wonder if that means 'little hills', or am I getting 'collettes' mixed up with 'collines'? It is the most glorious place. I wish I could live there and paint there. A family was picnicking near us; they looked so happy; their dog kept bounding back and forth over the blanket they'd spread on the grass, making muddy tracks, but it didn't seem to bother them at all; the parents lay on their elbows, watching the two little girls and a boy who were playing hide-and-seek around the olive trees. There are lots of olive trees here; I wonder if Renoir planted them or if they're older than that. I can hardly think of anything older than Renoir; he seems so primeval, like Eden. Those grey-green-silver leaves, I wish I could find exactly the right colours to paint them. I wonder if I'll ever get the chance? They change, too, depending on the light and the wind and the season. Anyway, I read the letter to Charles as he lay on his back in the grass. 'Hmmn,' he said, when I'd finished. 'What do you mean, "hmmn"?' I said. 'Nothing, just "hmmn". It's a rather nice letter.' 'Yes, I suppose it is.' 'So are you going to be a good girl and take your parents' advice?'

I had been saying no, no, no to myself all week, that not my parents or anything else would stand in the way of an immediate marriage, but the coolness in Charles' voice frightened me. Didn't he want to marry me after all? Maybe I was just a way of filling up the days—and nights—while he was here. And maybe, though I didn't want to admit it, my parents were right. What was the rush, and what would happen to my dreams of becoming a first-class painter? Sitting in that garden under the olive trees, and looking at the children playing and the tranquil bronze Venus that Renoir had sculpted late, late in life when he could hardly bend his fingers, there seemed no sense at all in taking a leap in the dark.

I felt very low. I sat with my knees drawn up, my chin resting on them. We sat there without saying anything for a long time. Far below us were the white buildings of Cagnes, and the Mediterranean, as blue as I've ever seen it—no green in it at all. I wonder if Charles sensed the change in my mood. He reached up suddenly and pulled me down to him and said, 'You knew I was only joking, didn't you, old thing?' He smoothed my hair back; I closed my eyes as he ran his finger

70

over my eyelids and down my nose. 'Of course, I want to marry you, Sophie darling, and you, me. And if you make me wait for you too long, you just might change your mind and leave me. Let's get married now. Do you think I could live in those wild woods forlorn without you?' His words startled me. 'What "wild woods forlorn"?' I said. 'London, London.' I looked at him, wondering whether he was playing with me again. But he wasn't. 'Stay with me, Sophie. Marry me. We'll go back to London together, Thursday night.' I closed my eyes again as he kissed me. This day has given me a lot to think about. I feel awfully tired.

Thursday, 6 July, en route to London, courtesy BEA. Charles and I were married this afternoon. Sophie Pierce is dead: Long live Mrs Charles Vivian!

NINE

I was looking up into silvery grey-green olive trees, but they were pushing down on me, enfolding me, their branches the sodden feathers of some drowned monster bird. The trunks were thick and twisted, the knot-holes deep as whirlpools; I felt myself being sucked into their black interiors. I awoke with a start; the sheets and blankets were twisted about me, half sliding to the floor. I could not think where I was; my head whirled. Then the room settled into place, my identity returned.

It must be late, I thought. There was no sound from the floor above; Patrick must already have left for school. The sky was ashen, grey with an undertone of green, and a cold wind was blowing off the river. I got up to close the window, and my foot skidded on something slick and papery. I looked down—Sophie's diary! The blue covers flapped open carelessly; the book must have slipped from my hand as I was falling asleep. The events of last night, and of six years ago, flooded over me. Why had I ever read it? What folly! And yet, it was not shame I felt, I told myself. Anyone would read an old journal that fell into his hands. But it was so immediate, so naked! The Sophie it disclosed was not wholly the Sophie I had known; the two Charles were even more unlike. The cold, deliberate man who had instructed me in my duties last evening—could he be the gambler who had picked up, bedded and married my sister in the space of a fortnight? The picture I had of Sophie, of Charles—and of myself—was somehow altered, thrown out of focus.

The face in the mirror that met mine looked white and unrested and plainer than ever. Would a man ever want me the way that Charles had wanted Sophie? I picked up a hairbrush and began brushing my hair. My hands looked old; the veins on my hands stood out; bony hands. I was twenty-nine years old and, whatever the year, for ever removed by circumstance and temperament from what Charles and Sophie had known. But could I ever have wanted that flouting of

72

reason and family regard, that haphazard coming together?

A knock at the door startled me, and the hairbrush dropped from my hand. Mrs Chalmers stood in the doorway, looking at me wonderingly, I who was usually up at seven and sharing boiled eggs with Patrick at half-past. It must be ten or eleven now. I had not the energy to amend my expression; I looked at Mrs Chalmers listlessly.

'There's a lady downstairs to see you. Madame Vassallo. She says she is in London only for the day and hoped to find you in.'

My mind struggled with the strange name. At last—'Oh, Madame Vassallo—yes, yes, she's my aunt.' Aunt Avery Vassallo. 'Tell her I'll be down in a few minutes, please.'

My sense of disorientation increased. What was Aunt Avery doing here? I had last seen her, thanks to Sophie, sitting in her Niçoise garden drinking iced tea under the pear tree. The world was too fast for me. I dressed slowly, cautiously, and went downstairs. A short, round woman with a fur toque on her head was standing in the parlour.

'Aunt Avery!'

'Sarah, my dear!'

We embraced and she drew away from me, still holding both my hands, to look at me. 'My dear girl, you look so peaked! What on earth have you been doing? I thought you were supposed to be having a holiday here.' Good old Avery, never one to spare feelings if she could help it. She did not wait for me to answer. 'I'm just passing through, Sarah. I flew home for your cousin Gerald's wedding in Marblehead. They told me you had come here, my dear, after poor Sophie's demise. Such a blow—so untimely! Quite unthinkable! I'm on my way back to Nice now, thank heaven. You have no idea what America is coming to these days!'

I might have told her that I had a very good idea of what it was coming to, having lived there all my life until six weeks ago, but I could see what Sophie meant, there was no use trying to stop the flow, one could only let it dry up by itself. She went on talking, through coffee and cakes, till I was caught up on all the family news (mostly disasters—Gerald's bride had caught her veil in the limousine door and nearly been scalped when the car pulled away and it ripped from her head—Uncle George's new swimming pool had been infested with frogs which, when exterminated, choked up the drains). She came to the end of her catalogue and suddenly addressed me directly:

'So, how are you finding life here, my dear?'

73

It took me a moment to realize that Avery was asking a question that actually required an answer.

'Oh, well, very pleasant. Patrick's no trouble, and London's marvellous. My life seems very peaceful after facing twenty little girls every day for seven hours at a stretch.'

'It does seem to me rather curious that you should be here, since I gather you never came once while Sophie was alive.'

'I wasn't invited until recently.'

'Hmmn. No, I wasn't invited, either. Sophie didn't put herself out much for other people, did she? But she was a sweet little thing, so pretty. What a shame! How is the boy taking it?'

'He seems all right. He's glad of a little company. That's why I came, of course. Sophie asked me to come, shortly before she died. And then Charles renewed the invitation. So I came.'

'You never were very strong-willed, my dear. But I guess Sophie made up for that—a true Aries!' Avery laughed heartily. 'Don't let yourself get sucked into anything, though. I'm sure that Charles Vivian would be only too glad to have you stay on as a kind of high-bred family governess to the boy—and probably more than that, too.' Her brown eyes quivered at me through the bleached fringe of her Anita-Loos bangs.

'What do you mean by that?'

'Well, my dear, not to mince words, you'd be quite a prize. Charles had the misfortune to have Sophie slip through his grasp just before she came into her inheritance. I don't suppose he'd let a second heiress get away.' I stared at her; she raced on, unheeding. 'You're a rich woman, what with half of your parents' estate and the direction of Sophie's share till Patrick comes of age, and when the day comes, as come all too soon it will, you'll have my money, too.' She spoke mournfully, and fingered the pearls on her broad purple bosom. 'I wouldn't want to leave it to your father's side of the family, heaven knows; they're no blood of mine, and Gerald is spoiled enough as it is. We talked about all the wills last week, at the wedding. Theale and Bissell and I.' She spoke of the Boston law firm that had handled our affairs for years as if it were composed of Siamese twins. 'They told me that if anything should happen to the child before his majority, you'd have everything. As it is, you must have well over a million now, haven't you? Theale and Bissell wouldn't tell me exactly.' She pouted at me inquiringly.

Her words, her thoughts revolted me. I responded coldly:

74

'I don't think you know what you're saying, Aunt.'

'Oh, but I do, my dear. You forget, I was there the first time around.'

'The first time around?' I said blankly.

'Yes, when Sophie and Charles met in Nice. While she was under my roof, I'm sorry to say. If only I'd known—but he seemed so nice, so proper, so Bostonian. And then, to run off like that, with little Sophie! To so beguile that young, innocent girl!'

'Sophie wasn't a child.'

'But she was only nineteen years old.'

'But she wanted to marry him—she wasn't carried off kicking and screaming. And you went to the wedding.'

'If you can call it a wedding, that hurry-up little job in a registry office off the Place Masséna. Dirt, pigeons, fish scales blowing about the alleyways. I never cease to thank my stars that I live at the clean end of Nice. Anyway,' Avery sniffed, overcoming the repugnant memory, 'someone had to represent the family. Sophie certainly wasn't going to wait for your parents to swell the throng.'

'Well, if Sophie wouldn't wait, I don't see how you can blame the marriage on Charles. It was her will, not his,' I said adamantly, with more decisiveness than I felt, for in my own mind I was not sure. What was one to make of that next to last entry in the diary, the conversation in Renoir's garden, when Sophie seemed to hesitate and Charles to apply the spur?

Avery spoke sharply: 'He wouldn't have married her if he hadn't known which side his bread was buttered on. He knew he had to strike while the iron was hot. He bowled over that little girl!' Avery talked in clichés when emotion gripped her strongly; it was her way of keeping it at a distance, I suppose. 'And, you know, I don't think he'd have gotten anywhere here in London if it hadn't been for her money. Her allowance, those grand annuities, went for raising his position, I'm certain. This house, too, this was Sophie's doing, you know.'

'What do you mean? This house belonged to Charles' father.'

'Oh, yes, it belonged to him, he owned it. But he rented it out to tenants years ago, when he went to live in the nursing home in Vence; he couldn't afford the rates and maintenance. What Charles brought Sophie home to was a shabby little flat in the Fulham Road. Charles always implied he had a lot of money, but he didn't.'

'He didn't imply it to Sophie. He told her straight off, in fact, that he had very little.'

'How do you know that?' Avery looked at me in amazement. 'I gathered that you and she had very little to say to each other after her marriage—or before it, for that matter.'

Thinking of my source of information, I was embarrassed for an answer. But Avery burbled on without waiting for one: 'His father had been well off once, I understand, but that was gone by the time Charles met Sophie. It was Sophie who took over the lease of the house shortly after they returned to London, and subsequently bought it. She wrote to me from time to time, not often—she was never much for letter-writing —but she did tell me about this house. She was expecting Patrick then, the first year of their marriage, and she was full of enthusiasm for domesticity—something I'd never have expected of her. She was restoring the house, redecorating, converting one of the floors for a nursery. I visited her here just after the baby was born—I wasn't invited, I just came— someone had to be a mother to the poor child. She was as perky as ever, treated the baby like a new toy, said she was going to have a whole houseful of children, she'd never guessed they were such fun. And the house looked lovely—new rugs, new furniture, flowers everywhere ...' Avery looked around her at the dark, grotesquely crowded parlour. 'It looks so different now; it seems to have gone downhill somehow— where did this awful furniture come from? And the walls— just look at them! The London air is so filthy, Sophie should have had them painted at least every second year.' She shuddered. 'I wonder what got into the girl, to let the place go to pieces like this?' I did not reply, for I knew the answer no more than she. 'And I doubt very much that Charles would have splashed into politics, got a nomination at first try, if it hadn't been for Sophie's money to pave the way. He lost, but I'm sure she wined and dined plenty of the right people to help him get the nomination.'

'Aunt Avery, surely no man is obliged to marry a poor girl. You weren't poor when your husband married you.'

'He had money of his own, and besides—' she twiddled her pearls—'he died before I did.'

'Well, leaving money out of it, don't you suppose that Charles and Sophie loved each other?'

'Love—*that*? A lamb and a wolf!'

Avery spoke so vehemently that I thought she would fly out of her chair; her pearls bounced on her breast like ping-pong balls.

'You're very hard on Charles, Aunt.'

'Perhaps,' she sniffed, 'perhaps I have spoken rather strongly.

76

Nonetheless, I am sure I am right in saying that he used his attractiveness irresponsibly. Well, it's all over now. Poor Sophie!' She sighed. 'Anyway, my dear, I'm glad I've had the chance to see you. It must be a good seven years since we met: do you remember when I came to collect Sophie in Cambridge and take her off to the Old World? Your mother and father acted as if they were sending a paper boat over Niagara —and they were, too. Dear, dear, how hard the years have been on all of us! You're not much different from what you were then, though. Older, I can see!' She grinned at me, baring her tiny, oblong teeth; she bore a remarkable resemblance to a rabbit, I thought, or a rat. 'But you've kept your figure. You'd never know you were on the wrong side of twenty-five. You and Sophie never had to worry about your weight—like your father in that respect—my side of the family always ran to fat!' She sighed again. 'Anyway, my dear, enjoy yourself, but take care. London's a good place to live in, but not to die in. You are going back to Mrs Lofting's soon, I trust?'

'Yes, in January.'

'Well, come see me on the Riviera before then, if you can. Just nip down, any week-end. Bring the boy, if you like. We're in one of the most sheltered areas, you know—it's a moot point whether we or Beaulieu have the mildest climate.'

'Thanks very much, Aunt, but I think I've done enough travelling for a while. And Patrick will want to be with his father over the Christmas holidays.'

'Oh, quite, quite, my dear, I understand. I'd rather like to see the boy, but he's in school at this hour, isn't he? Oh well, I'd probably scare him, a fierce old woman like me.' Avery's eyes looked suddenly sad and astute. Had I misjudged yet another human being? She got up to go, and I embraced her warmly. She went on talking as I saw her to the door. 'Teach the boy French, though, be sure to teach him French. There's no substitute for civilization, though Rome crumble about our heads! I must hurry now, Sarah dear. The plane's at one; I've kept the taxi waiting all this time. Good-bye, my dear! Say hello to Charles for me—I won't say, give him my love! *Au revoir!*'

She bustled down the path, her furry bulk receded into the cab, a flutter of a kid-gloved hand, she was gone.

I was about to close the door when a figure across the street caught my eye: there was something familiar about the lazy slouch and cocky, curly head of the man leaning against the Embankment railing. 'Fergus!' I called. He waved, and

77

bounded across the street, neatly dodging the Friday stream of west-bound cars.

'Hello, Sarah, you look like you've seen a ghost. What's up?'

'Nothing. Just a visit from a long-lost relative.'

'Sounds like you mean "well-lost", not "long lost". The old babe in the chinchilla? I think I met her once at your house a long time ago.'

'She's my aunt. She's all right. It's just that I feel a little shaken up this morning. Can you come in for a minute? I'd like to talk to you.'

'Can't now, sorry—the coach for Windsor's due in five minutes.'

'Windsor? You're living in high company.'

'I'm speaking to the local Conservative Club. Lunch, fare, and a few pounds for snooker tonight in Soho. Going to hustle a few games—set up some suckers. Want to come along? I used to take Sophie sometimes. She said she liked the "criminal element" in my character—such a change from her Cheyne Walk circle.'

I blinked at him. I never knew when he was joking. 'Not tonight, thanks. But I do want to talk to you some time, alone, without Gillian or Patrick.'

'Sounds delightful. What about?'

'Marriage.'

'You've got the wrong man, sweetie. I never talk about marriage. Never even think about it. It gives me the hiccups.'

'I mean Charles and Sophie's marriage.'

'Don't know a thing about it. Deep as a well, both of them. Two wells. Sophie deserved better than she got, though.'

'You're a loyal friend, aren't you?'

'I never said I was Charles' friend, only his colleague, sort of. Speaking of which, things are hetting up. Rumour is there'll be an election early next year, May or June probably. And rumour is that Charles wants the nomination that's open in Nottinghamshire.'

'So I've heard. Do you think he has a chance?'

'Might have. It's a marginal seat. He'll have to play his cards right. He has a way of stepping on toes. And he'll have to spread the money round a bit.'

'Money. I'm sick of the word.'

'So am I, old girl, but I learned it at my mother's knee. Other babies said "Mummy"; I said "Mu-mu-mu-mu-money". They're giving me five pounds for my talk today. Not much to hustle with, but better than nothing.'

'Why is Charles so set on being in Parliament?'

78

'A place of prestige, a place in the sun. No artisan he.'

'But it's not easy work, is it? And MPs don't make lots of money?'

'I don't think it's "easiness" he's after, or money as an end in itself. It's something else. He's probably as much of a gambler as I am, in his own way. But why all these questions? You can't plumb people for ever, you know, Sarah. You'll drive them crazy, and yourself along with it. Got to learn to float, baby, stay loose. Just like old Muhammad Ali says, "Float like a butterfly, sting like a bee." Hey, it's twelve-twenty now. I've got to dash. See you on the fifteenth!'

'Wait—what's the fifteenth?'

'Gillian's Christmas bash, of course. Hasn't she given you a ring about it? It'll be wild—her parties always are. Just be sure and eat something before you come—the gin punch is murder—and the only food you're likely to see is the lemon ring floating on top to mark the spot where the body went down! So long!'

Fergus gave me a nasty pinch, an outrageous pinch, and dashed across the street, barely getting there before the green coach for Windsor came charging down the Embankment. A last wave, and the coach whirled him away. I watched it take the rise and disappear round Whistler's Reach.

Avery, Fergus: no two beings farther apart. And yet both of them saw Sophie as an innocent, Charles as a predator, a judgment that I did not share. Charles was abrupt, unpredictable, demanding—but not, that I could sense, mercenary or malicious. And Sophie, I knew, was a past master at getting what she wanted, under any guise. Besides, how far could one trust the opinions of either Avery or Fergus? Avery was old-fashioned and self-deluding; Fergus was proud, jealous of Charles' status, and more than a little, it appeared, fond of Charles' wife. Whom could I trust, and what did it matter? As Avery had said, it was all over.

I turned back into the house. Mrs Chalmers was standing in the hall arranging a bowl of dried flowers, a monolithic figure in her black dress. I wondered if she had heard one conversation or both or none. We nodded at each other without speaking, and I made my way slowly upstairs to the safety of my room.

TEN

The afternoons drew in earlier, the haze in the air increased, ground frost rimed the grass in the mornings. Wreaths of holly and fir began to appear on the doors along Cheyne Walk, Christmas lights to shine from the windows. Occasionally, when I went walking with Patrick in the late afternoon, I would see gatherings of people moving about in carelessly curtained drawing-rooms under the winking lights of candles and chandeliers; a sight somewhat eerie to the onlooker to whom no sound penetrated, a grown-ups' Christmas panto-mime. At home in that season the festivities would have been the same but, because we were an old-fashioned clan, with more of an outdoor spirit: skating parties, sometimes as far afield as Wellesley or Waban, sleigh-rides, and excursions deep into the Lincoln woods to gather branches and berries. And, despite the increase of violence and vandalism in the very heart of Cambridge, so much so that only an unknowing visitor would wander alone across the Common at night, we still went carolling about the neighbourhood streets in the fort-night before Christmas, our breath coming in white, frosty bursts on the ice-cold air. In London, as the days grew short, I remembered these things, but I did not miss them.

What social life Charles was having at this time, I do not know. Perhaps he received invitations; the invitations he gave were nil. It was too soon after Sophie's death for him to be giving parties, he told me, and in his view the ordinary run of parties were a bore anyway, serving to disclose only how dull and petty and predictable people were. Nevertheless, he spent few evenings at home. Whether his club claimed him or other pleasures or 'homework', as he called it—for he did work diligently, I gathered, at his law practice and on the various civic committees of which he was a member—my presence apparently held little attraction for him. After our uneasy beginnings, I was surprised to find that I often enjoyed his company when he chose to grant it. For the most part, though, I was forced to find my own amusements, which was not difficult in London. By the time the second week of December came, Fergus' words had faded from my mind. Gillian apparently had changed her plans—whether about giving a party or about inviting me to it, I did not know or care. I was astonished therefore when, on one of the rare evenings we had dined together, Charles tossed his napkin on the table, pushed back his chair as if to leave, and then announced: 'We've been invited to a party on the fifteenth. Gillian Fox's "At Home". She rang up one evening when you were out. I accepted for both of us.'

'You might have told me!'

'I am telling you.'

'It's kind of her to think of us both.' My voice came down with unintended emphasis on the last word. 'But I thought you weren't keen on parties these days.'

'The difference, my dear Sarah, is that you have been invited, too. I shouldn't want to deprive you wholly of the pleasures of the season.'

I could not weigh the tone of his voice. Was there the faintest sneer in it? Always ready to imagine a slight, my instincts were to refuse the invitation, but I quelled them; I could not always be giving in to Charles, and I had had little enough gaiety since my arrival. It might be fun to go to Gillian's soirée, though I could not be said to shine in company (or out of it, as Sophie had once told me).

'Well, that's very nice of her. I didn't know she was a friend of yours. You've never mentioned her.' That was true enough; Gillian had spoken of Charles, but not the reverse.

'We've been thrown together now and then.'

'I see.'

'Why, Sarah, I believe you're jealous!' He laughed. 'Would you forbid me the company of women other than yourself?'

'Of course not,' I protested. 'Not that I have anything to do with it.'

'Oh, but you do. You're my chatelaine now, my keeper.'

'I am not your chatelaine!' I rose from the table angrily.

'Sarah—' he caught hold of my wrist—'I was only joking. You are entirely your own person, of course. But I should count it an inestimable favour if you would accompany me to Miss Gillian Fox's on Saturday the fifteenth of December.'

And so the matter was settled.

Gillian opened the door to us. She was wearing an Empire-line dress of crimson velvet; there was substantially more

81

empress than dress, however, and that of a creamy whiteness only redheads possess.

'Well—hello!' she said, smiling at both of us, but with a flirtatious note in her voice that was not for my benefit. 'How are you, darlings? Come in, you must be freezing!' She shook her coppery curls sympathetically; they were piled high on top of her head but I saw, as we followed her down the hall, that a few silky tendrils had been permitted to spill artfully down her neck. She shared a large, rambling South Kensington flat with three other girls; it was already filled with voices and smoke and the warmth of fifty or more bodies. She paused at the foot of the staircase. 'Now, Sarah darling, would you mind taking your coat upstairs, please—first room on the right? Charles, you'll have to dump yours in the larder— it's the only empty place! This way!' She turned on her heel, and Charles followed her. The scent of a rich, jasmine perfume hung on the air.

I came down the stairs, after leaving my coat, with some apprehensiveness. People had overflowed from the reception rooms into the hall, gesturing and talking like characters in a speeded-up old movie. I could not spot Charles or Gillian anywhere. I made my way towards what I took to be the bar in an adjoining room. A punch was being offered, though what was in it other than gin with a splash of pineapple juice and a few battered cherries, I could not tell, as I drank one cup quickly and then another out of sheer nervousness. There was no food; Fergus was right; a woman who gives a party can spend her time in front of the stove or in front of the mirror, and one had only to look at Gillian to know her choice. The room was crowded with people, not one of whom I recognized. I found myself boxed into a corner and almost sitting on the bar, a dangerous place to be.

'Sarah! you made it, after all! I was beginning to think that Charles had kept you in your cage tonight!'

I turned gratefully to the familiar voice.

'Oh, Fergus—I am glad to see you! Who are all these people? I'm nearly smothered.'

'Mostly television people, designers, married and unmarried girl-friends, a few business types for solidity. Foxie lacks money, but not style.' He dipped a pint mug into the punch bowl. 'Charles is living it up, I must say, in the midst of a bunch of beauties. Getting his old form back. Can't mourn for ever, of course, not even for Sophie.'

'Where is he? I haven't seen him since we got here.'

'Oh, off there, somewhere ...' He waved his mug in the

direction of the kitchen. 'Or maybe he's gone upstairs by now. There are parties and parties, you know.' He winked at me. 'Have a smoke?' He proffered a pack of gold-tipped Russian cigarettes, one of his few extravagances.

'No, thanks.' I did not let my mind linger over the prospect of Charles in a bunch of beauties. 'How did your talk at Windsor go?'

'Outstandingly, if I do say so myself. But I've made more on the horses recently than I have on the Tories. Picked two winners at Ascot today. They keep me in Sobranies, at least.' He flourished his cigarette elegantly. 'Charles was saying that if he got the nod up north he might have some work for me. Short-term, but I'm not proud. Who wants to work all the time, anyway? Besides, it's been my experience that people can't get along for long with a man of independent ideas.'

'Meaning you?'

'Meaning me, old girl.' He drained his mug exuberantly.

There was something endearing about Fergus. He loved the things that money could buy but would not put himself out to acquire it. In fact, I was not sure how he managed. He gave the impression that he skirted the edges of the underworld without quite falling in. I knew that he spent most of his evenings in Soho hanging around the pool rooms; he was good at pool, he had told me proudly, and had made quite a few pounds that way. Of course, he had added, that sort of place did leave one open to shady propositions. It was not hard to imagine Fergus lolling among the strippers and touts, the cripples, the hustlers, the drugged derelicts that filled the inner streets of Soho night and day; he seemed to feel at home among those who had failed in the eyes of society and who lived by their wits to outsmart that society. Yet he kept his innocence, or so I thought. There was something fresh and cheeky about Fergus, 'ornery' we might have said in the States. All very well at twenty-eight, I thought, but what would it be like for him ten years from now? The reflection saddened me as I looked at his rosy, sharp-featured face and flashing blue eyes. But what of myself in another ten years? It was a toss-up, I thought wryly, as to who would be the more pitiable.

'What are you looking so glum about, love? Drink up. Oops —punch all gone. Where's Gillian's bartender? She actually hired one, first time ever. Never mind, I'll get us a refill. Don't run away—back in a minute!'

'Wait, Fergus—' but he was gone, too. The smoke in the room was thicker than ever. All I wanted was a glass of water, no more punch. I turned to a man who had suddenly appeared behind the bar, evidently Gillian's missing bartender. 'A glass of water, please.'

'Really, my child? Whatever you say. Perhaps you'd prefer champagne, though? I do recommend the champagne; I brought it myself.'

Startled, I looked at him more closely. He was a guest, not a waiter. His tie was white, he wore a gardenia, and what I had taken for an ordinary evening coat was in fact a black cape which, I saw as he moved his huge bulk beneath the table, was lined in fiery red satin.

'Here we are!' he said triumphantly, emerging with a bottle of Bollinger's in each hand. 'I think I'd better keep hold of these. So careless of me to put them down,' he surveyed the crowded room, 'such riff-raff here—excluding present company.'

'Gillian has certainly packed them in, hasn't she? Though they don't look like riff-raff to me.'

'Oh, yes. Gillian always gives the air of knowing rich or important people, and since people who want to be rich or important like to find themselves in the company of those who *are*—' the cork popped out of the bottle and the wine foamed over the top—'Gillian's parties are always full of nobodies looking for somebodies. It's fascinating to watch. I simply *feed* on this sort of thing, do you?' He smiled a remarkably sweet smile, his face dimpling all over.

I stared at him open-mouthed. 'Well, I'm not sure I've ever been exposed to this sort of thing before. I don't know if I feed on it or not.'

'It's an acquired taste, my child. As all exquisite pleasures are.' He examined me swiftly from head to toe. I felt suddenly drab in my tailored green silk, though it was the handsomest dress I owned, and very expensive. 'No,' he said, continuing to smile at me kindly, 'perhaps this is not your milieu. What brings you here, may I ask?'

'I was invited along with Charles Vivian.'

His expression did not change, but the dimples went.

'Indeed? I understood that he had gone abroad, had been transferred to the Brussels branch of the firm after his wife's death.'

'Oh no, he has been in London all the time, so far as I know. Did you want to see him? I'll try to find him for you, if you like.'

'No, thank you, I'll find him when I want him, never fear. Don't trouble yourself.' His smile widened; the dimples were
84

back again. 'I gather you're an American. Are you any relation of the late Mrs Vivian, by any chance?'

'I'm her sister. I'm staying at the house on Cheyne Walk for a while, helping to look after her little boy.'

'I see. Yes, it must have been a shock for him. It was a very sudden death, wasn't it? I never heard the full story.'

'She fell off a balcony in the dark.'

'Dear me, how terrible! How excruciating!'

We gazed at each other helplessly. He poured out two more glasses of champagne. I plunged back to our earlier topic. 'And what about you? Are you rich—or important?'

He laughed. 'Oh, both, my dear, both, I truly hope and believe.'

'What do you do?' I persisted, drawn on by his bubbling manner.

'What do I *do*? How delightfully blunt you are, my child. To speak the truth, which I seldom bore people with, I don't do anything. I promote the activities of others, one might say.'

'A kind of charitable entrepreneur?'

This seemed to amuse him immensely. 'Exactly,' he laughed, his smooth face gleaming greenishly under the prisms of the chandelier, 'a charitable entrepreneur! Not that my enterprises always work out exactly as I plan them, alas!' He put down his glass abruptly. 'Ah, there's Freddie. Punctual to the minute.'

I followed the direction of his glance and saw a slight, mouse-coloured young man with pale, fixed eyes who stood stiffly by the door.

'Freddie's my chauffeur, my Neoptolemus. He'll do anything to drive my red Lotus. It's the pride of his life.' He winked at me, and I was more puzzled than ever, but grateful for his buoyant good humour. 'I must be going now, my child. Finish off the champagne for me, and do give Charles my fondest regards. Tell him he'll be hearing from me soon.' He began shouldering his way towards the door, his elephantine bulk moving with incredible grace through the swarm of bodies.

'But who *are* you?' I called after him, my voice drifting thinly above the crowd, lost.

But when he reached the door he turned back to me and pulled himself up very tall; he seemed to tower over the room. He pronounced two sharp syllables: 'Dil-lon.'

He was gone; the crowd overflowed the spot where he had been standing. Dil-lon. Dillon. Where had I met the name before? Dillon. Then I remembered: Sophie's diary. Dillon had been waiting for Charles one night in Nice. He and Charles were old friends, even then. A strange man. I liked him, though. His manner was gentle and funny, and he had taken the trouble to talk to me, which was more than I could say for my hostess or anyone else here, except Fergus.

Where was Fergus? He must have got lost while getting the promised refill, though someone, I saw, had supplied the lack for the punch bowl was full to the brim again, and a young man was cheerily holding out a cup to me. I did not want more alcohol. My face felt hot and my eyes were watering from the stuffiness of the room. I wondered where the bathroom was. Upstairs, probably, though it would be a struggle to push my way that far. Even the staircase was thronged with people now. I edged my way to it and up it, through glasses, ashtrays, hands, feet, stepping over maxi-skirts and mini-skirts till at last I reached the top. The upstairs hall was a relief, cool and empty though dark as pitch. I could make out several closed doors on either side of the long corridor. Luckily I found the bathroom at first try, splashed water on my face and arms and felt better.

As I came out, I heard voices from a room farther down the hall. The party, or part of it, had moved upstairs. My eyes were accustomed to the darkness now. The door was half-open. A faintly sweetish smell floated out, neither perfume nor tobacco smoke but partaking of both. Ten or twelve people were sprawled about the small bed-sitting room, but I only had eyes for two of them. Charles was sitting on the arm of a sofa, leaning forward talking to someone on the floor whose face I could not see. Sitting next to Charles on the sofa was Gillian; she lay back lazily against the pillows, her eyes closed, a cigarette in her mouth. But it was her right hand, startlingly white in the gloom, that drew and held my gaze. Her hand was resting on Charles' thigh. She did not move, her hand was motionless, but my heart sank sickeningly. The assurance, the repose of that hand declared the deepest intimacy between them. I do not know how I knew that; it was one of those things that one knows intuitively and undeniably. I could not move; I froze as an animal freezes when it senses danger to itself; I could not take my eyes away from that omnipotent hand. Then in an instant the tableau was broken. Charles turned from the person he had been talking to and leaned over to Gillian, his left arm sliding along the back of the sofa, his head inclining close to her face, her neck, her bosom; she laughed, and he straightened up, smiling. Her
86

hand had not moved from his leg. The communion was complete.

I could not look at them any longer. I hurried down the long corridor. My heart was racing, my breath was coming in uneven gasps, my whole body was trembling. I paused at the top of the tumbling staircase; the smoke drifted in wreaths below me. I was filled with nausea. I leaned against the wall in the dark, trying to steady myself, to stop the lop-sided feeling that had come over me. I knew in that moment that what had so afflicted me was the knowledge not of what I had seen in that room but of myself: I was in love with Charles Vivian. It was a fact as distinct and shocking to me as her hand on his thigh.

ELEVEN

To be in love, to know that one is in love, for the first time in one's life, is an overwhelming sensation; one feels that it must be obvious to the most uninquisitive eye, to complete strangers, above all to the person one loves. I hardly dared look at Charles as we drove home through empty streets in the small hours of the morning. My heart was pounding with exhilaration; but stabbing into that exhilaration was the memory of what I had seen in the darkened upstairs room. I did not know how I could endure such extremes of pain and joy. But, as with most things one has to endure, endure them I did; for Charles acted, oddly enough to my heightened sensitivity, as if we were exactly the same people who had driven north through those same streets a few hours earlier.

'Did you enjoy yourself, Sarah?'

'What?'

'I said, did you have a good time?'

'Oh ... well ... yes.'

'Sorry I had to leave you alone for so long. Gillian side-tracked me. She never lets go when she gets her claws into you. You seemed to be doing all right on your own, though. Fergus said he'd look after you.'

'Yes, he did, on and off.' I could barely recollect what I had done after coming downstairs again. In a state of nervous excitement I had talked to lots of people, about what I do not remember, with a boldness quite unlike me. I had even joined in the dancing. I remembered seeing Gillian dancing in another room, not with Charles. Charles had cut in on me while I was dancing with Fergus, and we had left shortly after. Gillian had waved good-bye to us from across the room; she was dancing with a wild grace, her curls, all shaken loose by then, streaming down her back.

We drove on in silence. The Battersea power station loomed up before us across the river, filling the blackness with golden-smoky plumes, a castle from a fairy-tale. Everything was transformed for me that night. I had to force myself to speak of ordinary things.

'By the way,' I said, 'a man said to give you his regards, and to tell you that you'd be hearing from him soon.'

'A man? How informative, my dear Sarah.'

'A fat man with a gardenia. I think his name was Dillon. He went off with a man called Freddie.'

The car swerved as I spoke, and we narrowly missed jumping the kerb.

'Dillon! Freddie Byers!'

'Yes, I guess so. He seemed to know you, and Sophie, too, but he thought you'd been in Brussels for some months.'

'What did you say to him?'

'Say to him? Why, I said you'd been in London all the time, so far as I knew. Isn't that the truth?'

'You little fool!' I was shaken by the ferocity in his voice. He added with more restraint but no kindness, 'Sarah, I should take it as a favour if you would not concern yourself with my affairs.'

Stricken, I looked away from him. The word 'affairs' reverberated between us. I thought of Gillian. The problem of Dillon seemed remote.

'I didn't know that your whereabouts was supposed to be a secret. Is Dillon not a friend of yours?'

'He's no friend of mine.' Charles' voice was cold as ice. He looked over at me and must have taken in my cringing state, for he said, more gently: 'It's all right, Sarah. You startled me, that's all. I suppose I couldn't put him off for ever, but I was hoping it would be later than sooner. There's no stopping him, though.' His face was grim again.

I felt the urge to comfort Charles and talk to him; but I was afraid to ask him any more questions. We drew up to the house on Cheyne Walk without another word.

Christmas was only ten days away. Jane, Mrs Chalmers, Patrick and I busied ourselves with Christmas preparations, and I had little time to brood on my happy and unhappy state. At the back of my mind was the knowledge that I must leave for Boston in mid-January, in time for the start of the second term; I had not been able to bring myself even to make a plane reservation. The thought of leaving this house was an anchor on my heart. It is true that Charles had asked me to stay longer, the very first day I had come to Cheyne Walk, but he had not spoken of it again. His need had decreased, while mine had grown out of all proportion.

Whatever my own turmoil, I was determined to give Patrick a happy Christmas. His school had recessed for the holidays, and we spent most of our time together. It is unusual for the season not to be a happy one, with children. The black moods that settle on adults are experienced by children, too, of course, but as a rule they lift more quickly. And Patrick, luckily, had a great willingness to be pleased. We walked, we shopped for Christmas presents, we went to performances of *Peter Pan* and *Toad of Toad Hall* (where Jane, whom we had taken with us, had bounced up and down in her seat as excitedly as Patrick), we brought home armfuls of holly and fir branches and mistletoe to deck the doors and mantelpieces throughout the house. The weather had stayed chilly but clear; Patrick and Charles had driven into the country one afternoon and come back with a huge, resinous, sweet-smelling spruce; we had set it up in the parlour and decked it with chains of cranberries and popcorn and rings of ribbon and coloured paper, with a shining, silver star on top. Patrick was enchanted; he said it was 'just like Mama used to do', but there was no sadness in his voice, and I was happy in his happiness.

With Charles' permission, I sent off Jane and Mrs Chalmers to their respective families on the twenty-fourth, not to return until after Boxing Day. I wanted to do all the cooking and final preparations by myself, to make it wholly a family holiday. The thought of leaving myself unchaperoned in the house did not trouble me for an instant, as once it would have done. I fed on Charles' every word and glance; I fattened like a hearth-side cat in the warmth of his presence. No, 'warmth' is perhaps the wrong word; his manner to me was not noticeably different from before—there were still the abrupt changes from sweetness to irony, familiarity to aloofness—but I had grown accustomed to his behaviour and revelled in his very unpredictability. And Gillian's name had not once cropped up between us in the days following the party, nor Dillon's.

On the afternoon of the twenty-fourth, as soon as Jane and Mrs Chalmers were out of the house, Patrick and I descended with anticipation to the kitchen. It was a region of the house he had little acquaintance with; Mrs Chalmers had strong views on where it was proper and where it was not proper for male children to venture. I myself was slightly intimidated, for I had never cooked a Christmas dinner by myself before. When Sophie and I had been growing up in Cambridge, the festive meal had always been in the hands of our Lithuanian cook, who succeeded admirably despite the last-minute flurries of criticism and advice that fell on her from my mother. Later,

90

after my parents' death, I had spent Christmas each year with one or another of my few remaining relatives. So it was with some trepidation that I propped up Mrs Beeton's massive cookery book in front of me, and Patrick and I, on an almost equal footing of ignorance and eagerness, began our tasks.

We decided to make the dressing for the turkey first. Patrick, working with great concentration, his tongue between his teeth, shredded two loaves of bread into crumbs; it looked enough to stuff three turkeys, though I found it was not. I chopped apples, onions and celery. Together we peeled a quart of chestnuts, approximately every fifth nut disappearing into Patrick's mouth. I set a pan of sugar and water and fresh cranberries on the stove for the sauce. Patrick sat on a stool, watching them, fascinated, as they began to pop and simmer skittishly, and giving them an occasional stir with a wooden spoon.

'Do you think Daddy will like my present, Aunt Sarah?'

'Oh yes, I'm sure he will. And he'll be pleased that you picked it out yourself.' I thought of our visit to the stationers', where Patrick had stood absorbed before a wall of coloured calendars. He had chosen a calendar with a motif of sporting scenes for Charles, mostly pictures of hunting and horse-racing. 'How did you decide to pick the one you did?' I asked idly, peeling strings off a stalk of celery and finding that very little remained of the stalk. 'Do you like horses a lot, Patrick?'

'Not as much as dogs, but Daddy likes horses. He used to go to the races a lot. He took me to the course at Brighton once. It was super! You could see the sea! And Dillon let me wear his binoculars.'

I dropped the celery. 'Dillon?'

'Yes.'

'Did you see him often?'

'No, just at the race-track. I don't think Mama liked him. He almost never came to the house. I liked him, though. He let me use his binoculars, and he bought me a stick of Brighton Rock almost as big as a cricket bat!' His voice was enthusiastic.

'Look out! The berries are boiling over!' I snatched the pan off the stove while Patrick brandished his wooden spoon helplessly in the air. Scarlet liquid was streaming down the side of the pan and dropping in great splotches on the stove and the floor.

'Are the cranberries all right, Aunt Sarah?' Patrick asked anxiously.

'Oh yes, they're fine, right as rain,' I said, with a certainty

91

I did not feel. 'We'll just let them stand a while to thicken.'

I quite forgot Dillon and Brighton as I mopped up the bright red stains from Mrs Chalmers' spotless floor. Patrick consoled himself with one of the unchopped apples from the basket in the pantry.

'Have you got a present for me yet, Aunt Sarah?'

'I certainly have. Tomorrow at this time you'll be playing with it!'

We smiled at each other, thinking of the day ahead. I had only just bought Patrick's present; I had dithered for days about what to get him. It was only by chance, a few days before, while I had been wandering down Regent Street, that I saw exactly what I wanted. Patrick loved dogs; more than anything else, he wanted a dog of his own. But Charles said he was too young to take care of one, and besides, they were a nuisance in the city, never got enough exercise. What I had seen in the Regent Street window was a giant stuffed dog, a foreign import, of chocolate-brown corduroy with floppy ears and soulful eyes and a wobbly tail. I hoped Patrick would like it; it was big enough and soft enough to cuddle and rough-house with; in any case it would have to do until the day that Charles deemed Patrick worthy of having a real dog. I scraped at a spot on the floor viciously, thinking again what despots parents are.

'Is anything the matter, Aunt Sarah?'

I looked up at him. He had found himself a perch on the counter beside the sink, safely out of the radius of any further explosions. But he appeared to be sitting right on the spot where I had been chopping the ingredients for the dressing.

'Oh, Patrick!'

'What is it?' Alarmed, he jumped off the counter, and pieces of apple, celery and onion shot into the air with him.

'Oh, nothing, my dear, nothing at all! Tomorrow is Christmas!' I caught him up and hugged him, and we both burst out laughing. Mrs Chalmers would never have recognized her kitchen.

And Christmas came. I went downstairs early to turn on the tree lights and brew the coffee and light the fire in the parlour fire-place. Sophie had added central heating to the house, but the old fire-places were not superfluous. Everything was ready. I looked at Patrick's stocking hanging from the mantel; it bulged mysteriously and exuberantly, like an ostrich that had swallowed a basket of fruit. The fresh, resinous smell of the tree was strong in the room; the lights glowed red, blue

92

and green. I opened the draperies; for once, there was no traffic on the Embankment. People had either got where they were going or had not yet begun their journeys. The Thames looked cold and grey in the early morning light. A handful of ducks floated slowly upriver towards Battersea Bridge: birds of calm, I thought, brooding on the charmed wave. Nothing had been settled, but in that quiet, happy hour I felt at peace, at one with myself and the two people I loved, still sleeping above me.

For a while that morning the spell was not broken. Patrick emptied his stocking, we breakfasted, we opened presents with much laughter and delight—until we came to the present I had bought for Patrick in Regent Street. It was the last thing he found, behind the tree, camouflaged in green tissue paper wrappings. He was entranced at the size of it. He tore at the ribbons and paper eagerly, and in seconds the giant dog stood free, wobbling on his splayed, corduroy feet.

'Oh, it's a—' Patrick's voice broke off sharply, the ribbon and paper dropped from his hand. He remained kneeling, looking from me to Charles and back again, his hazel eyes huge in his face and expressing, unmistakably, fear. Charles put down his coffee cup with a clatter. He, too, stared at me and then addressed Patrick:

'Well, aren't you going to thank your aunt?'

The corners of the child's mouth were trembling. 'Thank you, Aunt Sarah.'

'But what's the matter, Patrick?' I was as upset as he. 'Don't you like it? Did it frighten you?'

'No, it's just that ... when Mama was here ...' His voice trailed off miserably.

'When Mama was here—what?'

'Never mind, Patrick,' Charles said brusquely. 'It's a fine dog.'

But Patrick turned away from the present and began trying to fit together the new train cars and sidings that Charles had given him. Charles watched him impatiently. 'Here, let's take that upstairs and work on it. There's too much débris down here this morning.'

They left the room. I was in the midst of picking up the débris, and feeling distressed and bewildered, when the telephone rang.

'Sarah?'

'Yes?'

'Henry Hobbett-Gore here. Happy Christmas!'

'Oh, happy Christmas to you, too, Henry.'

'I'm calling from the country. Spending the holidays with my mother. Just wanted to wish you and the family greetings of the season. I can just imagine you this morning, enjoying a cosy domestic scene. Charles and the boy are certainly lucky to have you there!'

'Thanks, Henry. You have a good imagination. I hope you're having a nice holiday, too. Is your mother well?'

'Never worse,' he said cheerfully. 'Sarah, what I wanted to say—or ask, I mean—is whether you would come out with me on New Year's Eve? I thought we might do the town, y'know.' His voice rose jovially, full of self-congratulation.

'I'm not much of a party girl, Henry.'

'Of course you are, Sarah. You just need a little prompting. Mustn't hide your light under a bushel, y'know. Do come.'

I hesitated. But why shouldn't I go out with him? No one else seemed to find my company irresistible.

'All right, Henry. Thank you.'

'Fine! I'll pick you up about nine.' His voice was hearty. 'And give my regards to Charles. I'll be seeing him in a few days, of course.'

'Oh?'

'Selection board's interviewing the candidates here, y'know.'

'During the holidays?'

'Oh yes, best time to get everyone together. Say, maybe you'd like to come up with Charles and have a look round?'

'No, I don't think so, thank you.' I was not going to tell him that Charles had not even mentioned the interview to me.

'Well, whatever you say. This is the week of the big decision. Keep your fingers crossed! And don't do anything to bring scandal on the house!' he said jokingly.

'Count on me.'

'That's the girl! See you on the thirty-first then. Happy Christmas! *Ciao!*'

'*Ciao*, Henry.'

I drifted through the rest of the day listlessly. I hardly tasted the dinner that I had taken such pains to prepare. Patrick, though, appeared to have forgotten the distress of the morning, and ate and talked with good spirits, plainly delighted to be sharing a meal with his father and aunt together. Charles was polite but reserved, a manner of his that I knew well. After dinner he took Patrick out for a walk while I did the dishes, of which there seemed to be a great many for only three people. When I finally wiped the last spoon, I returned to the parlour and sat down wearily beside the fire. The tree looked bare after having been piled round with packages for the past week.

94

Only the big brown dog remained under it in homely splendour, his tissue paper wrappings slowly sinking around him.

It was not until night-time, when I was getting Patrick ready for bed, that he appeared to give another thought to the dog. He suddenly dashed out of the room, down the stairs, and some minutes later reappeared, panting, the dog peering out mournfully from under his arm.

'It's all right, Aunt Sarah. Daddy told me I could keep him for ever. He says it's all right this time!' He thrust the dog into his bed and jumped in after him. 'I'm going to call him "Pierce". That's your name and Mama's, isn't it? Or I might call him "George". He's a wonderful dog!'

I pulled the covers up over both of them and sat down on the edge of the bed. I looked down at the child gravely.

'But something was wrong, wasn't it, Patrick?'

'Well ...'

'Yes, tell me.'

'Well, Mama gave me a dog just like that.'

'I see.' No wonder the child had been dismayed when he first saw the dog this morning. 'So the dog reminds you of when she was here?'

'Well, you see, Mama gave it to me when she came back from a trip to France. Then Daddy pulled it away and it got torn and Mama got mad and I got taken down to the kitchen. I think they were about to have a terrible fight.'

'Over a stuffed dog?'

'Yes. Mama looked awfully angry when she took me down to Mrs Chalmers in the kitchen. When they let me come upstairs again, the dog was gone.'

He looked up at me anxiously. I replied quietly,

'No one will take this dog away from you, Patrick, I promise you that. Goodnight now, darling. Happy Christmas!'

He smiled then, his arms encircling the dog. Soon he slept, but murmured and groaned restlessly, as if re-enacting some ancient struggle. I stayed with him, stroking his hair, till he finally relaxed.

A five-year-old might mix up some of the details, I thought, but it was not a story he would make up. The account puzzled me, and I felt anger as well as puzzlement. It seemed that Charles and Sophie had treated their son as lightly and recklessly as they had the toy itself. But the fight over the dog could only have been the shadow of some other conflict between them. But conflict over what? It came home to me anew, and most disturbingly, how little I knew of Sophie or Charles and nothing whatever of their married life.

Patrick was breathing deeply and peacefully now. I walked as lightly as I could out of the room. The stairway was dark. I went down two flights and paused on the landing. I could see a crack of light under the closed door of Charles' study. Had he already shut himself up, without even saying goodnight? I wanted to talk to him, to have out this matter of the squabble over the dog. I hesitated, then descended to the ground floor without knocking at his door. The truth is, I suppose, I was afraid of him—or afraid of what he might tell me. I bolted the front door, checked that everything was put away in the kitchen, and went into the parlour. The coals were still glowing faintly in the blackened fire-place.

'Sarah.' I turned. Charles was sitting by the window, a bottle of brandy in his hand, two glasses beside him. 'I've been waiting for you. Sit down. Have a night-cap. There's something I want to talk to you about,' he said.

'There's something I want to talk to you about, too—that present I gave to Patrick today.'

'Oh, that ... that was just an unfortunate coincidence.'

'I know. Patrick told me about it when I was putting him to bed. He said that you and Sophie had a fight about it. Patrick, I gather, was caught in the cross-fire.'

'Yes, that's about it.'

'Why on earth were you fighting about a toy?'

'Obviously enough to anyone of intelligence, we weren't fighting about a toy,' he replied. 'Sarah—' he took a swallow of brandy, 'it's hard for me to talk to you about Sophie. She was your sister. And I don't know if you'd understand what I was talking about, anyway. You're so young.'

'Oh yes, four years older than Sophie.'

'Still young.' He drank off the rest of the glass. 'All right, then. We'll talk about the past, though I'd rather talk about the future. It's—well—you must have surmised the situation yourself, that first day here, when you asked if Sophie and I had been happy together?'

'I didn't know what I was saying. It was an ignorant question, a stupid question.'

'Ignorant, perhaps, not stupid. The intuition was dead on.' His voice was grave. 'We were happy together, in the beginning. More than the beginning—through four years of marriage. I suppose it was about two years ago that things started to go wrong. A very uncharacteristic lassitude came over her; she wanted to be by herself, and to paint; our usual life, public and private, went by the board. Then, briefly, she seemed to snap out of it, and we began to live a fast, busy life again.

96

But the trouble was still there, perhaps it had been there for a long time. Last October it came to light, the full horror of it.'

He paused, looked at me as if wondering whether or not to continue. Then:

'We were in the midst of my first national campaign; a by-election, for a seat in Warwickshire. Sophie was six months pregnant with our second child. She entered into the campaign —travelling, canvassing, meeting people—with as much gusto as she did everything else. Then, ten days before the ballot, she lost the baby. Went into premature labour. It lived for four hours. It—he—was too small to survive, lungs weren't working properly.'

'Sophie never told me!' I was aghast.

'I'm not surprised. Sophie was very proud, you know. She wouldn't talk about it to anyone. And she didn't look on it as sheer bad luck, something that might have happened to anyone. She blamed me for it. Said that I cared only about my own career, that I hadn't thought of her and the child at all.'

'Had you?' I, too, had experienced, in a few short weeks, something of this man's egoism. What must it have been like for Sophie in a time of anguish and loss?

'Of course I had! It was Sophie's idea, not mine, to throw herself into the campaign. She never wanted to be left out of anything. I think she looked on it as her election as much as mine. And she always played to win. We were alike in that respect, at least.'

'But you lost.'

'I lost. But I had a foot in the door. My name was known. And here I am again, going through the same gruelling business in Nottinghamshire.'

'So you do care more about getting into Parliament than anything else.'

'Anything else? What is "anything else"? What have I got left? Sophie's gone, the baby's gone. All I've got is Patrick, and I'm not even sure that I've got him.'

He poured himself another brandy. I had not tasted mine.

'No, election day came and I lost, but I had already lost Sophie. It wasn't simply the loss of the child. Or rather, I think the loss of the child made her feel how transient all things are, life itself. As the days went by, she got worse not better. Her grieving for the child turned to grief for herself. She began to feel, she became convinced, that only what one created by oneself—and for her that meant pictures, painting—had any

97

value and permanence. She said you could only count on what you did yourself, that you couldn't trust anyone else. She yearned for her old life, the days when she was "free", as she put it, and trying her wings as a painter. She made no secret of it to me'—his voice was tense with emotion—'that she looked on her marriage as the major mistake of her life.'

'That must have been—difficult,' I murmured, feeling suddenly an intruder into other, more passionate lives.

'Difficult? It was impossible. She spent hours, whole nights sometimes, locked up with herself in that attic studio, painting. And when she wasn't painting, she was scribbling away in her diary. She wouldn't talk to anyone—not that she'd ever been one for girly-girly friendships! Her diary was her only confidante. I came to hate the sight of those little blue books. She stopped caring about us, about the house, about her own appearance. She let everything go to pieces.'

'That sounds very unlike Sophie.'

'Everything was unlike what it had been. Our life together bore no resemblance to what it had been when we were first married. She virtually abandoned painting when we came to London. She was intent on nest-making and, I believe, on me. And when Patrick was born, that completed the idyll. She was wildly happy with him. I was delighted too, of course— my first child and a son.'

Insufferable man! I thought to myself, but jealous withal of Sophie for having given him such pleasure.

'That period seems incredible to me, looking back,' he continued. 'I can hardly believe it existed. It's like knowing that somewhere, under layers of pigment and varnishes, a perfect painting exists, to be discovered only by some suprahuman X-ray. Sophie obliterated our early life, quickly, irrecoverably. I can't begin to tell you what our life became, the layers of ugliness, deception, guilt, accusation. We began to argue about everything, anything. Patrick was one of our favourite means to club each other. Sophie, when she could be troubled to remember his existence, indulged him; she gave him anything, any time. She said she had had too many rules and restrictions in her own childhood; I doubted that; she probably had fewer than I did. In any case, I was very strict with Patrick, very demanding; I wanted decorum preserved. Sophie had Jane to help her, but she always refused to get a proper, full-time nanny for the boy. She said she wanted to raise her own child. In the early days, I hadn't objected.'

'You hadn't objected! I should hope not!'

'Sarah, don't be like Sophie, I beg you. I value you for your difference from her—your common sense, among other things —not for your likeness, God knows. Now keep a cool head, and let me finish.'

'Keep a cool head! You "value" me, do you? Are you thinking that perhaps you can employ me as that proper, sensible, cool-headed nanny that Sophie wouldn't have in the house!' I was furious. He could not know how he had stung me.

'Not at all. What I am thinking—though this hardly seems the time to raise the subject—'

'I don't want to know what you're thinking!' I stormed. 'What were you thinking of when Sophie was so sick and in need of help? Didn't you do anything to help her? Didn't you get a doctor for her, a psychiatrist?'

'I tried. For months she refused any professional help. She wouldn't even talk to her obstetrician. She said there was nothing wrong with her except me. You can't make someone see a psychiatrist if she refuses to go. And she wasn't insane, God knows, just angry, confused.'

'But couldn't you have made an effort to give her the time and closeness she needed?'

'I did. I missed I don't know how much work, how many appointments to spend time with her. But she didn't want me. I couldn't talk to her, I couldn't touch her. I certainly could not approach her bed; she left me in no doubt about that. She taunted me with tales of other lovers, liaisons with people I had known for years and with total strangers. She even implied that the dead child was not mine!'

'But the lovers were only in her imagination, weren't they? She only wanted to hurt you.'

'She only wanted to hurt me?' His voice was whip-like in its deadly mimicry of mine. 'Well, by God, she did hurt me! She cut me to the bone—and I returned the favour.' He paused. His face looked hot and flushed. The brandy bottle was almost empty. 'The best retort was sexual. Failing Sophie's bed, I went elsewhere.'

I stared at him, an uncontrollable anger rising in me. '—To Gillian Fox?'

'To Gillian, among others.' He returned my gaze coolly. 'Several others.'

'And you wonder that Sophie wouldn't let you near her? I just wonder how she stuck it as long as she did! I'll tell you this, as soon as Patrick goes back to school after the New Year, you won't see me in this house again! You can bring Gillian Fox to take care of all your needs—*all* your needs!'

My own voice, taut with fury, rang in my ears. I could hardly take in what Charles was saying to me:

'Sarah, for God's sake, listen to me! You're the one who wanted to talk about the past. Now hear me out.' His hand was on my wrist, encircling it, a vice. 'Some time before the end, there were signs that Sophie was coming out of it. In April she agreed to see a psychiatrist, and she and I began to—'

'I don't want to hear another word about you and Sophie or any other woman! You disgust me! What kind of man are you?' I wrenched my arm free and jerked to my feet. 'What woman could ever live with you?' My flesh burned where his fingers had dug into it. I stumbled from the room into the shadowy hall. The clock said nine, but Christmas was already over.

TWELVE

Henry's yellow Ferrari was plainly the latest thing in automotive design. It was as sinuous as a snake, and as low to the ground. Getting into it was a feat for a limbo dancer, which I was not, I thought ruefully, as Henry shut the door behind me and I examined the hem of my new white coat. Settling into the seat, I found myself sitting on genuine leopard-skin, with more of it underfoot. At least it did not have claws, I thought, as I slid back warily into place.

'Beautiful car, Henry!'

'You like my little motor, do you?' He patted the ebony dashboard appreciatively. 'It's my Christmas present to myself. You ought to see it on the open road—it really *goes*!' he said, as we accelerated from zero to forty miles an hour in approximately five seconds, and I struggled, too late, with my safety belt. 'Beats flying for getting up to Notts!'

Notts. Nottinghamshire. Charles. I had not talked to him since Christmas night. He had left for the north the next morning while I was giving Patrick his breakfast. I had gone over and over that quarrel in my mind, adding here, subtracting there, till I reached the conclusion I wanted: Charles was a martyr, Sophie a minx, and I was still desperately in love with him.

'Did the meeting go off all right? Did Charles make a good speech?'

Henry turned to me, his little grey eyes wide with surprise. 'Hasn't he told you all about it?'

'He isn't home yet.' And, though I did not say so, I had no idea when he would be coming home. There had been no postcard, no telephone call. I looked at Henry's face that was once more intent on the road—the blunt snout, the drooping jowls, the pink-skinned crater of his ear. He was as inscrutable as a pig. Had Charles got the nomination or not?

'I can't tell you the result of the vote, Sarah. Strictly against our by-laws—and women are the worst at keeping secrets, y'know!' He winked at me and laughed. 'It will be announced

101

officially next week. I can tell you that Charles was pretty impressive, though. Fielded the questions very smoothly. A bit too liberal, that speech, for my taste, but then I'm the original Tory squire—they don't come any squarer!' He laughed happily. He was not going to get any denial from me.

The traffic was light, and we tore through the West End at a breakneck pace, the wind whipping at the fish-like car. It must have been the coldest night of the year. I twisted the scarf that Charles had given me for Christmas more tightly about my neck. Why was I fated to spend New Year's Eve with the squarest of Tory squires? I resented Henry and his smug remarks. I wanted to be with Charles.

'What did you have in mind for tonight, Henry?' I asked indifferently.

'Oh, a little of this, a little of that. We're going to my place first. That's where we're all meeting.'

'All?'

'My crowd. Derelict aristocrats, y'know, escaping from their country houses.'

The prospect did not lighten my gloom, but I did not have much time to consider it, for we reached Henry's flat in Davies Street in a very few minutes. The street itself was deserted, the banks in mourning, the brokerage offices sealed and solid as a row of safes. Inside Henry's flat, the atmosphere was quite different. There were eight people—four men, four women—lounging about the living-room when he threw open the door. I experienced a mild, myopic panic: the women all looked alike to me, a flock of silver-sequinned doves that fluttered and giggled as Henry and I walked into the room. The men, dinner-suited mannequins, rose to their feet obediently. I was introduced all round, first names only: 'Bunny, Fiona, Diana, Sue—Jeremy, Nathan, Peter and George.' Henry wiped his brow as if the recital had exhausted him and disappeared with my coat into an inner room.

George, or maybe it was Jeremy, handed me a long glass and dropped a minute cube of ice into it. 'For you Americans,' he said, and smiled. I tasted it: neat Scotch.

'I'd like more ice, please, and some water.'

'Water here,' he said cheerfully, splashing a few drops into my glass, 'but I'm afraid we're all out of ice. Diana took most of it to make an ice-pack for Nathan's head. He's not over *last* night yet. Awfully careless planning, don't you think?'

I sipped nervously at my drink and looked at the man whom I took to be Nathan. He was lying on a sofa with rivulets of

102

water dripping down his forehead onto an aquamarine silk cushion. Everything in Henry's flat seemed to be aquamarine, orange or white; spare, modern and unsullied, except by privileged guests. My panic did not subside; I drank off half my glass in a swallow. Fiona—no, Diana—was leaning over Nathan and dropping what looked to be rolled anchovy fillets into his mouth.

'Just one more—down the hatch! That's a good boy!' Nathan gurgled a reply that was drowned out by Diana's high, fluty voice: 'No, no, fish oil is just what you need, darling. If you'd taken these last night, you wouldn't be feeling so rotten now!'

I watched in awe as she simultaneously rebalanced the ice-bag, prised open his mouth and unerringly shot an anchovy down it. Someone had refilled my glass; I had finished the first without noticing. Nathan, on the sofa, pulled himself up to a sitting position and promptly dropped back again.

'Disgusting, isn't it?'

'What?' I said. Henry was at my elbow, speaking to me. 'What's disgusting?'

'Drink,' he said.

'Drink? Don't you drink, Henry?' I looked at the glass in his hand.

'Bitter lemon only.'

'Oh.' I gulped at my drink defensively. There was less water and no ice.

'I don't approve of drinking, especially in women. It's degrading.' He looked at my glass reprovingly.

'Don't your girl-friends drink?' I asked, more loudly than I meant to, and the silver doves on the other side of the room whirred and tittered. Lowering my voice: 'Why do you go around with these people if you don't like what they do?'

'It's the price of popularity.'

He was paying the price, I thought, as I looked at his pained face, but had he gained the end? The beautiful people sprawled about the small sitting-room seemed to me no more than the careless tenants of an indulgent landlord. I had not seen any of them in conversation with Henry since we arrived. I felt little inclination to talk to him myself, for that matter. I moved closer to the mantel. It held serried rows of Christmas cards, a profusion of cherubs and angels, stars and poinsettias.

'What a lot of cards, Henry!'

'Yes,' he said proudly, 'I know a lot of people. And how about this?' He picked up a cardboard folder that held a large photograph: a row of chorus girls holding big balloons in

103

front of them—what Patrick fondly called 'shiny girls'—
beamed out at us with dazzling, identical smiles. 'My favourite
bunch,' Henry said, 'successors to the Windmill girls, the
greatest gang in Soho. Sweet of them to send it, wasn't it?
Autographed, too.' I bent closer to the photo; I would not
have guessed that the small inky marks at the bottom of the
picture had been made by human hands.

'You're quite the playboy, aren't you, Henry?' A devilish
streak, quite foreign to my nature, was rising in me. Was it
the Scotch? I finished the drink quickly, to be rid of it.

'Oh, I know them all, I know them all,' Henry said compla-
cently. 'They're quite a bunch. Much sweeter than they look.
It's a hard life, y'know. And they're always having to fight
off men.'

'Not *you*, I hope, Henry!' I said.

'Certainly not me!' he exclaimed, shutting the card emphatic-
ally and thrusting it back on the mantel. 'I admire them as
works of art, national monuments.'

I thought of the Junoesque figures imperfectly concealed by
the swelling balloons. 'Oh, I see. Quite.'

Henry leaned over to me confidentially; the smell of talcum
powder was strong and sweet. 'This crowd'—he gestured
around the room—'is really too free and easy for me.'

'Who's free and easy?' said Jeremy, or George, replacing
my empty glass with a full one but turning away without
waiting for a reply.

'You see what I mean,' whispered Henry. 'Thoughtless. But
a man must keep up appearances, y'know.' He sipped his bitter
lemon grimly. 'I wouldn't want to be thought a fuddy-duddy.'

The pathetic situation of the round little man all at once
shone through to me. He wanted to be liked, that was all; and
was temperamentally incapable of giving himself up to anything that smacked of sensuality—and intellectually unfit for
anything else. Not so different from myself, I thought, suddenly and humiliatingly. I sipped my Scotch morosely. My
green silk dress looked very flat across the bosom. I had no
need of balloons to hide my curves. I felt more than a little
dizzy. The room was hot and smoky.

'You're the kind of girl I really like, Sarah.' Henry was
breathing on me warmly. 'Not wild or aggressive. Too many
women don't know their place these days.' He sighed. 'No,
they don't make many like you any more, Sarah. You're just
like my mother, prim and proper.'

The devilish streak broke surface and would not be put
down. I had no intention of being lumped with this porcine

little man's mother. I drank off my glass at a gulp.

'Maybe I'm not so prim and proper. Wouldn't you rather I was a Windmill girl?' I said impulsively, waving my arms above me in what I took to be windmill fashion.

'Oh, no!' Henry said in a shocked voice.

'Well, can't we at least go dancing?' I implored. 'I thought you said you were a fiend on the dance floor.' I bared my teeth at him, clenched, as if holding a rose. Henry looked at me worriedly and then at his watch.

'Yes, it is getting on. Past the time of my reservation. I'll see if I can get the others on their feet.'

He succeeded, but they refused to go clubbing. They wanted to eat Chinese food; Bunny said she could not live through the night without shrimp foo yung. First, though, at Nathan's insistence, we all had to have one for the road. I had lost count of what number drink that was for me; whatever, it was too many, too fast. Then everybody was piling into cars. I was not in Henry's, I shared a single seat with two other people. It was Peter's knee, I think, that I was sitting on and his shoulder that I was being crushed into; Bunny, or Sue, cradled the other knee and shoulder.

Then we were sitting at a long table laid with a blindingly white table-cloth. Crimson dragons curled, humped, writhed their way around walls, lamp-shades, teapots and sugar bowls. My dizziness increased. I drank what I thought was Chinese tea from a tiny, dragon-wreathed cup; it was not tea, but more like raw brandy. It tasted fine. I drank up the cup next to me, too. Peter, or George, was insisting loudly to the waiter that we wanted a Peking duck to split between the ten of us; the waiter stood there helplessly, nodding his head affirmatively and waving his hand negatively; the proprietor came up to the table, and Peter repeated his command; the proprietor said that not even a *Peking* duck could feed ten people, his little joke, he said, bowing and smiling and denying us our duck. I am not sure what we finally did order—a little of this, a little of that, no doubt, for Henry was firm that we must each order something different since that was the only benefit of eating in a Chinese restaurant. What came was mostly rice, bowls and bowls of it. Jeremy said that we had to eat with chopsticks and scooped the cutlery off the table. Nathan said that anybody could eat with two chopsticks, the trick was to eat with one; we all had a go at that. The proprietor eyed us impassively.

What would Charles think if he could see me now, I wondered dizzily, as I balanced grains of rice like little white

105

fleas on a single chopstick? Damn it—what did it matter what he thought? Not so much as 'Good-bye, Sarah', not one word. He was probably nestled up to Gillian's velvety bosom at this very minute. I drank another cup of Chinese liqueur. George fed me curried crab solicitously.

Then we were all standing on the pavement again. The night was windier and colder than before. There seemed to be more of us, a devil's rout. We wove our way jaggedly across a street, another street. Then we were in a pub. Someone, a man's hand with hairs coming out of the back, was feeding me soggy crisps, and laughing. I was drinking beer now, out of a pint mug, and I remember thinking that ladies drank only half-pints. I smashed it to the floor. I was standing near a dartboard; someone was throwing darts, seemingly at me. I started throwing them back, and one caught Henry in the middle of his plump back. He turned round and gave me a baleful stare. Then we were outside the pub, in a street or square. We were holding hands; there seemed to be about twenty people now. We were dancing in a circle, round and round and back and forth; I felt myself being hugged and catapulted from one pair of arms to another. Then a clock was striking the hour, a lot of hours. There were hoots, cheers, the clapping of many hands, and the dancing became a swaying, sobbing chant of Auld Lang Syne. I had my arms around someone's neck and was swaying with him, telling him loudly that we didn't do this kind of thing in Boston. The pavement came up to meet me; I was picked up and whirled around; we were doing some kind of polka or schottische. I didn't know where Henry was; the man I was dancing with was taller, thinner; he had on a lamb's-wool sweater that was comfortingly warm and soft against my cheek; he smelled of tobacco and Guinness. I thought he might be Charles, but he wasn't.

Then we were back in Henry's flat. I was sitting on the floor of the bathroom, with two of the silver doves bending over me, talking to me in kind voices, holding out biscuits in their iridescent fingers, telling me that I ought to get something solid into my stomach. The rug was a terrible orange; the bathroom was carpeted. How could a bathroom be carpeted? 'Fiana—' I began.

'Not Fiana—I'm Diana, she's Fiona.'

I turned to the other sweet bird. 'Diona—' I tried again.

'No, no,' they giggled together: 'Diana! Fiona!'

'Fiana, Diona,' I repeated obediently, 'this rug is all wet. There must be frogs living here.'

'Only Henry,' they said, and collapsed in giggles.

106

'Oh, look, oh dear—' I pitched over flat on my stomach—
'The kitchen's carpeted, too! Unbelievable!' I was having a
very odd, possibly unique view of the flat. I saw an old rind
of cheese caught between the frame and the swinging door of
the kitchen. I saw carpet tacks sticking up like spikes where
the carpet had pulled away from the sill of the bathroom door.
How dangerous. Don't go barefoot, with naked foot stalking
in my chamber. Pierced by a carpet tack. Only Rilke knew
how to die, pricked by a rose in aromatic pain. I must get out
of this bathroom.

I was in the kitchen. My face grinned stupidly at me in a
dozen copper-bottomed pans that sprouted from the wall.
There was a wooden platter by the sink with a hunk of fat-
encased ham on it. I picked up the knife to cut myself a
slice. I came down hard. My thumb was bleeding. Cold water
was running on it. A white towel, turning pink, was being
wrapped about it. *Pâté thumb en croûte*, I thought, how
exotic. Then we, but only two, were outside again; fumes
floated up at me from a leopard-skin floorboard. I was aware
of Henry's squat figure beside me, hunched forward, like a
toad. He was staring straight ahead, as all toads do. Icy air
stabbed into my lungs. I felt for a moment revived.

'Where are we, Henry? Are we in lovers' lane?'

'We're in Park Lane. We're going home. You're going
home. You're a disgrace!'

The car plunged through the darkness. My euphoria
vanished. I felt sick. I knew that the Scotch and the beer, the
rice, the ham, the curried crab were not going to stay down.

'Stop, Henry. I'm going to be sick.' The car reeled on.
'Please stop!'

'I can't stop in the middle of Hyde Park Corner!'

He drove on relentlessly, the car swerving viciously around
one corner, another, another. And then I was sick, in helpless,
retching waves, all over his leopard-skin upholstery. I tried to
lean away, but there was no place to lean to in that tight
little cockpit.

The car stopped at last. Cheyne Walk. I was too weak to
open the door. Henry jerked me out. He held me as a police-
man holds a rioter, tightly, by the back of the upper arm,
and half-pulled, half-pushed me to the door. I found the key
in my bag, but could not see to put it in the lock. Henry
grabbed it away from me, stuck it in, and the door swung
open like magic. The house was as black as the night. I could
feel myself smiling moronically. 'Thank you, Henry dear.'

He pushed me into the blackness and pulled the door shut

107

behind me. My legs gave way and I slid to the floor, my back against the door. My head was reeling. I could smell the vomit on my coat. Charles' scarf was still wrapped miraculously about my head. 'Always true to you, darling, in my fashion'—the words of the old song ran through my head idiotically. I felt unboundedly happy and released. I got to my feet and fell straight forward. Sophie! I thought, and then nothing else.

Hands were picking me up, gathering my coat around me. I was being carried upstairs, all in a heap. I felt the comfortable hollow of my own bed under me, the softness of the eiderdown over me. Someone was washing my face with a rough wash-cloth. The figure above me was blurred, the voice came from a long distance:

'Happy New Year, Sarah!'

It was Charles. He was leaning over me, his mouth was on mine. He did not seem to mind at all what I smelled like. I could not stand it any more, these ups and downs. The tears were running out of my eyes and trickling into my ears. The absurdity of it all was too much. He was kissing me again. I was too tired to care.

THIRTEEN

Roads of sunlight lay across the room, widening and narrowing as the curtains stirred with the breeze. The light hurt my eyes; I shut them. That was no better. My head pounded, my throat was an empty well. Cinderella with her first hangover. But I was still dressed for the ball. My silk dress was a crush of wrinkles under me; I felt the dull abrasion of bracelet, earrings, stockings. Last night—how horrible, how humiliating! I rolled over into the pillow. But there was something else. Surely I was not dreaming. Charles had held me, kissed me. Remembering made my head hurt more. I lay there for some time, in a stupor of misery and excitement, before forcing myself to get up. I undressed, bathed, dressed again; every movement cost me a wave of dizziness. Had Charles kissed me out of commiseration, consolation, a sense of duty? I had known such kisses before—not many, but a few; they were not among the experiences a girl willingly remembers. I looked at the clock; the time was twelve. And the yellow Ferrari—had it turned into a pumpkin? Not likely. What was Henry thinking of me now? Oh dear! I threw myself on the bed again. I could hear Patrick and Jane laughing, on the stairs, coming closer. Patrick burst into the room.

'Happy New Year, Aunt Sarah!' He jumped on the bed and rocked back and forth happily. 'Aren't you ever going to get up? Jane's made pancakes! And I'm going to Gravesend!'

'That's nice,' I said. I wished he would get off the bed or at least stop shaking it. I looked at Jane, who was standing hesitantly in the doorway.

'Good morning, ma'am. I didn't mean to disturb you, but Master Patrick has been begging me to ask you.'

'Ask me what, Jane?' I hoped it was nothing requiring thought.

'Well, ma'am, my brother's here, and he said he'd take me and Master Patrick down to Gravesend for the day, for a little outing, to see the family, if it was all right with you and Mr

109

Vivian. I'm afraid I've been telling the child for a long time about the little ones at home, and he's keen on going, he is.' Jane twisted her apron nervously. She looked no more than a child herself.

'It's all right with me, Jane. Did you talk to Mr Vivian?'

'He went out early, ma'am. To his club, I think. And Jack—that's my brother—didn't know till an hour ago that he could have the car for the day. He drives for a family in Kensington. He's downstairs now. In the kitchen,' she added quickly.

I could not have cared less if he had been in the drawing-room smoking Charles' panatellas. Cars, driving—the very thought turned my stomach. Jane looked at me apprehensively.

'He's a very good driver, ma'am. Master Patrick will be perfectly safe, he will.'

'Of course, Jane, fine, by all means. That sounds splendid. Would you like that, Patrick?'

'Oh, yes!' He bounced up and down in enthusiasm.

'Then get off the bed, please, and be sure to put on plenty of warm clothes.'

'Oh yes, ma'am! I'll see to that!' Jane said, smiling as radiantly as Patrick. 'Um—ma'am, before I go, shall I get your lunch—breakfast, I mean?' she stammered, uncertain how to treat the strange hours I was keeping.

'No, Jane, nothing, thank you. I think I'll sleep for a while. I got home very late last night.'

'Yes, ma'am. We'll be back by eight at the latest. My mum'll give us tea. She makes lovely teas for company. She'll be pleased to have Master Patrick.'

'Can we have crumpets, Jane? And currant buns, and those little cakes with nuts on top? Can we? Can we?'

'Come now, Master Patrick. Your auntie don't want all this noise and bother.' She led him by the hand out of the room and shut the door very gently behind her. Jane was wiser in the ways of the world than I had given her credit for, I thought gratefully.

And I did fall asleep. When I awoke, the sky was darkening with storm clouds and the onset of evening, though the luminous hands on the clock by the bedside pointed to just past four. I felt much less queasy than I had in the morning; I saw things better. The familiar objects in the room seemed to stand out more distinctly as the darkness increased: next to the stuffed white cat, the blue glass eyes of the china-headed doll glowed at me from the rocker; the red roses that Avery had sent for Christmas intensified in redness and shapeliness,

110

like living things about to spring out of the vase that held
them.

A knock on the door made my heart leap. Charles walked
into the room, carrying a tray.

'Good morning, Sarah—or afternoon—whichever you
prefer.'

'Hello.' I felt myself blushing. I looked at the floor; I could
not look at him. I heard him set the tray on the table. The
smell of coffee mingled with the roses.

'Are you up to eating?'

'Coffee only.'

'Yes, I can imagine you're thirsty.' He poured a cup and
handed it to me. 'You acted as if you'd put away a whole
bottle of whatever it was you were drinking, or perhaps
several.'

'Oh, Charles!'

'Oh, Sarah!' His despairing tone mimicked mine. 'Don't be
a foolish girl. Everybody gets drunk some time. Now tell me
all about it.'

'I made such a fool of myself last night. I drank too much
and threw up all over Henry Hobbett-Gore's car, and when I
got home, you were there—you *were* there, weren't you?'

'Yes, I was.'

'And you saw me all sick and drunk. Oh dear!' My voice
was close to breaking.

'Yes, you were sick and drunk. That's certainly the case.
Don't you remember anything else?' He sat down on the bed
and took my hand in his. His voice was gentle. 'Silly old thing.
I think you'd better stay here, you know.'

'Stay here?' I repeated stupidly. I had lain here all day;
I knew I would have to get up some time.

'Yes, stay here. Stay in London.' He looked at me intently.
His voice had an urgent note I had never heard before. I did
not know how to respond; perhaps I was afraid of responding.
I looked away from him.

'I'd have to give up my job,' I said finally. 'I'd have to find
a new job. That might not be so easy to do.'

'No, it might not.' He dropped my hand and stood up, his
voice aloof. Somehow I had erred; the moment of closeness
was broken.

He walked over to the window, his tall figure darker against
the dark sky. The clouds were thick and low; the rain was
imminent. Across the river the broad-lettered sign on the paper
mill was barely visible, but I knew what it said: 'Thousands
of Pounds Wasted Daily'. Gulls swirled over the empty barges

111

like bits of grey-white paper. Battersea Bridge rested heavily on its curved, stony flanks. The sober sister of Albert Bridge, I thought, as I was the sober sister of Sophie. No arcs, no lights, no sweet prolixities. Suddenly the white globes of the Embankment lamps lighted up, quartered by their black iron frames, blotting out by their brightness the river and the farther shore.

'Thank you for bringing me breakfast.'

Charles turned. 'No trouble. Don't you want your cinnamon toast? It's my speciality. I used to make it for Sophie.'

'All right,' I answered faintly, 'I'll eat it.'

Charles, leaning against the window frame, smiled enigmatically as I bit into the cold toast, which I could hardly chew. 'What happened last night? It must have been something unusual.'

'Henry doesn't drink. Nothing at all.'

'I know.'

'Why didn't you tell me?'

'I hardly thought it newsworthy.' There was laughter in his voice. 'But do go on.'

'Well, Henry wasn't drinking, doesn't drink, and he made me uncomfortable, some of the things he said, especially about women, so the more he didn't drink, the more I did.'

'How perverse of you, Sarah! I shouldn't have expected it.'

'It wasn't exactly deliberate,' I defended myself. 'In fact, it wasn't deliberate at all. It just happened. I felt alone. I didn't want to be there.'

'Where did you want to be?'

I hurried on, not answering that question. 'There were a lot of people, girls in silvery dresses and feathered capes, and a lot of men. I danced in the street, outside a pub. I don't know where.'

Charles laughed heartlessly. 'I wish I'd been there!'

'I wish you *had* been,' I said bitterly.

'Do you really?'

He was taunting me again. And yet he had kissed me. What kind of game was he playing? Had he guessed how vulnerable I was?

'Your friend Henry should have looked out for me,' I said hotly. 'He shouldn't have let me drink so much.'

'My friend, is he?'

'Yes, of course!'

'He didn't ask me out on New Year's Eve. I thought he was your friend. And I may remind you, Sarah, that I asked you to

112

be especially nice to Henry. He carries a lot of weight in the constituency.'

'He carries a lot of weight, period.' I got the last bite of toast down with an effort. 'What did you do to celebrate New Year's Eve, by the way? Sing Auld Lang Syne with Gillian?'

'I was here, waiting for you. I had something to discuss with you, but, as it turned out, you were in no state to discuss it.' He yawned. He could not have had very much sleep, I thought, thanks to me. 'No, Sarah, I'm very much afraid that you've disgraced me for ever with Henry Hobbett-Gore.'

'Oh, Charles!' This time my voice did break, and tears of shame and exhaustion streamed down my cheeks.

He did not move from the window. 'Well, my dear, it really doesn't matter. I've got the nomination.'

'You've—got—the nomination?' I sobbed. 'Why didn't you say so before?'

'I was waiting for the right moment.' His voice seemed to come from a great distance, out of the darkness. He spoke evenly, deliberately. 'I've worked for this nomination for a long time. Now it has come to me and it means, the Labour majority being a small one, that I may be in Parliament in a few months' time. I am glad to have you to share it with.'

His words sank into me. I hardly dared interpret what he meant by 'sharing' his life's ambition. I traced Sophie's monogram with a trembling finger over and over on the border of the linen sheet.

The rain that had been threatening began to break against the window. I had loved the sound of the rain since childhood, when the nor'easters would sweep down from Cape Ann, and Sophie and I would huddle together on the window bench of the nursery, watching the rain beat against the panes of the high, round window; the bench was our ship, the window our port-hole, we rode out a thousand storms. The rain was beating harder now. My tears subsided.

'Sarah—'

Charles' voice startled me. For a moment I had forgotten that he was in the room. He, the sky, the river were invisible, or rather of a uniform darkness; there was nothing distinguishable but the sound of the falling rain.

'Yes?' My voice was calm.

'I want you to be my wife.'

I had imagined these words night and day; I had waited for them as I used to wait for the rain when the thunderclouds gathered. But now that they were spoken, I felt no release. I was out of the habit of having the gods bend to my will.

'Well, Sarah?' Charles was standing over me. 'Are you disinclined to dwindle into a wife?' His voice was half-serious, half-bantering again. A picture from Sophie's diary flashed into my mind, Charles standing over the body he had just risen from, buttoning his shirt, looking down at Sophie and telling her that he just might marry her. Was the same pattern of mockery and tyranny repeating itself? Or was it mockery and tyranny?

'Sophie—' I began.

'Yes?' I had never heard the word spoken less acquiescingly.

'Sophie was so—' my mind groped—'extraordinary.' The word came out haltingly, in fragments. I felt as if I had only then discovered how to put syllables together, to use language. It is a fearful thing to speak honestly.

'Sophie is dead.' His voice was unfathomable. He moved away from me, back to the window. 'You think I compare you with Sophie, is that it? I have watched you very closely over the past few months, Sarah—playing with Patrick, reading, sewing, talking to Jane. Can you not sense that I find a peacefulness in your presence, a warmth, a tranquillity that I find with no other woman?'

Still I did not answer. I could not.

'Yes, Sophie was my wife for six years. She gave me certain things that I doubt are in your power to give, thank God. Things I do not very much care for any more.'

He sounded tired, and I could not bear the heaviness, the pain in his voice. But even so, something in me protested and I was afraid. My sister, I had begun to suspect, had been more than a sensual, ambitious girl, and Charles must have known that, too. Yet how quickly, how cold-bloodedly, it seemed, he dismissed the one sister for the other. But we shut out from our mind what we do not want to admit. One cannot be honest with oneself for very long at a stretch: it is too exhausting, it is as if there were no glass between oneself and the beating rain.

'And you must be aware, Sarah,' Charles was saying, 'that Patrick loves you very much.'

'Do you?' I asked, in a whisper.

'As much as I can love anyone.' His voice was fainter now, too, his face turned away from me.

'Oh, Charles, I do love you!'

I had wanted to say those words for so long, longer than I had known. I did not want him to be so far away. I got up and ran to him and threw my arms around his neck and this time, when he kissed me, I did not draw away.

FOURTEEN

The cold weather that had set in on New Year's Eve, after our fair and extended autumn, worsened; wind and snow swept Cheyne Walk; the temperature sank; people wondered if the Thames would freeze over, as it had not done in living memory. But I was as insensible of winter as a bear in a cave. The weeks from January to May were probably the happiest of my life. I lived very much within myself; I could not share my new-found happiness with anyone—hardly, at first, even with Charles. I was shy in his presence, unused to giving or receiving caresses, though he and our approaching marriage were all my thought.

It may have been that in spite of my trance-like contentment I was still somewhat afraid of him, or perhaps of marriage itself. I had no one to talk to about my situation, even if I had been able to overcome my reticence. The few girls whom I had once felt close to had been married for almost a decade, and although in Boston we met for lunch or a concert occasionally, their domestic lives had removed them from me. They seemed, when I met them, tired and preoccupied, and more than one had told me, needlessly, that I simply had no idea what it was like, coping with three children under six. Were they, I wondered, looking for sympathy or merely trying to explain why we found less and less to talk about? I did sympathize but I also felt, which they seemed not to sense in their preoccupation with their growing families, if not envy then sadness, as I viewed a sphere of human existence that seemed to be receding slowly but certainly from me, Miss Pierce, with every year that passed. Their little children delighted me when, and that was not often, they brought them along to our appointments. I loved the pleasure that children took in any novelty that came their way, whether it was a taxi-ride or a dragonfly: a capacity for joy was something I rarely met with in people my own age, myself not excepted. In restaurants—for I ate out alone much of the time—I always looked for the tables with children. I became

115

accustomed and more or less resigned to being an observer of other people's families. Now, at a stroke, with a midnight kiss, a New Year's summons, all that had changed: I, too, was to come in out of the cold.

But still there was a period of waiting to be got through. Charles thought it not politic to marry so soon after Sophie's death, or even to announce our engagement; it might not sit well, he said, with his constituents or his law partners or the party. I agreed, of course, as I agreed with everything he thought and said then. I wrote to Mrs Lofting simply that the situation in London required my staying on for a while and that I would write to her again soon about my plans. I discovered that lying—or concealment of the truth, as I preferred to think of it—was not so difficult when one's personal happiness was concerned. Only to Patrick did I say that I would be staying on in Chelsea, with him, for ever. He did not act ecstatic or even surprised; 'for ever' does not have the significance for a five-year-old that it has for a newly reprieved spinster. When, somewhat disappointed at Patrick's matter-of-fact reaction, I told Charles of it, he laughed and said I lacked the hard shell that a parent develops after years of being taken for granted.

In regard to being taken for granted, he could have added 'fiancée' to 'parent', for I saw even less of him during the winter months than I had in the autumn. He seemed edgy, and with reason, I suppose, for his trial as well as mine was approaching. It was rumoured that an election would be called for the spring, and though the campaign would not officially begin till a month or so before Election Day, the candidates and the constituency associations were gearing themselves for combat. The result was that Charles worked at his office till eight or nine in the evening in an effort to get ahead of the work that would pile up in his absence, and frequently at week-ends he went up to Nottinghamshire to map out with his agent the strategy and tactics—canvassing, speeches, literature, publicity—for the coming campaign.

I was not wholly neglected, however, for Charles decided it was time to enlarge my social life and extend my English education. We invited some of his law partners and their wives to dinner, and received invitations in return; I also met a few of the younger Conservatives who were particular friends of Charles. Among the people I did not see was Henry Hobbett-Gore. I had written a note of apology to him after the New Year's Eve débâcle but had received no reply. Charles, though, had seen him and said that my note had mollified him—Henry had concluded that I must have been suffering 'delayed mental stress' because of the death of my sister. Whatever, I had quite frightened him away, and I confess I was not sorry.

Occasionally I met Charles at his club for dinner, where, on my first visit, I left a tip for the attendant in the ladies' room only to have it returned to me on a silver tray by a porter with an impassive face; Charles informed me, with sly gravity, that one never tips in a London gentlemen's club. I think it amused him, though it did not always amuse me, to attempt my education as a proper English wife. So far as I could judge from watching Charles' married friends, an English wife showed her skill by plotting an orbit for her life that crossed her husband's as little as possible; the aim was to achieve parallel courses that served, ideally, the interests of both but, practically, the interests of the husband, with a thousand light years in between.

It struck me that the English always wanted to get rid of each other: husbands, wives; parents, children—and the other way around. I saw little affection, tenderness or even interest between most of the couples in their thirties or forties who came to sit in our grand, faded drawing-room, and I wondered whatever happened to the friendly, playful demonstrativeness of the boys and girls who sauntered arm in arm up and down King's Road? The old custom of the women withdrawing from the men after dinner was, I began to realize, simply an outward and visible sign of an inward, invisible remoteness between the sexes. But even as I caught myself making the observation, I reflected that I had seen Americans drift into the same division of an evening. And why not? It is something of a relief, wherever one may be, to get up and stretch one's legs and talk to a different face in a smaller group. But what I found puzzling and annoying, though to a lesser degree than Sophie must have, was the arbitrariness of the customs I encountered, the lack of allowance for individual cases, for spontaneity. Just once, I thought, it would be nice to sit at a dinner-table and continue a conversation to its natural end.

I was not cast for the rôle of iconoclast, however; the manners I observed perplexed rather than angered me. In the long run, I suppose, I liked living in a country that was polite, non-violent, civilized, whatever vipers lurked underneath. England neither expected nor invited dazzling displays of ego; in a nation where, in contrast, it is believed that any man can do anything—and ought to, with as much razzle-dazzle as possible—some man will pick up a rifle and blast a President's head off. I had never heard of a politician being assassinated

117

in England—Ulster, of course, was something else—in modern times. Perhaps that was why the political scene in England was so fascinating to observe, the covert play of personal ambition against the ancient, mammoth spiderweb of code and custom.

March turned into April and in the third week of the month, the Prime Minister issued the expected statement to the press: a General Election in the last week of May. Parliament was dissolved; Charles prepared his election address and went north to be formally adopted as candidate; there was a lull of about a week while the parties gathered themselves for the full offensive.

I had already begun reading everything I could find concerning the election and British politics in general, including a number of articles and reviews that Charles had written during the last few years. He wrote well, with grace and incisiveness; I was impressed by how much better an educated Englishman writes than his counterpart in America. I said so to Charles on his return from the north, but he brushed it off with a laugh. He said that any such facility was from being obliged to participate in debates at school from a very early age; the training had produced in him not only fluency but a conviction of the relativity of all principles and commitments. Take the issues of the current election, he said—inflation, unemployment, immigration, taxes—he could argue the side of his Labour opponent on all of them with as much truth and cogency as his own. If that was the case, I returned, why was he so devoted to making a career in Conservative politics? He answered: 'Sarah, my dear, I pursue politics because I've led a very sheltered life—it's a way of breaking out. All gambling is. And gambling with the Tories is more fun.' His answer was no answer at all—at least, not to me, unable to shake off my New England earnestness—but it was not the first time that Charles had left me floundering.

He did not say this in the presence of his agent, who had returned with him from Nottinghamshire. The agent was in London briefly to get special last-minute instructions from Central Office, for the party was of course very keen on winning a marginal seat. The agent was a talkative little man, with a face like Terry Thomas'. He had flashy gold teeth, pocked cheeks, a whinnying laugh, and in his tattersall jacket and yellow, mock-suede waistcoat he looked less like a promoter of the Tories than of the sporting life. Despite or because of his jaunty, ebullient air, he did not have the look of an agent who was used to winning; but Charles said that he had done

118

an excellent job in the last campaign, and the constituency organization had been diligently maintained and shored up in the period since. That was important; local organizations, I gathered, were as fragile as old houses, likely to fall to pieces between elections, and it was impossible to restore them in the four or five weeks that a formal campaign allowed.

The excitement of the race began to communicate itself to me—largely, I suppose, because Charles was in it but also because an interest in politics is as natural as breathing to someone born and bred in Boston. For generations Massachusetts had managed to throw up, and sometimes out, politicians of the first order as its contribution to American life; and though my father had always been more concerned with ancient Chinese emperors than with our local, golden Irish lads, I had, nonetheless, a predisposition to be caught up in the drama of any political contest. Charles invited me to come up and have a look at his constituency once things were well under way, and I awaited the trip impatiently.

For the most part the planning and activity of his campaign took place outside my view, in Nottinghamshire, but occasionally some of the younger Tories would gather at our house in Cheyne Walk in the evening. Fergus was among the most frequent visitors. Although the constituency association had officially only one agent to serve it, and though the money a candidate was allowed to spend on the campaign was regulated, I drew out of Fergus that Charles was paying him a considerable amount to serve as a kind of personal assistant— driving him about the county, assisting with the canvassing, jollying along the voters who were already in the Tory fold. Watching the two men together, I could not imagine what had ever brought them together in the first place. Perhaps Fergus' seeming dissoluteness complemented Charles' seeming propriety, the one's loquaciousness the other's taciturnity. Their relationship at this time was certainly not equable. Charles was peremptory with Fergus; the authoritative, not to say bullying, side of his nature came to the fore. Clearly Charles liked to be in charge of things, to snap his fingers and make others jump. Better Fergus than me, I thought; I was content to observe and keep out of the way. Fergus, I knew, was proud and prickly, but he needed money, and his hunger to belong to the greater political world was so intense that he put up with the cut to his spirit. I suppose he lived vicariously in Charles' contest and anticipated triumph. At any rate, he seemed to accept the master-servant relationship that Charles forced upon him. The two of them spent hours before a huge

119

chart that Charles had tacked up on the wall of his study; there, arguing continuously, they plotted their canvassing raids, alighting with blue-headed pins on houses of committed Tories, hovering with red-headed pins above areas where the inhabitants were as yet uncommitted to either side.

Two or three times Gillian came along with Fergus. Charles greeted her, the first time she turned up, with a cool nonchalance. I imagined I could see surprise in her eyes, but she gave nothing away. We sat down to coffee in the parlour while Charles and Fergus went upstairs to study their chart.

'What's up?' Gillian said, declining sugar.

'What's up?' I looked at her innocently. I had never before been in a position of tacit superiority over another woman, and I confess I enjoyed the novelty.

'Between you and Charles.'

'Nothing's up.'

'You're looking different these days. Prettier. Who's the man?' I smiled, sipped my coffee, and said nothing. 'I thought you were going back to the States in January. Overstaying your leave, aren't you?'

'I seem to be serving a useful purpose here,' I said. 'Patrick needs me.'

'I see.' She twisted a long, coppery curl around her finger. 'You're not his type, you know.'

She did not mean Patrick, and formerly her bluntness would have cowed me. But times had changed; I had the confidence of a courted woman.

'Oh, what is his type? I hadn't noticed he was particularly attracted to any girl in London.'

In the days that followed Gillian did not mention again the tacit liaison between Charles and myself; she seemed to accept it, or perhaps she was merely biding her time, waiting for my own words to turn back on me. I saw her frequently in Fergus' company, though seldom at our house; he looking happy and buoyant, she somewhat sulky and bemused. Considering the men I had seen at her Christmas party, I speculated that she could have latched onto a more affluent and prominent young man than Fergus, but affinities are hard to divine; it may be that she found Fergus comfortable, familiar, and he for his part doted on her. His arm was always around her waist, he hung on her every word, his fondness plain for all to see, though it struck me as a decidedly one-way relationship. It did not occur to me that an observer might have formed the same impression regarding Charles and me, with the rôles reversed. For myself, I had no doubt at all that Charles was

120

as much in love with me as I with him.

While the election campaign gathered steam, my own hopes and dreams kept pace as I pottered about the house on Cheyne Walk filling up the day with one small task after another. Every room I walked into, every cup I held, every book I picked up and put down again, restlessly, seemed filled with Charles' presence. The days were lengthening now, the afternoons stretching out. There was that stillness in the air that precedes the dawn, spring itself. The snows of January and February had long since gone; the garden, though still more brown than green and the ground heavy with recent frosts, gave signs of awakening. Crocuses broke through the ground; hyacinths showed their pale, curly heads; and daffodils began to take shape on their sturdy stems, filling out in yellow-green plenitude. Already from Cornwall and the Scillies, flowers heaped the stalls in Sloane Square and the carts and barrows along King's Road—great bunches of daffodils, narcissi, jonquils, anemones and deep-hued violets. I looked out at our long, narrow, high-walled garden and dreamed of the future: I would plant more vines and creepers and perhaps some rambling yellow roses to clothe the bare brick walls, mouldy and dark with two centuries of London air; I would bring in dogwood and honeysuckle and more lilacs, the sort we had at home; and perhaps I would have a small summer-house built at the bottom of the garden. I had plans for the interior of the house, too. I would refurbish the parlour and the drawing-room, repaper the halls, the staircase. I was full of plans as winter turned into spring. I understood better how Sophie, for all her ambitious independence, could have given herself up to shaping a house, a life, for someone she loved. And I would not make Sophie's mistake of letting the whole thing crumble.

I spoke of my schemes to Charles, and he listened to me patiently, though he made no suggestions himself. He said, however, smiling, that I must not be extravagant for he was only a solicitor of average means, after all, muddling along on more the appearance than the substance of wealth.

'But I have lots of money, Charles,' I said eagerly. 'Clear and free, and not on an annuity basis, either. I'm a *bona fide* heiress, after all, and the money's doing nothing but mounting up in the bank.'

'What a delightful thought!' he laughed. 'Gold coins rolling out of the chinks of the First National Bank of Boston. How sweet to have an heiress under one's roof! Don't spend your

121

money wildly, though, my dear. Save enough to buy me a Cabinet post someday.'

He was teasing me again, and I wanted him to be serious. My chrysalis stage had ended; I wanted to talk to him about everything, and to share everything I had with him. It was intoxicating to be able to do things, give things, to one's future husband.

'I really think I ought to put my money into your hands, Charles, or at least make you co-holder of everything.' He did not reply. I looked at him anxiously. 'That's a common arrangement, isn't it, for husband and wife to be joint owners of all money and property?'

'It's common enough, Sarah, but you're overlooking one thing.'

'What's that?'

'You are not yet my wife.'

'Does it matter?'

'Oh, let us say that it might not look well if an aspiring MP were made the beneficiary of a millionairess he had only just met. I might be indicted for seduction, or criminal hypnotism.'

I smiled at him.

'Mind you, though, I intend to claim it all when we're married. I might even abandon my law practice entirely.'

'That would be nice—then you might be able to spend a little time with me for a change.'

His smile was grave, almost sad. 'I know I'm not much good to you at the moment but hang on for a while, will you?'

The answer, of course, was 'yes', and his apology sweetened by a kiss. He was not importunate as a lover. Knowing something of his relations with Sophie and Gillian I was half-expecting more. But it was almost as if there were a weariness in Charles; in the few evenings we had to ourselves we sat together in the parlour and read or wrote, and he was content to give me an occasional pat or caress, his kisses gentle, undemanding. I did not mind. I was not experienced in love-making and at heart, I suppose, I was thankful not to be called on for more than I could readily give.

As the weather improved, I began to spend more time in Sophie's attic. The attic was quieter and warmer than the rooms on the Embankment, and I liked looking out at the burgeoning garden. I had set myself the task of mastering French, for Charles spoke it like a second tongue, and my knowledge of the language had faded with my schooldays. His law work sometimes sent him to France, and he had promised to take me there, and I was eager to please him. Certainly I had plenty of time for study. Other than the two days a week I spent doing volunteer work for the Red Cross, I had few demands on my time. Mrs Chalmers and Jane carried on the work of the house between them, and I was too diffident to interfere with their customary arrangements. I limited myself to a little gardening—while trying to keep out of the way of the gardener—and looking after Patrick. He was willing now to join me in the garret, to play quietly with his cars or colouring books while I laboriously practised my French with silent mouthings. He had gradually lost his fear of the room that had seen the last of his mother; it seemed that he had shut out of his mind the dark ending and remembered only the happy days when his mother had painted there and they had taken tea. The room was almost bare now; I had had Sophie's easel, her books, her canvases and painting supplies removed to the basement, leaving only the old horsehair sofa and chair, which I planned to re-upholster, and the huge roll-top desk.

For weeks I had put off clearing out the crammed desk, though it was an irritating reminder to me every time I looked at it of Sophie and her volatile, untidy life. Charles said that he had been through her papers after her death but, if so, he had not taken the trouble to put them in any discernible order. Finally, one day in May, the day before I was to go up to Nottinghamshire for my visit to Charles' constituency, I decided to put off the job no longer.

In the spring sunshine the desk loomed large and golden; the persistent rays of the sun seemed about to warm it into life like a lump of commonplace matter that medieval alchemists thought to convert to gold. I wondered if it was in fact the same desk that had belonged to my grandfather; I did not know how Sophie had disposed of her share of his possessions. It was certainly very like. One of my earliest memories was of sitting on Grandpa Pierce's knee in the study in Quincy, and his taking out and explaining to me slowly, painstakingly, the contents of this and that mysterious crevice in his neatly ordered desk. And Sophie, hardly more than a baby, sitting on the floor, playing with boxes of paper-clips and rubber bands and propping up Webster's unabridged dictionary before her, placing her tiny fingers in the alphabet-notches of the volumes as if playing on a papery spinet.

I looked at the old desk critically. How could Sophie have made such a rat's nest? She was so careless, so untidy. But then, she always had been; she collected things just as she

123

collected people and treated them with the same negligence. The desk was stuffed with old letters, papers, snapshots, string and ribbons, torn envelopes, broken pens and gnawed pencils —Sophie had always gnawed things, including her fingernails, her one unglamorous feature. I resolutely set about sorting out and rearranging the chaos she had left.

I left the snapshots until last. There were piles of them, mostly of people and places I did not recognize, many of them signed with affectionate scrawls on the back. How had Sophie managed to inspire affection, not to say adoration, in so many people? The little cheat! All that surface warmth and gaiety, and how ill-tempered and selfish underneath! Well, no woman is a heroine to her sister, I mused. Among the unknown faces a familiar pair suddenly stared out at me: Mother and Father, snapped in the back garden in Cambridge. They were sitting on a bench under the apple tree that bore bushels of apples every year, all of them wormy despite my mother and the gardener's best efforts; Sophie and I had eaten them anyway, tucked away in our hidden tree-house from which Sophie had once pushed me out and I had plummeted to the bench below —the bench where my parents sat in the picture—and broken my nose, giving character along with pain, my father consoled me, to my stiffly regular Pierce features. Mother sat rigidly on the weathered bench, glaring at the camera, or the camera-man more likely, the diamond pin on her dark crêpe blouse making a blur of white on the glossy print; Father, in his old-fashioned linen suit, long hands drooping over his knees, pale eyes vacant, looking as if he were in another world, and he probably was. They both looked straight ahead, not touching each other, neither seemingly aware of the other's presence. What had they talked about after thirty years of marriage? Not much that I could recall, and I wondered if one of the reasons that Mother never stopped talking to us, her daughters, was to fill up the silence of his presence. Marriage was a strange business, certainly—but it would be different with Charles and me!

And here was another, of the four of us and Avery. It must have been taken at the end of the summer when Sophie was about to leave for Europe. I was standing at the top of the porch steps behind the others, frowning. My hair was done in the same way then, seven years ago, as it was now, and how unbecoming it was I saw with dismay, pulled back so tightly like that, wrenching my eyes into slanted almonds. Avery looked unchanged, too, fondling her pearls, smiling her know-ing, rabbity smile, her bleached pouffed hair sitting on top of

124

her head like a grounded dirigible. And Sophie, leaning back nonchalantly on the steps, her legs crossed, one sandalled foot kicking some imaginary obstacle in the air, her skirt hiked up to cool off or show off her shapely legs, ready to conquer Europe.

Well, that was the lot. I had been through all the drawers now. The desk was empty. I looked down at the miscellany on the floor. What does one do with relics of the dead? I could put them in the cupboard of my bedroom for the time being, though that, too, would have to be cleared out soon, I thought with a sudden thrill, to make room for Charles' things.

I was about to pull down the barrel-top lid and wash my hands, grimy from the sorting and clearing, when I had a flash of *déjà vu*, of my grandfather at his desk in Quincy saying, 'Now, Sarah, I'll show you some magic. Put your finger under this panel'—guiding my stubby child's hand to the left side of the desk—'say, "Open Sesame", give a push, then a pull, and see what happens.'

My hand on this May morning glided, as if propelled by an invisible force, to the same spot; I repeated the magic ritual; a spring gave way; the hidden compartment shot out. And there it was: a blue notebook, of the same sort I had found in Sophie's dressing-gown. I picked it up, my hand trembling, and read the words on the dusty cover: 'Sophie Pierce Vivian: Her Book'.

FIFTEEN

Wednesday, 15 August

We came down fast—I'd forgotten what it's like—swooping
in just above the waves—you think you're not going to make
it—then the plane gives a last little lunge and you're over the
beach at last and touching, running, settling, all engines spent.
In the war, planes often didn't make it. They'd wobble home
to their carrier all shot up and then swish right over the edge,
unable to manage the landing. I've seen old films of it. It's so
horrible it's almost comic, a drunk's routine out of a silent
movie. I don't know why they release coverage of it so many
years later. You feel so helpless, watching. Oh hell, I don't
know why I'm so morbid, except that I'm getting awfully tired
waiting for Charles to turn up!

It was great this afternoon, coming into the terminal, French
booming over the loudspeaker and the smell of the beach and
pommes allumettes and everybody looking bare and brown
and sexy. I kind of wish Charles had been there to meet me,
but of course he didn't know I was coming and I don't know,
anyway, how he's going to take my little surprise visit. I was
so mad at him I just wanted to swoop down and annihilate
him. But now that I'm here, it's getting away from me. Maybe
what I really wanted was just to get away for a while, to be
alone with him, free, London behind us. It's awfully hard to
stay mad on the Riviera! I wonder if that's because I met
Charles here and we fell in love and I was happiest. Dr C. says
that sometimes people get sort of frozen in their minds about
a place that meant a lot to them. Nice for me is always sunshine and flowers and palm-trees and tearing around the hills
in an old Peugeot and making love. And heat—my God, I'd
forgotten that! The poor old air-conditioning just can't compete. I had to keep the taxi windows rolled down all the way
coming in from the airport even though I just about got blown
to pieces. That taxi-driver didn't turn a hair. Stopping at a
traffic light he turns round to me, waves a little package in
my face and says, '*Voulez-vous des cigarettes, mademoiselle?*'

126

'What's this?' I said, looking at the 'High Flyer' label. '*Ah, ne connaissez-vous pas cette espèce de cigarette, mademoiselle?*' 'No,' I said. I was about to take it anyway but he snatched it out of reach and put it back in his pocket. '*Il n'importe pas, mademoiselle. Elles sont peut-être un peu fortes pour vous.*' Thinking about it now, I wonder if they were marijuana. Avery says the Riviera's a big centre for drug-trafficking now, not just the soft stuff but cocaine and heroin, too.

Avery! I'll be damned if I'm going to let her know that I'm in town. I know the first thing she'd say: 'How peaked you're looking, dear girl!' *Peaked* is one of her favourite words. And I don't need her to tell me. Nervous sprains, strains or crack-ups don't exactly leave you looking like an ad for Revlon. Well, at least the taxi-driver took me for a 'mademoiselle'—that's some comfort in my old age. And I've got back some of the weight I lost—the old bras are filling out nicely again. Charles always was a great one for bosoms.

Nine o'clock and he's still not here. Of course, people keep such crazy business hours around here. I'll give him another half-hour and then go downstairs to La Rotonde for a bite. Not that I feel very hungry, I ate so much at Georgie's. Quite a change from my usual nursery fare, boiled eggs and tinned apricot halves. That's all that Patrick will eat for lunch these days. I wonder what he's doing now. In bed but not asleep, probably, and making Jane read 'Winnie the Pooh' to him. It's an endless job, keeping him amused. I wish he had some playmates, but kids don't *play* on Cheyne Walk. He likes that little easel I made him so he could paint alongside me in the attic, but it hasn't been much help to me. I've still got to watch him every minute with all that turpentine and copal lying around. And he's always knocking things over. It just about drives me out of my mind—how can I concentrate on what I'm doing when I have to concentrate on what he's doing! He won't stay with Jane for long when I'm around, wants to be with me all the time. I guess I gave him a good scare last winter, poor thing! Oh well, it'll be better next month when he starts school. Then I'll really be able to get down to work. Got to get the new balcony put up, though. There's hardly room for a sitting cat there now. I wrote to Newby, but he said they couldn't do the job before October; I'll have to find someone else.

Well, if I have to twiddle my thumbs, this is a good enough place to do it. Charles certainly isn't stinting himself on my money. This must be one of the more luxurious rooms in the

Negresco, and I bet ain't none of 'em too scrawny. Not like the room he used to have in that little *pension*, where the floor squeaked and the faucets dripped, and the sheets on the bed were so thin you put your toe through them if you twitched a muscle. I like the big 'N's on everything here, makes me think of Napoleon and imperial grandeur. I wonder if Napoleon ever had a nervous collapse or if Josephine ever walked off with all his annuity—if emperors get annuities? They did love each other, though. Not that it ended very well.

Gee, the view from the balcony here is nice. High enough up not to hear the traffic, just the sea glittering and the bathers coming home across the Promenade and the umbrellas on the beach standing out with that last extra brightness things take on just before they fade into the night. I wish I'd brought my paints. Keeping a diary isn't a very good substitute for painting, but it's something, I guess. Funny, I can't shake the need to set things down, to write them if I can't paint them. Maybe it's because I've got nobody to talk to except that creepy psychiatrist. Anyway, Mr Argos used to say that a painter ought to make notes on *everything* because 'accurate observation is the basis of all art'—I can just hear him whining at us from the lectern! The only trouble with him was, he was so busy observing things—especially his girl-students—he never got round to finishing one good picture. *Quelle* fate!

The light's almost gone now. They're folding up the umbrellas on the beach. I could at least have bought a box of water-colours at the shop. I was in such a hurry, so silly, there's really time for everything, but you never think so at the time. I wonder if there's going to be a *nuit scintillante* tonight? Part of the Promenade's blocked off to cars, and it looks like stacks of benches set up on the centre island. I used to love those *nuits*, years ago, the floats and flowers and fireworks. People didn't have to *will* themselves to be happy and silly then, they just were, we all were. Now, I don't know, because finally the rockets would all go out and the flowers fall, no matter how much wine you drank or how hard you danced. I can't take too many fireworks and dying falls these days.

But it's going to be different now, I feel it, I'm getting better. I'm painting again—not that crazy stuff I turned out last winter after the baby died—the little oil I did last week of the garden is first-class, I know it—at least, it showed *sense*. Painting's the one thing I do that the Great White Doctor seems to approve of. He calls it 'therapeutic', the silly ass. He sees everything, whether it's painting or screwing, in terms of health and

128

sickness. Can't he realize that I paint because I want to, because I like making something as perfect as I can, something that will last? Nothing living lasts, does it? And yet, you want to make the painting itself live, come to life. And it does live, if you're good enough, if you don't let other things get in the way and beat you down. But it's going to be different now. I am getting better—if only Charles wouldn't go and pull a silly trick like this on me! Well, the hell with him. It's great to be in Nice again!

Later

Almost midnight, and he's still not back. I'm beat. Maybe it's the Negresco; you have to be riding high to take this place. I was walking back from the bar just now, feeling pretty good after a second brandy; the corridors were deserted; I don't know where everybody is at this hour of the night—out promenading or *nuit scintillante*-ing or still lying on those hard, pebbly beaches? The corridors seemed so dark and empty all of a sudden. I think the tunnels of ancient Egyptian tombs must have been like this, the heavy pillars and the rich flatness of everything. I walked by the bridge-room, the tables shrouded, past the lighted showcases filled with silk cravats and gold-enamelled spoons and doll's house reproductions of Monet and Renoir on miniature easels. Maybe it was those showcases that set me on edge, all that rich stuff floating in the void. Anyway, I was almost to the end of the hall when I saw a boy, a bell-hop, sitting on the marble base of one of the pillars. He looked worn out; maybe only his stiff, gold-laced uniform was holding him up; his eyes were closed, he had dozed off. He looked so—I don't know—forlorn? sitting there alone, sleeping, in the midst of that blackness, that painted Egyptian tomb. As I walked by, his head jerked up, he opened his eyes—he looked as if he'd come from a thousand miles away, out of the Babylonian starlight—and in a second he jumped to his feet and smiled and bowed, his whole length alert and resplendent in his plum and blue and gold-laced uniform. I smiled back, but instead of feeling pleased or reassured that everything was as it should be, I felt the whole weight of things come down on me. What must it be like to be seventeen years old and spending your days and nights bowing to strangers in a fancy hotel? Why should he be nodding and bowing to me, rich brat that I am? What are his family doing now—sleeping four to a bed in some crummy tenement in the Vieux Port? It's funny I should feel this way —I've never felt guilty before about being rich.

129

Maybe it's worse having money for a while, and then not having it, the way it was for Charles' family. Maybe that's why he acts the way he does, stinginess alternating with extravagance—on my money, of course! He didn't even want to have the new balcony put up, though he'll spend a hundred pounds on a custom-made suit. But it's not just money—there's something else about Charles. Even when he's most reserved and calculating, he's always looking for excitement. For a while, I was his excitement, I guess. But there's an odd streak in him, something that loves the great gamble. Politics is only the polite side of that coin. It's something I sense rather than know. Imagine being married to a man for six years and not knowing what makes him tick! I wish Charles' father were still alive—I need him, I need to talk to him—but he didn't even live long enough to see Patrick born. Ah, I feel low tonight, I can't figure things out.

The doctor said I should expect to feel this way sometimes; depressions aren't cured overnight, and there are setbacks, even though he has finally cut me loose from therapy and pills. But just being told it doesn't help very much. Standing on the balcony earlier, watching the people down below, it might have been the promenade in any little Mediterranean town the way the figures meet, swirl, part again, the girls and boys gliding together, *les patineurs*, the sharp blades gliding, cutting, cutting out, to die, to sleep ... but you can't paint that scene. Too much blue, too deep a night, no *belles étoiles*. The night the baby was born was the worst, though. I knew it wasn't going to live; I could tell from the way the nurses scurried around and kept sticking their stethoscopes against my belly, never leaving me alone, one rushing in when the other rushed out, it might have been a relay team for the Olympics. And then Charles leaning over me, telling me that the baby was born and well—a boy—breathing, the tiny chest pounding in and out—but I knew he was too little—they hadn't even weighed him, just whisked him away into the isolette—and then they gave me gas, but I can still hear my own voice, coming from far away, not from me, the Wizard of Oz behind a screen, saying over and over, 'But he's too little, he's too little'. And he was.

That's how it started, the depression. The doctor says it had been coming on for a long time, but shrinks always say that, it's their stock line. They're afraid to take the plunge of saying that any one thing matters, so they say that everything matters. What matters is *death*, after all. I'm not afraid to say it. The child died; he never even had time to touch me. Pure loss. The
130

purest loss. It all seems like death sometimes; everything fades, goes. How could we have been so happy once?

Thursday, 16 August

He finally came in, just after midnight, his arms full of packages and a big stuffed dog. I can't say his face lighted up when he saw *me* sitting on the bed. 'Sophie!' he says. 'What on earth ...?'

'Surprised? I came to catch a thief.'

'A thief?' For once I'd managed to startle him; all the stuff he was holding dropped to the floor.

'Oh yes, I went down to our friendly local bank to talk to our friendly local bank manager, thinking I would transfer some money from our regular account into savings, only to find we have no money to transfer—you'd withdrawn the whole amount of my annuity cheque that came in last week. A little matter of ten thousand pounds.'

'You came all the way to Nice to tell me that? Good Lord! I was going to put it back in a few days. I needed it right away, Sophie dear. I should think you could have trusted me. Did you think I'd filched it to run off with another woman?'

The bastard. But I'd made up my mind to keep my temper. 'I would've given it to you,' I said sweetly, 'if you'd asked. I've always given you money when you wanted it.' I couldn't resist sticking the needle in a bit. But he shoved it right back:

'Oh, you would've given it to me? The way you've been acting, I don't have any idea what to expect from you any more.'

His words were so cold, so detached, they really sliced into me. What the hell *had* I been thinking of? That by plopping myself down in Nice I could tell him off and lie in his bed at the same time? I felt as if I'd been split into a thousand pieces. Bluff it out, I thought, bluff it out. Don't let him see how easily he can crush you, kill you.

'Well, I see you've bought something for Patrick anyway out of your big haul.' I reached out towards the dog.

He grabbed it up and put it in the wardrobe. Silence. I knew the next move would have to be mine. He never apologizes, for anything.

'All right, Charles. I didn't suppose you'd stolen it, of course, only borrowed it.' I'd be damned if I was going to apologize either.

He took off his tie and shoes and sat down on the edge of a silly little gilded chair and looked at me for a long minute. 'Well,' he said, 'now that you're here, you might as well stay a while. Have a drink.' Warm Cinzano Bianco isn't my idea of a drink, but I took it as a peace offering. I should've known he wouldn't let me down that easily, though, because the next thing he said was: 'And what have you done with Patrick?'

'What have I done with Patrick? What the hell do you mean by that! And since when have *you* been concerned about being away from him?'

'I'm not his mother.'

'Nor his father either, are you implying? That's what you said about the baby, isn't it?'

'Oh, no, Sophie, not that again. We've been through that scene. Fergus and the others were only "pals"—wasn't that your word for it?'

'Yes, they were pals. It's a good word. You weren't, God knows. All you could think of was getting ahead, getting elected.'

'That's not quite how I remember it.'

'No, it wouldn't be. I was just something to throw down and screw when the mood moved you—not that it often did.'

'As I recall it, you didn't want me. You were off on your painting spree. And even when I thought you were back to normal again, and when you insisted on electioneering with me, the walls were up. And after the baby was born—'

'And died—'

'And died ... we couldn't be in a room two minutes together without fighting—when we were speaking at all, that is.'

'It doesn't seem to be much different now, does it, in spite of my "psychotherapy"? No, not even in the bridal suite of the Negresco or whatever this is. Pretty fancy fittings you've got here. Bed comfortable?'

'You ought to know. It looks as though you've been living in it.'

I saw what he meant. Movie magazines, *Figaro* and *Nice-Matin*, cigarette wrappers, the contents of my travelling kit were strewn over the coverlet. I slumped back against the pillows. He always manages to put you in the wrong. I tried once more:

'I didn't really come here to scold you about the money. I thought I did but I didn't. I just wanted to be with you again, alone, free, the last two years washed out.'

I had made him a present of the truth, a truth I hadn't known until I got here, but he didn't seem very keen on having it. He just looked at me and said wearily, 'All right, Sophie. But this wasn't the time. You know I'm here on business. I have to be in Marseilles tomorrow and Cannes the day after.'

'O.K., I'll come with you. I've never been to Marseilles.'

'It's a big, dirty city.'

'Fine, sounds just like London.'

'It's not. And you can't come with me. I've got too many people to see, too much business on hand.'

'What business? Why don't you ever talk to me about what you're doing? We never talk any more.'

'Nothing worth talking about. My elderly, expatriate clients wouldn't interest you. You wouldn't understand. I wouldn't want you to understand, anyway. Things happen to people's lives that they can't predict.'

'Something's happened to this marriage that I couldn't predict.'

'People can't always live like Byronic lovers.'

'I know that.'

'I don't think you do.'

'I do. All I want is for us to be happy together.'

He sighed then. 'You're still a romantic. I never was.'

'But you were, you are!'

'Sophie, I'm just a worn-down, middle-aged man. I'm doing what I have to do, I'm following where life has led me. I alternate between wanting to be on top and wanting to be nothing. A burnt-out case.'

'You make it sound as if everything's finished.'

'Well?'

'You still want to get into Parliament, don't you?' He didn't answer. 'Is it your work that's tiring you out? You seem to have more clients than ever. I thought that once you were a senior partner you could relax.'

'And live a little?'

'Yes, and live a little. Why do they always give you all the work in France to handle?'

'I asked for it.'

'Well, ask for it back.'

'I asked for it years ago, when I wanted a change from England. Now I can't get out of it. I'm their man on the Riviera.' He sighed again, and I noticed for the first time how deep the lines were around his mouth.

'When I come into my inheritance next spring, we could go anywhere. You could do anything you wanted to.'

He smiled briefly. 'I'm an old work-horse. Work-horses aren't up to dashing escapes. Shall I give up the law firm, and politics, too? Or do you think I could be an absentee MP, residing in Nassau, perhaps, or Boston, Massachusetts? Well, maybe that's no farther away than living in London and

133

representing a constituency in Nottinghamshire. Not, perhaps, that I'll have to worry about it, the good graces of Henry Hobbett-Gore notwithstanding. In the last ten years I've got exactly nowhere.'

'I don't care where you get to or don't get to. Couldn't we at least try to have more of a life together?'

'Oh yes, my dear, we could try.' He ran a hand across his forehead. 'Let's turn in. I'm tired.' He looked tired; his eyes were lifeless; he might have been a wooden puppet sitting on that silly little chair. 'I may be through with the Cannes and Marseilles business by Saturday night. I can't promise. If I am, we can spend a couple of days here and fly back to London on Monday night. I have one appointment here on Monday afternoon. Now, sweep that junk out of the way and let's go to bed.'

So we went to bed. We lay apart, careful not to let our bodies touch, even by accident. I could hear noise and music through the closed shutters. My mind kept going over what we had said, I couldn't sleep. But Charles' breathing deepened and slowed. I had forgotten how easily, whatever the circumstances, he fell asleep. It was a long time since we had shared the same bed. I reached out and put my arm across his chest. He was dead to the world. But then he rolled over and pulled me close to him and began to kiss my body. It was almost like the old days, when Charles was new and love was new and there was nothing old under the sun.

Friday, 17 August, London

Like the old days—what a joke! I wrote that twenty-four hours ago and now everything's changed again. You pay for everything, even for one night; I've always known that, but retribution seems to come faster these days. Charles had already left by the time I got my eyes open yesterday. I was sitting up in bed writing away in this journal, feeling pretty pleased with myself and the way things had turned out during the night, and eating lovely warm croissants and wondering whether I had the energy to go for a swim before it got too hot, when the phone rang; it was the desk, saying there was a telegram for Mr Vivian and would I take it or did I wish to have him notified at the Marseilles address he'd left. I said I'd take it. That was a mistake—maybe! The sleepy-eyed bell-boy I saw the other night, or one who looks just like him, brought it round. I licked the butter off my fingers and opened it without a second thought. I've never had scruples about reading other people's mail, Sarah would turn over in her

134

grave, the prissy old thing. Don't interfere, she says, respect people's privacy. There's something very off-putting about Sarah's righteousness, she makes you feel like a criminal somehow, just because you're interested in other people's lives and want to be part of them. But she has her points, I've come to see that. Anyway, I am part of Charles' life, and I guess I've always felt that anything that belonged to him belonged to me, and vice versa. Well, maybe this time I should've played it her way because I got a shock when I read that telegram: MEET ME AT THE COTTAGE TWENTYTHREE HOURS SEVENTEENTH. BRING PRESENT. CANT WAIT.

Not my idea of a love letter, but the message was loud and clear. There's only one reason for meeting somebody at eleven o'clock at night! And there's only one place that Charles and I call 'the cottage', the week-end house in Sussex. Oh yes, that would be just the spot for a comfy little bedding-down. No name, no address, but I've got a pretty good hunch who would write to Charles in such a know-it-all, demanding way. Dear Old Foxie—Miss Gillian Fox, the slut! And what a nerve—'bring present'! That's just the sort of thing she'd say. I've never known just what happened between her and Charles last winter, but I know she's got brains for only one thing. No wonder Fergus took to hanging around me; I guess even Foxie doesn't have room in her bed for two at once. I'll tell her a thing or two! Will she ever be surprised when it's MRS Vivian who keeps that tryst!

But now that I'm back in London, I'm getting cold feet. Charles will wonder where in blazes I am when he gets back to the hotel tomorrow. *Tant pis* for him! But what will I say to her? And what'll I say to Charles—if I say anything? If I scare her enough, maybe she'll keep her mouth shut. No, Foxie would never keep her mouth shut. But what if it's not Foxie? What if it's a woman I've never met? I'll threaten her; and if I have to, I'll pay her off, if she's the kind that can be paid off. What I feel like doing is bashing her head in!

Oh dear, poor Patrick, as soon as I get here, I'm gone again. He was so glad to see me—only two days away and Jane said he'd been mewling the whole time. Well, kids ought to learn to be alone; they're not going to have their mothers around for ever! I'm glad I brought him that dog that Charles bought, though; didn't have time to shop for anything else. He loves it. We really ought to get him a dog. Oh Lord, what if I'm all wrong about the telegram? Dr C. says that it's easy to imagine evils when you're depressed, that you tend to see

135

anything out of the ordinary as directed against you personally. But I don't think I am wrong. In four hours, I'll know.

Saturday, 18 August

The worst is over. Or at least last night is over. I hope I never have to go through a night like that again. But I learned what I had to.

When I set out I was so nervous it's a wonder I didn't run somebody down; I'm pretty sure I went through at least one red light. In the country it got worse, not better. The roads looked strange to me; the moon was full, the shadows made it difficult, the trees along the side. I thought at first I wasn't going to find it; it was a curious sensation, as though I'd never been there before. I'd always looked on the cottage as our refuge, our special place—not because it was bought with my money but because it's where Charles is at his best, relaxed, unpreoccupied with how much work he's got to do (though even there he insists on having an extension phone in the bedroom—we never get away completely from his damn business!). The only place he wears old clothes and doesn't mind carrying a broken-spoked umbrella; picnics with Patrick, and pub-lunches and flying kites on the Downs. All that was as if it had never been. I went past the Baileys' place without even noticing it; I would've gone on past our lane if it hadn't been for the big oak jutting across the turning. That whammed me into focus again and I made a sharp turn—there was an awful crackling noise and I thought for a minute I had hit the fence, but it was only the tyres going over a big branch lying across the road. I would've missed the lane altogether if it hadn't been for the tree. Maybe I wanted to drive right by; they say you do things sometimes that seem accidental but aren't really. Anyway, I got there, finally, in one piece.

There was no light on, I hadn't expected there to be; I wanted to be sure to be there first. My hand was shaking when I put the key in the door. It stuck when I pushed it; we hadn't been there since June what with Patrick's chicken pox and one thing and another. Inside it was hot and stuffy, and there was a smell of rotting fruit. One mystery was solved: where Patrick had left his bag of tangerines that last week-end. I switched on the light. It was 10.45, a quarter of an hour to wait. How well did she know the roads? How well did she know Charles? Yes, well, I knew the answer to that one, too. I couldn't sit still, I walked from one room to another, turning on lights as I went, no dark doorways for me. I went into the kitchen. All those cold, white appliances, it might have been
136

a morgue, the white enamelled table a dissecting slab. I went into our bedroom; the huge soft bed, white again, another morgue, where once—no, better not think about that. I went into Patrick's room. There was his bookshelf full of tattered books, his alphabet-lettered quilt, a few stuffed animals that were just that much lower in his affections not to be carted back to Cheyne Walk. I felt sick. Was Patrick to be the only survivor of this marriage? I looked at my watch. It was after eleven. Maybe she wasn't coming? I suddenly thought that it was a mistake to leave on all the lights, she might suspect something and not come to the door. Did I want her to come? My courage failed. I was ready to run, to disappear; I couldn't face it out. I stood there, leaning against Patrick's door, paralysed. But if we do nothing, then something is done to us. I have always been one to take fate into my own hands, whatever the consequences. Sarah calls it recklessness, but I've never been able to live any other way.

I turned off all the lights, and seconds later I heard the crunch of tyres over the fallen oak branch. Oak leaves always hang on the longest; I remembered that from Cambridge days. I could hear the Baileys' dogs barking, a long way away. A car pulled up at the side of the house and parked. I waited in the darkness for the knock on the door. It didn't come—but the door was swinging open—and a figure stood out blackly against the moonlight. I walked forward boldly and flipped on the light. My hand froze on the switch. Standing on the threshold was a man, no more than a boy, gaping at me as moronically as I must have been gaping at him. A voice called from the darkness: 'Freddie!' The boy turned. A large figure filled the doorway behind him. We stared at each other. It was Aubrey Dillon.

'Mrs Vivian!'

'Dillon!'

'Charles didn't tell me he was bringing you along on this trip. What a surprise!' He stepped into the room, blinking at the brightness.

'I wasn't expecting you, Dillon.'

'Nor I you, my dear. How charming! Just we two, then? No Charles?' He looked around inquiringly, at all the open doorways.

'Charles is ... I'm afraid Charles didn't know I was coming.'

'Indeed?' Dillon raised his eyebrows, his round face sleek as a seal's. 'Freddie—' the boy had not moved, slouched against the wall, his cigarette ash getting longer and longer as he looked from one to the other of us—'Wait in the car. We

137

shan't be long.' Dillon turned back to me. I took a deep breath and said:

'Charles is in Nice. It must have been you, then, who wired him?'

It seemed to me that he hesitated before answering. 'Wired him? Did he say something to you of a wire?'

'I was in Nice, too. He wasn't in the hotel when the telegram came. I took it for him. He doesn't know anything about it. I thought it was from someone else. A woman.' Should I have said that? I didn't want to reveal any more of the tangle than I had to.

'Ah,' Dillon smiled sweetly, 'I see. You thought it was a matter of a lovers' tryst—and you thought you would take matters into your own hands. Such touching wifely devotion! But it was rather naughty of you, wasn't it? I wonder what Charles will make of it?'

'I'll settle with Charles later. What are *you* doing here is the question?'

'Why, I'm on my way to Brighton. I'd planned to see Charles on the way. I'm afraid you have caused me considerable inconvenience, my dear Mrs Vivian. Ah well, can't be helped. I hadn't made allowance for domestic passions interrupting our little business meeting.'

'Business? I didn't know you had any business with the firm.'

'Oh, I don't. It's a different thing entirely. A sideline, a mere sideline.'

'What sort of a sideline? Does your being here have anything to do with Charles taking ten thousand pounds out of the bank?'

'Oh, my dear, did he do that? How dreadful, how perfectly dreadful!'

'He said that he needed it right away and that he'd get it back in a few days. You do have something to do with it, don't you?' The relief I'd felt in not finding Foxie here was giving way to anger. Dillon sat down in a window-seat and ran his thumb along the knife-edge creases of his trousers. 'Dillon, you had better answer me. Coming to meet Charles like this, in the middle of the night—you'd think you were a pair of criminals or something!'

At that he looked up at me and smiled. 'And if we were, what would you do?'

'I'd call the police.'

'My dear young woman, on whatever grounds? It's no longer against the law for two consenting adults to get together, no
138

matter what the hour of the day or night.' He laughed a tinkly, malicious laugh. 'Why don't you ask Charles the reason for our meeting?'

'I will, never fear. I will make him tell me the truth.'

'Ah, the truth, my dear Mrs Vivian. A dangerous thing to have in one's possession.' He examined me coolly, no laughter in his eyes or voice now. 'And who knows? You might just be capable of obtaining it from Charles. Every man has his breaking-point. He has been under considerable strain. I've lately thought that even ... yes, you're a surprising woman ...' His voice trailed off, his eyes lingered on me. Slimy old thing. Dillon has always given me the creeps.

'All right, Dillon. Let's have it. What's going on?'

He sighed, a put-on sigh if ever I heard one. 'Very well, my dear. It's probably better that you hear it from me than from Charles at that. I assume you know about Charles' passion—' he paused '—that perhaps unfortunate passion—for the equine sex. Not sex, I mean, race, species. Dear, dear, isn't language tricky? His passion for the horses is what I meant to say, betting on the horses. The fact is, we had a little transaction due on that account. That's why I am here.'

'Do you mean that Charles owes you money?'

'Hmmn ... I wouldn't want to upset you. I see that he has not said anything to you about it. Ah well, that is perhaps something a loving husband wouldn't impart to his wife. No, I don't suppose he would. He probably wanted to get it all cleared up without troubling you.' He paused. 'I was very sorry to hear that you have not been in the best of health in recent months. Your nerves, I understand?'

I wasn't taking any sympathy from him. 'They're getting better. I'll be perfectly all right if I don't have to put up with too much.'

'Young children are so wearing, of course. Not that I have any, but I have been exposed to children'—he said this as if speaking of cholera on the P. & O. Line—'heaven knows how many times!'

'I asked you, does Charles owe you money?'

'Oh, well, yes,' Dillon shrugged. 'He owes me something. He was going to deliver it to me here. A mere trifle.'

'Such as ten thousand pounds?'

'Well ...'

'Have you been placing racing bets for him?'

'It's nothing, my dear, truly nothing, a trifle. Charles did ask me to place some bets for him, rather sizable bets, at the meeting at Goodwood last month. He thought he had two

139

sure winners. He didn't have the cash he needed, so I offered to lend him some at a very small rate of interest. He took the loan; he bet; he lost. I need the principal and the interest, paid now. I have other investments, other parties to represent.' He leaned back against the casement, his fat flesh overflowing the narrow window-seat. 'There, my dear, the whole sordid story.'

'That was my money he took to pay you with, the annuity that comes to me from my parents' estate.'

'Dear, dear, how thoughtless of Charles. But I'm sure he will repay you. He's very faithful, really, in his fashion. He hasn't disappointed me yet.'

'Dillon,' I said—I could hardly bear to look at him—'I don't want you to take any more bets for Charles or to make him any more loans.'

He laughed. 'I don't know how one obliterates the urge to gamble, my dear. I sometimes think it's a congenital curse. It is with me—the prodigal son of a horse-mad, alcoholic Irish peer. And I don't gamble only on the horses. Or only for money!' He laughed again. I felt lost. 'Now, now, my dear, Charles is in tender hands with me. Some of the people I know in this line would positively rip him to shreds. Better that he fall into my hands than theirs!'

Was that supposed to cheer me up? I wondered how far I could trust Dillon. He was slippery as an eel. And yet, I so much wanted to talk to someone about Charles. But Dillon was babbling away about race tracks:

'You know, my dear, you ought to come with us to a meeting some time. There are many lovely courses here in the south—Epsom, Ascot, Brighton. Goodwood is particularly charming, I think. Such nice trees bordering the course. Speak-of trees, that oak at the head of your drive is rather perilously placed, if I may say so. Freddie almost ran right through the fence because of it, and a horrible dog came prancing along the road, barking at us, a veritable Cerberus. Anyway, as I was saying, Goodwood is charming and there's a delightful inn near by—they do an excellent sole, poached and served with a little butter and lemon, not drowned in a fussy sauce.' Dillon gazed out of the window dreamily.

'Oh, Dillon, why is Charles like this? Why should he need to gamble? We have enough money now, and we'll have tons when I come into my inheritance next year.'

Dillon did not answer right away. Then he said: 'Money's part of the reason, no doubt. For many years Charles didn't have enough; it's a kind of deprivation one never quite recovers

140

from if one has luxurious tastes; now he wants to pile up treasure in the midst of plenty, like Heidi hoarding white bread under her pillow.' He shifted his huge bulk so as to face me more directly. 'Charles has always gambled, as long as I've known him, ever since we first met at Cambridge. He came into a little money then, when his mother died, and he took up the horses seriously. In a small society such as Cambridge, gamblers tend to find one another very quickly; Charles was eager for company and advice. I was glad to oblige!' Dillon smiled and fingered a large diamond on his left hand. 'I'm not sure he does it for the money any more. The urge to cut out, to take risks, to do something not quite within the approved pattern—it's not so unusual, is it? Especially amongst us proper Englishmen—and Anglo-Irish, if I may include myself. We are made to conform at such an early age—to obey, to be respectable, to queue up at Nanny's orders even to wash our hands. Alas! The personality, the ego, will take its revenge, in one way or another. Look at Lawrence, Burton, Doughty—the fascination that India and Africa and Arabia have always held for people on this snug little island—we have to explore, to experiment, preferably with black magic, not white. And the permissiveness of the present age is an illusion. Nearly everything we do in the world nowadays is prescribed for us, by computers if not by nannies. It can be rather suffocating. It can fill one with panic, as a matter of fact.'

I couldn't follow everything he said. There was so much, and some of it ... I looked at him. It was hard to reconcile the idea of panic with that smooth-faced shark. 'Are you filled with panic, Dillon?'

He smiled. 'Who knows? We all have our tensional outlets, as the psychologists say.'

'Oh yes, the shrinks. They have a name for everything. I've had enough of them for a while!' I was as close to feeling companionable with Dillon as I ever had been.

'As for Charles' gambling, it has its virtuous side. I'm sure it's the same urge that drove him into politics. Perhaps he'll be the saviour of the government some day, if he doesn't fall prey to Crockford's or William Hill first!' He laughed shortly. 'No, I don't mean to be frivolous. I suppose the gambling is a pity, since it distresses you so much. But what is the answer? If we knew the secrets of human behaviour, we could cure all the moral unfortunates of the world, n'est-ce pas? Alcoholics, perverts, drug addicts? Do you know Blake's lines, "I mark in every face I meet, marks of weakness, marks of woe?" Charles' weakness is comparatively harmless—at least so long

141

as he is married to a rich, and discreet, woman.' He laughed again, and I felt the joke was on me. My fellow-feeling for him went.

Suddenly I could not bear any more talk. Dillon was right, the truth is dangerous. He had placed his arrows too well; they fell on me as well as on Charles. I, too, had gambled with life, more than once. Wasn't my coming here tonight itself a gamble? And wasn't it the streak of wildness in Charles that had drawn me to him in the first place?

I offered Dillon a glass of vermouth, all that remained in the liquor cupboard, by way of farewell and took one myself. Was it only two nights ago that I had been drinking Cinzano with Charles in the Negresco? I wanted him with me. If only we could have settled down for the night, there in the cottage, and I could have begun to give him the trust and understanding I had failed him in for so long! But he was not there. The moon filled the sky. It was almost midnight. Dillon's Lotus gleamed like a dark plum in the moonlight; Freddie Byers leaned against it, the tip of his cigarette glowing redly. He seemed to be smiling at me idiotically. Dillon's words came back to me, 'marks of weakness, marks of woe'.

SIXTEEN

Yellow-orange lights were all I could see as the train rushed
north into industrial England. The fog seeped into the carriage itself, deepening the grime of the worn, grey seats and
the uneven floor. Above the finger-smudged mirror the webs
of the luggage rack sagged and swayed, empty but for my
one small bag. I watched it nervously as the train rocked
around a curve. We must be heading west now, north-west,
towards the coal-mining country. I had looked forward to this
week-end, to visiting Charles in his constituency; but Sophie's
diary had done its work, eaten into my mind as destructively
as acid.

Another half-hour, if the train was on time. The fog was
beginning to thin, though the day remained dark. Now and
then I could see slag heaps rising up like small mountains,
and the gigantic spines of mining machinery, steel dinosaurs
frozen in their tracks. I thought of my grandfather's abandoned New England mills. Vitality, productiveness, waste,
decay. Was there no escaping the cycle?

I got off the train in what seemed to be a deserted town.
There were no taxis at the station. I looked around me, at the
streets straggling up and down the sides of a winding ridge.
I would have to walk. I knew that Charles could not meet
me; he was speaking at the other side of the district. We were
to meet at the hotel where he had booked a room for me;
'the town's leading hotel,' he had said, and added, 'the only
hotel.' Rows of raw brick houses—not the brick of Cheyne
Walk—flanked the hilly streets, their chimneys and television
antennae tangled against the sky. There was no traffic; the
place was noiseless, a ghost town. The shops were unlighted,
some of them shuttered. I remembered Charles saying that
Thursday was early-closing day here. A little boy sitting on
a doorstep stared at me open-mouthed; two young girls,
chattering at a bus-stop, fell silent as I walked by. I felt suddenly
conspicuous in my fashionable coat, my expensive shoes and

handbag. I walked faster, I was almost running, when a voice cried out behind me:

'Hullo there! Sarah!'

I whirled around. A curly head leaned out of a car window.

'Oh, Fergus, I'm so glad to see somebody!'

'Humpf! You might've said you were glad to see *me*.'

'Well, yes, of course. It's just that you surprised me, I wasn't expecting anyone. I thought that Charles was out in the country this afternoon.'

'He is. He sent me to pick you up, but I didn't quite make it in time. Never knew that train to be on time before. Sorry. Anyway, hop in, and I'll buzz you over to the hotel.' He scooped up a pile of campaign leaflets and posters from the seat beside him and tossed them in the back. 'What do you think of this town?' he asked, as we chugged slowly up the hill.

'I don't know. It's not ... much like the south. I haven't seen much of England, of course.'

'Well, you're in the heartlands now. Charles' spiritual home, we hope, after Election Day.'

His words gave me pause; I could not imagine Charles committing his future to this bleak place. Or was he committing it to the prestige-filled benches of the Commons? And where did the Charles of Sophie's diary fit into the picture? I picked up a leaflet off the floor of the car. Charles' face, unusually affable, smiled from the wrinkled page.

'How are things going?' I asked.

'Oh, you've seen one campaign, you've seen them all. More television spots now, and the publicity releases get bigger and glossier each time round.'

'It doesn't look like Tory territory here, somehow.'

'No, wouldn't be,' Fergus answered, 'except that everybody's going broke. They're so desperate, they'll try anything—even a Tory. That's what we're hoping, anyway. Several mines have gone under, and the farmers and the small industries can't compete successfully on the foreign markets. And strikes—all the time! Even if the stuff gets produced on time, it usually sits round for weeks, months even, waiting to be transported.' The car shuddered as Fergus jerked it into second gear. 'Yes, I've got to admit it, we are lazy buggers. Swill the tea and shaft the efficiency experts—but kick like hell when the money doesn't come in!' His voice was gloomy. 'Charles is working at it, I'll give him that. I guess I know every committee room and assembly hall in this constituency. Speeches, rallies, debates, canvassing—Charles never stops talking.'

144

I somehow could not imagine my reserved and elegant fiancé addressing himself to the public. I looked down at the leaflet in my lap and smoothed out the creases in the familiar face. Familiar when I saw it in front of me. Oddly, I could never exactly remember Charles' features when he was out of sight. 'Is he a good speaker?' I asked.

'You'll find out for yourself tomorrow night—there's a big meeting at the Town Hall. Labour candidate's speaking, too. And a Liberal—first time they've put up a candidate in this constituency.'

'Do they have a chance?'

'Not a snowball's chance in hell! But they ought to help us. They're more likely to cut into Labour's vote than ours. Thank God for third parties!'

'What will Charles be speaking on?'

'Everything, old girl, everything. Same old stuff. He'll pull out all the stops with the election only two weeks away. The audiences have been pretty good on the whole, receptive. I think the women kind of like having a handsome young widower for a candidate. Not that the candidate makes all that much difference, really. People will vote the way they've voted for twenty years—unless they're hurting in their wallets. Which they are here, I'm happy to say.'

'Fergus, what a cynic you are!'

'It's not cynicism, it's statistics. Study the figures.' He turned and grinned at me. 'Still, if it's any consolation to you, the agent says there are more women volunteers for the party organization this time than they've ever had before. Charles' blue rosettes are all lovingly hand-sewn, you can bet.'

It was not a consolation to me. I did not like the thought of Charles being lionized by a flock of women while I was a hundred and fifty miles away. I scowled at my reflection in the windscreen and said nothing.

'I'm picking him up at six. He said he'd take you out to dinner—down to dinner, rather. The hotel's got the only decent dining-room in town. And here it is!' Fergus pulled in to the kerb and stopped.

'Are you staying here, too?' I asked, looking up at an unprepossessing grey building with a half-furled canopy over the door.

'Fat chance! My digs are down the street,' he said, jerking a thumb backwards. 'Boarding-house. Bubble-and-squeak and one ounce of meat. Want to shack up with me? More fun than Charles.' Fergus laughed nastily and pushed open the door. 'Well, see you *mañana*. Sweet dreams, princess.'

Fergus swung around and was gone. I registered at the desk and followed the porter up the stairway of the old hotel. It was not the Negresco. The glass cases along the walls held only fire extinguishers and coiled hoses. Burnt-orange carpeting flowed over the stairs and through the halls like a river of ancient lava. The walls were a dull beige, punctuated with brass brackets that must once have held gas lamps but which now flickered with tiny electric bulbs masked by silk-fringed shades. At least the place was clean. The woodwork smelt of wax and disinfectant; the windows were streakless, unopened and, I discovered, unopenable. I hung up my few clothes, kicked off my shoes and lay down on the bed. Sophie's diary, briefly displaced by Fergus' conversation, filled my mind.

The next few hours did not dispel the tenseness I felt. Charles turned up for dinner accompanied by the chairman of the local party organization, a Mr Twombly. He was a pleasant man who chatted about Nottingham churches and the decline of the countryside, but I found it difficult to take an interest in the county landmarks, despite his invitation to visit one of the stately homes with his wife the following afternoon. We dawdled over the last of our coffee in the lounge. It was only eight-thirty, but the dining-room and the lounge were deserted, cigar smoke the only trace of the largely male clientele. A television set boomed from an adjoining room, cutting noisily into our conversation. Mr Twombly made an early departure. Charles suggested a night-cap in his room, and I assented half-heartedly. The moment I had feared had come: I was alone with him.

When he had closed the door behind us, he put his arms around me and kissed me as if he meant it.

'Sarah, I'm glad you're here! I've missed you!' He drew back and examined me. 'You're looking tired.'

'Oh, a little.' What could I say to him that was not a lie? 'And it'll get worse before it gets better. Patrick's half-term holiday starts next week. We'll be on the go all the time.'

'I can imagine.' Charles poured himself a whisky from a bottle on the dresser and handed a glass to me. 'Why don't you take him down to the cottage in Sussex? Take Jane with you. It's nice down there at this time of year with the weather warming up. And Patrick has a great time with the Bailey children, our neighbours. They'll keep him occupied, and it will give you something of a rest.' He smiled at me. 'If you find you like it, we might spend our honeymoon there. Much more relaxing than the Continent.' He sat down on the bed and leaned back against the knobbed brass bedstead.

146

'I don't think I would like it there.'

He looked up, startled. 'Why not?'

I could not keep it to myself any longer. 'I don't think I'd fancy sleeping in a place where you'd taken your mistresses or your gambling friends or both.'

'What in blazes do you mean by that?'

There was no turning back now. 'Sophie kept a diary. I found it in the desk in the attic. She said you had taken her money to pay off some racing debts. Dillon told her about the gambling. She met him in the cottage one night last August. She had expected to find a woman there; Dillon had expected you. But you were still in France.' I ran my finger round the rim of the glass; I could not look at Charles.

'What else does she say?' he asked coldly.

'Isn't that enough?'

'Let me see that diary. I'm sure you haven't let it out of your sight.'

It was in my handbag. I drew out the blue book and handed it to him. He turned to the last page first, then glanced quickly at the other pages. He tossed it on the dresser and poured out another shot of whisky. My head reeled with a sense of *déjà vu*, of Sophie confronting Charles in the hotel in Nice. I waited for the explosion, but all he said, quietly, was:

'I thought I had weeded out her desk. I went over everything, got rid of all her scribblings.'

'The desk has a hidden drawer. You press a concealed spring at the left side and the drawer shoots out, a sort of secret compartment.' I wanted now to wash my hands of the deed. I rushed on, eager to explain everything. 'I knew how the desk worked, you see. We had one like it at home.'

'At home?' The two words snapped and fell like icicles. 'Were there even amongst the Pierces a few sins that had to be kept out of sight, a little money hoarded, a few compromising papers?' His voice rose angrily. 'What was your purpose, my dear Sarah, in throwing this diary in my face? Was it to display your own cleverness—and sneakiness? It appears that the Pierce sisters are not so unlike as I thought—meddlers, traitors, both of them.' I felt as if I had been struck; I cowered against the dresser. 'Or did you just want to let me know, as if it were news, that I've been a gambler and a sponge, hardly a man to admit to one's house, much less to Parliament? Or did you simply want to reproach me for being cruel to your sister— for I suppose you think I *was* cruel?'

He looked at me wearily and slumped back against the bed.

'I haven't gambled since I left Cambridge. There were a

147

bunch of us then, including Dillon. We used to go off to the races whenever we could. Dillon's father bred race horses—as a sideline to being a lord. Dillon got us all hooked. It didn't last, though, any more than my money lasted. When I took my degree and came back to London, that world—Cambridge—betting'—he shrugged—'disappeared.'

I said in no more than a whisper, 'But the diary—it's all there.'

'It's all there according to Sophie.'

'What do you mean?'

'Didn't it strike you as a rather odd journal, Sarah?'

'Yes. I've never heard of such bizarre happenings in my life!'

'And didn't the author herself strike you as somewhat—bizarre?'

'I'm not sure what you mean. Sophie has always had her own view of things. And she has always been a little mercurial.'

'Mercurial!' Charles snorted. 'That diary is the diary of a woman who had been under a psychiatrist's care for four months. She was under his care because she had had that nervous collapse following the death of the baby. It was something that could have happened, that does happen, to a lot of women, but Sophie took it as a personal arrow of fate against her. And this developed into a broader sense of being persecuted; everything was a burden to her, everyone was conspiring against her happiness. I had married her for her money, I had discouraged her painting, I was dissipating our—her—fortune. Her imagination knew no bounds. Those months were hell, let me tell you!'

'Do you mean ... are you saying that Sophie was not in her right mind when she wrote those things?'

Charles looked at me levelly. 'What do you think?'

I did not know what to think. I wanted to believe him, and yet, how could I discount the explicitness of my sister's words? I said faintly, 'You didn't take the money from the bank then? And Sophie didn't follow you to Nice? And she didn't meet Dillon at the cottage?'

'Wait a minute, one question at a time. Yes, I took some of her annuity—I had to, to pay for all her bills and expenditures. She threw money around as if it were straw. And, yes, she went to Nice. She "followed" me only in the sense that she took a plane later than mine. We had agreed to have a few days together *pour le sport*, as we used to say in the old days, though I warned her that the time would be mostly taken up with my business appointments. I think she spent a good part of the time simply wandering round the hotel corridors,
148

or sitting in that tomb of a bar drinking brandy alexanders. She went back to London before I did because Jane was due for her annual holiday.'

'And the telegram?'

'I received a telegram, which she signed for, but it was on business of the firm's.'

'And the visit to the cottage, the talk with Dillon?'

'Can you really believe such stuff?' He waved his glass angrily. 'Fabricated, the whole fantastic episode.' He paused. 'So far as I know, anyway. Neither she nor Dillon ever said anything to me about it.'

I felt as if the ground had been knocked from under me. Charles was pouring more whisky into my glass. It was the last thing I needed. My head swam. Was his story true? Was it more plausible than Sophie's was the question. Was my sense of truth always to depend on how other people saw things? I was weak as water; indeterminate; floundering. But it was plain, on the evidence of the diary alone, that Sophie had been in a precarious emotional state. And besides, why would Charles lie to me? What would be the gain, other than to preserve the heroic image I had of him? Could he—so self-assured, so imperious—care what I thought of him? Of course, if he loved me. So it came down to the fact that whether he was lying or telling the truth or something in between, he said what he did to safeguard our relationship. In that moment I felt more than reprieved—I felt happy. And I could not help thinking, with an unsisterly satisfaction, that whichever version of those few August days was accurate, one thing was sure: Charles and Sophie had been barely hanging together in their marriage.

I sat down beside him on the bed and put my head on his shoulder. I was too tired to move. He put his arm around me. We did not say anything. I must have closed my eyes, for the next thing I knew he was shaking me and saying:

'Wake up, sleepyhead. Why are you always falling asleep? Are you pulling another New Year's Eve bit on me?'

I answered drowsily. 'At least I'm not drunk this time.'

'That's something. Never rape a girl when she's drunk, I say.'

'Man of honour, aren't you?'

'Not entirely.'

He pulled me closer to him and slid his hand under my breast. His hand was warm, comforting. I felt myself relaxing, surrendering to his kisses. I half-protested:

'Ah, Charles, it's all so rotten.'

'What's rotten?' he murmured, barely lifting his mouth from mine. 'What is life without a consummated passion, as they say? I think it's very nice. And about time, too.'

'I mean, it's so rotten, my falling in love with my dead sister's husband.'

'Second-hand goods, you mean?'

'I'm the one who feels second-hand. Second-best.'

'But I hadn't even met you when Sophie came along.'

'But if you had ... You did love her, didn't you?'

'I'm not sure if you want me to answer yes or no.'

'I suppose you're right.'

I nestled farther into his shoulder. I felt at peace all at once. His hand was unbuttoning my blouse, sliding underneath, stroking me. I felt sleepy as a cat beside a fire. I put my arms around him. Why had I been afraid of him, of this, for so long?

A knock at the door, and Charles was up in an instant. 'Yes?' he snapped. I hurriedly buttoned my blouse and moved from the bed to the chair. Charles opened the door.

'Well, hi!' Fergus grinned at us from the doorway. 'Not interrupting anything, I hope? Thought I'd better let you know, Charles, they've moved up the time of the talk at the colliery tomorrow. I'll have to pick you up at eight. Better get an early beddy-byes.'

I could not stand the smirk on his face. 'Come in, Fergus,' I said, as nonchalantly as I could manage. 'We were just— talking.'

Charles glared at Fergus, looked at me, relented, poured out a drink and handed it to the intruder. 'Yes, talking,' he said, 'about the future. Here's to us'—raising his glass to me— 'Keep it a secret, Fergus, even from Gillian: Sarah and I are going to be married.'

Fergus and I both stared at him. It was the first time Charles had spoken of the event to anyone. And it was the only time I saw Fergus spill a drop of whisky.

150

SEVENTEEN

Going south was better than going north, I thought, as we dropped over the edge of the Downs just past Westerham. The Kent countryside was a fresh, rolling green around us; great stands of oaks and beeches lined the rims and hollows of the hills, and over all lay the mild warmth of the first fine spring day. It seemed as if we had been coasting, floating downhill, all the way from London. We had followed the A21 as far as Bromley, then branched off towards Westerham and into the country rather than taking the more direct route via Sevenoaks and Tonbridge. I felt as if I were breathing fresh air for the first time in months. Hopfields showed new, green shoots under their poles and trellises; here and there, hedges of white-blooming hawthorn intersected the fields and pasture lands. Patrick inched forward on the seat beside me, eagerly pointing out familiar landmarks as we neared our destination. The cottage lay just over the border, in northeast Sussex.

'Here we are!' he cried.

I made a sharp turn at a towering oak tree, the memory of Sophie's diary shuddering into my mind, and we rode down a gravelly lane towards a small, timbered house of white-washed stone. Dogs were racing about the car, barking wildly, and as soon as we stopped Patrick bounded out of the door and hugged them excitedly. They were all over us. I wondered if they smelled the bacon sandwiches in the bag in Patrick's hand or if they were simply glad to see newcomers in their midst. A man and a woman and three children came up over the rise east of the house. They were waving and gesticulating, but at that distance I could hear nothing; the dogs responded as if to a supersonic whistle and raced back to join them. In a few moments the whole party was upon us. Introductions followed; these were the Baileys, as I had surmised, and, though they could not have expected my coming, they did not seem to find it at all surprising that I was Patrick's aunt and that we had come to spend a week in the country. They welcomed us

151

unquestioningly. I was grateful. I had had my fill of inter-
rogations, direct and indirect, in the last few months.

Ann and Hugh Bailey helped me to unload the car, and the
children and the dogs trailed us happily into the large, bright
kitchen. The Bailey children skirted Patrick in age: a girl of
nine, a boy of seven, another boy, four. They were shaggy,
brown-haired and merry-eyed, like their parents. Hugh Bailey
laid and lighted a fire for me in the living-room fireplace;
May was a deceptive month, he said, it might feel like November when the sun went in. The children rushed outside to
carry in more logs from the shed, and Ann Bailey and I put
away provisions on the kitchen shelves. They were easy to get
on with, the Baileys. In a very few minutes I had accepted an
invitation to join them for church and midday dinner the
next day, had been told where to buy groceries and newspapers,
which butcher had the best meat, who sold the freshest fruits
and vegetables, and where the nearest doctor was in case of
emergency (the last emergency had been two years ago, when
the middle Bailey child got himself inexplicably wedged
between the seat and the back of a kitchen chair—and came off
with nothing worse than scraped shoulder-blades).

They took Patrick back to their farm with them for the
afternoon. I watched them as they disappeared over the rise,
a mêlée of running dogs and children. Did children under ten
always run, I wondered, as soon as they hit open country?
Patrick was plainly overjoyed to be with them. I longed to
give him brothers and sisters of his own to play with. Surely
thirty was not too old to start a family—my mother had been
over forty when Sophie and I were born! I made myself a cup
of coffee and sat down at the kitchen table, feeling too lazy
and contented even to unpack the suitcases. The sun poured in
through the high, wide windows and glistened on the white-
washed walls. So this was the place that Sophie had imagined
as a trysting spot, the cross-roads of hidden liaisons. I smiled at
the thought. It was hard to envision a homelier, simpler place,
or one more remote from affairs of any kind. I wondered what
Charles was doing at that moment. Saturday—there would be
another candidates' debate in the Town Hall, I remembered.
He would be good at that. I had heard him speak, and
applauded him, and he had said to me afterwards that he was
good at making the worse reason appear the better. He was
right, too, I thought, sipping the steaming coffee gingerly. At
least, he had always had the last word in any dialogue that I
had ever had with him. Not that I begrudged it to him any
more; I liked the feeling of being taken in hand, supervised, if
152

that was the word for it. Sophie never had—too bad for her! I stirred more sugar into my coffee. Only six days till Thursday and the election. And then, when it was over, whatever the outcome, Charles would have a respite and we would have the summer before us, just the three of us. And at the end of the summer—the wedding! I longed for Charles to be here already. He had been right: this was the place for a honeymoon.

Sitting in the sunny kitchen of that peaceful cottage, looking out at the open countryside that undulated in green waves on either side, I felt ashamed that I had felt the need to check on Charles' story. But the doubts had come back to me. On my return to London I had called up Dillon—his voice on the telephone had been disconcertingly like Charles'—and invited him to tea. He had come, only yesterday, promptly at four, emerging from his red Lotus like a fat, ambling Buddha. Mrs Chalmers had shown him into the parlour, their thick, dark-clad figures looking remarkably alike and intimidating to me in the shadowy room. It was some time before I could bring myself to speak of the matter that had brought us together.

'My sister made a reference in a journal she kept to meeting you at a cottage in Sussex last August, shortly before her death.'

'Meeting *me*? My dear Miss Pierce, I am not in the habit of making assignations with young married women in lonely country cottages.'

'No, no,' I stumbled, 'I didn't mean anything like that. Sophie said that you had planned to meet Charles there, to collect a debt from him.'

'You've discussed this with Charles, I presume?' Dillon said, helping himself from a plate of meringues.

'Yes, his view is that it was complete fantasy on Sophie's part. But—I had to ask you. Because she might have gone to the cottage without telling Charles. And a week later, she was dead. It's too puzzling. I don't like it hanging over me.'

'I sympathize. One hates to feel that one is being shadowed, especially by the dead.'

Neither of us spoke for a moment. Then I said, half-apologizing, 'Please, Dillon, don't for heaven's sake, tell Charles that I've been asking you about it.'

'Never fear, my dear. I long ago discerned that any continuing relationship between a man and a woman entails—deception. I plume myself on having remained clear of such entanglements.' He laughed, but the word 'deception' stung. 'Anyway, my dear, I can assure you that I was nowhere near Charles' cottage last August. I visited the two of them there

153

only once, the first year they were married, having received a note from your sister to the effect that she would like the chance to know me better. It was an invitation that, I believe, she regretted. The truth is, your sister did not relish my acquaintance with her husband.'

'Why not?'

'Have you no idea?' He smiled at me over the rim of his teacup. 'My dear Miss Pierce, how delightfully tolerant you are—or naïve? Give me an American every time.'

I took no notice. I was past that kind of insult, if insult it was. 'Charles did tell me, when I saw him in Nottinghamshire last week-end, that the two of you had been part of a racing and betting circle at Cambridge.'

'Ah, yes, the excesses of youth!'

I looked at his pale, sagging face and wondered what excesses had replaced, as some clearly had, those of youth, as he had put it.

'I have the impression,' he murmured, 'that you do not know your future husband very well.' Now it was my turn to be startled, for Charles had been very firm about keeping our engagement a secret; the admission to Fergus the other night was the first time, to my knowledge, that he had broken the silence. Dillon, as if he had been following my thoughts, said: 'It is quite plain from the tone of your voice, your concern, which way you and Charles are heading. As a matter of fact, I flatter myself that I divined your feelings for him even before you did—the time we first met.'

'Oh, yes, at Gillian Fox's.' I had not forgotten that December night, either.

'A charming girl, Gillian. *Très festin.* A shade *déclassée* to hold the interest of a man of taste for long, perhaps.' He spoke softly, knowingly, the silky antennae of his perceptions playing with the situation. We might have been the spider and the fly sitting in the parlour, though which of us was the spider and which the fly it would have been hard to say. 'I consider it inevitable that you and Charles will marry,' he continued. 'It is logical, from every point of view. I congratulate you. And I feel certain that you will bring a fresh moral fervour into his life, if I may say so.'

'Why do you say so?' I said, suddenly truculent. I was not willing to have Charles criticized by anyone but me.

'Oh, nothing, my dear, nothing at all—the impulsive speech of a jealous man, perhaps! Why is it that no good woman has ever rescued me?' He swallowed another meringue, whole. 'But, to go back to your question, Charles has shown, as you

154

have learned, a tendency to involve himself with unsavoury characters—'

'Meaning you?'

'Yes,' he smiled, his dark eyes widening with pleasure. 'Of course, that's all in the past, the gambling, the dissipation. Charles has made a most respectable career for himself in the law. And it is not something he will throw over carelessly—he values position and prestige. Compared to the man I knew at university, he has become decorous, discreet, conventional to the point of stuffiness.' Dillon rolled his eyes in mock dismay. 'But the flaw is—perhaps you have not yet had time to remark it—he craves excitement. He should have been a courier, perhaps, a spy, a mountain-climber, a mercenary in Africa—anything but a London solicitor!'

His words made me uneasy. Had he not said almost the same things to Sophie, according to her diary? But if he had said these things to her, surely he would not be so reckless as to repeat them to me? I looked at him; he was gazing out of the window, his face as untroubled as the mist-shrouded Thames. The teacup looked no bigger than a thimble in his large, fleshy hand. He turned to me:

'The craving for excitement, for violence even, is not uncommon, of course. The problem for men of our position is finding respectable channels for such a drive. And if the channels were respectable, they would most likely, alas!, lose their appeal for Charles.'

'You speak as if this compulsion were still present, not something in the past.'

'One doesn't outgrow one's temperament, my dear.' He smiled at me benevolently. 'But perhaps politics is the happy answer to the problem.'

'Politics?'

'My dear, nothing is more exciting than politics, or more violent. I am thinking of violence in terms of an act of will, not its physical manifestations. Why should any reasonable person engage himself in politics? It is a game of chance but more than that, for it entails grim and strenuous competition. For winner and loser alike, it is warfare, it is murder.'

I stared at him. His words were completely incongruous with the languid figure he presented as he dabbed at his lips with a cambric napkin.

'You tax my imagination, Dillon.'

'And your patience as well?' He laughed. 'Never mind, my dear. Allow me to compliment you on your tea. It is exquisite. It wafts one to the very slopes of Assam, to those "isles of

155

Ternate and Tidore, whence Merchants bring their spicy Drugs ..." But I see that my wanderings alarm you. How careless of me to think aloud—not of Milton, but of your intended husband. Please forgive my error. But truth is best between friends, don't you think? And I do hope we shall be friends. Now, I must go. Freddie is waiting, and he's in a no-parking zone as it is. Let me say once more, to set your mind at rest, I did not meet the first Mrs Vivian in Sussex last August for any reason whatever.'

'It's not only on account of Charles that I asked,' I said, as I rose with him and saw him to the door. 'I suppose it's that I still can't realize that Sophie is dead, that she could have died so suddenly, so—freakishly. Though I've had cause to wonder, even about that.'

'Whatever do you mean?'

'Oh, nothing.' I looked down, abashed. Certainly I had better not say anything more about Sophie's diary, her illness, her delusions. 'It's my thoughts that are wandering now, I guess.' I smiled at him as he turned at the gate and tipped his hat to me, and felt with a stab at my heart the truth of his remark that deception between a man and a woman is inevitable.

My coffee had grown cold while I had gone over in my mind the conversation with Dillon. I got up and poured it into the sink and sighed. Such a beautiful afternoon. Getting chillier, though, Hugh Bailey was right. Perhaps I ought to walk over to the Baileys and see how Patrick was getting on. I could just see the twin chimneys of their farmhouse poking up over the hill. But why should I bother him? He was probably glad to be out from under my eye for a few hours. I picked up a dust-cloth and drifted from room to room, more in the interests of exploring my small domain than of cleaning it. I was glad, after all, that I had not brought Jane. It was good to be alone for a while. How peaceful it was here, how quiet, after the press of London and the busy suburbs that we had driven through in coming south. The cottage had only a few rooms, three bedrooms, snug and low-ceilinged, all of them facing south over the Weald. I dusted off chairs and tables and book-shelves absent-mindedly. The furniture was old and nonde-script, a place for people to be comfortable rather than stylish. No wonder Sophie and Charles had looked on this cottage as a refuge. What was it in most people—in city-dwellers, at least—that required a tension of opposites? Weren't any of us, ever, all of one piece? I paused at Patrick's small, white-washed
156

room. His diminutive bed was spread with a quilt that had been on Sophie's bed when she was a child—'Jack and Jill went up the hill'—coloured appliquèd figures stitched on a white ground and bordered by appliquèd letters of the alphabet. In one corner of the room stood a small rocking-horse, hard-ridden, the left runner broken off just under the foreleg. There were dozens of books lying haphazardly on the shelves of a low, white bookcase, many of them with their covers ripped off, their spines cracked by a child's careless handling. I sat down on the floor and began sorting them out and straightening them. I was still very much my parents' child, I thought wryly, with my mother's horror of disorder and my father's reverence for the printed word. *Mother Goose*, a facsimile of the first edition, with the dear old illustrations; *The Owl and the Pussycat*, in French and English—how elegant! *Little Black Sambo*—there had been talk of banning that from the library at Mrs Lofting's, on the grounds that it showed racial discrimination. What idiocy!

I had worked down to the bottom shelf, sorting and dusting, when I saw it. My heart froze. A blue notebook, with Sophie's name on the cover. I could not have been more shocked if I had seen a scorpion crawling along the shelf. I forced myself to pick it up; I turned to the first page: *Sunday, 19 August* was the heading. I flipped it shut. I felt an almost physical revulsion from it. August the nineteenth. That would have been one week to the day before her death. Her last journal. But what was it doing here? Of course, she had been staying in the cottage in the last part of August—until the night she went up to London, and to her death.

The fire in the living-room suddenly crackled as a burning log broke and fell. I picked up the blue book and walked towards the fire as if in a dream. Had Sophie not always come between me and what I wanted? Was she not doing it now, even in death? My impulse was to fling the book into the fire, which was now burning furiously. But I did not. I went to my bedroom, opened my suitcase and put the diary in. I would not read it; I could not bring myself to read it; but neither could I destroy it. Violence, wilful destructiveness was alien to my nature. And to burn the notebook would be, in a way, to burn Sophie. Dillon was right: violence is an act of will. I shoved the suitcase back under the bed. I would give the diary to Charles when the election was over, when he returned from the north. He could do with it what he wanted. After all, it was his property now, wasn't it? A husband's claims were greater than a sister's.

157

The next morning the burden of my discovery still weighed on me. My mind was only half on what I was doing as I dressed Patrick and myself for church. I did not think I could face the convivial Baileys and their energetic children, much less the scrutiny of the God I had been taught to believe in. At church the prayers and psalms floated above me; the congregation might have been chanting in Assyrian for all I knew. I became fully aware of the service only when the minister began to read the marriage banns of a couple who were to be married in a few weeks. The solemnity of Christian marriage hung over me, yet my own impending entrance into that state seemed as unreal as a fairy-tale. But the week had been fixed upon, the wedding-dress ordered (for I had wanted to make everything as formal, as ceremonious as possible, in contrast to Sophie's hasty, improvised yoking), and in two weeks I had an appointment, with Charles' permission if not blessing, to talk to a cleric at Chelsea Old Church about the event. Two lives to be joined till death them did part. Oh, let it be different with us, Charles, I prayed. Let it not go downhill, into boredom, quarrels, depression, silence. What marriages had I known that were truly happy?

I looked across the aisle to where the Baileys sat, elbow to elbow in the short pew. They looked happy enough, I thought. Good planning, or pure luck? On the other side of me, Patrick was fidgeting, cracking his knuckles. There was no Sunday School here, and he was not accustomed to an adult service. He had been content for a while, listening to the singing and watching the gowned figures move about the lighted altar. Now he was as restless as I was, and busied himself with stacking and unstacking prayer-books and hymnals on the railing in front of us. Were people of Pierce blood never at peace with themselves, I thought irritably?

By the time we had eaten our way through Ann Bailey's Sunday dinner, I had recovered my spirits somewhat. One could not be long with the Baileys without catching some of their gaiety and good humour. We drank coffee and chatted companionably as the children finished off the apple pie. With the last bite and a mumbled 'Excuse me, please,' the young ones were up and out, into the yard and off towards the orchard, the dogs racing after them in frantic delight.

'Nice, aren't they?' Ann Bailey said, with cheerful pride and pleasure. 'I should've reminded them to put on their Wellingtons. So muddy in the fields now. We've had rain for weeks.'

'It was a good idea you had, bringing Patrick down for the

158

holidays,' Hugh Bailey said, puffing on his pipe. 'I think he's always liked being here, in the country.'

'He likes your children, that's plain to see.' I smiled at him. I could not begin to tell them how much I, too, despite my earlier misgivings, liked being here, out of the haunting associations of the house on Cheyne Walk. Even Sophie's last diary seemed distant, eradicable. I had forgotten what it was like to be part of a family again.

'Have you found everything you need in the cottage?' Ann asked. 'We can lend you some extra blankets if you need them. There's no heating in the cottage other than the fire-place and a couple of portable fires—as you must have discovered! It dropped to the low forties last night. Supposed to stay warm for the next few days, though, thank goodness!'

'We've been very comfortable, thanks.'

'Your place looks to have stood the winter well,' Hugh said. 'We had to put a new roof on ours. Worst winter in years.'

'Everything seems to be in good shape, as far as I can see. Charles arranged to have the water and electricity turned on before we came down. All the house needed was a little dusting and airing. I guess it hasn't been used since'—I hesitated, for they had avoided mentioning Sophie except for brief condolences at our first meeting—'since Sophie was there last August.'

'No,' they said together, too quickly. They looked embarrassed. I had learned that death embarrassed other people, especially the kind ones. Hugh leapt in to fill the silence: 'There's the fence, of course. I meant to call Charles' attention to it last summer when he came to pick up Patrick, but it slipped my mind. He ought to see to it or stray sheep and cows will wander in and ruin the grass. I nailed a couple of boards over it as a temporary measure, but it needs a whole new section with proper posts. After the election, that is. We know he's busy now.'

'The fence?' I asked blankly.

'Yes, haven't you noticed? Near where your lane joins the main road, by the bend. A car rammed into it last summer. Coming too fast, I guess. Misjudged the turning.'

'A car?'

'Yes. It couldn't have been Sophie or Charles. They know the road too well—even though Sophie always did drive as if the devil was after her! Ann saw it, as a matter of fact. She was out rounding up the dogs. There was a full moon, it always drives them mad, I don't know why. They sounded like a pack of wolves that night.'

'What night?'

'A night last August,' Ann said. 'A few days before your sister came down to the cottage with Patrick. Couldn't miss it. It was a smashing car. Just the sort of sporty job that Hugh's been pining for for years.' She smiled at her husband fondly. 'A red Lotus.'

'A red Lotus?' I stared at them stupidly. They sat there sipping their coffee as if Ann had said nothing out of the ordinary.

'Yes,' Ann said. 'I only saw it for an instant. The car hit the fence, reversed and shot off down the lane. It must've been going to the Braddocks'—their cottage is about a mile past yours, to the south. We didn't give it much thought. We figured it couldn't have been a burglar, in a car like that!'

The coffee was bitter in my mouth. A red Lotus. The pride of Freddie Byers' life.

> The man in the moon
>   Came tumbling down,
> And asked his way to Norwich.
> He went by the south
>   And burnt his mouth
> With supping cold pease-porridge.

'Where's Norwich, Aunt Sarah?'

'Oh, in the north somewhere. Norfolk.'

'Where Daddy is?'

'No, not there.'

'How could he burn his mouth if the porridge was cold?'

'I don't know, Patrick. It's a riddle. That's how riddles are.'

'Not real?'

'Some of them are real.'

'I like riddles. Let's read some more.'

'Aren't you tired after all that tree-climbing?'

'No, I'm not. Please read another one.'

So we read another, and another and another. Even the old nursery rhymes took on sinister meanings for me that evening. I wished I had brought Jane with me. I wished I could go back to the Baileys. I even wished, passingly, for Avery and her harmless, mindless gabble. For some minutes more I read to Patrick, but before long he, too, left me, his eyelids drooping lower and lower and finally closing in sleep. I smoothed the quilt over him, turned off the light and opened the window. The May night was soft and warm and full of the

160

scent of pear and apple trees in blossom. Under the climbing moon the slopes of the Weald rose and fell whitely as far as I could see, an ocean becalmed.

I knew what I had to do. I shut Patrick's door quietly, walked into my bedroom and pulled the suitcase out from under the bed. I pushed open the clasps. The blue notebook was lying where I had left it. Had I thought it would magically disappear if I turned my ring three times? I took it into the living-room, switched on the light by the rocking-chair and sat down. I opened the notebook, my hands and feet cold despite the warmth of the night, and began to read.

EIGHTEEN

Sunday, 19 August

It's all down the drain, so quickly, gone. I should've known better than to trust Dillon. I'm scared. And there's nobody to talk to. That's the trouble with being an egotist—it's fine, so long as all you need is you. But even if Sarah were here— and my invitation probably hasn't even got to her yet—she'd just sit back and tell me I've made a mess of things. I have, too. But it's not just me—there are others to blame, or something to blame. It's not fair! And I was so ready to try again, to forgive, to understand, to be good.

The day started well enough, though I was tired and didn't have Jane to help me. She left after breakfast for her fortnight's holiday—gone to Blackpool—*quelle joie!* But I got through the morning without snapping once at Patrick; I took him for a walk, I set up his easel in the attic and let him paint alongside me till noon, and then we took a picnic lunch over to Battersea. Mrs C. gave us her usual mournful stare when I told her we were going picnicking, as if we were going to shed all our clothes and frolic *sur l'herbe*. Might've been a good idea, at that; I'm sick of the sight of these English wrapped up in their macintoshes from one end of the year to the other. Not like France; they take pride in the body there; even the sixty-year-olds walk with a kind of swagger—in Nice, at least. But then, the climate's better there; running around half-naked makes sense on the Riviera. Nothing makes sense here. Mrs C. is up to no good; I'm sure she's manipulating the household accounts. But then, I'm awfully ready to suspect people these days. The doctor said it's all in my mind. That's funny, coming from a psychiatrist.

It was nice going along the river. I've got so I just tune out the noise of the traffic. We took some bread to feed the gulls. They have such sharp, fierce eyes. Funny, they make me think of Mama's eyes—not that Mama ever stooped to pick up crumbs! Patrick never seems to get the idea that you have to stand away from the birds and toss the crumbs to them. He runs right into the middle of them and practically sits on them,

162

and of course they all fly up squawking. This time they came down one after the other onto the Embankment railing, in a line, heads facing east, as if they were queueing up for the No. 39 bus. The sky was so blue, they looked washed out against it. Patrick asked where the moon was. I said it had gone away. 'Oh,' he said, 'the moon has gone to work—like Daddy.' That gave me a start; it was truer than he knew. I don't know how he can worship his father so, when Charles gives him so little time. Maybe some men just aren't cut out to be fathers. Papa never seemed to be very close to us; he didn't play games with us or take us places; but you still felt that we, Sarah and I, were all he really cared about—except for a few Chinese poems from the ninth century, maybe! Charles just doesn't seem to care about his own child. No, that can't be true. Now, knowing what I do, I think it might be an odd kind of honesty on Charles' part, refusing to let Patrick depend on what may someday forsake him. But Patrick does depend on him, that's the terrible thing. Any crumb that Charles tosses to him he treasures. When I told him that it was his daddy who had bought the big stuffed dog for him, he wouldn't let it out of his sight. There was hardly room for the two of them in the bed last night! Funny how kids will do everything they can to make up for what they sense is lacking. They seem to know that love is how things should be. It's hard to imagine that Charles was ever Patrick's age, with a child's willingness to trust, to love. When does it all change, and why?

We sat on the grass at Battersea and ate our sandwiches, and I tried to figure out what I would say to Charles. Should I tell him about the talk with Dillon or not? Not, I decided. I'd make up some story about why I left Nice early; I'd say I had a call from Jane about Patrick or something. Not a very good way to begin *la vita nuova*, with more lies, but it seemed better to me than telling the truth. Charles can't stand to be humiliated. As for Dillon, I'd let him wiggle out of it as best he could. I didn't think he'd be too eager to tell Charles about his own part in bringing me in on this. It was hard trying to think, though, when I had to keep dragging Patrick away from the river's edge. He's going to drown himself someday, darn kid! I thought I'd have the whole week-end to sort things out; Charles had told me in Nice that he wouldn't be coming back till Monday night. But he telephoned while I was out with Patrick this morning; Mrs C. took the message; he was coming back on the 1 p.m. flight, the first he could get. I wonder if my leaving without telling him had anything to do with it. After lunch, Patrick wanted to go for some rides in the Fun Fair, so we did. I waited until three to tell him that his father would be home by tea-time; if you tell kids things too far in advance, they won't give you a minute's peace—everything is *now* as they see it. That was probably the only thing that could've dragged Patrick away from the bumper-cars; he loves those violent things, they just about rip me apart. As soon as I told him, we had to race back across Albert Bridge and set up a tea-party, 'for Daddy'. You'd think Charles had been away ten months instead of ten days!

I had Mrs C. put the tea things in the parlour; it's cooler there now than in the attic, except at night. Patrick arranged the cups and saucers to his liking, in a circle, and put a tin of orangeade and the teapot in the middle, though I told him that Daddy would probably rather have Scotch than tea. Then he opened a box of chocolate mallows—they're his favourite, so he supposes they're Charles' favourite, too. The new dog was invited to sit in the little wicker chair. When everything was ready, Patrick climbed up on the back of the sofa and watched out of the window. I was as excited as he was. I tried to collect my thoughts, what I was going to say to Charles, but all I could think about was the chocolate mallows melting in the heat and making a sticky mess.

It must've been about four o'clock when Patrick let out a shout: 'There's Daddy!' I rushed to the window. It was Charles, all right—but he wasn't alone. My heart turned over. Dillon was with him. How could I face him after Friday night? They stopped at the gate; they seemed to be arguing about something, but I couldn't make out over the traffic what they were saying. Patrick leaned out of the window: 'Daddy! Daddy!' Charles looked up, startled. His face was white and strained; I'd never seen him looking so haggard. When he came into the room, Patrick ran to him and jumped into his arms. Then he pointed to the tea-table and said, 'See, we're having a tea-party for you, Daddy. He can come, too,' he added, looking at Dillon in the doorway. 'Dog is here, too. He has his own chair. I haven't named him yet. He's a wonderful dog— thank you, Daddy!' Charles looked around at Dillon, questioningly, and Dillon sort of nodded his head, unsmiling. Charles said, 'Yes, he is a nice dog, Patrick, but I've got something else for you instead.' He undid the green-striped shopping bag under his arm and took out another stuffed animal; it was a giant teddy-bear, covered in the same chocolate-brown corduroy as the dog. Patrick didn't know what to make of it. He looked at Charles and his mouth began to wobble at the edges and he ran to the dog and clutched him in his arms: 'No! This is my
164

dog! You can't take him away! This is his home. You can't take him away!' Charles looked back at Dillon, a look of hopelessness on his face. Dillon said, 'Take the dog.' Charles went to Patrick and started to lift it from his arms. Patrick clung to it. His father said, 'Give it to me, Patrick. I said you could have the bear.' 'No!' Patrick shouted, and, holding onto the dog, he jerked away from Charles and tripped backwards over the wicker chair. There was a tearing noise, cloth ripping apart, the seam of the animal's underbelly split open, and suddenly there were trails and mounds of fluffy white powder and some small plastic bags lying on the carpet. Patrick let go of the dog and began sobbing. Charles' hands were shaking as he tried to scoop the bags and the powder—it looked like baby talc—into the shopping bag.

'Charles, for heaven's sake, what are you doing? Let Patrick have the dog—it's only a toy!'

Charles didn't look at me. 'Get Patrick out of here,' he said.

Dillon hadn't moved from the doorway. He stood there, twisting his hat in his hands, an odd smile on his face. Patrick was clinging to me now, sobbing.

'There, there, Patrick,' I tried to soothe him, 'it's all right. Daddy has brought you something else.'

'I don't want it, I want my dog! Look what they've done to him—he's all broken!'

The torn dog lay on the floor, looking up at us lop-sidedly, white powder trailing out of his insides. I didn't know what to think, but Charles was right, this was no place for Patrick. I lifted him up and carried him down to the kitchen and dumped him in Mrs Chalmers' lap. She held onto him and for once kept her mouth shut, too astonished to say anything.

When I got upstairs again, Dillon had gone, and the dog and the powder and the bags with him. Traces of white stuff were still on the rug. Charles had the hearth broom in his hand and was trying to brush them into his handkerchief.

'Charles!'

He stood up abruptly. His hands and the cuffs of his dark suit were white with the powdery stuff.

'Sophie, I didn't mean this to happen. It's finished now, believe me.'

'What's finished? What is this all about?'

'It's done with, I said. Don't ask me any questions.'

'I certainly will ask you questions. Why didn't you let Patrick keep his dog? What was in it? What was in those plastic bags?'

165

'Don't ask me anything. Be thankful for what you don't know. You're not involved.'

'Not involved? Good God, how can I not be involved, with you and Patrick at each other's throats! And all the rest of it! Listen to me, Charles. I met Dillon at the cottage on Friday night. He told me everything.'

'Yes, he told me. I know what he told you.'

'And was it true?'

'Why not?'

'Why not?' I was shaking with anger. 'How long have you been lying to me about your life? And what is it now? What is all *this*?' My toe swept a circle through the stuff on the rug.

'Don't let Patrick up here till I've picked it up.'

'What is it—poison or something?'

'I can't tell you.'

'You certainly can tell me.'

'I was going to wait until tonight when Patrick was asleep to take the dog. But Dillon wouldn't wait. Couldn't wait.'

'What has Dillon got to do with it? He's always hanging around us.'

'God, yes!'

'I'm asking for an explanation. We're not leaving it like this.'

'Yes, we are.'

'Let me see that powder.'

'No!'

'Yes!'

He wrenched away from me and stuffed the handkerchief back in his pocket and ground what remained of the powder into the rug with his shoe.

'Look, we'll talk about it later, Sophie. I have to get out of here now.'

I stood between him and the door. I would not be tossed aside like the dog; if he wanted me out of the way, he'd have to push me from the spot. He didn't push me. He held onto me by the shoulders, looked down at me with horror-stricken eyes—no, not horror—his eyes were empty, the eyes of a blind man. I think it was then I knew that there would be no new life for us, no second beginning. The strength drained out of me; I shrugged off his hands. After he had gone, I sank down on the floor and cried. I don't know how long I lay there. Sounds from the kitchen drifted up to me, Patrick's thin, high voice mingling with low grunts from Mrs Chalmers. Patrick must have been playing at the sink; pans rattled, and the old pipes reverberated with the gurglings of running water. My mind

166

slowly unclenched; I opened my eyes. I found I was looking at one of the small plastic bags, opaque, cloudy, filled with the white powder. It was lying under the olive velvet chair; Charles must've overlooked it in his clearing up. I grasped it, held onto the chair and pulled myself up. The traffic had increased to a roar on the Embankment as people streamed back into the city from Sunday outings. The neon sign of a mill across the river threw spinning coils of red and blue light upon the water. 'Thousands of Pounds Wasted Daily'. All at once I knew what I held in my hand, and what Charles had been doing in Nice, what Dillon and he had been doing for the last six years, or longer, back in some unbelievable time when my life had not yet been twisted together with theirs. I looked down at the bag in my hand. The stuff of death.

I picked up my handbag, dropped the bag into it, and walked out the door. I knew of one chemist's shop that would be open on Sunday; it was the one where I usually had my prescriptions filled. I walked up Old Church Street, turned right, and walked towards Sloane Square in the darkening summer dusk.

Monday, 20 August
Mr Pringle had said he'd try to have it analysed by four o'clock. I could either call him up or come by the shop. When the time came, I couldn't phone him, I didn't have the nerve. It was like phoning up to find out if a pregnancy test was positive or negative, the kind of moment that took years off your life.

A splendid afternoon. Old men were sitting on benches in the public garden across from Chelsea Old Church, sunning themselves, and for once that silly statue of Persephone did not look out of place, raising her bronze arms to the sun. In Paulton's Square some children were digging in a sand-pile under the beech trees, their *au pairs* idling near by, chattering in Spanish. Only the line of old flats by the Rolls-Royce garage looked out of key, discoloured, unwashed, with broken windows and peeling doors.

There was one customer ahead of me at the shop. He was asking for an aspirin that really worked. Mr Pringle kept saying they were all the same, all the same, unless he wanted something to help with his digestion, too. I hid behind a revolving stand and fiddled with shower-caps and sun-glasses while the two men compared five different brands of aspirin as if they were tiaras at Tiffany's. When the man finally left, Mr Pringle went into the back of the shop. I went up to the counter, but I didn't ring the bell for service. I wanted to know

167

and not to know. I waited some minutes before Mr Pringle came out again, a frail, white-haired man with gold-rimmed glasses. His head bobbed in greeting, jerkily; he had told me once that he had Parkinson's disease; his hands shook slightly and his head bobbed on his long thin neck like a ball juggled on top of a fountain of water. It might have been disconcerting to a stranger, but I was used to it. Besides, if he had the shakes, so did I.

'Good afternoon, Mrs Vivian.'

'Good afternoon.'

'You've come about the powder?' His head nodded up and down, answering his own question, and he looked around as if afraid we'd be overheard, though no one else had come into the shop. 'Have you any idea what it is?'

'I—I'm not sure. No.'

'Possession without a prescription is a criminal offence.'

'It's not mine. I just—found it.'

'I'll have to turn it over to the police.'

'Oh, no! Don't do that! They'll ask too many questions.'

'I'm afraid questions have to be asked, Mrs Vivian. Where did you get it?'

'I just found it. That is, my little boy found it. While he was playing.' I had thought out beforehand what I would say, but I could hardly get the words out. 'Behind the wall on the north edge of the public garden off Old Church Street. Where those seedy old men wander around.'

Mr Pringle frowned at me over the top of his glasses. 'I've seen plenty of strange things round here, Mrs Vivian. I've been a chemist in the King's Road for forty years. What people will do for thrills these days, it's past believing.' His head bobbed more violently than ever. 'The things that go on round here now, right under our noses. I remember when Chelsea was quiet and peaceful, nothing wilder than a painter's tea-party or two. It was like a village. Some people kept chickens in their back gardens. Times were, you could hear a cock crowing at daybreak. Didn't even have many crimes against women then. You had to go to Soho and the East End for that.' It seemed to me he spoke with a kind of relish. I was getting impatient.

'But what is the powder, Mr Pringle?'

He came back to the present reluctantly. 'Better keep an eye on your little boy, Mrs Vivian. If he had got any of that powder into him, it would've killed him. And looks sort of like icing-sugar, doesn't it? The things that go on round here, right under our noses. I tell you—there's no penalty too hard

168

for the people who bring in this stuff!'

'But what is it, Mr Pringle?'

'Heroin.' His voice was stern. 'High quality, too, eighty-seven per cent pure. When they cut it—the dealers always dilute it, to make every penny they can—it'd be worth thousands on the black market. Just the few ounces in that little bag.'

Heroin. I got out of the shop somehow, backed out, I seem to remember, with Mr Pringle staring at me over the top of his gold-rimmed half-glasses till I was out the door. My mouth was dry. I kept swallowing and swallowing. Heroin. Charles and Dillon. For years. Those business trips to the South of France three or four times a year, so convenient. Things I had read, things I had heard, from Avery and others, came flocking back to me. Marseilles, the biggest dispatching port for drugs in Western Europe. Into Marseilles by land and sea, opium smuggled in from the Middle East and processed in secret laboratories on the Riviera. All the hills and inlets of that beautiful region, filled with villas concealing laboratories as hidden as sparrows in ashes. 'Laboratories'—what a fine, scientific term for the caves of death! And then from Marseilles or neighbouring ports, by a thousand devious means, to Britain, to America, everywhere. Charles' 'clients'—oh yes, no doubt there were some *bona fide* ones, clients of the law firm, but they were a mere cover for a more profitable business. And how had he done it? With playthings, toys—stuffed dogs, teddy-bears, drums, music-boxes—the sort of thing he'd been bringing Patrick for years. I could just picture his affable, slightly embarrassed air if the Customs people bothered to ask him about the things he carried with him off the plane. Oh yes, for my young son, can't come home empty-handed to the little ones, you know; I could just hear his plummy, Oxbridge accent—it gets them every time. And, yes, the innocent gifts got to Patrick all right; the loaded ones went—elsewhere. Until a few days ago, I thought bitterly, when I snatched up the dog in the Negresco and carried it home myself. And what if Patrick *had* accidentally got some of the powder into him? It could have happened so easily, Mr Pringle was right. I shuddered; I felt so dizzy I could hardly walk; I had to sit down on the steps of the Chelsea Town Hall. People walked by with hardly a glance. Just another crazy Chelsea type.

Midnight

Charles hasn't come home. I waited up for him last night,

169

too, till one in the morning, till I finally flaked out. When I came downstairs in the morning, I stopped at his study. He wasn't there, but at least he had come home; his bed was unmade, rumpled, blankets and pillows spilling over to the floor. I hurried down to the dining-room. Mrs Chalmers was clearing his place. Mr Vivian had just left, she said.

But tonight I would not fall asleep. It was impossible. And he must come home, he must. I called his office twice today, once before I went to the chemist's and once after. He had not been in at all, his secretary said, and would I like to leave a message? Nothing fit for her ears, I thought, and hung up. I keep asking myself—why has he done it, why, why? He likes the good life, God knows, but he makes a decent amount of money from his law practice, far more now than he did when we were first married. And I've always shared my annuity money freely with him. He's certainly no drug addict himself, I know that. He likes—or used to like—a lot of sex and a lot of booze, but on that reckoning I guess a lot of us would have to be accounted addicts! Oh Lord, I don't know what to do or what to say to him. I didn't get much satisfaction out of Dillon, the snake. When I called him tonight, all I had in mind was finding out where Charles was. I went up to the study to make the call, so snoopy old Mrs C. couldn't hear me. It rang six times. I was just putting the receiver down when I heard Dillon's voice breathing heavily into the phone: 'Yes?'

'Dillon,' I swallowed, 'it's Sophie Vivian speaking.'

'Ah, Mrs Vivian,' he panted, 'pardon my breathlessness. I've just come in—up rather. All these stairs! Our filigree lift is very pretty but quite useless!'

'I want to speak to Charles. Is he with you?'

'Why, no, I haven't seen him since our little tea-party yesterday afternoon. Incidentally, I hope your son likes his new animal.'

'No, he does not.' I had had a hard time getting Patrick calmed down the night before. 'Do you know where Charles is?'

Dillon's voice was cool. 'I am not your husband's keeper, Mrs Vivian.'

'Are you not?' I was getting angrier by the minute.

'I thought we had settled that at the cottage on Friday. You're not fretting over that little contretemps yesterday afternoon, are you, by any chance?'

'Yes, and not by chance, Dillon.' I hadn't planned to say anything more to him, but his supercilious tone made me
170

mad. I charged ahead: 'I know what was in that dog, Dillon.'

Silence at the other end of the line. Then:

'Stuffing, I presume?'

'Heroin.'

'Heroin. Gracious! What on earth leads you to that fantastic supposition, my dear?'

'I found some of the powder under a chair, one of those plastic bags, after you and Charles had left. I had it analysed by a chemist. I got the report on it this afternoon.'

Dillon's voice was suddenly lower, fainter. 'If that is the case,' he said slowly, 'then it is obvious why Charles was so anxious to reclaim the animal.'

'You were in on it, too, Dillon! You've been trouble in our lives for as long as I can remember. On the Riviera, before we were married, you were there even then, getting Charles to do your dirty work.'

'Ah, the toad at the dear one's ear, do you mean? *Quelle dommage!*'

'*Quelle dommage* for you! I won't stop here, you know. I'll go to the police!' I said that in a rush; it hadn't entered my mind before that moment.

'You have no proof.' His voice was icy. 'That bag you took to be analysed—so impulsively, so unfortunately—can't be traced to me. No one would believe your unlikely story. No, Mrs Vivian, you have no proof whatever.'

'I have enough evidence to alert the police,' I flamed on. 'I can have them track every move you make, every letter, every phone call. I'll expose you for the snake you are!' I felt a tremendous exultation as I spoke, and I meant every word.

When Dillon replied, his voice was back to normal, controlled and even: 'I hope you enjoyed your little tirade. It may cost you dearly.'

'What do you mean? Are you threatening me?'

'I never make threats—such a barbaric practice. I would simply put a question to you: Are you ready to expose Charles to the authorities along with me?'

His words stunned me. He was right, of course. I could take no action against Dillon without involving Charles. Whatever the upshot of an official investigation, his career would be ruined—not to speak of our marriage, if anything was left of it. But I could not stop: 'You're the one responsible for this business ever getting started. I'm sure of it. Charles would never have gotten into this on his own. I don't know what your

171

hold over him is, but I know he wouldn't have done it on his own.'

'Why people act the way they do is not the court's prime concern. In fact, my dear, if you will forgive my bluntness in saying so, you are remarkably ignorant for a woman married to a lawyer. A man is prosecuted for what he has done, not for what he or another has had the idea of doing. "Evil into the mind of man may come and go, and leave no spot or stain behind ..."'

'It won't end here, Dillon!' His suavity drove me wild. 'I'm going to the police. I'll make you pay for this. You won't get off scot-free!'

'And neither, I fear, my dear, will you.' His voice was soft, treacherous. 'But I'm sure there's no need to repeat myself—such a bore. Please excuse me now, I must go. I have a party on this evening. Freddie is waiting. *A bientôt!*'

There was a click on the other end of the line; the phone was dead.

That was more than two hours ago, and still no Charles. Oh—there's the front door. He's home!

22 *August*

It's Wednesday now and we're at the cottage, but I still can hardly bear to think about that scene two nights ago—

I rushed out onto the landing. Charles was standing at the bottom of the stairs, looking up at me.

'Come into the parlour, Sophie.'

'Let's sit on the balcony. There's a breeze now.'

'I prefer it here.'

'I prefer the attic.'

'Come down here.'

Funny how people will argue about things like that when their lives are at stake.

We went into the parlour. Charles poured himself a brandy from the decanter on the mantelpiece. He didn't offer me one. He stood by the window, looking out. It was a dark night, the sky had clouded over. The river was invisible.

'It was all I could do to come home last night, Sophie. I couldn't face you or Patrick. I suppose you've guessed what it was?'

'I didn't guess. I came across a bag of it you'd missed. I took it to a chemist for analysis.'

'You can still surprise me.' He didn't sound surprised; his voice was leaden. 'I didn't think you'd get a professional analysis. Not that it matters. So you know everything?'

172

'Not everything. How could you do it, Charles?'

'What can I say? It's finished.'

'But how, why, did it ever get started?'

His face was still turned away from me. 'It started at Cambridge. I went through my mother's legacy very quickly, gambling on the horses. Dillon loaned me a lot of money. At first I won more than I lost. But the luck went. For it is luck —you can study the form sheets till you're blue in the face— it's still a mug's game. I began to lose, consistently, heavily. I went to Father first, but he couldn't help me; the business had been failing for some time, though he'd kept it from me. I think he wanted me to have a good life, to do the things— especially going to university—that he hadn't been able to do. But even if he'd had the money, I don't know if he'd have bailed me out—he was always harping on "personal responsibility". Anyway, I got no help there.' He stopped, and poured himself another brandy.

'So what did you do?'

'About that time I took finals and managed to come up with a First. It landed me an articleship with one of the top law firms; I was to work at their branch office in Nice— it was disbanded eight years ago—for the first two years. I asked Dillon if I could pay the debt in instalments. He said no, but that if I'd do him a favour he'd forget the money. I said, what kind of favour? I hadn't lost all my senses then. He said I only had to bring back something from the Continent for him. That's how it began. The "something" was newly processed heroin. Dillon was and is an addict. I didn't know it then. I've learned a lot about drugs since then. He's a registered addict on the Home Office roll; if he were to try to smuggle it in himself, they'd be on him in a flash. But he didn't get into drug-trafficking simply to supplement what he's officially allowed; he's in it for the money and for— well—the perverse satisfaction of manipulating others, of putting something over on a society that he despises.'

'But why did you go on doing it? You say he said that you only had to do him the one favour.'

He sighed. 'Why? I've asked myself that a thousand times. When I went to Dillon after the first trip and said I'd done my duty, he said all right, I was a free man again. And then he laughed, sniggered, I suppose, is a better word for it, and asked me if I wanted to make some money for myself. "Doing that?" I said. *"Oui précisément."* "Not on your life." "Think about it," he said. "All right, I'll think about it." In fact, I

173

avoided thinking about it for some time. But then—' he shrugged helplessly.

'Then what, Charles?'

He turned on me viciously. 'Then what, Sophie! My God, you spoiled little brat! You've never had to lift a finger for money all the days of your life. You don't know what it's like—there's no way it could enter your flip little head—to work yourself to the bone and see the world slipping away from you, the things you'd counted on, the things you wanted.'

'There are plenty of people in that boat. They don't take to drug-trafficking as a way out! Necessity is the devil's excuse!'

'You little prig! I feel like bashing your face in sometimes!' He grabbed me by the shoulders.

'Go ahead, you crummy coward!'

He let go of me then. There might've been ten miles between us instead of the length of his arms. He went on quietly, more as if talking to himself than to me:

'It's not easy, living on the Riviera with no money. The salary I was getting from the firm then was a pittance. Everything was dear, the necessities as well as—'

'—the luxuries,' I concluded. 'Like gambling. Like the Hippodrome at Cagnes, and the casinos at Cannes and Nice and Monaco.'

'Yes, like all that,' he said wearily, and sat down on the sofa.

'So you took Dillon up on his offer?'

'Yes.'

I poured myself a brandy. Charles was already on his third. 'How did you work it? What was the routine?' It was as if my curiosity was a thing apart, detached, floating. My voice seemed to be coming from the other side of the room, not the chair where I was sitting.

'Instructions were given to me by scrambled telephone messages. I never saw any of the people I was dealing with in France. The heroin—sometimes cocaine or hashish, I think, but usually heroin—would be waiting for me in some pre-arranged place and disguised in some unlikely container. Never more than three or four kilos at a time, often less.'

'How much is a kilo?'

'A little over two pounds. It doesn't sound like much, but it's worth a fortune. A wholesaler will pay five thousand pounds or more for a kilo of relatively pure heroin. He'll cut it, adulterate it, and sell it to distributors for at least one and

174

a half times as much—say, eight thousand pounds per kilo. And the price goes up all the time.'

'And you used camouflages like the stuffed animals to get it into the country?'

'Yes. I was a very unlikely suspect, of course. I had *bona fide* business in France, a home office in England, and my family and friends were here. It was only natural that I should bring home various gifts and personal effects from time to time.'

I snorted at that. Charles took no notice.

'Dillon revelled in thinking up unlikely vehicles for the stuff: boxes of talcum powder complete with puffs; toys of all kinds; an occasional chess set, the pieces hollowed out and refilled; quilted table-mats, tea-cosies, skirts of Provençal cotton—the padding being provided by the powder, of course. Nothing so ordinary as a false-bottomed suitcase for Dillon's tastes.'

'And when you got it here, to England, you delivered it to Dillon?'

'Not to Dillon himself. I left the package or packages at a pre-arranged place. I don't even know if they all went to Dillon—he's undoubtedly part of a larger operation. Most of it probably goes to the States—the market is bigger and the prices are higher there. Last Friday would have been the exception to the rule of my never delivering the goods to him personally. His orders had apparently been changed at the last minute; he had to get hold of the consignment on Friday night rather than on Tuesday, as had originally been planned. But I didn't get the telegram about the change of plans— you did. He had hit on the cottage as a convenient meeting-point—he had been there once before, years ago, you remember—because he could continue on to Brighton from there. From something he let drop, I gather that Brighton was where his connection was.'

'But why had you taken my money with you to Nice? What had that got to do with it?'

'The result of another foul-up in that particular operation. It's a primitive business in its way—tit for tat—for all its sophisticated disguises and manoeuvrings. Every time I picked up a consignment in France I left a specified amount of money, again in an appropriate disguise, in its place. The money was supplied to me anonymously through the post. But this time it didn't arrive. I phoned Dillon, I was frantic, just before I left for Nice. He disclaimed all responsibility, said he didn't know anything about the money and that he was not going to hazard any of his own for my benefit. He said I'd have to sort it out for myself. So I sorted it out—I took your annuity. I assumed I'd get my usual pay-off in a few days, as always.'

'Have you got it?'

'Not yet,' he said drily. 'Of course, they'd only have received the stuff yesterday at the earliest, after Dillon left here. Or perhaps they—whoever they are—have discovered that the shipment is one bag short. Not that I supposedly could be held to account for that. It's not my business to know the exact amount in each shipment—that's their worry!'

'And when I came into your life—that didn't make any difference?'

'Yes, it made a difference.' He twirled the brandy glass in his hands and smiled ruefully. 'I trafficked even more. I wanted to impress you. And I didn't want to rely on your money to live in a style to which you—and I, increasingly—had become addicted. For you are an addict, you know, Sophie. You're addicted to luxury and to having your way and to making heads turn if not roll. Even when I first met you, you had not the faintest resemblance to the impoverished art student you liked to imagine yourself as. Not the faintest. You've never done an honest day's work in your life! And that's why your painting shows talent but no character,' he added, twisting the knife.

'That's not fair!'

'Perhaps not. It doesn't matter. I wanted you. I wanted to please you. I'd never been so attracted to a woman sexually. You needn't wince—I've known you not to scorn that side of things. In fact, I've always thought that that's where your true talent lies—in bed.'

'The hell with you!'

He laughed. 'And that's another part of it. Sex covers a wide ground. I liked your sauciness, your "spunk", to use one of your American words. I was tired to death of Englishwomen. They're either earnest and hard-working—"useful" as we say of certain horses—or they're tarts. Maybe it's the result of our caste system.'

'We have our caste system, too,' I murmured.

'Perhaps. But it liberated you. England's didn't liberate me. It didn't liberate Dillon, either. He has a taste for dirt, I have a taste for gold. It's the same thing in the long run.' He laughed mirthlessly.

I didn't want to hear anything more. There was only one last question,

'What now, Charles?'

'Oh, Sophie! My God, what now? What a laugh! What do you foresee, my faded little fire-ball?'

'I don't see much of anything.'

'Neither do I.'

'It's late. Almost two.'

'Yes, it's late.'

'Are you coming up?'

'Coming up where?'

'To bed.' I added in a whisper: 'I don't mean the bed in your study.' I wanted to lie in his arms and forget everything. I guess he'd been right about me. He was always right. I hated him, I wanted him.

He didn't answer. I felt as if I'd been turned to stone. I had spoken out of my heart; the rest didn't matter.

I didn't look at him as I got up to go. But at the door I stopped and turned to him and said: 'By the way, Charles, I rang Dillon tonight. I told him I knew.'

That got a rise out of him. 'No!' he exploded.

'But why does it matter?' The expression on his face frightened me. 'It's because of him that we're in this mess. I hadn't planned to tell him—I was only trying to find out where you were—but I did. And I told him I was going to the police.'

'Good God!' He collected himself. 'You shouldn't have done that, Sophie.'

'I didn't mean it. I wasn't thinking. I just wanted to tell him off; I always have. It was emotionally satisfying, as they say—I should think that you of all people would understand that!' My voice was bitter. 'Besides, as he pointed out to me, no one could prove anything, there's no evidence.'

'No evidence,' Charles said slowly, 'of anything we've done in the past. But you've threatened his lifeline, Sophie. If you went to the narcotics division with what you know, they'd be on him in a second. His name is already down as a registered addict. And he probably thinks you know—or will find out—more than you're telling. He has a curiously high opinion of your intelligence, despite his patronizing way of patting you on the head. I think you frighten him. I think all women frighten him, for that matter.' He ran a hand across his eyes and groaned. 'Oh, Sophie, what have you let me in for now?'

'What have I let *you* in for? My God! What did you let me and Patrick in for? Patrick might have been killed playing with your deadly toys! Not to mention all the poor drugged bastards I'll never set eyes on! My God, Charles!'

177

I burst out sobbing. 'What am I going to do now? I can't think. What shall I do? I can't think!'

He stood up and walked over to me. He didn't touch me. 'I think you'd better go away for a while, Sophie. Go to the cottage; take Patrick. Things have piled up on you here. I want to be alone for a while, too.' My head barely came up to his shoulder; I dared not look at his face; his voice told me nothing of what he was feeling. 'I have to go to Brussels for a conference later this week. When I come back, Thursday week, we'll settle it.'

'Settle it?' The tears were running down my cheeks, salty in my mouth.

'Cheer up, old flame.' He barely touched my chin with his hand. 'We're not dead yet.'

Sunday, 26 August

I've gone round and round. What's the use, what's the answer? Of course I wouldn't go to the police. It's not that the whole drug-trafficking business doesn't sicken me. But I'd never turn Charles in, never. Dillon's another matter—but I can't accuse one without bringing in the other. The real problem is, what to do about this marriage? Is marriage always a leap in the dark? I ought to leave Charles, I know that. I could just go away, cut loose, with Patrick. But cut loose to what? I don't want to cut loose. 'Entreat me not to leave thee, or to return from following after thee ...' That was one of the passages that Mama liked to read from the Bible. I never used to understand it when I was little, I just liked the sound of it, the way the words repeated and doubled back on each other, I wasn't quite sure if they were saying yes or no. The Book of Ruth. Ruth, funny word. Do I have it in my heart or not? I want to be forgiven, too. If Charles will meet me half-way ... but there's not much sign that he will. 'We're not dead yet.' What kind of a crack was that? Or did he mean that everything will turn out all right for us?

This room, Patrick's, is the quietest in the house. Those Bailey kids always make so much noise when they come over to our yard to play. But I can't send Patrick over to their place all the time—he's practically lived there since we got here on Tuesday morning. They're out front now, I can hear them yelling. They've been running the hose all afternoon; the lawn's awash with three inches of water. Our unmowed grass is sticking straight up like those Japanese paper-flowers that open under water. Say, there's my missing tennis shoe, what do you know! Missing since last summer. The water

178

must've floated it out from somewhere. The things that turn up in my life! It's too absurd. Life really is absurd. Oh, there's Patrick now, the little monkey, and Ian with him. I shouted at them to turn off the water but they didn't hear. I suppose they're going back to the farm to play with the new kittens. It's a wonder the poor things are still alive, the way they maul them so without meaning to. Well, thank heaven for a little peace and quiet. I can get in some painting before the light goes. I'll show Charles what character is! Oh, here's Patrick back again—and there's the phone!

NINETEEN

The kettle came to a boil, whistled with a piercing scream.
My mind echoed it as I lifted the kettle off the stove and filled
the teapot. Seven o'clock in the morning. Sunlight was edging
across the valley, scouring the depressions of the eastern hills.
The kitchen lay still in shadow; the grass outside the windows
looked dank, wet, as it had looked to Sophie on that last
August afternoon. Was it only I who had changed? Last night's
dishes cluttered the table, unscraped, unwashed; a half-eaten
banana, Patrick's dessert, was smeared across the red-and-
white oilcloth. I felt disoriented; I seemed to have no relation
to the objects around me. I stirred the tea, poured it, sipped
a burning mouthful. What was I doing, what had I been doing,
all these months? I had no distinct memory even of the last
few hours. I must have slept, but my mind had kept tossing up
fragments of Sophie's diary the whole night through—the torn
corduroy dog, Charles' cuffs white with powder, Mr Pringle's
bobbing head, Sophie's missing tennis shoe, 'Entreat me not
to leave thee ...'
  'Aunt Sarah! I want my breakfast!' Patrick padded into
the kitchen, blue felt slippers in his hand. 'Is this the right
foot?' he asked, wedging the right foot into the wrong
slipper.
  'No. Yes. Here, sit down.' I took a small foot in my hand
and slid it into the right slipper. 'There. Do you see the way
your foot curves there? And the way the slipper curves in
the same place? That's how you tell.'
  'But it's hard to tell, Aunt Sarah. Both feet curve. How
do you tell left from right?'
  Or right from wrong, or true from false, or love from hate?
The curve of the thing, the way it hit you. The way it whirled
around and came back at you like a boomerang. Charles'
drug-trafficking, Charles' duplicity ...
  'Ian said the Braddocks are going to drown their new
kittens. Why are they going to do that?'
  'Because they can't find homes for them, I suppose. Because
180

they can't have twenty cats running around.'

'Why not?'

Why not, indeed? What did it matter, what did anything matter?

'Couldn't we take one, Aunt Sarah?'

'I don't know. We'll see. Your father isn't very fond of animals.'

'Oh, please, Aunt Sarah, let's do take one!'

'Don't pester me, Patrick,' I answered shortly. 'Eat your breakfast. Here's some juice. Do you want cornflakes?'

'No, I want *that*.' He pointed to another box of cereal. 'It's got a magic ring inside.'

'A magic ring?'

'It's here somewhere.' He dug his hand into the box, scattering cereal over the table.

'Stop that! We aren't going to empty the whole box just to find the magic ring.'

It was there, somewhere. What was it she had said? 'I'll show Charles what character is!' Not the words of a woman about to commit suicide. Not the tone of one given to fantasies. Sophie had not lied; Charles had lied, Dillon had lied. I had chosen to believe Charles because I had wanted to. And yet, Sophie for some months had been ill, depressed, at times on the verge of hysteria—I had her own word for that. But that last diary was the diary of a totally sane person—wasn't it? When Sophie went up to London that Sunday—it could only have been a few hours after she wrote the last entry—she had had no intention of killing herself. So, then, her death was an accident, as I had assumed in the first place. Sophie had always attracted accidents—and caused them. She had been bad news in well-run lives. But she had always come out on top, ahead of the game, as when she had fallen through the window in Cambridge and come back flaunting her new stitches and her rabbit-fur muff. Yes, she had always had the rabbit's-foot of good luck. Until the last. But freakish accidents, fatal accidents, did happen. Hadn't I read somewhere that more people died each year from accidents at home than from any other cause? But what had taken her up to London so suddenly? There was no evidence in the diary that she had been planning to go anywhere. I gathered up the dishes from the table, scraped the leavings into the dust-bin. It must be there somewhere, the lead, the clue. I got out the washing-up bowl from under the sink and turned on the tap hard.

'I'll wash the dishes for you, Aunt Sarah.' Patrick had climbed up on the stool beside me and was contemplating the

181

billow of soapsuds and steam rising from the sink. 'Can I wear the rubber gloves?'

'No, you dry, I'll wash,' I said firmly. We had lost more than one dish with Patrick as dishwasher.

'I won't break any this time, I promise. Please, can't I?'

Weak-willed as always, I stepped aside and shoved Patrick's stool in front of the sink. He looked like a sorcerer's apprentice, combing the soapsuds with the long, dangling fingers of Sophie's blue rubber gloves. I picked up a tea-towel and began wiping the half-rinsed dishes.

'Patrick, last summer, when you were here with your mother —that day she went up to London and you stayed with the Baileys—do you remember?'

'Oh, yes, I slept in a bunk bed, the top one. Ian had the bottom. It was fun! I wish we had bunk beds, Aunt Sarah.'

'Yes, yes. Before your mother took you over to Ian's, did anyone come here? A visitor?'

Patrick steered the dish-mop like a boat among the suds. 'I don't know. I don't think so. Nobody ever came to see us here.' He groped for the bar of soap in the water. 'Fergus came sometimes. And Gillian once.'

'Fergus? Did Fergus come that day—or Gillian?'

'I don't remember. I don't think so. No.' He found the soap; it squirted out of his hands and landed on the floor. I picked it up with a sigh. If only I could put my finger on something, something.

'Here, Aunt Sarah, you can do the rest. It's no fun when the bubbles are gone.' He slipped off the stool and thrust the dish-mop at me. 'Ian said they're putting up a new loft in the barn today. Can I go over and watch them?'

'A new loft?' I repeated mechanically, taking the dish-mop.

'Yes. The old one's falling down. Ian's daddy said we shouldn't jump on it so much.'

A new loft. That was it. The new balcony. Sophie had said that the builders couldn't come to do the work until October. Sophie had died on the twenty-sixth of August.

'Aunt Sarah, you're dripping water on the floor!'

I looked down. Water and suds were oozing from the mop suspended in my hand; I was standing in a soapy pool. Patrick was looking at me anxiously.

'It's all right, Patrick,' I said, wiping it up. 'The loft. Yes. We'll go over to the Baileys' this morning. In fact—how would you like to stay with them tonight?' I spoke with a cheerfulness I did not feel. 'I have to go up to London. You'd
182

rather stay here, wouldn't you, than go up to London with me?'

'Are you going up to London?' His voice was uncertain, then exuberant. 'Yes, I want to stay here! I hope I can have the top bunk again!'

Later, the chores done, I telephoned Ann Bailey. If she was surprised at the turn our conversation took, she gave no sign of it. It was only I who spoke with apprehension.

'Ann, the day last summer that Sophie went up to London —the last day—what time did she leave?'

'About eight or so it must've been.'

'Did she say why she was going?'

'No, she didn't. She just said that she had to go up to London unexpectedly and would we mind keeping Patrick for her? I would've asked her what had come up, but she seemed in such a hurry, and I was in the midst of getting the kids to bed. She just sort of shoved Patrick in the door with his pyjamas under his arm, kissed him and dashed out again.'

'Did she say when she'd be back?'

'Well, no, not exactly. She did shout something to us when she was getting into the car—"See you tomorrow!" or something like that. We didn't see her "tomorrow", of course. We never saw her again.' Ann's voice was suddenly solemn.

'Ann, could you help me out? I've got to go up to London unexpectedly'—I realized with horror that my words repeated hers, Sophie's—'and I wonder if I can leave Patrick with you? I'll be back tomorrow. I know he'd rather be here than in London.'

'Certainly, Sarah. The kids love having Patrick here. So do we. And we're putting up a new loft in the barn—that'll keep them happy!' She paused. 'But you will come back tomorrow, won't you?'

'Oh, yes,' I said grimly, 'I'll come back.'

I put down the receiver with difficulty; I had twisted the telephone cord into a corkscrew.

The chemist's shop was empty except for a pimply-faced boy in a white apron who was shifting dusty, cellophane-wrapped boxes of perfume from one shelf to another. He looked up expectantly, perhaps thinking I was about to relieve him of a dozen bottles of *Ma Griffe*.

'Is Mr Pringle here?'

His face dropped. 'He's mixing a prescription. Want him?'

'Yes, I do. Tell him it's Miss Pierce.'

In a few moments Mr Pringle came out alone from the back of the shop, his bald head gleaming under the overhead lights. He looked like the picture of Humpty-Dumpty in Patrick's nursery-rhyme book, his egg-shaped head nodding precariously on his frail body.

'Good afternoon, Miss Pierce. What can I do for you? Didn't those hay-fever pills help you? They're our most popular line.'

'No, I didn't come about the hay fever, Mr Pringle.'

He peered at me over the gold-rimmed spectacles, taking in my agitation. He waited. Chemists are patient, like doctors.

'It's about my sister, Mrs Vivian.'

'Yes?'

'Did she—did she come to you last summer with some powder to be analysed?'

'Yes, she did.' The glare of the lights turned his spectacles to ice.

'Was it heroin?'

'Yes, it was. She brought it in shortly before her death, not more than a week or so before.' He looked at me curiously. 'How is it you have reason to ask about it now? Haven't found more of the stuff, have you?' He bared his teeth in what might have been a smile.

'Oh, no, no. I was looking over something she'd written. She mentioned it. It seemed so odd.'

'Yes, it seemed odd at the time. Person doesn't just *find* bags of heroin lying around. Still, this is an odd neighbourhood —drugs, mugs, gangs, music that blasts your head off—right in the King's Road! Just listen to that place across the street!' He pointed a shaking finger towards a boutique that looked like an Arabian bazaar, rock and roll music pouring from its beaded portière. 'I have to listen to that stuff ten hours a day! Cracked one of my crystal jars last week!'

A vein in his skull pounded under the light; his liver-spotted hands clutched the counter angrily as he bent towards me:

'Chelsea's not what it used to be. Not the Chelsea I knew!'

I stepped back involuntarily. 'Mr Pringle,' I said timidly, 'was my sister taking any drugs herself that summer?'

'Not the kind she brought in, if that's what you mean.' The vein in his head subsided. 'I rightly shouldn't discuss what medication a customer's taking. But seeing she's dead, I suppose it can't do any harm—or any good, either,' he added morosely. 'I filled a number of prescriptions for her that year, mostly for anti-depressant pills. She was taking them pretty regularly. Prescribed for her by her psychiatrist. They have

184

a funny effect on people sometimes.'

'What do you mean?'

'Oh, my impression is—I'm not a psychiatrist, of course—they sometimes send the patient swinging from one mood to another with no rhyme or reason, the very condition they're supposed to cure.' His voice was melancholy. It occurred to me that his zest for his profession was mitigated by a native pessimism.

'You think they had that effect on her?'

'Perhaps. She was a whimsical lady. A lady, though.' His head bobbed approvingly. 'But they couldn't have affected her the last month. She'd stopped taking the anti-depressants. Told me so herself—burst into the shop one day and said, "Burn the prescriptions, Mr Pringle! I'm cured—or almost! The Great White Doctor says so!" That's what she always called her psychiatrist to me, "the Great White Doctor".' He laughed shortly. 'She looked mighty perky that day, her blue eyes snapping and dancing—flounced in here in a saucy little skirt shorter than my own granddaughter's!'

More Sophie-worship at work, I thought, with a stab of the old jealousy. I asked coolly, 'Who was her psychiatrist, Mr Pringle?'

His face became stern again. 'I really shouldn't pass on that kind of information, Miss Pierce. Mr Vivian could probably tell you if you wanted to know.'

'He's away now, campaigning in the north.'

'Standing again, is he?'

'Yes.'

'Hope he gets in. The more Tories get in the better. Perhaps they can get rid of *that*—' he pointed a menacing finger at the shop across the street. 'That came in under Labour.'

'Yes, yes, but about my sister's doctor, Mr Pringle—I do want to talk to him. Now.'

He studied me. 'All right, Miss Pierce. I can look his name out for you. I didn't burn those prescriptions, of course. Got prescriptions on file from forty years back. Just a minute, please.'

When he reappeared a few minutes later, he handed me a slip of paper with a name, address and telephone number written on it. The Great White Doctor was a Dr J. A. B. Calder of Ebury Street.

The black leather chair swivelled round on its shiny chrome legs. The psychiatrist's body curved with the chair, a curving reed, concave, resilient, its length and leanness accentuated

185

by a suit so dark it was almost black, the sort of suit an under-
taker might wear. His face was startlingly white and unmarked
above it. How could he be so at ease, dealing with despair
every day?

'Your sister was my patient for only four months, Miss
Pierce. From April to the beginning of August.'

'You had been treating her for depression?'

'Yes. That term is often misunderstood. Let me make it
clear that she was not a manic-depressive, she was not psy-
chotic. She was nervous and troubled. A "cyclothermic"
temperament, we call it—a person of ups and downs.'

'A lot of people are like that,' I said. 'They don't go to
psychiatrists.'

Something in his manner set me on edge. Perhaps it was
the smoothness of his voice or the way his long, white fingers
climbed up and down, making churches' steeples with each
other. And he looked so young, probably no older than I was.
Why had I always found it difficult to accept the wisdom of
old people but had no conviction that the young had anything
better to offer?

'No, that's true, a lot don't go to psychiatrists. But perhaps
they ought to.'

'Oh?'

He smiled at me, sensing my hostility. 'Because a psychiatrist
would listen to them. Often people are unhappy to the point
of desperation simply because they have no one to listen to
them.'

'What did Sophie say she was unhappy about?'

'The baby she had lost. Her marriage. Her "erraticness",
as she put it, as a mother. Her sense of time wasted, as a
painter. The erosion of her self-confidence.' He paused. 'Some
of those things she told me, others I divined from what she
didn't tell me. That's my job.' His words were diffident, but
something of a finely-honed intelligence shone out. I realized
that I had underestimated the man. I had been prepared to
dislike him, to take out on him my own feelings of frustration
and perplexity in regard to Sophie's death.

'That takes in a great deal,' I murmured.

'Yes. They were real problems, not ones that she invented
to win attention and sympathy. Even if they had been invented,
of course, they would still have been problems.' The leather
chair squeaked as he rocked backwards.

'You were not surprised, then, to learn of her death? You
thought she was leaning towards suicide?'

The spine of the chair snapped forwards again. 'By no
186

means! She was making a strong and, I believe, successful effort to get the better of her problems. By the time she ended her sessions with me'—his voice was authoritative—'she was incapable of suicide.'

'So you think that her death was an accident?'

'I have no doubt it was an accident. A stroke of fate.'

'I didn't think that psychiatrists believed in fate.'

'Is "chance" better? Or why give what happened any name at all? She fell from a height involuntarily—that is my description of the event. But why are you asking me these things, Miss Pierce? And so long afterwards?' His fingers started walking again, white praying mantises.

I answered in a low voice: 'I can't get her death out of my mind.' I looked away at the floor, bare, golden, so highly polished that the legs of the furniture gleamed in it. His chair squeaked again.

'You figured in her thoughts quite a lot.'

I looked up at him then. 'I did?'

'On the whole she admired you, though she was somewhat afraid of you. She tended to measure herself against you. She contrasted her failures with your success.'

'Her failures—my success?' I repeated stupidly.

'She felt you had "consolidated your inheritance". That was a phrase she used once. It has stayed with me. She didn't mean it in terms of money—though she was worried about that, too; she half-dreaded the wealth that was going to descend on her when she turned twenty-six. What she meant, I deduced, was that you had put your roots down, flourished, produced something useful—both by teaching and by remaining loyal to the old ties of family, friendship, place ...'

'Good Lord! Sophie was the one who dared to break away, to make an independent life. She was the one who got out from under the burden of the past. What a queer view she had of *me*!'

'She might think your view queer, Miss Pierce.' His voice was gentle, not scolding, almost as if he were giving a benediction. I felt as if someone had suddenly opened the door at the top of a dark cellar. 'In the long run,' he continued, 'a mature human being makes a style equal to his will. In the eyes of another person, one may be over-reaching or under-reaching, dependent or independent. That doesn't matter. What one thinks of one's self matters.'

'And you think Sophie was doing that, towards the end, making a style equal to her will?'

'She was getting there.'

'She didn't come to see you shortly before her death?'

'No. Her last visit here was during the first week of August. She felt strong enough to go it on her own. I acquiesced—no, that is the wrong word—I agreed. Besides, it was plain that she was experiencing a negative reaction against me. It's not unusual. And usually it is—as it was in this case—a good sign. It means that the patient is willing to take responsibility for her own life again. Of course, it would've been better if Sophie's husband had come for counselling, too, during the months she was my patient. I met him only once. He brought her here for her first visit.' My surprise must have been evident, for he added, 'In any troubled marriage, Miss Pierce, there are two people involved.'

'Yes,' I said, 'I guess that's obvious.'

'It's not always obvious, or acceptable, to the couple concerned.' He shifted in his chair. 'I wrote to him after I saw the notice of her death in the paper. I invited him to call on me. But he didn't come. I understood.'

'Understood what?'

'His distress, and the guilt he must have been feeling.'

'*Guilt?*' I looked at him incredulously.

'It is almost inevitable when a wife or husband dies for the partner who is left—and often other relatives as well—to feel some guilt. No life is lived singly.'

'I see,' I murmured, 'yes, I understand. Well, thank you, Dr Calder. Thank you for seeing me this afternoon. I'm afraid I must have held up your next patient.'

'No, I have no more patients today.'

'Well, thank you again.'

I wrestled myself into my jacket, picked up a fallen glove, hooked my bag over my shoulder. But Dr Calder did not rise, as physicians usually do to indicate that an interview is at an end. I waited awkwardly on the edge of my chair. He had picked up an ivory paper-knife from his desk and was turning it in his hands, his long thumb exploring the intricately carved handle.

'Sophie's death was no one's fault, Miss Pierce. I have the impression that you believe that you, too, failed her in some way. Let me assure you, you have no reason to reproach yourself. You were one of the few stable points of reference in her life. It may have taken—it did take—a long time for her to fathom her feelings in regard to her family. People of Sophie's nature often have difficulty in coming to terms with the things they love; it's as if some centrifugal force drives them away from what nurtures them most. At one of our last

188

meetings, Sophie told me that she was going to write to you, to ask you to visit her. That was a tremendously significant overture from a psychiatrist's point of view—and it should be from yours, too.'

So saying, he did rise, smiling, and I took my leave. I walked out into Ebury Street, liberated, exhilarated, floating.

But that passed, too.

The musty, worn smell of the hall struck me anew, the same as when I had first entered the house eight months ago. Jane's voice, singing in a high soprano, quivered up to me from the basement. Jane was one of those, I had noticed, who make up for a lack of contact with others by expanding vocally when alone. I walked up the dark staircase as lightly as I could, not that there was much chance of her hearing me over the ringing trills of 'Santa Lucia'.

I paused at the first floor. The grand, faded drawing-room held the last light of the sun; the crimson chairs and draperies sagged with their own rich weight; a regal room, for mercantile kings and queens. Charles' study was dark. I went on, past my room, past Patrick's, Jane's, and up the last, narrowing flight to the attic. I entered, and walked over to the french windows. The garden below was a darkening rectangle, its new spring greenness fading into the night. There was a brief twitter of birds from the stunted lilac shrubs. At home our lilacs had been twenty feet tall, had swept the air with their sweetness. How far away they were! I turned the key in the lock and tried the doors, but they would not give. I saw they were bolted top and bottom. What would have prompted Sophie to open the doors and step out on what she thought to be the balcony? Or had the doors been open when she entered the room? What had brought her to this garret on that August night? I looked about me. The dark, empty room could yield nothing new. And yet, suddenly, though I am not a superstitious person, the room was filled with presences—no, not presences so much as a kind of resonance, the shuddering of strong wills in conflict.

I hurried out of the room and down the stairs. Jane's thin but earnest voice was still holding forth. It did little to cheer me, but I needed human companionship.

'Oh, Madam! You did give me an awful fright!' Jane, scrubbing the kitchen floor, jumped up and whirled around at the sound of my step. 'Is anything wrong, ma'am? Not Master Patrick, is it?'

'No, Jane, nothing's wrong. I'm sorry I frightened you. I

189

had to come up to London to—keep a few appointments. I'm just here for the night. I'll go back to Sussex tomorrow.'

'Have a cup of tea, ma'am. We don't have no proper dinner prepared. Weren't expecting nobody.' Jane wiped her hands, flustered, and poured out a cup from a steaming pot. As she handed it to me, I saw that her thin young arms, exposed by her rolled-up sleeves, were red and roughened to the elbow. How little I knew of any of them, I thought. How little effort I had made to know them.

'Jane,' I said, after I had politely sipped the tea for a few moments, 'where were you the night that my sister died?'

'I was in Gravesend, ma'am, with my family. I'd just come back from Blackpool. It was my two weeks' annual holiday. Didn't know anything about it till a note came from Mrs Chalmers—we haven't got a telephone at our house.'

'Had my sister said anything to you about having the balcony pulled down?'

'Well,' Jane said doubtfully, 'not "pulled down". I don't recollect her ever saying that. "Built up" was her words, I think. 'Course—' she grinned toothily, 'I guess it'd have to be *pulled down* before it could be *built up!*'

'But she did speak to you about having work done to the balcony?'

'Yes, ma'am, many times. She said it was too narrow and shaky, and the railing was too low. She wanted a bigger, stronger place, where she could set up her easel and things she was painting, and where the boy could play without danger of falling off.'

'Do you know what firm of builders did the work?'

'I don't rightly recall, ma'am. They was only here for a couple of days—didn't take 'em long to put up the new balcony. I wasn't here, of course, when they took the old one down. I think it started with a "W"—Wallace or Willis or something. It was painted on the side of their van, had some of the letters missing, I think.' Jane frowned, squinting up her face as if the effort would conjure up the van again. But her face relaxed and she said sadly, 'I just can't seem to see it in my mind's eye.'

'Never mind, Jane. Maybe it will come to you. Did you know that the workmen were scheduled to come that particular week?'

'No, ma'am. Mrs Vivian didn't say anything to me about it. But she didn't talk to me much about appointments and such. She talked to Mrs Chalmers. Mrs Chalmers sort of looks on this as her own house, anyway. She'd been housekeeper for

190

old Mr Vivian for years and years, and she stayed on with the
tenants he let it to before young Mr Vivian came back with
his new bride. Mrs Chalmers knows everything there is to
know about this house, I reckon!'

I sipped my tea slowly, thinking about what she had said.
'Where is Mrs Chalmers?'

'She's out on some errand. Went to the chemist's, I think.
She's got one of her headaches again.' Jane lowered herself
to the floor, scowling, and started scrubbing again. 'Don't
know why she should get headaches—I'm the one who does
the work in this house!'

'Will she be back soon?'

'I reckon so. She don't like to be out after dark. She's
afraid of attackers.' Jane giggled. 'Don't think any man would
get the better of her!'

'No,' I smiled back, 'I don't think so either.' I thought of
Mrs Chalmers. She loomed in my mind, as she often did in
reality, huge as a Sumo wrestler, her dark hair pulled back
and sworded with lacquered skewers. 'Mrs Chalmers is a very
unusual person.'

'Oh, she is, Madam!' The unusual intimacy of our tête-à-
tête went to Jane's head. 'And, you know, ma'am—she drinks!'
Her voice dropped to a vengeful whisper, 'That's what she
does—she drinks!'

'Really!'

'Oh, not a lot, ma'am.' Jane subsided meekly into truth.
'A glass of sherry before lunch. From the decanter in the
parlour. I've seen her. When you and the master aren't here.
She sits right down in a chair there, looking and nodding and
waving her hand round, just like she's carrying on a conversation with someone.'

I stared at Jane. Did this house breed madness in everyone?

'Did she and my sister get along all right, with one replacing
the other as mistress of the house?'

'Oh, well, ma'am ...' Jane looked down and scrubbed
intently at an invisible smudge on the floor.

'Go ahead, Jane, tell me.'

'Well, ma'am, since you ask, there was no love lost between
them. No, none at all, I suppose. They didn't see eye to eye,
you might say.'

'How do you mean? In what way?'

'Well, ma'am, it's a bit hard to say. Young Mr Vivian has
always been the apple of Mrs Chalmers' eye, of course. She's
been with him since he was a baby'—that's no guarantee of
affection, I thought—'and he's always been very nice to her—

gives her extra money and lots of time off. She doesn't have to do any housework really. Me and the men who come to wash windows do all the work!' Her voice was indignant again.

'And very nice the house looks, too, Jane,' I said, not wholly truthfully. But it was not Jane's fault that the panelling was warping or that the walls needed painting or that the only fresh thing in the whole house was Patrick's laughter—responsibility, I realized, had been abandoned in this house long ago ... 'Yes, Jane, very nice.'

'Thank you, ma'am. Anyway, ma'am—when your sister came home with young Mr Vivian from the Continent that summer—I'd just come on as help six months before—and took over the house again, it was a real shock to Mrs Chalmers. She didn't have no advance warning, you see; nothing. It shook her up. And her and Mrs Vivian didn't have the same ideas about how to run a house; no, nothing the same at all. Mrs Vivian was always flinging doors and windows wide open, and bringing in armfuls of leaves and flowers and such and strewing them round just anywhere. And she didn't keep to mealtimes that Mrs Chalmers had set up years ago; and she painted most of the walls white or light, and was always carting new furniture in and out. At the beginning, leastwise. Last couple of years, Mrs Vivian just seemed to lose interest in the house, treated it careless like, let everything go. Both ways, Mrs Chalmers took it as sort of an insult.' Jane glanced at me hastily. 'Not meaning to speak too strongly, ma'am.'

'No, no, Jane. I quite understand.'

'And then,' she went on, 'if you'll pardon me saying so, Mrs Chalmers thought there was hard feelings between the master and the mistress after a while, and she blamed the mistress for it. Master could never do wrong in her eyes. She thought Mrs Vivian didn't kotow enough to Mr Vivian, didn't make him comfortable the way that she, Mrs Chalmers, always had, and the way she thought every woman ought to treat him.' Jane paused, breathless, sitting back on her heels, then added: 'And I reckon she's right about that, too. Mr Vivian has always treated me awful kind, and I try to do the same by him.'

I looked at her sharply. Did every female in this house fall in love with its master?

The garden gate slammed, and there was the faint bump-bump of a shopping-cart along the back path. Jane looked up in alarm. 'Oh, that must be her now—and I haven't got her floor done yet! She'll be furious!' She dropped to her knees again and began scrubbing vigorously.

192

'Jane, would you please tell Mrs Chalmers to come up to see me when she has a moment?'

'Yes, ma'am. I hope you aren't going to tell her—'

'No, Jane. There's just a question or two I want to ask her about the house. I'll be in the parlour.'

Upstairs, I walked up and down nervously for some minutes till there was a knock on the door and Mrs Chalmers' black form filled the doorway.

'You wished to see me, Miss Pierce?'

'Yes. Please sit down, Mrs Chalmers.'

She settled herself in an armchair facing me, her wide black skirt rustling about her imperiously, as if she, not I, were the mistress of the house. And perhaps she was, I thought, for what Jane had told me of her pride and possessiveness towards the house—and towards Charles—had brought on an attack of my old deferential timidity. She could not have been unhappy when Sophie had taken her final leave of this house. I addressed her apprehensively:

'Mrs Chalmers, I'd like to ask you a few questions about last summer.'

Her black eyes were unblinking; she was watching me as a snake watches a rabbit.

'Do you happen to know which firm of builders dismantled the balcony?'

'By a curious chance I do.' She leaned forwards, resting her broad arms on the arms of the chair. 'Mrs Vivian had told me I could take a week off, after Mr Vivian left for Brussels. He left on Thursday midday and would be gone for a week; she and the child had gone to the country two days before. So on Thursday afternoon I took the train to my sister's in Ruislip. That's where I usually go when I have some time off—to try to bring some order into her household. Six children she has!' Mrs Chalmers' face was stern; from the tone of her voice 'children' might have been synonymous with 'delinquents' or 'dust catchers' or both. 'Well, I got as far as Sudbury Hill when I discovered that I'd forgotten my petit-point—I was working a chair cover for my eldest niece's wedding present—so I hopped off the train'—it was hard for me to imagine Mrs Chalmers hopping off anything—'and onto another, and came back as fast as I could. When I got here, there was a blue van in front of the house, one I'd never seen before, a shabby-looking thing. "WELWOOD, Designers and Builders" it said on the side; and there were pieces of board and lengths of iron pipe sticking out of it, and some lying right in the middle of the pavement. Well, I never! I've heard of thieves coming in and moving things out in broad daylight, just as if they were acting on commission, while the owners are away. I rushed into the house, but there was no sign of anyone. Just as I came out again, a man in painter's overalls came swinging through the side gate, bold as brass, carrying a long piece of black-scrolled iron—part of *our* balcony!'

Her voice shook with vexation. She pulled a flowered handkerchief from her sleeve and coughed into it violently.

'Do have a glass of sherry, Mrs Chalmers. It helps to clear the throat, I think.'

She took the glass without a word, as if bestowing a favour on me, and continued:

'I stepped right up to him and informed him that I was the housekeeper and asked him who he was and what was he doing here. He didn't even tip his cap. He spat on our walk! Then he said he was here to take down the balcony and put up a new one. "By whose orders?" I said. "Lady of the house," he said, "Mrs Vivian." Well, there was nothing I could do about that, seeing as it was on her orders. I hurried round back to see if they were making a mess of the garden. They were. But I never did like those puny little lilac shrubs that Mrs Vivian had put in at the edge of the terrace. Never grew well, didn't get enough sun; anybody would've known that.' She sniffed and took a large swallow of sherry. 'They were just starting the taking-down part. They'd finish the rest of it the next day, one of the workmen said, and then come back the next week to put up the new one. But, of course, as it turned out, with the funeral and all, they didn't put up the new balcony for a good two weeks. We had enough on our hands without them traipsing round the place!'

'So you had no idea they were coming when you went off to your sister's that Thursday?'

'None at all. And they upset me so, I went back to Ruislip without the petit-point I'd come for! That's why I came back again on Monday—I hadn't planned to!' She drank off the sherry. 'I knew that Mrs Vivian was planning to have the work done, but she hadn't bothered to tell me when. I wasn't prepared; it just about gave me a fit, seeing that man coming out of our gate!'

'Oh, dear!' I said helplessly.

Mrs Chalmers fanned herself with her handkerchief. The whites of her eyes were cross-hatched with angry red lines.

'Mrs Vivian had some strange notions, toying with this house as the fancy took her. It was her house by marriage only.

194

It wasn't part of her blood, her upbringing. She was only an American.' Her eyes were bold on mine. 'Anyway, there was nothing I could do. I told Welwood, though, that they weren't to set foot in the house itself. He said they had no intention to, sassy-like, but I went in again, anyway, to make sure that everything was locked up tight. Including the doors in the attic. I can still see one of those idiots grinning at me from his ladder, through the glass!'

'You're certain, then, that the french windows were locked?'

'Locked with a key, and bolted, top and bottom. Just as always.'

'As always?'

'Yes. I'll say that for Mrs Vivian. She took no chances where Master Patrick was concerned. She always bolted the french windows when she left the garret. The child could turn the key in the lock, but the big bolt at the top was too much for him.'

'But hadn't Welwood nailed a board across the windows, anyway, outside? Surely that would've been an elementary safety precaution?'

The contempt in Mrs Chalmers' voice was scarcely camouflaged as she replied, 'Fine precaution! Haven't you noticed— they open *inwards*!' And then: 'No, I'll give the builders that much. It wasn't their fault, the accident. Mr Vivian talked to them, of course, right after. At least, I suppose he did. I'm sure he did. He asked me to look out their address in the directory. He'd had no idea they were coming either. Imagine, she hadn't even told *him*! But then—'

'Then what, Mrs Chalmers?'

'Weren't many words passing between them that summer. Might've been a pair of strangers living under the same roof.'

I made one last effort, my courage failing.

'But if my sister had ordered—and very shortly before her death, it appears—the reconstruction of the balcony, how could she have been so—forgetful—as to open a bolted door and step out?'

Mrs Chalmers haughtily poured herself another glass of sherry from the decanter at hand before answering me.

'Meaning no disrespect, Miss Pierce'—her expression belied her words—'your sister was, especially towards the end— how shall I put it?—a bit flyaway, frivolous. She'd flutter round the house, upstairs and down, the child whining at her heels, forgetting from one minute to the next what she was about. She'd be laughing one minute and sobbing the next—even in front of me and Jane! She was not, if I may

195

say so, a very stable force in this household!'

Mrs Chalmers threw back her shoulders and sat up very straight—unmistakably, a stable force.

I crossed over Beaufort Street to the west and walked towards that stretch of the river known as Whistler's Reach. Gulls flapped and screeched about the houseboats clustered in the mud of the northern shore; their hulls were just beginning to lift with the incoming tide, giant water-plants floating on iron-stemmed anchors. Something about the great bend of the Thames filled me with awe: the sudden widening, the coming back in a gallant turn, the angle of the bridges as they spanned the banks—Wandsworth Bridge looking as if it would converge with an extension of Battersea Bridge at some not distant point to the south—the two holding all between them in a firm yet generous grip. On either shore, the chimneys of factories, mills, water-works and gas-plants thrust into the brightening morning sky; and though the skyline had been different, I reflected, the river, the bend, the barges, the boats, the changing tones of sky and water had been the same when Whistler and Turner had painted them from this spot a hundred or more years ago.

As I turned north towards the Fulham Road, my sense of exhilaration lessened. Blocks of a housing estate blotted out the river view. Dirty shop-fronts and boarded windows alternated with tarted-up old houses. The air was thick, gritty. Fashion and civic funds were fingering but had not yet wiped out the blowziness of western Chelsea. After two wrong turnings, I found the street I was looking for. Half-way up it was parked a blue van, the left side noticeably lower than the right, tilted like a grounded houseboat. 'WELWOOD, Designers and Builders' was grandly lettered on the side of the van in flaking white paint. I looked through the door of the shop it was parked beside. Beyond the dirt-veiled glass was a cluttered room, with no one in it; then I saw that it opened out into a courtyard about three times the size of the room itself. A man in paint-spattered overalls was bent over a long board set up on sawhorses. With sweeping strokes he was painting it an indescribable and, one might hope, unrepeatable shade of puce.

'Excuse me,' I said, stepping into the courtyard, 'are you Mr Welwood, the builder?'

'Nobody else.' He straightened up and looked at me with some interest. 'Want some work done, do you?'

196

'No, I'm afraid not. I—I'm here to ask you about some work you did for someone else.'

'Oh,' he grunted, and bent to his painting again. I spoke to his back for most of our conversation.

'Do you remember putting up a balcony at a house on Cheyne Walk last summer?'

'Of course I remember. August. Hot. Rained most of the summer, and then that ruddy hot spell at the end, just when things ought to be cooling off.'

It seemed that he was a man to whom whatever was said would come as a challenge to take the opposite tack.

'You hadn't been employed by the Vivians before, I take it?'

'We'd never done no work before, not for anyone, in that part of Chelsea. Not on Cheyne Walk.' He drew out the last two words in a way that was at once caressing and sneering. 'It was a nice house. Didn't see much wrong with the balcony. Could've just shored up the joints a bit, whole thing didn't have to come down. She wanted it bigger, though—wider 'specially.' He plunged his brush into the pot of paint. 'Way it turned out, it wasn't wide enough.'

'How long before—her death—had she made the arrangements with you?'

'Just a few days.' He slapped down a blob of paint. 'Couldn't believe she was dead a few days later. Terrible thing, that. People just don't think. Terrible. Her husband come running like a scared rabbit to see us, after. I told him we done just what she said. But he was upset, I tell you, shaking all over. Felt sorry for him, of course. But we done exactly what she ordered.'

'What exactly had she ordered?'

'As I recollect, she wanted it about three feet longer and four feet wider, and the railing raised. And she wanted it done right away, while she and her boy were out of the house. She didn't want him fooling round while the work was going on, y'see—thought it wasn't safe, I s'pose. If we couldn't do it right away, she'd get someone else, she said.'

'So it was very much a hurry-up job,' I mused, half-aloud.

'You can bet we weren't going to turn it down!' Welwood snapped. 'We don't exactly have jobs waiting for us from morning to night every day of the year. Properly, we're designers and builders, like it says on our van there'—he nodded towards the grimy window—'but money's tight these days. Haven't designed or built much of anything in the last five years. Lucky to get the chance to mend a ceiling or level

197

off a floor or do the odd painting job. Had to let two of my boys go last winter—no way to keep 'em on regular wages. Just me and Friday left now.'

'Friday?'

'Found his footprint in a paved walk we laid—his first job —been "Friday" ever since.' He squatted back on his haunches and grinned at me. 'Ever read a book called *Robinson Crusoe*?'

'Oh—yes. I see.'

'So we were real glad to get that job on Cheyne Walk. Not a big job, of course. I figured it would take us two days at the outside to take the old balcony down and prepare the boards for the new one, another two or three days to put the new one up. Not a big job. But she said we could name our price.'

'When she talked to you about it, did she seem at all— nervous—uncertain?'

'Oh, we never *talked* to her.' He spat carelessly over the sawhorse.

'You never talked to her? What do you mean—you never talked to her face to face, just over the telephone?'

'We never talked to her at all, period.' He stood back and surveyed the hideously glistening board. 'She wrote us a letter.'

'A letter?'

'Yep. Just about the only time I ever got a piece of work 'specially ordered, on fancy, thick writing-paper, and from Cheyne Walk, at that. We started the work the same day, soon as we got our tools together.' He thrust his brush into a jar of turpentine; the clear liquid turned blood-red. 'I've still got that letter, somewhere.'

'Would you mind if I had a look at it?'

He wiped his hands on a puce-coloured rag and went into the shop. I followed. There was no reason to expect new light on the accident from a business letter, but I felt strangely agitated. Everything that I had read by Sophie in the last few months had sent my mind spinning.

Welwood rummaged about in an old, two-drawer, grey metal filing case. I heard the clank of hollow glass as he investigated the top drawer. It was evidently a repository for empty beer bottles. Then he tugged at the bottom drawer; it slid open reluctantly. I could just see into it over his battered work table. It was full of papers, filed horizontally. Welwood huffed and puffed, his considerable stomach bumping against the cabinet as he prised up the strata. At last he stood up and dropped a

198

blue envelope on the table in front of me. An unusual filing system, I thought, that filed letters in their envelopes. I picked it up hesitantly and took out a sheet of blue stationery. It was the same sort of paper that Sophie had used for her last letter to me, engraved at the top with her name; the letter was typed in élite type with a worn, blue ribbon. Sophie had carted that ancient typewriter with her from one side of the ocean to the other. Her signature, in black ink, stood out vividly at the bottom of the page.

Dear Sir

I wish to have the present balcony of my garret removed and a new one put up in its place. The present balcony is shaky and too narrow; I wish it to be replaced in the same type of wood, and with the railings placed higher. It should have these measurements: 14 feet in length, 8 feet in width.

I shall be on holiday until 30 August, and the work must be completed before my return, as I do not want my small son to be on the premises while the construction is going on. If previous commitments do not allow you to do the work immediately, please ring me or leave a message as soon as you receive this letter, so that I may make arrangements with another firm.

I shall pay any price that you consider appropriate for the immediate completion of this work.

Yours truly,
Sophie Vivian
(Mrs Chas. A.)

At the bottom left-hand corner she had typed her address, telephone number, the postal district and the date.

I looked at the letter, read it over twice, three times. It seemed straightforward enough, though the language was different from that of the diaries. But it was a business letter, of course, not a private journal. But if she had been in such a hurry to have the work done, why hadn't she telephoned Welwood instead of writing to him? Still, she had written to the other builder, Newby, too, the one who couldn't do the job before October. Perhaps she preferred putting commissions in writing; many people were like that, after all. And yet there was something, something—I studied the blue page in my hand—that was not quite right.

'Just what I said, ain't it?'

I looked up. I had forgotten Welwood. He was sitting on the edge of his table, picking at his teeth with a matchstick.

'Oh ... yes.' I started to hand it back to him, but stopped. 'Could I keep this letter, Mr Welwood?'

He looked at me warily. 'Think I'd better keep it myself. Never know when a chap's going to take it into his head to lay charges—negligence, or something. Don't want no criminal suit and no defence.' He paused, reconsidered. 'Tell you what, though, you can make a copy, if you want.'

So I put the letter down on the scarred table and copied it, word for word. I was down to the last lines when my hand froze:

London, S.W.3
22 August

The twenty-second of August. Sophie had died on Sunday the twenty-sixth. The twenty-second would have been a Wednesday, five days before her death. But on Wednesday the twenty-second Sophie and Patrick had been in Sussex, at the cottage. They had left London on Tuesday—Mrs Chalmers had told me that, and Sophie herself had mentioned it in the diary. So how could she have written to Welwood on Wednesday, from London?

But perhaps she had misdated the letter; perhaps she had written it before leaving for the country and had left it with Charles or Mrs Chalmers to post. No, she couldn't have done that, for neither of them had known anything about the builders coming. She must have posted the letter herself. But perhaps she had written the letter after getting to the cottage, and had simply put her London address on it unthinkingly, by habit? I looked up from the letter, perplexed. The blue envelope, lying on the edge of the table, caught my eye. I stared at it. Suddenly the virtue of Welwood's filing system, which preserved envelopes as well as their contents, came home to me. I snatched up the envelope. Except for a smudge over the year—probably the imprint of one of Welwood's beer bottles —the postmark was plain as day: 'Chelsea, S.W.3, 2:15 p.m., 22 Aug.'

My hand shook as I put the letter that Sophie did not write back into its envelope. I returned it to its recipient, who was unconcernedly gazing out of the window, still chewing on his matchstick.

TWENTY

A mind that has, by all training and instinct, excluded violence from its preoccupations, does not readily admit the jagged fact of murder. Murder happened to other people, never to one's acquaintances, impossibly to one's sister. But Sophie had been murdered. She did not write that letter. She had no idea that the balcony had been removed when she stepped out for the last time. Or had she stepped out? Had she not, in fact, been pushed? The garret was invisible from the houses on either side; the garden was walled; the hour had been late, the summer twilight gone. There was very little likelihood that anyone could have witnessed her fall—except the murderer.

The murderer would have had to be someone acquainted with the plan of the house, with Sophie's habits, with the whereabouts of the servants—or one who would have been able to obtain that acquaintance on short notice. Several people, perhaps more than I knew, qualified on those counts. But knowledge of the intimate details of someone's life does not prompt normal human beings to extinguish that life. Normal human beings! They seemed to be in short supply in Sophie's circle. Charles, Dillon, Fergus, Gillian, Avery, Mrs Chalmers, Dr Calder, Sophie herself—all of them had more sides and turnings to their personalities, for good or ill, than I in my smug wisdom had credited them with. Perhaps it was my conception of normality that was at fault. Perhaps I was the abnormal human being—one who, for some thirty years, had never acted out of passion or wisdom nor recognized them in others? Charles' compulsion to gamble, Dillon's need for drugs, Gillian's voracious desire for Charles and her jealousy, Fergus' pride and his frustration at being no better than a mercenary in the hire of others, Mrs Chalmers' fierce possessiveness towards a house and its head: passions had been revealed to me in the last few months that I had never encountered or allowed myself to encounter before. Were any of those passions strong enough to kill for?

These questions I turned over and over in my mind in the forty-eight hours following my return to Sussex on Tuesday afternoon. Thursday was Election Day, and Patrick and I would be driving back to London on Friday to meet Charles on his return from the North, to congratulate or console him as the balloting indicated. In the last days of the campaign, the radio and the newspapers were unceasing in their commentary on the election; but whereas before I had followed every word, weighed every prediction in regard to Charles' chances, it all seemed to me now curiously distant, irrelevant, as if the contest were being fought in another country, another universe, by beings that were no more than atoms of dust. And yet I longed for Charles' return; the secret I bore was too much for anyone to bear alone. But when, unexpectedly, I heard his voice over the telephone on Tuesday night, I could not say a word to him of my discovery. He had telephoned, he said, just to 'keep in touch'—he had never been one for writing letters. Over the wire he was his usual brusque self, alternately charming and impatient, solicitous and patronizing. He paid attention to one, I realized, only when one was with him. It was impressive but chilling, his ability to shear off one part of his life from the rest.

On Wednesday and Thursday I took Patrick and the Bailey children for long walks along the river and into the band of woods that bordered our land to the west. The countryside was fresh and green, the ground springy underfoot from the recent rains. We stumbled across vines of wild strawberries, the fruit not yet ripe; and here and there, in the dark, mossy places of the woods, we found clusters of violets, and bluebells nodding on their slender stems. I needed to walk, to explore, to wear myself out, to distract myself from the terrors of thinking. I circled away from the problem only to return to it, my mind winding tighter and tighter about it, Ariadne's thread rolling in reverse. It had to be Sophie's discovery of the drug-trafficking that had precipitated her death. And if it was, the two suspects, then, were Dillon and—the idea was as hard for me to admit as that of murder itself—Charles. But Charles, thank God, had been in Brussels, had returned to London only when summoned by Mrs Chalmers' cross-Channel telephone call. Dillon, then. He had shown himself in Sophie's diary as having neither scruples nor tenderness towards other people. He had known both Sophie and Charles for years, had been involved with drugs and drug-trafficking even longer; Sophie had told him of the chemist's report, had threatened to expose him and he in turn had, despite his denial, in effect threatened her. And
202

yet, I had seen for myself that Dillon was indolent by nature, slow-moving as a domesticated cat, fastidious, disdainful of strenuous undertakings—not the make-up of a murderer. But what did I know of the make-up of a murderer? For that matter, what if Sophie's discovery of the drug-trafficking seven days before her death was simply a coincidence, had nothing in fact to do with her end?

On Thursday evening Ann Bailey came over to the cottage to listen to the election results with me. The polls did not close until ten o'clock; reports from the north came in slowly and erratically. Patrick, although he did not quite know what an election was, knew that it was something that mattered very much to his father; he kept popping in and out of bed and jumping onto my lap, begging to be allowed 'just one more minute' to stay up with us. He was plainly more excited than Ann was; by eleven o'clock her yawns became more frequent and less camouflaged; she had come, I knew, only out of kindness, to keep me company.

'Ann,' I said, 'there's no need for both of us to be sleepless wrecks tomorrow. Why don't you go on home now?' I added with a forced lightness, 'I'll send up a rocket flare if Charles wins—you can watch for it from your window!'

'All right, Sarah,' Ann smiled. 'Hope I can keep my eyes open that long. Sorry to be such a wash-out. That's what the simple country life does to you.'

The simple country life, I thought, as she left. Lord, what a blessing! I tucked Patrick into bed for what I hoped was the last time and went into my own bedroom. I put the small portable radio down beside the telephone on the bedside table and lay down for a few minutes' rest. In the course of the day I had walked and worried myself to the edge of exhaustion. Crisp voices unreeled figure after figure out of the radio, on and on and on. It beat counting sheep as a way to oblivion, I remember thinking—they ought to make tapes of it for insomniacs—and then nothing more. I was walking in the Lincoln woods at home, and in my hand I held the pointed flowers of white trillium; they were ringing, vibrating with energy, trying to talk to me. I was too sleepy to answer, but the ringing continued, in insistent bursts. I looked about me groggily, wondering what to do about it. My eyes focused on the white telephone by the bedside. It was the telephone that was beating upon my consciousness. I yanked the receiver off the cradle and pulled it towards me.

'Sarah?'

'Charles!' I was wide awake instantly.

'It's all over.'

I knew immediately, from the tone of his voice, the outcome. 'You've won!'

'Yes, we won. Labour will call for a recount. The margin is less than three hundred. But I think we've done it—at last.' His voice was strident with strain and exhilaration.

'That's marvellous. What are you doing now?'

'Celebrating—as you can hear.' He must have turned the receiver outwards: I could hear voices, laughter, scuffling, a door banging in the background. 'I'll be home tomorrow—today, I should say. It's already Friday. Thank God it's over.'

'You don't sound very pleased about winning.'

'Of course I'm pleased. I'm just worn out. Don't mind me, Sarah. You don't know how wearing these last few days have been.'

'Oh, yes, I do,' I said, and my voice trembled. I wanted to tell him everything, then and there, but the distance, the static, our common weariness kept me from it. 'I'll be in London to meet you. What time will you get in?'

'Late-ish. Nine or ten, probably. Have to do some sweeping up here, so to speak.' I could hardly hear him over the noise in the background. A broken chorus of 'For He's a Jolly Good Fellow' swelled over the line.

'All right, Charles. Till tonight, then.'

'Till tonight, darling.'

It was the first time he had ever called me 'darling'. I put the phone down slowly and lay back on the bed. The voices on the radio were still droning out statistics, blotting out all sensation that elections were made by living beings. It was some time before I could force myself to get up. But there were lights to be turned out, papers to be picked up, as well as some two hundred pieces of jigsaw puzzle that Patrick had been trying to put together, unsuccessfully, on the living-room floor. As my last duty, I went into Patrick's room to make sure that he was well-covered for the night, or what remained of it, for the sky was already lightening towards the eastern edges. He was rolled up in bed like a little hedgehog, the corduroy dog beside him. I bent over him and removed a fire-engine and a plastic trumpet from his arms. Suddenly he rolled over, his eyes wide open, and smiled at me.

'Daddy's won!'

'Yes, he has,' I smiled back, 'but how did you know, you little monkey? I thought you were sound asleep.'

'I heard him. I was making a peanut-butter sandwich in the kitchen, and the phone rang, and I listened. I heard him
204

talking. Just like last time.'

'Last time?'

'When Mama was here. The day she went away and didn't come back. You *will* take me with you when you go to meet Daddy, won't you, Aunt Sarah?'

My heart must have stopped beating for the space of his question. 'You heard him on the phone the last day your mother was here? Are you sure? Are you sure it was your father?'

'Oh, yes, I know Daddy's voice. He said, "Meet me at the house at eleven o'clock tonight. Don't say anything to anyone." And Mama said, "How could I? I'll be there," and then some other words, I didn't know what they meant.'

'Why didn't you ever tell anyone this before, Patrick?'

'No one ever asked me.'

His head fell back drowsily on the pillow. In a moment he was deep in a sleep that the dawn did not bring me.

TWENTY-ONE

The summer lights of Battersea Pleasure Gardens flickered among the trees across the river, here, there, gone, appearing again as the foliage shifted with the breeze. The parlour windows were wide open to the warm, windy night. The Albert Bridge and Cadogan Pier also glistened with lights, and excursion boats and pleasure craft of one kind and another glided up and down the river as London gave itself up to yet another season. And yet the city was never exhausted. It was as if it renewed itself, gathered its stamina in the winter months, the working months as I thought of them, and so could surrender itself without impairment to the thousands of visitors that surged into it, tested, examined, admired and trampled it between June and September. London encompassed everything.

'Sarah, my dear, must we have the windows open? I'm positively congealing!'

I turned around. I had forgotten Avery, I had forgotten everything, for all of sixty seconds.

'Sorry,' I said, shutting the windows. 'Not quite Riviera weather, I guess.'

'It's certainly not! But I suppose it seems warm to you.'

I shrugged. 'Warmer than it has been.'

'Well, I should've known better than to trust English weather. It's always risky, venturing out of one's own domain. I was watching a movie on television last night at the hotel, *Lost Horizon*, with that marvellous Ronald Colman. But what happened to that beautiful young girl when she ran away from Shangri-la with him—I could hardly bear to watch!'

Avery grimaced and twisted her pearls fretfully. I regarded her not wholly with amusement.

'But you ventured out, Aunt Avery.'

'I? Oh, well, coming to London is nothing really. I just like to complain, I suppose—I have nothing else to do. London is really the only place where one can get sensible clothes and well-made shoes.'

'No, I mean forty or fifty years ago or whenever it was—venturing out of New England to marry your Frenchman.'

'Oh, yes, that.' Avery looked at me vaguely, her wrinkled, powdered face frowning and creasing into more wrinkles, as if she were struggling to place something as remote as Shangri-la. 'That just happened. I didn't mean to. Anyway, my dear'—she was suddenly brisk again—'is he *never* coming? My plane's at eleven-thirty and it's half-past nine now. I shouldn't have stayed on, but when I phoned you this afternoon and heard about the election and all—well, it really is rather thrilling!'

'Is it?'

'My dear girl, I don't understand you. The last time I saw you, just before Christmas, it was plain that all you could think about was Charles Vivian!'

'Was it that plain?'

'Yes, it was,' Avery said petulantly. 'You were as bad as Sophie. You young girls, you're all alike!'

What further comparisons I might have been treated to were lost as steps and voices sounded on the front walk, and a moment later the thick, oaken door swung on its hinges and closed with a thump. Gillian Fox's coppery head poked around the door of the parlour, Fergus behind her. I could see Charles' long legs disappearing up the stairs.

'Hi, gang!' Fergus said. 'We're home! Conquering heroes and all that.'

'Hello, Fergus, Gillian. Aunt Avery, have you met these people? Gillian Fox and Fergus Howell?'

'Oh, yes, my dear, Sophie introduced us ages ago. How are you both?' A barely perceptible trill had come into Avery's voice, the archness of aged vivacity. Avery had always liked an audience.

'We are—outstanding!' Fergus answered blithely, and plumped himself down in an armchair. 'What's this I see? A bottle of Fortnum's own reserve cooling in the ice-bucket?'

'Yes, my little contribution to the occasion,' Avery simpered. 'I really don't approve of drinking, but a man doesn't get elected to Parliament every day!'

'Lovely,' Gillian purred. 'We've been on the road for ever. Charles wouldn't stop for anything but a beer and a sandwich, and that was ages ago. The traffic coming into London was simply awful.' She twisted a silky curl around her forefinger and tugged at her skin-tight jersey. 'I do think champagne is soothing—more like food than drink.'

'Do you, my dear?' Avery leaned forward to peer at this

207

exotic bird more closely. 'Well, if that's your usual diet, you do seem to thrive on it.'

Gillian smiled graciously and patted her sleek middle. She flicked a glance at me as if to say, that's one up on you. But how could she have known that neither she nor any woman could make me jealous again?

Mrs Chalmers strode into the room with a tray of coffee, cakes and sandwiches. She had taken off her usual apron, and her black silk dress rustled importantly; she looked unwontedly festive and good-humoured. Jane followed close behind her with cups and cutlery and set them down awkwardly, blushes coming and going on her face at finding herself in the midst of so many people. She retreated hurriedly from the room. I heard her voice and Mrs Chalmers' talking excitedly in the hall, and a male voice—Charles' voice—answering.

In a moment he walked into the parlour. His eyes sought mine at once. He was smiling, expectant; a Tory-blue rosette shone glossily on his lapel. I did not move from the window, but I returned his smile, being now as adept as he at pretence, and motioned with my eyes towards Avery. He turned and greeted her and immediately everyone was talking at him, congratulating him all over again. Fergus uncorked the champagne, glasses were filled, toasts drunk, and Charles and Fergus between them retold, at Avery's request, the campaign from beginning to end.

I hardly listened; I watched the river. There were fewer boats as the hour grew late. Only now and then the brisk, efficient sally of a police launch, and once a broad freighter passed, its stern and starboard lights gleaming in the darkness. The darkness lessened as the moon rose higher in the sky. It was almost at the full, extinguishing the stars at the edge of its bright periphery.

I could feel Charles looking at me, puzzled by my aloofness. Let him look, I thought, and suddenly turned to him, meeting his gaze directly. He faltered for a second in what he was saying but as I dropped my eyes again he resumed good-naturedly, having won from me, I suppose he thought, the customary submission. We sat there for a long time, Gillian and Fergus getting shriller and drunker as a second bottle of Fortnum's own reserve was emptied, Avery more arch and anecdotal, Charles more expansive and imperious. Avery at last brought the celebration to an end by informing us—cooing at us, rather, like a happy mother-hen—that poor Charles must get some rest and she must get to the airport and we all had tomorrow to think about. That some of us did not have a tomorrow to

208

think about was something she did not know and could not have credited. Fergus lurched to his feet, dragging Gillian up with him and offered to drive Avery to the airport, but Charles broke in:

'Before you go, there's one thing more that needs celebrating.'

He looked at me, winked, smiled. Horror rushed over me as I realized what he was about to say. I opened my mouth to protest, but no words came.

'Lacking any parents or fairy-godmother to make the announcement—though Avery might do for the latter in a pinch—it falls to me to say, with the greatest pleasure, that Sarah and I are going to be married.'

I did not attempt to assess the reactions that greeted this announcement. The party went on for at least another quarter of an hour, complete with felicitations and back-slappings, embraces and toasts and a few underhand comments from Gillian that presumably no one heard but me. Charles, released from the stresses of the campaign, was in a fine exuberant mood. If Avery had not finally seized Fergus firmly by one hand and Gillian by the other, we might have gone on partying all night.

When at last they were gone, Charles pulled me towards him. He let go of me abruptly when he felt my stiffness.

'What is it, Sarah? You're not yourself tonight. Was my announcement too sudden for you?'

'No, it's not that.'

'It seemed the right moment, but perhaps I'm too much in the habit of making unsolicited speeches. It's a common failing of politicians.' He was smiling, though I had drawn away from him.

'I have to talk to you, Charles.'

'Well, talk then.' He sat down on the sofa and looked at me calmly.

Just then Jane came into the room and began to gather up the débris of the evening. She looked from one to the other of us nervously, and dropped spoons and forks in retreating. Charles leaned over and helped her to pick them up. Mrs Chalmers, I noticed, was in the hall, sweeping, despite the lateness of the hour.

'All right,' Charles said. 'I can see you're on edge. Let's go upstairs to talk. You've obviously got something on your mind that's meant for me alone.' His voice was still indulgent, though there was a note of impatience in it, too. 'Yes, let's go upstairs. This room stinks of smoke and drink.'

209

I turned without a word, dodged Mrs Chalmers' large form in the hall and started up the stairs. It was second nature to me by then to watch my step on the frayed carpet and sagging wood. Such a small rottenness—what did it matter? Was it only last autumn that I had first climbed this ancient stairway? All the way up to the top of the house. Light from the hall shone faintly into the narrow, attic room. I fumbled for the switch on the light above the desk, but Charles stopped my hand.

'Leave it like this,' he said softly.

I withdrew my hand from his and walked over to the french windows. The wind had died down; the leaves of the trees, silvery under the moon, were motionless in the still air. I unbolted the doors and opened them and surveyed the night. Still I could not speak. I heard Charles drop heavily onto a seat behind me. I turned around. The room was flooded with moonlight, so bright as to disorient the senses. I felt bodiless, shafted by light. I began to speak in a trance, not daring to premeditate my words for fear I should not be able to say them. I told him all, piece by piece, as I had learned it, as it had come to me, ending with the knowledge that Patrick had given me the night before. I must have talked for a long time; the clock at the bottom of the hall was striking midnight as I finished.

TWENTY-TWO

'You shouldn't stand so near the railing, Sarah, you might fall over.' The voice came out of the darkness. Charles was sitting on the sofa against the further wall, where the moonlight did not reach. I had never heard such a cold voice; it chilled me to the bone. 'No one knows these things but you. We can't afford to lose our star witness.'

'We?'

'A manner of speaking. There is a part of me that approves and applauds your industry—your perseverance in building up a case, your labouring loyalty to a sister you hated. Tell me, how could you have kept silent till now? Why didn't you shout it out to everyone—the Baileys, Avery, Fergus, Gillian, the police—the moment you had put the last nail in place?'

'I loved you,' I answered in a low tone.

'And you don't now?' The voice was mocking. 'Do you really think that our affections are changed by what the loved one does? Don't you remember that love is not love which alters when it alteration finds? I admit that there are some of us—pragmatists in all things—whose affections change according to circumstances. We would sacrifice any relationship, however loving it might once have been—as mine and Sophie's once was—if it brought us or even threatened to bring us misery, anxiety, public or private humiliation. But you are not a pragmatist, Sarah. You play the rôle badly. You don't quite believe in the evidence you have pieced together—because you are still in love with me.'

'No.'

'I don't believe you. I have observed you with some interest over the past months. You are in love with me, and I have asked you to marry me, yet there is no end to your need to be hurt, to imagine yourself slighted or neglected or the object of criticism. What saves you from being a masochist—and masochists are such bores, after all—is your childlike delight in having the hurt removed. Your view is the same as Patrick's when he scrapes a knee or an elbow: "Kiss it and make it

211

well." If I were to take you in my arms right now and hold you and tell you, though offering no evidence to back me up, that what happened to Sophie was none of my doing, you would accept my words without question. The truth is, you like to think that you have made an assay of justice, but you end by believing what you want to believe.'

His words stunned me, but they no longer had the power to confuse me.

'You're wrong. What I *want* to believe is beside the point.'

I walked to the middle of the room and switched on the green-shaded bulb hanging from a cord above the desk. The vehemence of the gesture set the cord swinging; light fled in crazy circles round the walls. I wanted to see Charles' face. But when the reeling movement stopped, his face told me nothing.

'So you truly believe I murdered Sophie?'

'What else?'

He shrugged, looked at me levelly, sighed.

'So little faith.'

'Faith! My God, Charles, you're a fine one to talk!'

'Oh, yes, I know.' He half smiled. 'But it was Dillon. If Sophie hadn't told him what she knew, she'd still be here.'

I stared at him. I felt a miraculous relief. Of course, it had been Dillon, just as I had first thought. It was Dillon who had written the letter to Welwood, and Dillon who had telephoned Sophie at the cottage. Patrick had been mistaken—the voices of Charles and Dillon were virtually indistinguishable on the telephone—I had discovered that myself, the time that I had called Dillon after coming back from Nottinghamshire.

Charles went on talking, counterpointing my own thoughts. 'I went to see him that night, Monday, as soon as Sophie had told me that she'd told him. He said she had to be disposed of. Yes, that was his phrase, "disposed of". If she went to the police with her story, Dillon's career came to an end. More than his career; drugs were his whole life. Sophie's testimony would have put him—us—our travels, activities, communications under constant surveillance. Dillon would've been a natural suspect, being already on the registered addicts' list. He was adamant; he said she had to be disposed of, and that it had to look like an accident.'

'But Sophie would never have gone to the police! She said so to you, she said so in her diary. She loathed Dillon, but she would never have exposed you.' I smiled at him wryly. 'She didn't revere justice any more than you say that I do.'

'No, she wouldn't have gone to the police. But I couldn't

212

convince Dillon of that. He didn't trust her. She had already pulled that trick of intercepting the telegram and turning up at the cottage. He simply didn't trust her—and if there are degrees of trust, I'm sure I'm right in saying that no one is less trusting than a drug smuggler.'

'But how could Dillon have imagined she'd go to the police? It was he himself who pointed out to Sophie that exposing him meant exposing you—and he made it clear that he didn't think her capable of that.'

'Yes, that's what he implied. But the irony is, he did think her capable of exposing me, perhaps even anxious to expose me. He thought that our marriage was on the rocks. He thought she might well take her revenge on me, on what our marriage had done to her life, by publicly humiliating me, naming me as an accomplice in the drug ring.' Charles stretched out his long legs and leaned back against the sofa. 'And Dillon hated Sophie. She stood for a lot of things—beauty, talent, courage, ambition—that he could never command and so despised. To obliterate her was, for a moment, to obliterate them.'

'But why didn't you stop him? Why didn't you warn Sophie that she was in danger? He must have learned from Mrs Chalmers that Sophie was in Sussex and that the house would be empty that week-end. How could you have left her, how could you have gone off to Brussels with the situation unresolved?'

Charles got up and walked over to the windows.

'You ask a lot of questions, Sarah. I thought you had all the answers. You were in no doubt of them a few minutes ago.'

I hung my head. 'I was—hasty. Oh, Charles!'

I ran to him and threw my arms around him.

'Forgive me, Charles!'

I shall never forget the tenderness with which he disengaged my arms from about his neck. He did not drop my hands, but held them, and looked into my eyes:

'No, Sarah, you weren't wrong. You had the answers.'

I studied his face anxiously. I could not make sense of his words.

'What do you mean, I wasn't wrong?'

He dropped my hands and leaned against the window-frame.

'I wrote the letter to Welwood. I met Sophie here that night.'

'You!'

'Yes, how unlikely, how—monstrous. But so it was. I had let Dillon make up my mind for me, as I have always let him, I suppose. He left me little choice. It was her life or—ours. Mine as well as Sophie's.'

213

'Charles!'

'That day, Tuesday—Sophie and Patrick had left for Sussex in the morning—I was in a daze. Don't ask me how I persuaded myself to do it. I don't know. Perhaps Sophie and I could have run away, somewhere, to another country. I don't know. There seemed no way out then. And, since at long last we are each speaking the truth, Sarah, perhaps, perhaps— though I cannot now accept it—perhaps I wanted to be rid of Sophie. The only thing, I gather, that her diary does not make plain—it couldn't, for it was her diary, not mine—was how unendurable I, not only Sophie, had found the last two years of our life together.'

I could not see his face as he spoke. He had turned from me, was looking out into the night.

'I had no idea how to go about it. She refused to take pills, wouldn't touch even aspirin since giving up the anti-depressants a few weeks before; poison I knew nothing about anyway, and besides it would've been discovered in an autopsy. Guns, knives—impossible. I was sitting up here on the balcony on Tuesday night when the idea came to me. She didn't care about the rest of the house, but she was keen on having the balcony enlarged to give herself more painting space. I knew she had recently asked our usual builders to do the work, but they couldn't take it on before October; she had a bee in her bonnet that she wanted it done during the summer holidays. So it came to me, why not have it done for her? Only—have the work only half completed—the balcony taken down but not replaced. If, by some unlikely chance, she had returned to the house before Sunday night and seen the work in progress, I'd simply have told her that it was a little surprise I'd planned for her. I knew it would be easy to get a small, local outfit that could do a quick job and be glad to have it and not ask too many niggling questions. The seamy end of Chelsea has plenty of that sort to choose from. I picked out an address from the yellow pages and wrote to them in Sophie's name—I knew her signature as well as my own.'

'But what if the builders hadn't been able to do the work right away?'

'I'd posted the letter on Wednesday. I knew they'd get it on Thursday. They didn't ring me then to say that they couldn't—I waited round a few hours to make sure. Then, knowing that things were in train, I left for the conference in Brussels.' Charles rubbed his cheek. 'The conference in Brussels! Yes, there really was one—not that I had any very cogent suggestions to make to the assembled legal minds about

214

the EEC problems that we had met to deal with! Anyway, if Welwood hadn't been free, I could easily have found another crew—small builders are ten a penny. But Welwood was free. I knew he'd not be able to do more than take the old balcony down in what remained of the working week.'

'But it was an awful gamble!'

Charles gave a bitter laugh. 'Haven't you heard, Sarah? I'm a gambler!' He turned to me as if to read my expression, but I looked away from him, withdrew into the safety of the room. 'Oh, yes, there were several gambles involved, for that matter. Although Mrs Chalmers told me that Sophie had given her a week off, what if she had decided to spend part of her leave here? Her quarters in this house are more spacious and private than at her sister's, I'm sure. Or what if Sophie had refused to meet me when I telephoned her on Sunday? Or what if, contrary to my instructions, she hadn't come to the house alone? What if she had brought Patrick along with her? Oh, yes, my scheme was full of gambles. And, who knows, perhaps I liked it the better for that!'

I was sick at heart. There was not much more I had to know.

'So when she arrived at the house that Sunday night, you were already here. You made sure that the balcony was down. You opened the french windows. You left the garret dark, as you did tonight, except for the light from the hall.'

'Yes.'

'And when the two of you came up here, talked a bit, perhaps, stood by the windows, you simply—pushed her?'

'Pushed her? My God! What do you take me for?'

There was no answering that.

'We were sitting here, talking. Sophie said that of course she wouldn't go to the police, that she had said she would only to taunt Dillon. And then she told me in effect, in her proud, stubborn way—there was never anything of the suppliant about Sophie—that she still loved me and that though our marriage was a shambles, she thought we could put it right again. She said these things very coolly; she might have been appraising one of her own paintings. She amazed me; she always amazed me. I'd been expecting a scene. It would've made it easier. I didn't know how to answer her. She looked very beautiful, formidably beautiful; even in the half-darkness, her eyes were hard and bright as sapphires—she looked no older than on the day I'd first seen her, sitting on a bar stool in Cap Trois Mille.' Charles straightened his shoulders and arched his back wearily. 'We sat in silence for some minutes. Then she got up and

215

stretched, as if she'd become cramped sitting in that chair—where you're sitting now, Sarah—and sauntered over to the open doors and stood there, breathing in the night air. In that instant I knew I couldn't go through with it. I was petrified. "Sophie!" I said. "Yes, Charles?" she answered, her back to me. "Sophie, come here!" But she didn't turn round. She said—she must have been smiling, I could hear it in her voice—"No, if you want me, you can come to me." And then she simply—stepped out.'

'Oh, Charles!'

'There was no sound, not even the beginning of a scream, only the faint thud of the body landing. I couldn't look. No one could have survived that fall—five storeys down, onto a paved terrace. I was panic-stricken. I was out of the house in seconds. I ran up to King's Road, flagged a taxi, got to the airport and was back at my hotel in Brussels before three a.m.'

'You just—left her there?'

'What could I have done? Stayed to pick up the pieces?' He fingered the ribbons of the blue rosette that was still pinned to his lapel. 'I know, in retrospect, how helpless the people at Chappaquiddick must have felt. It was too late. Too late for everything.'

'Charles. Charles.' I could only repeat his name. I spoke it as a lament, not a question, not an imprecation.

He looked at me.

'I knew she had written to you not long before, asking you to come for a visit. One might think that that would've been the last thing I wanted after her death. But that wasn't so. I wanted you here, not only for the help you could give me with Patrick. Perhaps I needed something to hang onto, too. Perhaps—I don't know—I thought, through you, somehow to atone for her death.'

'And now?'

'And now?' His voice was mocking again. 'That's up to you, isn't it, Sarah? You have Sophie's diary. You know where to put your hands on the Welwood letter. You have heard me confess to premeditated murder. It's up to you, isn't it?'

I felt sick, drained.

'Yes, it's up to me,' I said very faintly. And then: 'Do you love me, Charles? Did you ever love me?'

'You asked me that once before.'

'Yes, I remember. On New Year's Day. And you said, "As much as I can love anyone."'

'Yes, that's what I said.'

He was standing by the windows, looking out into the night.
216

His face was profiled against the moon, which had already begun to slip downwards.

I left the room, and groped my way unseeingly down the staircase.

TWENTY-THREE

We are almost ready. The house has been listed for sale; I am leaving it in the hands of an agent, and the furniture will be sold, too. Charles' sister did not want any of it, said she never could stand the heavy old stuff: I gather she lives spartanly and happily among her dog kennels in Leicestershire. I have saved a few things to take home—the pinewood rocker, the roll-top desk, Sophie's stuffed cat and china-headed doll and the vermeil-enamelled vanity set. And one or two of her paintings. I told Jane to take what she wanted from the closets full of clothes, but she, shy gawky thing, took only a couple of evening frocks; she will wear them to her Scottish dancing, if she can find such a group on the other side of the water—as surely she can, Boston being what it is, God help it. She will be able to look after Patrick on days I have to teach late, and she can see him to and from school, for if one thing is certain it is that Mrs Lofting's School for Girls will not adjust its rules to admit Patrick. Mrs Chalmers has found another place: a young family with new-born twins; she says their household is in a state of chaos, but that she will bring order into it. I tremble for them, though I gave her a good recommendation.

I have almost finished the packing. There are a few last-minute things to put in. My wedding dress is still hanging on the closet door, casting watery shadows as the room lightens. What to do with it is a problem; perhaps I will just leave it hanging there. Our plane leaves at noon. The light is increasing fast now; the lights on Albert Bridge will soon snap off, as someone somewhere throws a master switch and the lights go off all over London. It has been a quiet, unbroken night here, the first night this month that Patrick has not awakened, crying out from nightmares, and stumbled shivering and sobbing into my room.

Despite the quiet, I have been sleepless for most of the night, as I was on that night four weeks ago when Charles and I last talked together. I had heard no sound then, either, nothing at all. He had not even turned to look at me as I left the garret. Jane and Patrick were sound asleep when I looked in at them; I went to bed but I slept badly, awakening many

218

times before the dawn breeze stirred the air and the gulls began wheeling and screeching along the Embankment. I could not lie still any longer; I got out of bed and went into the hall. Not a sound. I wondered if Charles was as sleepless as I—Sophie had said he could sleep through anything. My mind was no more decided on a course of action than before; the shock to my emotions had been such that I was incapable of planning the day in front of me, much less the course of my whole life. The light in the hall was still burning, though we usually turned it off at night. Had Charles gone to bed, or was he still in the attic, as restless as I? I went up the stairs. The door was ajar, as I had left it; the green-shaded bulb over the desk glowed faintly in the early light. One of the french windows swung to with a bang, caught by the quickening breeze. I went over to lock it and paused, looking out at the peaceful, grey-green, misty garden embraced by its dark red wall, the sharp line of the top and corners blurred by the morning mist. How familiar that tiny rectangle of London had become to me! As I turned to go, something on the edge of the terrace caught my eye. I stepped out on the balcony. The dark shape on the terrace was a man, lying almost where Sophie must have fallen. His head on the pale pavement was haloed with blood. Oh, God—no! I had to clutch the balcony railing to keep from fainting with dizziness. I could not look. I forced myself to open my eyes. The ribbons of a bright blue rosette fanned out against the grey stone. It was Charles.

It has helped, though I am not sure why, to write out these things during the past few weeks. Perhaps writing, as fully and accurately as I can, is as close as I shall ever come to what Charles called a consummated passion. But what piece of writing is ever complete and accurate? For completeness, truth, depends on comprehension, the comprehension that the reader brings as well as the writer. Even now, I am not sure that I fully understand Sophie's diaries, just as I did not understand Sophie while she lived. Or Charles. Or Dillon.

Dillon is still alive, of course. A week or so ago I sent a letter to the police division that deals with narcotics; I told them what I knew of Dillon's activities, leaving Charles' name out of it, and my own. I do not know if they will follow it up— no authority that I have ever had anything to do with has shown much relish for anonymous letters—but I have no wish to involve myself further with the forces of justice or of corruption.

No doubt there is much that neither the police nor our decorous neighbours on Cheyne Walk will ever puzzle out.

219

Charles' death itself, for instance. The police questioned me rigorously enough about that, but got nowhere. Two sudden deaths in less than a year, in the same house, by the same means, an inexplicable fall. An accident, a suicide? Oh, no, the talk must go—not that it has come to my ears, for people treat me very gently these days—not a suicide. Charles Vivian was a newly elected MP, had a solid solicitor's practice, was engaged to an American heiress. No, surely not a suicide, for despair does not enter the houses of the rich and well-beloved.

What will it be like to go back to Boston now—the school-girls' tea-parties, Saturday nights at the Symphony, picnics in Concord and Lincoln? At least I will have Patrick, and that cheers me somewhat. My own little boy, or as close as I will ever come to having a child of my own. How fast the night is going. I can see my reflection quite clearly in the mirror now. I look old, faded. Imagine my thinking that I should ever have been a bride—what dreams of joy and glory! Had Charles ever loved me? I have not been able to bring myself to consider that question in the past few weeks. Had he ever loved anyone, even Sophie? He had not said he loved her; he had described his feelings for her in oddly assorted, even contradictory, ways. As for me, he had not—not disliked me. He had found me agreeable, helpful, docile, perhaps. And rich, of course. And our marriage would have gone down the drain even faster than his and Sophie's.

But people go on getting married. Fergus told me only last week that he and Gillian were going to 'tie the knot'. Insouciant Fergus! How will they fare, I wonder? Who knows? Sophie said that marriage was always a leap in the dark. It's not a leap that I any longer have hope, expectation or desire of making.

The lights have just gone out on Albert Bridge; it is a great, grey giant lying across the Thames, its colours not yet visible. I hear they are thinking of tearing it down, despite the work that has gone into strengthening it over the past few years. It is a gay, graceful thing, for all its size—but when have grace and gaiety ever insured longevity? I must get up and finish the packing and write a note for the men who are coming for the trunks tomorrow, though Mrs Chalmers said she would see to everything. The night is almost gone. It looks as if we will have a clear day for flying. The fog is thinning; ribbons of mist are blowing upwards, drifting towards the northeast. I must not sit here dawdling any longer. Patrick will be waking up soon and rushing into my room, his sweet face rosy with sleep, his eyes dark with the terror of half-remembered dreams.